Secret of the Sixth Magic

2nd edition

Lyndon Hardy

Volume 2 of Magic by the Numbers

Bartizan Press
Los Angeles

Second edition
Version 1
Print ISBN: 978-0-9971501-7-9
Library of Congress Control Number: 2016940435

Other books by Lyndon Hardy

Master of the Five Magics, 2nd edition
Riddle of the Seven Realms, 2nd edition

Visit Lyndon Hardy's website at: http://www.alodar.com/blog

Cover by Tom Momary http://www.tomomary.com

Map by Ana Maria Velicu http://facebook.com/ancart7

1. Fantasy 2. Magic 3. Wizard 4. Sorcerer 5. Alchemy 6. Adventure

To my mother, Zell

Contents

The Laws of Magic   1

Map   2

Part One *Puzzles for the Wordsmith*   3

Part Two *The Postulate of Invariance*   89

Part Three *The Axiom of Least Contradiction*   191

Part Four *The Verity of Exclusion*   259

Author's Afterward   331

What's next?   336

Glossary   339

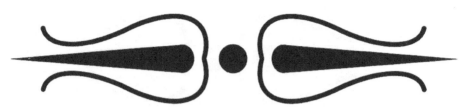

Part One *Puzzles for the Wordsmith*

1	The Navigator's Cube	5
2	Landfall	7
3	The Master's Hut	10
4	The Proposition	17
5	Practice by Rote	24
6	The Trader's Tent	28
7	The Tyro's First Spell	34
8	The Persistence of Vision	41
9	Storm-flight	45
10	A Well-cast Charm	51
11	Sorcerer's Gambit	57
12	Delia's Talent	63
13	The Wordsmith's Reward	69
14	Into the Hall	72

15 The Purging Flame   77

16 Inconceivable   81

17 A New Direction   85

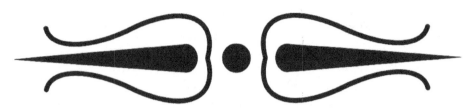

Part Two *The Postulate of Invariance*

1 Whispers of Memory 91

2 The Contracting Cube 96

3 Augusta 101

4 The Vault in the Grotto 107

5 A Matter of Scale 115

6 Sleight of Hand 121

7 Scentstones 128

8 Panic in the Market 131

9 The Three Adventurers 136

10 Trocolar's Keep 141

11 Perseverance and Threshold 146

12 Melibar 149

13 Seven Exactly 153

14 The Magic Sword 157

15 Stuck in the Stone   162

16 Fleeting Treasure   168

17 High Tide   177

18 The Final Tally   185

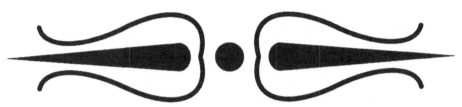

Part Three *The Axiom of Least Contradiction*

1 Homecoming   193

2 Spring Harvest   197

3 Tread of the Ambulators   202

4 Fugitive's Choice   209

5 Intertwined Journeys   213

6 Which Way To Turn   217

7 Drums and Weights   221

8 A Chain Reaction   227

9 Strength in Numbers   230

10 Avalanche   233

11 Torpordust   237

12 Manipulants and Rock Bubblers   241

13 Growing Rebellion   246

14 The Door into Elsewhere   253

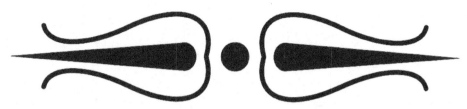

Part Four *The Verity of Exclusion*

1 Skysoar   261

2 Saga of the First among the Navigators   266

3 Attraction and Repulsion   274

4 Foul Air   280

5 The Metamagican's Key   286

6 A Gift Freely Given   293

7 The Archimage   297

8 Counterattack   304

9 A Portal between Realms   308

10 Memory's End   312

11 The Final Puzzle   314

12 Duel of the Metamagicians   319

13 A New Beginning   325

The Laws of Magic

Thaumaturgy

The Principle of Sympathy — like produces like

The Principle of Contagion — once together, always together

Alchemy

The Doctrine of Signatures — the attributes without mirror the powers within

Magic

○

The Maxim of Persistence — perfection is eternal

Sorcery

◉

The Rule of Three — thrice spoken, once fulfilled

Wizardry

The Law of Ubiquity — flame permeates all

The Law of Dichotomy — dominance or submission

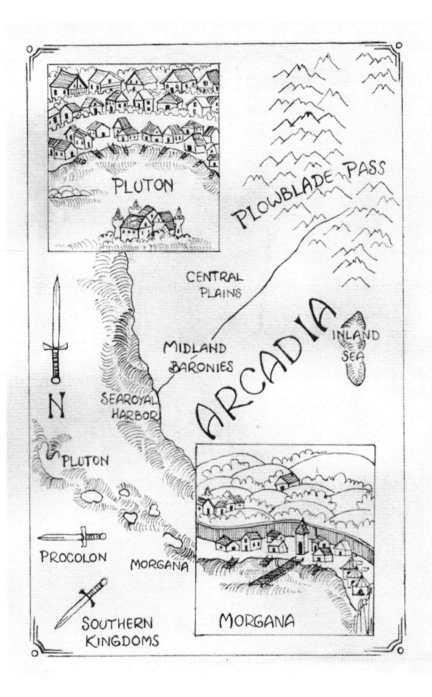

PLUTON

PLOWBLADE PASS

CENTRAL PLAINS

MIDLAND BARONIES

ARCADIA

INLAND SEA

N

SEAROYAL HARBOR

PLUTON

PROCOLON

MORGANA

SOUTHERN KINGDOMS

MORGANA

Part One

Puzzles for the Wordsmith

The Navigator's Cube

THE WHIRLING behind Jason intensified. On a puff of wind, the three masters were flung into the nearest of the open cubes, bouncing off the walls. Then strong gusts swept him from his feet His changer ripped from his belt with the slash of an airborne knife. With no way to control his motion, he jerked across the terrain, bobbing like a butterfly but heading unerringly for the box. With a mighty blow from the rear, he slammed into one side, head pointed towards the ground.

The cube was mounted on a platform with legs of unequal length so that they provided a level base on the slope. Jason grabbed at a bottom edge, trying to resist the blast of air pushing him towards the opening at the top, but the wind increased to a roaring gale. Churning dust mingled with the stink of the vapors, blinding his sight. He was stretched into a painful thin line, feet directly overhead. The muscles in his back knotted from the strain. He tightened his grip as best he could, but his fingers slid from the smooth surface of the cube like bark pulled from a tree.

In a rush, he was hurled high in the air over the top of the container. Then the gale slowed almost as abruptly as it had begun. He plunged back earthward into the gaping opening now beneath him.

The masters scrambled out of the way as he crashed into their midst, but he paid them little heed. He jumped and grabbed the upper edge of the box, swinging his leg in a wide arc, attempting to find some purchase so that he could climb back out. But the top was too high. He could not hook his foot over the edge. In final desperation, he chinned himself and stared at the navigator's smiling face.

"The cube is an excellent idea from the practitioners of your arts," the navigator said. "Of course, your magic no longer works, so my manipulants have had to build them based on the law I have moved into its place. The device is not quite the same. The walls are as thin and light as bread, rather than built of thick metal that cannot be moved. Each contraction is less, a few arm's length at most and not a reduction by a factor of two. But it is as secure as the original.

"In the end, the result will be the same. The cube compresses whatever is inside into a pulp that drains through a small hole in the bottom. A sip of your marrow will be my first taste of victory."

The navigator tilted his head back and laughed. With a flourish, he pointed to one of his manipulants, and the lid of the box rotated on its hinges. It slammed onto Jason's head and began to force him down into the inside.

Jason savored the last sights, whatever they were. The masters and men-at-arms who had followed him up the hill were all scattered in bloody disarray on the slope. Pillage continued in the royal tents. The navigator was now marching in triumph down the hillside. Manipulants slumped to one side of the cube, exhausted from the heat. The portal on the other side opened onto Ponzar's lithon, and heavy brown vapors spewed through and contaminated the air.

With a gasp, Jason released his grip and fell to the bottom of the cube. The lid slammed shut. In the sudden darkness, he felt the vibration that meant the start of the first contraction. This could not be his fate, he thought in disbelief. Not for a wordsmith who seldom ventured from the cozy comfort of his library. The trip to the island of Morgana was to have been no more than a chance to get past whatever was blocking his inspirations. And it all had started less than a year ago ...

Landfall

JASON'S PULSE quickened as he stepped from the creaking gangplank onto the firmness of the pier. Finally, he had arrived at Morgana, the island of sorcery. He was far from his comfortable nest with its comforting scrolls that stacked to the ceiling on almost every wall. But after a dozen days or more of contemplation, he had decided. He would do it. He was even more anxious now about having to experience the unfamiliar, but, back in his den, he had not been able to think of anything better to try.

As the other passengers disembarked from the skiff, Jason hesitated a moment longer. He drew his threadbare wordsmith's cloak tight against the onshore breeze. His hair was raven black, combed back straight above a square and unlined face. With sea green eyes, he scrutinized whatever he saw, seeming to bore beneath the surface to discover the secret of what lay within. He had the broad shoulders of a smith, but pale skin and smooth palms marked him as one who did not toil in the sun. Around his neck on a leather thong hung a smooth disk of gold, the features of the old king long since worn away.

At the end of the planking stood a brightly painted gatehouse guarded by two men-at-arms who collected a copper from each one who passed. On either side, all around the small harbor, rough beamed buildings crowded the shoreline and extended precariously over the water on makeshift piers. Warehouses and property barns, canvas mills and costume shops, tackle forges and mirror silveries, and all the services for both the sea and the inland mingled in disarray.

The land rose behind the harbor, first to a wide ledge and then into a jumble of vegetated hills and valleys that hid the lairs of the sorcerers.

Jason dug into his meager purse for a coin and joined the end of the orderly line paying the landing fee. "Which path to the hut of Farnel the Master?" he asked the guards as he dropped his copper into the pot.

"There are many trails up into the interior, and he is the one I must find."

The guard on the left shook out of his bored lethargy and scowled as if he were too important to be bothered. "All visitors are confined to the shorelands, lord and bondsman alike. Stay among the houses of the harbor or on the path that runs from the bazaar to the keep. The hills are for the masters and tyros only." He stared at Jason. "For your own protection, they are forbidden."

"Then how does one meet a master?" Jason asked. "How do I engage Farnel in conversation?"

The second guard looked up from his tally sheet and laughed. "To come eye to eye with a sorcerer other than in the presentation hall is not something that most would wish."

"Nevertheless, I must," Jason said.

"Then wait near the entrance to the presentation hall." The guard shrugged. "Wait in the hope that Farnel decides to come out of the hills this year and give a performance. He is less apt than most, but it would be your only chance with safety. Along the shore, all of the masters have sworn to cast their illusions from the stage and nowhere else."

Another skiff banged into the pier, and the guards' faces warped in annoyance. One returned his attention to completing the tally sheet and the other motioned Jason on through the gate.

Jason started to ask more but then thought better of it. He turned to follow the rest of his landing party through the gatehouse and onto the beach. In a slow moving queue, he crossed the narrow stretch of sand and climbed the wooden steps placed in the hillside. Several tedious minutes later, he reached the broad ledge, some ten times the height of a man above the level of the sea.

The native rock of the ledge was covered with a bed of crushed white stone that led away in two directions. To the south, the path angled around the bend of the island to where Jason knew stood the keep and presentation hall for the lords. To the north, the trail ended against a cliff of granite that thrust into the still waters of the bay.

On the beach to the immediate south stood the bondsman bazaar. Two wavy rows of tents stretched across the sand. Some were grandiose and gaudy with panels of bright colors supported by three or four poles, but others were no more than awnings covering rough podiums, counters, and simple frames. The path between the tents was deserted and the cries of the hawkers silent. Nightfall was still six hours away. In the distance, beyond the bazaar, the hazy outline of mainland Arcadia could just barely be seen.

8

After looking about for a moment to get their bearings, most of the landing party headed south, carrying goods and trinkets. A few soon disappeared into the paths leading upwards into the hills, chattering like small birds about last year's glamours and what had caught the fancy of the high prince. Jason though for a long while trying to decide which way to go, then finally started in the direction of the presentation hall, but with a much slower pace than those who preceded him.

The advice of the guard was not at all what he had wanted to hear. Waiting for Farnel would mean going deeper into the village and getting lodging beyond the bazaar. He could have to idle away the rest of the season, and the coin in his purse would not last that long. And worse, the master might not come down from the hills at all.

Convincing the sorcerer to accept him immediately had been what Jason had hoped to accomplish. As Farnel's tyro, he would study glamours and enchantments, rather than incantations, formulas, ritual, or flame. Then, when the instruction was complete, he would be able to enchant himself, enter that mystical state that led to the discovery of new charms, to rid himself of the inability to write that had lasted for almost an entire year.

If one wanted to study sorcery, then Morgana was where he should come. Nowhere else was the craft of illusion practiced so freely. Nowhere else could Jason receive so much instruction in so little time. And by looking through the popular broadsides as well as the arcane scrolls, he had deduced which master more than any other would need what he had to offer — if only he could get to Farnel before it was too late to prepare for this year's competition.

Jason stopped his slow pacing. The pathway was quiet. Those up ahead were not to be seen. The entire skiff load behind him had gone on to the bazaar. No one else was on the trail, and the flanks of the hills cut the gatehouse from his line of sight. To the left of where he had stopped was a path that wandered away from the bed of crushed stone up into the notch between two cliffs.

After a few more moments of thought, he took the first step. "I will just have to ignore the warnings," he said aloud to reassure himself. "The sooner I can see Master Farnel, the sooner I will know if he will agree or not."

Without looking back, Jason clambered up the path.

The Master's Hut

THE STUBBY shadows of midday grew into the slender spires of evening while Jason followed the random patchwork of paths through the hills. He encountered no one, and the signposts were few and well weathered. It took him many hours to find the one that pointed in the direction of Farnel's hut.

The sun slid toward the jagged horizon as Jason climbed the last few lengths to his goal. As he did, he became aware of angry voices from some point farther up the trail. His view in front was blocked by a boulder tumbled onto the path and resting in a litter of smaller stones and snapped branches. The scruffy underbrush on the hill face to the left bore a slashing vertical scar that marked the huge rock's passage. The rise on the right was not as steep, but the vegetation was sparser, with stunted trunks and tiny leaves growing from fissures in a monolithic slab of rock.

Cautiously, Jason approached the barrier and squeezed between the dislodged boulder and the adjacent hillside. Up the trail, a group of youths surrounded two older and taller men who alternately waved their arms and pounded their fists to emphasize the words they were hurling at each other.

The encircling band all wore simple robes a shade grayer than white, the mark of the tyro, and the two they surrounded were dressed in master's deeper charcoal. On one of the masters, the logo of the sorcerer's eye was old and faded. The other's emblem sparkled with embroidered gold. Behind them, all stood a small structure of planks haphazardly assembled together like a pile of windblown sticks. Thin sheets of mica filled lopsided window frames, and a curl of smoke snaked from the top of a mud-brick chimney on the side.

Farnel's hut, Jason thought, and the master is probably one of the two who are arguing in front. He had done far better than waiting at the hall. He crept closer to the edge of the boulder. As he did, the others did not spot him. They all were engrossed in the loud conversation.

The more plainly dressed master growled with a husky voice. His face was rough and wrinkled like crumpled paper. A fringe of white circled his bald crown. Age should have bent his back and stooped his shoulders, but he stood straight as a lance, refusing to yield as a matter of principle.

"Simple thrills and no more," he snorted. "Pockmarked monsters, low-cut necklines, spurting gore. Your productions are all alike, Gerilac. An instant of sudden shock and then they are done. Nothing of substance to add to the legacy of the craft."

"Like your renditions, I suppose," Gerilac answered. "With colors so mute that even the tyros fall asleep." He stroked his precisely trimmed goatee and smoothed his shoulder-length hair into place. On the mainland, he could have walked in the company of the lords and none would have noticed. "By the laws, Farnel, it is well that everyone pays your antiquated theories only polite notice. If all were to follow your lead, the rich purses from the mainland would have stopped coming long ago. No one chooses to pay a sorcerer who is a bore."

"But it is not art," Farnel shot back. "We do only cartoons of what was performed a decade ago. In another, stick figures jerking around the hall will capture the accolade."

"And how valuable is this art of yours?" Gerilac fingered Farnel's robe. "Sewing your own mends. Rationing your meals between payment for the private charms in the off-season and the charities of your peers. Compare that with the elegance of my chambers and the number of tyros at my disposal. I have won the supreme accolade for the last three years running, while you entered no productions at all. Is it because you choose not to compete, or perhaps because you cannot, even if you tried?"

"I was first among the masters of Morgana long before you earned your robe," Farnel growled. "If you doubt it, look me in the eye. I still can stand as well as you in the chanting well in any season."

Gerilac flung his arm across his face. "Strike out again, and Canthor and his men-at-arms will see that you spend more than a single night in the keep. You know the agreement among the masters. Lack of control is bad for the reputation of the island. And the traffic from the mainland that rides with it."

"Drop your arm, Gerilac. Another few nights on a cold slab just might be worth it."

Suddenly, one of the tyros cried out. "I see a shadow moving near the boulder. Come out and reveal yourself!"

Jason did not move.

"Come out or we will drag you out!"

Reluctantly, Jason stepped forward. He began to rub the coin around his neck. The plan was to speak to Farnel without a large audience, not like this.

The sorcerers stopped circling one another. All eyes turned to see who was among them. One of the tyros, older than the rest, tugged another on the sleeve. "Get Canthor," he said.

The second nodded, bolted from the circle, and in an instant disappeared around the next bend in the trail. Then the ring of light gray robes dissolved and regrouped in a line between Jason and the sorcerers.

"I am Erid, lead tyro of Master Gerilac," the one in the center pointed a thumb to his chest. "And my master does not take kindly to interruption." He leered a crooked smile. "For my own part, however, I welcome the opportunity —before the bailiff comes to snatch you away."

"My dealings are with Master Farnel," Jason labored to say. "A tyro will not do."

"You should have heeded the warnings and stayed within the confines of the harbor," Erid said. "Here in the hills, we practice glamours of our own choosing." His smile broadened like the rising sun. "Even if you have a taste for art, you might find the experience somewhat, shall we say, unsettling ..."

Laughter raced across the line, and menacing smiles settled on the tyros' faces. With explosive force, Jason's chest tightened within an unyielding vice. His heart raced. His gut began to churn.

"My intent is not to provoke," he said as firmly as he could. "I did not come to be the subject of your experimentation."

"Then your prowess is remarkable indeed," another of the tyros said. "Tell us how you plan not to look one of us in the eye or keep your ears always protected against a whisper."

"Enough. Leave him be," Farnel cut in. "You do your master no credit and waste what is most precious besides. Your talent should be channeled toward pleasing the moneyed lord, not baiting a bondsman who wanders away from the bazaar."

"I am no bondsman," Jason tried to take a deep breath but could not. His words had become forced. "My, my knowledge of the lore of Arcadia can be of great value to you, Master Farnel." He took another breath and then another. "Let me speak more of my merit. You will be convinced."

"I am the one you seek," Farnel said. "But I see not merit but folly in

12

whomever wanders here alone. It is true that all the masters of Morgana strive to dispel the reputation of fear that sorcery enjoys elsewhere. The livelihood of our small island depends upon it. The lords of the mainland would not come and pay good gold for our entertainments if there was a hint of greater risk involved.

"But our craft must be experimentally manipulated as well. Only near the harbor have we forsworn all glamours. Only in the presentation hall do we enchant with consent. Here in our private retreats, one must rely on the good judgment of whomever he encounters. The tyros cannot be kept under constant watch to ensure that they stay within the bounds of prudence."

"And your luck today was not the best." Farnel turned and cast a frown back at his peer. "You may be noted for your prizes, Gerilac, but your students set no high standards by their conduct."

"An easy thought for one who has no tyros of his own," Gerilac flicked some dust from the rich velvet of his robe. "Although with no accolades in a decade, not even a minor mark of merit, one can understand why there would be none to attend to you."

Farnel ignored Gerilac's reply and turned back to Jason. "Come, I will escort you to the harbor. It would not be well for you to be found by one of Canthor's patrols.

"I have a proposition for you," Jason persisted.

"Not now." Farnel waved down the path. "Let us get to the harbor without delay. Gerilac has babbled at me all afternoon, and I do not care to hear more of his plans to bedazzle the high prince."

"Discussion of the relative value of your skills and mine brings you discomfort, does it not?" Gerilac said.' "Go ahead. Take advantage of your excuse while you have it. Further talk will not change your worth in the eyes of the other masters."

Farnel's face clouded like an approaching storm. He whipped back to stare at Gerilac without saying a word. Again, Gerilac flung his arm across his face. Then, after a moment, he lowered it to return the stare. Like gladiators in an arena, the two sorcerers closed upon each other, the first words of enchantment rumbling from their lips.

As the masters engaged, the tyros exchanging hurried glances. "This one talks of dealing only with a master, but now we will see how well he likes the skill of a tyro," Erid said.

Farnel and Gerilac circled one another, arms across their eyes and shouting to drown out each other's charm. Jason took a half step backward.

The tyros rushed forth. The alternatives flashed in Jason's mind: something from the scrolls of manual combat in his library, run back the way he had come, throw a fuselage of rocks, ...

Before he could act, the tyros crashed into him and hurled him to the ground. One stone scraped against Jason's cheek; another scratched a ragged line along his bare arm. With a jarring thud, his head cracked against the large boulder that blocked the path. In a fog, he slammed his hands against his ears.

"And now the enchantment," Erid panted. "Perhaps one that will engender a little more respect."

Jason tried to shake his head clear, but the other tyros held it firm, ripping his protecting hands away. "As for the fee," Erid pointed at Jason's chest. "This bauble of gold will do."

Jason struggled to free himself. His senses reeled. Erid's image danced in duplicate. "Seize the coin at your peril," he managed to gasp. "For fifteen years have I carried it. Even though I would have to track you to the northern wastes, I will have it back."

Erid looked into Jason's eyes and hesitated. The fire that suddenly smoldered there was not to be dismissed lightly. "Perhaps not worth the trouble of taking," he mumbled. "But if it carries with it the memories of when you were a boy, it will make the enchantment all the easier. Think of the coin, hapless one, while you look into my face."

Jason slammed shut his eyes, but the tyros forced them back open. Unable to avoid Erid's stare, he heard the beginnings of the sonorous chant that dulled his consciousness.

He tried to defocus Erid's face into the blur of sky behind, but his thoughts became sluggish and like massive oxen lumbered away on their own. The tyro's eyes loomed larger and larger until they blotted out everything behind, finally engulfing Jason's will and swallowing it whole. He felt the events of the morning wash into indistinct nothingness and then the day and the week before. With accelerating quickness, all his travels folded and tucked into small compartments of his mind that he could no longer reach. He was a youth of twenty, fifteen, and then ten.

Jason felt the constraints that held him fall away, and he took a step forward. The hillside shimmered and was gone ...

He found himself in a dimly lit hovel, still hot from the blazing sun and choking in slowly settling dust. He heard a weak cough from the cot and saw the strained look on his mother's face as she gently placed her palm on his sister's forehead.

Hesitantly, he offered the coin in his hand back to his father. "But this

14

brandel will pay for the alchemist's potion," Jason heard himself say. "It will make her well. I can take the examination next month or even next year if need be."

"The next month or the next year we will still be here, Jason." His father waved an arm around the small room. "And no more sure of a coin of gold then than now. Take the payment for the testing. Even master Milton says you have a head for it. He remembers no one else in the village with your sharpness."

The old man's eyes widened and he looked off in the distance. "An apprentice thaumaturge. It is the first step to becoming a master. And then, after Milton passes on, you will be the one who nurtures the crops for Lord Kenton and ensures his harvest. You will sit in honor at his table. And when you wear that robe, this will be but a memory for us all. There will be purses full of coins, why, even tokens from the islands! Jason, your sister wishes it as fervently as I."

Jason looked to the cot and grimaced. His sister did not care about apprenticeships and fees of the master. She was too young to know. All she wanted was to get well, to play tag again, or to ride on his back and laugh. He was taking away the one sure chance she had for a cure, leaving her and gambling that the fever might break on its own accord. Was a robe of brown worth so much that the choice was as easy as his father made it?

"Go, Jason, his father said. "Milton gathers the applicants in the square before the sun passes its zenith. Being late is not an auspicious beginning."

Jason felt the upwelling doubt. But looking in his father's eyes, he could not find the courage to speak again. He clutched the coin, nodded, and turned for the door.

Then the imagery of the glamour blurred. Days passed in a heartbeat. No sooner had he left the hut than he seemed to have returned. He was back outside his doorway, staring at the rough cloth that covered the entrance. How long he stood there, he could not recall. The sun had set, and even the lights in the other shacks were long since extinguished.

"Jason, is that you?" His father pushed aside the drapery and motioned him inside. "The four days of testing are done. You were to have returned by noon. Your mother could stand it no longer, and I was just going to look."

With reluctant steps, Jason entered the hut. A single candle cast dancing shadows on the rough walls. He saw the rumpled covers and the empty cot but felt no surprise. He had heard at noon after Milton had discharged him in the square. Shyly, he looked at his mother, kneading her hands in an endless pattern and staring into the darkness.

Jason's father followed his gaze and lowered his own eyes. "It was for the best," he said with gravel in his voice. "For the rest of us all, in the long run, it was for the best."

Jason opened his mouth to speak, but his throat was dry as old parchment. Numbly he followed the sweep of his father's hand to the small stool near the table.

"But do not dwell on that now," his father said. 'There will be time enough for tears. Tell us of your test. To which journeyman will you be assigned? Was it Aramac? They say he is the swiftest. Certainly, Milton would pair the best with the best."

Jason shook his head and unclenched his fist. He bit his lip as he looked down at the gold coin sparkling innocently in his palm. He saw his father's eyes widen in amazement and felt the beginnings of the sobs that would rack his body for hours to come ...

"Canthor. It is Canthor!"

The yell cut through Jason's spilled memories. The image of glinting mail and stern faces suddenly mixed with the receding dark shadows of his father's hut.

"To the keep. Take the intruder to the keep!" a voice bellowed above the rest.

Jason strained to separate the confusion, but he could not escape the charm. The last he remembered before collapsing into oblivion was choking the painful words to his father. "They collect no fee from those who fail."

The Proposition

THE FIRST rays of the rising sun slanted through the high window. Jason frowned and shielded his eyes. He rolled on his side and stretched awake. The thin layer of straw had done little to soften the hard stone floor, and it seemed each muscle in his back protested the movement.

Except for the one shaft of light, everything was in soft darkness. It took several minutes for him to see his surroundings. The room was shaped like a piece of pie with the central tip bitten off. The gently curved outer wall contained the only window. Descending sunlight illuminated dancing motes of dust and splashed on the rough flagstones of the floor that was held together by crumbling mortar. An iron grating prevented exit to a corridor to the interior. In the dark shadow beyond was the outline of a spiral staircase that led to other levels of the keep. Across the cell, hands resting on crossed legs, sat the master sorcerer, Farnel.

"Any enchantment broken in the middle can produce undesired effects," the sorcerer said. "Even one that tries to make you act as you once were. I decided to come and watch you through the night to see that you recovered well."

Jason shook his head to clear it of the cobwebs of memory. He rose to sitting and centered the coin on his chest. Grimly, he pushed the old images away, back to where they had been hidden. He turned his attention to Farnel, who was patiently watching him like a mother awaiting the arousal of her youngest child.

With a final deep sigh, Jason focused his thoughts on the present and what he wished to do. He pushed away a last minute hesitation. "Perhaps it is just as well that events transpired as they did. Your attention is what I sought, and now it looks as if I might have it."

"Do not bore me with your proposition, whatever it is," Farnel raised his hand. "I am satisfied with my surroundings. I do not care for some reckless adventure for a lord from across the sea, regardless of the number of tokens dangled my way."

"Yet you have not won any prize in the competition for a decade, nor even bothered to enter in the last three."

"A worthless exercise," Farnel snorted. "A mere shadow of what it once meant. Before the high prince assumed his regency, the supreme accolade and the rest of the prizes were decided on merit, artistic merit. The old king may have ruled with too light a hand, but he could distinguish between a vision of true depth and a shallow thrill."

"The high prince is not the only judge. Don't all the master sorcerers vote on the compositions of their peers as well?"

"Swayed by the easy coin, everyone," Farnel dismissed the words. "Once the visits of twenty lords were enough. They appreciated the images that we placed in their minds and paid fairly for the entertainments we gave them. It was not much, but we lived in adequate style."

Farnel rose to his feet and began to pace about the cell as if he were the prisoner rather than Jason. "But then, on some idle thought, the high prince and his followers came one year to see what transpired in this corner of the kingdom. In one visit, They left more gold than we received from the rest of the year combined. And with his bulging purse, he placed in our heads images as sharp as any of us could have formed with our craft: robes of smooth linen, soft beds, not one tyro, but a dozen.

"Now none has the strength to vote his conscience. They all fear what would happen if this one small group were displeasured. The lesser lords, the bondsmen who accompany them, the principles of artistic composition — they do not matter as long as the high prince continues to add hundreds of tokens to the prize sack for the supreme accolade."

Jason nodded and chose his next words carefully. "The works of Farnel have remained cast in the traditional forms; this is well known. But is it because of this that they are now held in low esteem?"

Farnel scowled at Jason. "You have received an ample portion of my good nature. Do not presume it gives you license to judge."

"But I do know something of the artistic images you make with your craft. *The Antique Pastoral, Calm Sea in Winter, Mountain Sunlight,* and many more. My library is quite complete. There are few scrolls which record your feats that I do not have a copy."

"My works of a decade ago!" Farnel stared at Jason as if he saw a long-lost relative returning from the dead. "I see you have not sought me out unprepared."

The sorcerer closed his eyes and ran his tongue across his lips, savoring the memories. For a moment, there was silence, but then Farnel snapped back. "But they won no prizes. The drift to shallow forms and empty expression had already begun."

"I know also of what the others said of your works," Jason rushed on. He had to be convincing. There may not be another chance. "Bold in principle and mood, but flawed in historical or geographic fact. Incorrect costuming of the period, a jutting sandbar in the wrong place, reflections from an impossible direction."

"Excuses, all of them. The works of Gerilac were the new sensation in the eyes of the prince."

"But had yours not been built on error, what then?" Jason persisted. "Without the nagging irritants, how might the artistic education of the high prince have proceeded? And who now might also wear a robe of velvet?"

"Your tongue is glib. I grant you that, but the sand has already run through the glass. What is done is done. It is a matter of style, and our craft suffers because of it." Farnel paused. "But I wonder. You show passion in all of this. What does the doddering of an old sorcerer matter to you?"

"I am a wordsmith," Jason held his hand to his chest." I have earned my bread by creating new scrolls, not ones of fact but of fancies instead. Similar to what you do here on Morgana. The lords are entertained by having my creations read to them."

"Hmmm, that sounds most inefficient. With a single enchantment, we can put images in the minds of many all at once. Surely, copying scrolls over and over must be a drudgery that consumes much of your time."

"No, that is not my problem," Jason shook his head. "When I finish a new scroll, I pass it to a nearby thaumaturge. With his craft, he connects a hundred or more quill pens to act as one. Then by tracing what I have put onto the original, my words are transcribed to the others and then they are offered for sale. We share in the profits that ensue."

"That does not explain your interest in dealing with me," Farnel said.

"To create new scrolls over and over again, I have assembled a large library. From it, I get the seeds from which my own scribing grows."

It was embarrassing, but he had to continue. "That is to say, up until last year that is what I did. It was all very comforting, really. Snug in by own den by a warming fire, I would think and write, spinning tales that others found to be amusing. I was content. I needed nothing more. I had no desire to venture out into the far reaches of the world and engage in some great quest worthy of the sagas.

"Like most other wordsmiths, I worked with a routine. Breakfast, then settling down at my writing desk, sharpening my quills and dipping one into the inkwell, I waited for the thoughts to come. If they did not immediately, I would distract myself with something else for a while, solving a puzzle mentioned in one of my scrolls, and then return to scribing.

"But about a year ago, the coming of new seeds slowed to a trickle. Ones that did proved to be barren. The wait for the ideas lengthened. My distractions became longer and longer. I began to spend more and more time scouring my scrolls seeking more brain teasers to solve, and then, even more hours working on their solutions."

"I would imagine," Farnel stroked his chin, "that the number of such trinkets to be small."

"There are more than one might think. The alchemist transporting a imp, flask of acid and bag of silver coins across a river, the wizard covering a square box of nine dots with four straight lines as part of a ritual, five magicians dividing a chest of gold coins —"

"And the distractions began to fill your day more and more. You could not stop wasting time solving puzzles and concentrate instead on your livelihood."

"Yes!" Jason exclaimed. "Exactly! How did you guess?"

"Part of the art of sorcery is listening carefully to others," Farnel shrugged. "Inferring their inner makeup makes the casting of charms much more effective."

"Things have continued to the point that my flow of ideas has completely stopped," Jason lowered his head, too embarrassed to look directly at the master. "No new tale have I passed to the thaumaturge in over a year! My purse is almost empty. Soon I will be reduced to begging in the street to perform simple scribing in exchange for food."

Like a great weight, Jason's words pushed down on his shoulders. Saying more was hard. "I do not know what to do, how to restore things to the way they once were. Despite having to confront the new, I decided that I must make the trip. You are my last chance."

"I do not see how my craft would help," Farnel spoke like a judge rendering his final verdict.

"The ideas that you sorcerers use for your presentations must come from somewhere. I have read in one of my scrolls that there is a charm that you sometimes use on yourselves — to discover what you could not just by labored thinking alone."

"Yes, there are such spells," Farnel conceded. "One opens our minds to discover new charms that are hitherto unknown. Another is used by many here on Morgana to get the inspiration for new presentations. I myself have never felt the need for such a crutch."

"The themes of your presentations are second to none, Master Farnel. It is in the execution details where you falter."

Farnel frowned, and Jason rushed to continue. "In the course of assembling my library, I have learned many things that can serve you well. For example, two centuries ago, the capes of the lords hung just to their waists, and their faces were clean-shaven. The high tide covers the sandbar in the Bay of Cloves. In the morning, when one is looking down into the valley beyond Plowblade Pass, the shadows are on the left."

Farnel looked at Jason in silence for a long while. He ran his hand over the back of his neck but said nothing.

"Knowledge," Jason broke the quiet. "Knowledge to remove the inconsistencies from your works, the imperfections that seem to bother the other masters so. All that I have learned I will share if you take me as your tyro and teach me the one charm so that I can enchant myself."

"I can perform such an enchantment on you a single time now. Perhaps it will give you the next seed for you to grow."

"No, not *one* time!" Jason cried. "I need something that I can use whenever I have the need after I return home. I want the ability to cast the spell myself. Just the one spell. That is all that I ask."

"It is not as simple as that." Farnel laughed. "Charms are not in a catalogue from which you merely select which to use. You must learn the fundamentals first. Perform the more simple glamours and cantrips. Gradually build up to be able to do what you ask."

"Yes, I expected as much," Jason said, "How long —"

Jason started to say more, but the jangle of a key in the lock distracted his attention.

"Canthor, you come half a day early," the master rose to his feet. "I thought the penalty for wandering in the hills ran at least from sun to sun."

Jason slowed the rush of his thoughts as the figure swung open the grating. The bailiff wore leggings and a sleeveless tunic. The skin of his arms was smooth and taut. Short bristles of hair, struggling back from a daily shaving, covered a shiny head. Only his face showed any aging. His eyes swam in a sea of wrinkles from a perpetual squint.

"The crude pranks of Gerilac's tyros are punishment for any man." Canthor chuckled. "I dare wager that this lad will no longer take our

21

warnings so lightly. No, now is the time to depart. Before Erid and the others think of coming here and sneaking in more practice."

He waved Jason to the corridor with one hand and grabbed Farnel by the arm with the other. "And as for you, my unbending friend, far less bother for me if the masters set decent examples for the tyros to follow. Gerilac told me of what you were attempting when I was summoned."

Farnel shrugged. "If what he built had some merit, it would not matter."

"A soldier is measured by his most recent battle," Canthor said, "no matter how glorious were the ones that came before. If you wish to challenge Gerilac's ascendancy, it must be in the presentation hall, not with hot words shouted outside its walls."

"Sage advice from one who has not raised a sword in true anger in many a year!" Farnel snorted back. "If that is so, why are you here instead of taking a side in the growing unrest in the northern plateau of the mainland? The high prince has need of men at arms."

"The difference is that I am at peace with my lot," Canthor replied. "As long as there is sufficient bread on my table and pulling masters apart does not occur too often, I do not care what the others may say behind my back."

Farnel frowned and began to pace again. "It is too late in the season," he muttered, "and for too long have I not dabbled with the themes and forms."

"Spend time in the bazaar," Canthor said. "Listen to the bondsmen prattle about their lords' latest fancies. You know that pandering to the popular tastes is how Gerilac achieves his successes. You could learn in a few nights what he guesses at for the entire year."

"Yes, yes, I have pondered that idea often enough myself. But masters do not thread their way among the hawkers and imitation delights. That is a job for a tyro, and there is none who would care to accept my tutorage."

The master stopped, and his eyes narrowed in thought. He looked at Jason. "I suppose an alchemist would say that some of the random factors have aligned".

"Very well." Farnel continued. "As Canthor says, it would be better than mouthing more words of protest that the others pay little attention to. I accept your proposition. I will begin your instruction, as you desire. In exchange, you will spend part of each day in the bazaar. Use the skills of your craft to befriend the bondsmen and learn the latest gossips of the mainland. We will work together for a presentation to the high prince."

"But the bazaar would be something unfamiliar and new," Jason said. "I was thinking instead to provide you knowledge from my library."

"Canthor has made it quite clear," Farnel shook his head. "It is the current gossip of the streets that I need to know, not dull facts from dusty scrolls."

"Visiting a strange bazaar was not part of my original thinking," Jason protested. "It was to learn from you in the confines of your hut. Enclosed dwellings, or wide open unpopulated expanses — they give me no pause. But unfamiliar public places — places with all the *people*, all the — all the *noise* ..."

"So, you are saying — what?" Farnel asked.

Jason did not immediately reply. He folded his arms across his chest and closed his eyes.

"Well?" Farnel insisted after nothing more happened for almost a minute.

Another minute passed, and finally, Jason reopened his eyes and took a deep breath. "I have decided. There still is no other choice. I must be able to resume my craft."

Farnel glowered, his patience wearing thin at the indirect answers.

"I did manage to survive the hardships of the journey here," Jason said. "And I had no discomfort with the bazaar near my own den once I learned enough about all of its nooks and crannies — where the crowds usually were and where there were not. I suppose that a market here is much the same as everywhere else."

He took a second breath and then spoke with more conviction. "I understand and accept that I will have to learn basics first. How long will the entire process take?"

Farnel placed a hand on Jason's shoulder. "The agreement is that I will teach. I can promise no more. It is up to you to marshal the talents that are needed."

Practice by Rote

JASON SLUMPED down on the stool in Farnel's hut. The last few months had been a blur. Almost like a magician's automaton, he had worked from sunrise far into the night, following Farnel's instruction, gathering information in the bazaar, and helping to prepare their audition.

It had not been as bad as he had first thought. By visiting the bazaar at dusk when others were still few, he could concentrate on the surroundings rather than be overwhelmed by the crowds. At first, he could only manage to venture to the tents closest to the harbor, but then with each trip, he was able to explore farther and farther along the road that led to the presentation hall and the keep. Tired, yet at the same time mentally exhilarated, things were working out. He was on the path of ridding himself of his accursed inability to write.

"A battle scene." Farnel shook his head as he jotted a final note and tore the full sheet from the easel. "Who would have thought that I would dabble in something so explicit and mundane?"

"But the whispers in the bazaar point consistently and clearly," Jason said. "Once you piece them all together, a pattern emerges. The high prince is troubled about the unrest in the Wheatlands, and the crushing of the rebellion at Plowblade Pass three generations ago would be an excellent salve."

He scooped up the outline as it fluttered to the floor and pinned it in line with the others already filling the walls In Farnel's small hut. A bed of straw, hearth of smoke-blackened brick, and bowl-cluttered table were at the far end. The coarse blankets under which Jason slept on the floor were pushed into a corner like discarded rags. On the longest wall, thin planking supported by tiers of stone sagged under the weight of bound parchment and furled scrolls. The rest of the space was a jumble of wadded paper and stacks of properties used in illusion making: model dragons, silks and furs, cameos of billowing clouds and stormy seas, glass trinkets, and sun-bleached bones.

"Yes, yes, I understand." Farnel slid from his high stool and stepped over the pile of swords, axes, helmets, and other weapons lent by Canthor to aid in the suggestions. "Your sojourns to the bazaar indeed provided the focus for the path we should take. And your knowledge of the historical event has been impressive. The agony of the commander before ordering his followers to their death gives me sufficient scope to project something of a deeper meaning.

"I wonder, though," he continued, "with all of this scribing, perhaps your mental block has been removed. Surely, you have had to exercise your wordsmith skills to construct the battle to such detail."

"The details are nothing new," Jason shook his head. "They were extracted from a fancy I created some years ago — but they will seem fresh to the high prince when presented as an enchantment."

"Still, I am uneasy," Farnel said. "We started so very late compared with the others. They have had time to polish their offerings to a high luster while we are not quite done with a complete structure from end to end. Had we been, I would have shown a rough outline to the other masters in the hall this evening. Already they are deciding which to reject and which to keep for presentation to the prince. And when he comes, there will be little time left for more auditions. He is here for a week only. If one is not ready for him, there is no point in continuing further."

The master scratched the back of his neck. "Yet, there are signs of hope. Even Gerilac must have some concern that I am competing again. He was almost civil as he sat next to me at the council meeting when we had our morning meal."

"Perhaps he begins to wonder what profit comes from my travels," Jason said. "I have noticed Erid and the others following me from time to time. But it will do them little good. Tonight will be the last. I have only one more tent to visit, that of a trader named Drandor, at the end of the row."

Jason wrinkled his brow. "He is a rather peculiar sort, to hear the others talk, not connected in any way with the affairs of the prince. But everyone also says the visit is worth it — just to get a look at his assistant, if nothing else."

"I admit the value of your trips," Farnel replied, "but sometimes I wonder if so many have been necessary to achieve the same result. Ordinarily, a tyro's afternoon is spent practicing the charms his master has taught him during the morning"

"I *have* been studying," Jason protested. "Everything you have explained to me I have committed to memory. But first, I intend to honor my part of our bargain as faithfully as you have honored yours. Rote and repetition can come later when there is more time. For now, I should be expanding the outline into more detail and help select the charmlets that will be used. Then we would feel more confident about the final impact that the presentation will have."

"Why, most of this outline is already explicit enough." Farnel frowned and looked at the jottings covering the walls. "The basic idea is not to use a fine brush when a mop will do. The sorcerer should only suggest. The viewer will fill in a much more vivid scene with his own imagination."

"But why risk the random thoughts that might come into their minds when you can direct the precise image with certainty?"

"You already know enough to answer that. What is the basic law of sorcery?"

"The Rule of Three," or 'thrice repeated, once fulfilled.' Each charm must be spoken in its entirety three times without the slightest error, or it will come to nothing."

"And the more detailed the illusion?"

"The longer and more difficult the glamour." Jason paused for a few moments. "Ah, yes, I understand what you are saying. In Procolon across the sea, where sorcery is a sinister weapon of state, the length of the charm does not matter. But in a presentation hall, under the lightest of glamours, the words must be swift, or else the lords will hoot and ask for the next production."

"It works for the benefit of the master as well." Farnel began to scrutinize the last sheet of the outline, cramming cryptic notes into the margins of what was already there. "Each charm robs something of the life force of the sorcerer; there is only so much power within him. And the simpler he can make his glamours, the longer will he prosper. Why, it is for that very reason that the sorcerers of Arcadia forswore the deeper cantrips ages ago and retired to Morgana to deal in nothing more than simple pleasures.

"But enough of that. I want to run through the broad outlines before we go. There will be sufficient time to select the details, once we have been chosen for the final program."

The sorcerer turned to the first sheet and studied its contents. "Let me see, the high cliff walls that define the pass, the hint of a storm in the morning, and the last meal in the camps. Perhaps Alaraic's *Foreboding*, followed by Magneton's *Walls of Closure* and then *Aroma of the*

Hunters. Yes, they should be sufficiently close."

"Would not *Dark Clouds* and Clinton's *Granite Spires* be more to the point?" Jason asked.

Farnel cast Jason an appraising glance. "You learn fast, tyro, but in this case, that combination will not work. Dark Clouds finishes on too low a syllable to connect onto the Clinton charmlet smoothly. I am a practiced master, but even I would not risk mouthing such a transition."

"A small *Hint of Curiosity*, then *Around the Roses*, and finally *The Unexpected Garden* sandwiched between the two will line them up perfectly."

"Hmmm, yes, perhaps you might be right," Farnel said after a moment's thought. "How did you come up with that possibility?"

"Well, I have not been able to stop thinking about puzzles completely. I saw an analogy between connecting necessary charmlets with a word ladder and was able to come up with a solution. You see, each charmlets can be represented as a series of distinct spoken tones, and if one —"

"Never mind about that. A master sorcerer is known by the charms he speaks, Jason, no matter how well he can shuffle things around in his head. Believe me, the first time you misspeak, and the spell goes awry, the sickness that follows will make you wish you had doubled your practice."

"But the rote is so boring. It is just a matter of putting in the effort to do it."

"Exactly so. There is more to success than making a fuzzy plan that leads in the general direction of the goal. At some point, each step must be executed to the finest detail."

Jason frowned. He did not like the way the conversation was going. Soon Farnel would be insisting he pass up exploring the last tent and spend the evening running through simple recitals. And surely, he could do that easily enough. The time would be wasted.

"The sun is setting," he said, "and it might be better if I visit this Drandor soon before the bazaar gets too crowded. The traders are more willing to talk if their tents are not filled with customers."

Farnel looked outside at the growing dimness and then back at Jason. "In sorcery, a master can only suggest. It is the tyro who ultimately must force himself to attempt the tests. Yes, yes, go on. I see in your eyes how much you want to investigate some more. I will dabble with what we have and perhaps even be ready for a first trial when you return."

The Trader's Tent

JASON STEPPED onto the bazaar pathway and avoided the few others that were already there. He had walked the distance from the hills to the shoreline in under an hour. He felt relief to be away from Farnel's hut and the sorcerer's all-too-accurate observations. To Jason's left, a hawker in a tunic of gaudy red and green touted sketches that leapt from their canvases. On the right, the moan of a faraway whistle promised to conjure up rare creatures of legend. Down the path were the other displays: multifaceted mirrors, rotating checkered boards, and vaults of total darkness where one would seal his ears with wax and dip his hands in a numbing salve before entering.

Besides the usual taverns and stalls, after dark the bazaar would be crammed with peddlers of cheap illusions. They had nothing to do with real sorcery. That was banned in the harbor area by decree of the masters. But with their lords traipsing off to the presentation hall to fill their minds with the artfully constructed images, the bondsmen hungered for a taste of the same thrills. They paid their coppers for the risqué sketches, the touch in darkness of the slimy tentacle, and the dizzy heads from spinning in the small cages hung from a rope.

Jason meandered down the pathway, and finally, he reached the end of the row where stood a medium-sized tent, set apart from the rest. This was Drandor's, the last to check. The pavilion was constructed from three smaller ones, inexpertly sewn together, with excess fabric hanging in disarray where they joined. The colors had long since faded. No pennants flew from the pole tops, nor did any peddler challenge the passerby to come inside. It was like what a lord's child would have constructed for play in the courtyard of a keep.

Jason ducked to enter the low opening. It was dark inside, illuminated only by two small candles, their flames unprotected by any sort of bowl.

"What do you sell?" Jason asked, as the slight figure behind the high counter began to take on detail. "Your brothers in the other tents are much more boastful of their wares."

"Exercises for the mind," a melodious voice responded. "Journey with these and you can create illusions of your own making."

Jason adjusted to the flickering light. A young woman with curls of golden hair that cascaded about her shoulders like eddies from a waterfall stood behind a counter in front of him. Her features were drawn with the deftness of a sculptor. If not for the tension in her face that pulled the skin tight and wrinkled the corners of her eyes, she would have been judged most fair. From a loop around her neck fell a free-flowing gown that sparkled in a subtle iridescence. On her left arm wound a thin band of dull iron, the emblem of an indentured servant.

The counter in front of her supported a scatter of small works of metal, twinkling in the candlelight, webs of intertwined wires and burnished flatwares intricately pieced together.

"Your tent has been placed in the wrong position." Jason appraised the woman's beauty. "The more traditional entertainments are closer to the entrance by the harbor."

"It is as I have told you," she responded after a quick look over her shoulder to the curtain that partitioned the tent. "Entertainments for the mind. Please, buy one. It will help me a great deal."

Again, Jason marveled at the voice, tinkling softly like a chime in a light wind. "My name is Jason," he said without thinking. "What is yours?"

"Delia," she replied. "But that is unimportant. Please examine what I have to offer."

Jason studied the contents of the countertop and grabbed at the tangle of wire that was closest. "Ah, you mean puzzles," he said with sudden pleasure as he recognized the objects. "I am afraid you will find that few of the pages and runners will care for such things. However, with me, you are in luck. I have studied such baubles for — for much too long. Unfortunately, I seem to have some knack with them, and I am drawn to their challenges. Watch how swiftly this one can be undone."

Jason closed his eyes for an instant to recall the sequence of moves he had deduced from examining the diagrams in his library. He grunted in satisfaction that the memory was still there. Then he deftly whirled the wires through a blurring pattern and, with a dramatic flourish, dropped the puzzle onto the counter. The wires tingled dully but remained in a tangle.

"Let me see that again," he said in disbelief. "I must have made a wrong move. It has been some time since I worked this one in particular." Jason picked up the puzzle and scrutinized the bends and runs. "Yes, there is a difference here. The outer loop on the larger wire whirls to the left rather than to the right. That means …"

His voice trailed off as he shut his eyes and ran through the sequences again. "Very clever," he opened them again with a grin. "It makes the ending the mirror image of what one would expect."

With a rush slightly slower than the first time, he completed the altered moves and tossed the decoupled pieces back onto the counter. "Most unusual. Do you have any more like that? I thought I understood all there was to be found in Arcadia."

"Have him pay or make room for the next." A deep voice sounded from behind the partition. "Your job, girl, is to sell the merchandise, not bat eyelashes at the patrons. Melibar wants a filled purse in a fortnight. No less will do."

The curtain swept aside and a short, dark-haired man entered to stand beside Delia. His large head was in grotesque proportion to a diminutive frame. One eye seemed swollen shut from a wart that covered most of a jowl and sprouted three coarse black hairs as thick as nails. The upper lip pulled up in a wide grin revealing yellow-stained teeth and whitish gums.

He grasped Delia's bare arm in a vise-like grip. Although the flesh paled from the pressure, she bit her lip and did not speak.

"This evening we must do better, Delia. On the other islands, they were poor and a token was hard to pry loose. But here, we have the jangle of copper and silver from the mainland. Why even this gentleman displays a coin of gold about his neck. Tonight there will be no excuse. Fill the purse as you have been directed or else you will learn more of my pastimes in the room behind."

Jason contemplated Delia's frozen expression, wondering if he should do something. On one hand, it was none of his business. On the other, he did not like this Drandor's menacing hints at all. Perhaps he should just get up and walk out. Perhaps he should … No, this just was not right! He made his decision and wrestled with his near-empty pouch to produce a coin.

"Here, let her go," he said. "She has served her purpose well. It is because of her that I buy one of these trinkets. From you, there would have been no sale."

"I am Drandor, the trader," the small man stretched his smile even further as he released his grip. "And I see you are a gentleman of discerning taste. Perhaps some other item from far away would pique

30

your interest as well."

He swept his arm in a large arc while making a bow. "Here in the back are the better items that cannot be bartered for less than true gold or tokens of the islands."

Jason watched Delia rub her arm, her lips still set firm. "You have no cause," he said. "It is not her fault that your tent is not abuzz with gawkers like the others. Raise up a flap or two. Add some light and sound."

"My partner, Melibar, wants buyers, not ones who only look and then go their way. And do not waste any thoughts on the girl. She is not a bondsman with rights and privileges, but fully indentured, no different from a lute, a painted vase, or any other item I have to sell. I can do with her what I will."

Drandor followed Jason's eyes back to Delia and grunted. "Unless, of course, the gentleman is sufficiently smitten to bargain for her as well. Although I warn you, the price will be dear. She cost no less than fifteen tokens in the exchanges at Pluton. And it would take much more to compensate for my lost pleasures if she were to go."

Delia reached out her hand and placed it on Jason's, which was resting on the counter, her eyes opening wide in sudden expectancy. He peered into their deepness and sucked in his breath. Only with a determined effort was he able to will his faltering attention back to Drandor. "You mentioned items from faraway lands. Perhaps there will be something more to my liking."

Drandor grunted and pulled aside the curtain. Jason hesitated, but finally, his curiosity became too intense. What was behind there anyway? He rounded the counter and stepped cautiously into the rear portion of the tent. Bolts of cloth, stacked precariously, towered on one side of the entrance. Cases of spices, their aromas competing for attention, framed the other. Huge bottles filled with dense green swamp gas lined the far wall in front of another flap that must lead to a final compartment beyond.

A small furnace with coals still smoldering stood beneath a large wooden frame, from which hung a collection of shackles, spikes, and chains, pokers, and tongs, their tips, thrust into the cooling sand, still glowed a dull cherry-red. Scattered about were sketches of terrified women straining against their bonds to avoid the touch of searing iron. One drawing was draped over the body of a small rodent, its limbs bound to a small wooden frame by tightly turned loops of thin wire and its crushed skull lying in a pool of blood.

31

Near the center of the tent, stringed instruments and long, hollow reeds lay in a jumble on top of a pile of small drums, their heads pulled tight by tiny weights spaced around their rims. A long roll of parchment, almost gauze-like in transparency lay on the floor. From a cage in a far corner cloaked in shadow came a canine growl, followed by another deeper than the first. Instinctively, Jason froze and held his breath. He had encountered large mastiffs before, but somehow these guttural rolls touched a primitive nerve. It had been a warning, and he knew he would not be given another.

"Not now, my pretty," Drandor said. "This is for business." A single paw thudded against the framework in defiant protest, and then there was silence. Jason let out his breath. He peered into the pen, trying to see what could shake a crate so large and stoutly built, but except for two burning eyes, there was only blackness. He smoothed the short hairs on the back of his neck and glanced over the other stacks and containers.

"And what is that?" Jason pointed at two lattices to his left, one flat on the floor and the other a waist-high scaffold of thin struts all at right angles outlining what appeared to be a three-dimensional array of randomly stacked and touching cubes.

At each vertex, a small sphere adorned with three patches of color encompassed the six struts that met there. Although each color repeated many times throughout the lattice, the combination at each vertex was unique. On both of the lattices, a small braided loop of gold entwined one vertex in particular.

Jason reached to touch one of the curious structures, but a high-pitched voice cut him short. "Property of my master, property of Melibar," it said. "I am a guardian, and you must not touch."

Jason glanced upward. The light from one of the lamps was not produced by a flame, but by the incandescence of a tiny imp, flittering brightly in a glass prison. Like a newborn baby, its skin was soft and unwrinkled. Gossamer wings buzzed behind dangling delicate limbs.

"An imp in a bottle," Jason wondered aloud. "Why, after the archimage battled the demon prince years ago, I thought all wizards abandoned such indiscretions. You deal in marvels indeed."

"Like the lattices, there are a few items not for sale," Drandor glanced at the flap leading to the third compartment and then spoke as if he were on a stage, enunciating each word so that everyone listening could hear. "They are the private property of my partner. He stores them here while — while he rests. The pet is a gift from him to me."

Drandor watched the tent flap, apparently awaiting a reaction. The

32

canvas rippled slightly and a wave of cold air rolled underneath the gap above the floor rugs like a sluggish wave, but nothing else happened. The trader let out his breath and turned his attention back to Jason. "But no matter. What else, what else?" he suggested. "State your pleasure. I can satisfy a prince with what I have in stock today."

Jason watched the flap a while longer as the cold coiled about his ankles, but the canvas hung straight. Except for the gentle breathing of the mastiffs, there was no more sound. With a shrug, he turned back to what had originally attracted his interest. "I have only copper," he said as he studied first the imp and then the lattice underneath. "The gold around my neck I will not part with for any of this."

"Only copper!" Drandor exclaimed. "Copper and no gold! I am to show these choice wares only to those willing to pay, and in a discreet manner besides. Melibar wills it so. Take your imposturing to another tent, where they are more gullible and less prudent with their precious time."

Drandor grabbed Jason by the arm, but he shrugged the trader off. "A moment, just a moment more. There is a puzzle here. What do the vertices represent? What do the colors indicate?"

"Be gone, I say." Drandor reached for Jason a second time but then stopped, as a blast of trumpets suddenly pierced the air.

"The high prince." A muted cry soaked through the heavy canvas of the tent. "The high prince. He disembarks in an hour. Bondsmen of the prince and his retinue, attend unto your lords."

Farnel and his sorceries popped back into Jason's mind, and he knew that time enough had been spent at the bazaar. Puzzles were not why he had come to Morgana. He wanted to break his fascination with them, not be drawn in deeper. Despite a sudden reluctance, he must go back to Farnel's hut. There would be little time left now in which to prepare. He looked at Drandor's scowl and again at the cage in the corner. Intriguing, but nothing to aid Farnel in his preparations. With an irritated wave, he indicated that he was going.

"I will return, Drandor," he surprised himself calling out as he passed through the front tent. He cast one glance back at Delia, standing like a statue behind the counter. "There are things here that interests me. Yes, things that I would like to know much better."

The Tyro's First Spell

"TONIGHT!" FARNEL growled. "We must present what we have tonight. My peers will determine the final list at the end of the audition session that is taking place now," he scowled. "They will make the selection and be done with it so that the winners have time to prepare."

"But as you have told me, we are not quite ready," Jason replied, just barely into the hut. "Only the barest of sketches with no substance behind any of them."

"It cannot be helped," the master waved away the words. "Get the stool and observe what I have put together. Note the jumpy transitions and any other major flaws. If it holds together well enough, we will go to the hall immediately and demand to be heard."

Jason climbed up on the stool. Farnel stood at the opposite side of the room, adjusted his robe, and then, without preamble, rattled off the glamour. With surprising quickness, the sketch on the first sheet seemed to spring to life. The mountain felt real. The distant thunder forewarned of the approaching storm. Jason saw the blur of troops and heard the oration on horseback and the yell as two seas of men poured toward each other. In rapid succession, the images flitted by, each indistinct and lacking in detail, but somehow capturing the depth of feeling that ultimately would be there.

Through it all, Jason was keenly aware of his real surroundings. The hard stool was uncomfortable. The smells of yesterday's meal still hung in the air like visitors who had outstayed their welcomes. In the periphery of his vision, the disarray of the hut had not gone away. He felt the freedom to engage or ignore the images as he chose. Idly, he broke focus and sought out Farnel to see how he gestured as he ran through the charm. Once Jason concentrated on looking, the sorcerer sprang into view, his eyes wide and staring.

Then, without warning, Farnel's eyes bulged even further. He grabbed at his throat, and a dry rasp like a file scraping against flimsy metal escaped instead of a sonorous tone. In an instant, the spell was broken. The mountains, the lightning, the cavalry, all vanished in a flash. Jason saw only Farnel in his hut, the master falling to his knees and emitting retching sounds as he sagged. Jason sprang from the stool and ran to where the sorcerer had collapsed into a tight ball, clutching his throat with one hand and holding his other arm to his stomach.

"Master, Master Farnel, what happened?" Jason yelled. "How did you lose control?"

The sorcerer's eyes twitched from left to right and back like a runaway metronome. He lolled his head to the side. "Gerilac," he croaked. "The reason for the restraint at the meeting. I should have known. A few drops of some depressant in the wine would have done it. Enough for me to lose my voice and falter. He knew the prince would come today and that it would be our very last chance to audition."

Jason stepped back, giving Farnel room, and then helped him struggle up on one elbow. "He fears my entry into the competition, the sorcerer said. " He fears it! Now more than ever, I must go on."

The master rose to sitting, and Jason offered an arm to pull him up. The sorcerer wavered and then lowered himself back to the floor with a groan. "It is not done yet," he said weakly. "I can feel the backlash stirring in my head. It will be several days before I can attempt another spell."

"But the selection. You told me we must hurry or be too late to be considered."

"*You* will have to cast the glamours. Gather up the outline. I will accompany as best I can."

'The glamours! I do not know a tenth of what is needed."

"You told me you had practiced," Farnel growled.

"*Studied*, yes. Studied but not practiced. It is an entirely different thing."

The feeling of what suddenly was being asked of him began to bubble inside. Of course, he knew he finally must prove his capabilities to Farnel before moving on to the charm he really wanted to learn, but not like this, not until he was ready.

"It is only a quick skim-through," Farnel insisted. "Just set up the stage and cast a light *Power of Suggestion*. It is the first one that I taught you. The masters have seen many such outlines. They will be able to extrapolate to the quality that will be there."

Jason started to say more, but from the look in Farnel's eyes, he knew that further argument was useless. Moving like a snail born three summers ago, he gathered up the sheets and bound them to an easel board.

"Rest on my shoulder as we go," he said. "Perhaps your strength will return enough so you can cast the charm yourself."

Farnel coughed and waved Jason to the door. The sorcerer grabbed a torch and teetered after with a shuffling step. Without speaking, they started on the path.

After an hour of stumbles and rest stops, they arrived at the wooden building that was illuminated by a ring of torchlight at the end of the trail. It was the largest structure on the island, larger even than Canthor's stone keep. Weathered cedar covered the exterior — a quilt of planks running in different directions, as new extensions were hastily added to accommodate the increased entourage that the high prince brought with him each year. Originally a two-story rectangle of modest size, the hall sprawled in an ungainly array of annexes, corridors, and lofts.

Jason and Farnel entered through the low door cut in the rear and ascended the half-flight of stairs that led to the stage. Behind the first few rows, the seats were not arrayed in a regular pattern. Instead, they clumped in groups of twos and threes, some with tables and lounges close by. Between each group, threading back and forth across the upslope ran a confusion of partitions that blocked the view of one group from another, while not obscuring the stage.

"The Maze of Partitions," Farnel croaked as he waved at the sprawl of paneling. "Getting to a seat from the entrance in the front of the hall is like one of those puzzles you babble about."

Jason ignored the master's frustrations at the turn of events. He had his own concerns to deal with now. He examined the muted tapestries on the outer walls that absorbed even the echoes of midday to produce an unnatural silence. From a well at the foot of the stage, an almost painful light leaped up to hit the array of faceted mirrors overhead. Beams of white blankness reflected throughout the theater, into the recesses off the luxury boxes along the walls, and down the corridors to the more private suites branching in random directions.

Besides the well-beams, the hall glowed from a scatter of candles and oil lamps tucked into odd crannies, the ones closest to the tapestries above buckets of sand or water, in case they should catch fire. One stretch of paneling was streaked with smoky black from an apparent accident long ago. Others danced with frescoes and mosaics, pale reminders of popular glamours cast over the years.

Traveling with Farnel had been a help, but the familiar feeling of panic had begun to well up within Jason the first time he was jostled in the now crowded bazaar. Now, inside the hall, it was getting even worse — the racing heart, the labored breathing, the churning gut. The edifice was too large, too grand, potentially too bursting with people. Hundreds could be here at the same time.

"And so from this dozen we must choose the four to present to the prince."

Jason felt Farnel's elbow in his ribs. He blinked and looked about. From somewhere in the hall, one of the masters had addressed the others.

"As usual, a difficult choice. They all have merit. But we cannot expect the lords to sit through more than four and still retain their good humor."

Farnel elbowed Jason again and whispered what he should say in his ear. He struggled to put the anxiety aside and began rubbing the coin around his neck. It was not as bad as all of that, he reasoned with himself. The hundreds were not here. That was only a possibility. Now, no more besides the masters and he could not even see one of them from where he stood. He tried to focus on the words that he was to speak.

"There is yet another," Jason called out. "Master Farnel breaks his long absence with a submission for consideration by his peers."

"It grows late," Gerilac shouted from wherever he was hidden. "Besides, the master must have had decided at the last minute to withdraw after all."

"For this selection, I will cast the glamour." Jason forced out the words. "Master Farnel will observe with the rest of you, in order to gain a better critique of the results."

"A tyro, and one who has received instruction for less than a year? Most unacceptable," Gerilac said.

"But Farnel's coming out of his withdrawal should be encouraged," another replied. "Have with it, tyro. I am curious as to what your master has to offer."

Jason nodded and relayed the instructions to the runners for which properties to fetch and position. A few minutes later, the stage was alive with activity. While the fabric boulders and mountain skyline were pushed into place, Jason descended into the chanting well. He placed his sandals in the footprints painted on the floor as Farnel had instructed and slid his forearms onto the rests.

He blinked at the strong light and turned his head slightly so that the glare was not directly in his eyes. In the proper position, an image of his face reflected up onto the mirrors overhead and then was projected to all the recesses of the hall.

The curtain closed. After a moment, the final scrapes and thumps behind it halted. In the silence that followed, the distress in Jason's stomach intensified. Why did he have to do this here rather than in the master's hut? Why hadn't he spent some time practicing the words to the simple charms? At the time, it had appeared so easy. He should at least have gone through them once to cement them in his memory. Now, instead of the studied calm that Farnel said was so necessary, visions of hurried flight streaked through his mind. He tried to concentrate on utter blackness and to push the extraneous thoughts away. But like minnows swimming through a large net, they passed through his barriers with ease.

The curtain opened. Jason grabbed for the first word of the charm. He opened his mouth to speak, but then hesitated and frowned. Somehow, the way it formed on his tongue did not feel quite correct. If he spoke, something subtle would be wrong. He strained to recall the proper enunciation, as Farnel had taught it to him, but the sharp edges that made all the difference blurred. He raced forward in his mind to the second word, hoping by association to recover the first, but it, too, dissolved into a meaningless garble. With a feeling of sudden helplessness that mixed with nausea, he mentally tore through the first stanza, searching for some phrase that remained firm and solid, but as he did, it all slipped away, until not a single syllable remained.

"Well," Gerilac boomed out, "we are waiting for the effect. At least something to cover the seams and rips in the properties. They are meant only to be a hint. The glamour is to carry the burden of it all."

"The first scene is morning in Plowblade Pass," Jason called back. "From the west come the lightning flashes of a storm."

"Ah, opening with a riveting display," someone said. "Eye-burning bolts of yellow, claps of thunder that hurt the ears. It seems that Farnel has come around at last."

Jason tried a final time to recall the glamour, but it was totally gone. His mind was blank.

"Come, come, the lightning," the voice persisted.

"No, that is not the main effect," Jason called out in desperation. "You see, Master Farnel intended to focus on the commanders." He shuffled through the easel sheets. "Here, I will show you the outline. It begins in the second scene — *The Thrill of the Storm.*

"It is not directly in view." Jason raced up the stairs in a flapping of papers. "Just muted rolls and brief flashes at the periphery of vision.

38

More of an ominous foreboding to set the mood. It is later that the principle theme is brought forth."

"The prince will not sit still for such empty art!" Gerilac exclaimed. "There are three or four here with much more interest and impact."

"If you could see the effects and how they mix together, you would better understand," Jason said weakly.

"Understand, understand!" Gerilac shot back. "It is for you to understand, tyro. We pick the four to present to the prince on the merit of what we see here and now. No credit is given for hasty preparation and promise of improvement later on."

Jason scanned the area. Gerilac was not alone. *All* the masters were here in the same compartment with him. He began to fell dizzy and the onset of chills. Down the row of solemn masters, the faces were as stern as cliffs of granite. One or two nodded in agreement with Gerilac's words.

"Master Gerilac is right," one of them said. "It would be unfair to the others to judge on scribbled notes alone. At the very least, there should be some *Power of Suggestion*. Why even a tyro of a week should know it well. Return home with your master. There is nothing more here that you can do."

Farnel pushed forward, but then staggered, clutching his stomach. He strained to launch a protest of his own, but no words could he force out. The master's discomfort had a different cause, Jason understood, but the knowledge did little to help how he himself felt.

No one spoke. After a long silence, the master's shoulders slumped. With a deep sigh, he grabbed Jason's arm and turned for the stage door, a look of bitter disappointment clouding his face. Jason pulled himself free but did not protest further. In a daze, he followed the master out of the hall. For a long while, the two walked the path of white stones in silence, Farnel with his hands clamped in a tight knot over his stomach.

"Gerilac and the supreme accolade," the master whispered as they approached the hut, the deepness of his voice beginning to return. "Again it is a possibility." He grabbed at a branch that poked onto the trail way and snapped it in two with a savage twist, hurling the free piece up the hillside. "Gerilac knew the prince would come today and acted accordingly. Incapacitating my voice for a few hours was enough. I should have been more alert during the instruction. The signs were there, but I was distracted by the preparations. You absorb a lot quickly, Jason, but not once did I see you try even the simplest of charms."

"No!" Jason broke out of his reverie. "I will do better. We have an agreement. My help in a production in exchange for your instruction on self-enchantment." He felt drained from the disappointment in the hall and did not like where Farnel's thoughts were leading.

"The opportunity of this year's production has been lost." Farnel shrugged. "It again will be Gerilac or some other bragging at the feasting when it is done. But that is not any different from what it has been so many years before. Somehow, I shall find the will to endure it. I will go and raise my tankard with the rest and look them all in the eye — if they dare to return my stare."

Farnel's eyes narrowed as he studied Jason before him. "But as for you, trust the experience of the master. The end of season celebration should be avoided. No, not for you the festivities.

He turned back in the direction of his hut. "You can stay until after the official end-of-season in a week. With you still about, Gerilac might wonder if there is some scheme of my own that is hatching. The uncertainty is the least I can repay." He glanced a final time at Jason. "And after that, we will see, we will see if there is any profit in instructing you further."

The Persistence of Vision

AS HE sat on the cliff above the harbor, Jason pulled his arms tighter around his knees to shut out the onshore breeze. The wind whipping up and over the precipice seemed to whisper dark secrets as it sped by. The moon was full, shining in a gap in a cloud-filled sky. Cold and sterile light cast pale shadows among the dark buildings below. The man-made lights were all out. The ships of the prince had left hours before.

He was despondent. The week after the failure in the chanting well had been a total waste. Farnel had said no more about the future. It was clear enough that Jason would have to prove he could at least cast simple charms if he were to stay and learn more.

Since Farnel was no longer preparing a presentation, there had been opportunities to try, but each time, Jason shrank away from the attempt. Just like when he tried to write, a puzzle would pop into his mind — an old one, one for which he had forgotten the solution perhaps, but a distraction nonetheless. He did not want to risk a miscasting and spent his time reconstructing the solutions instead.

Only in the presentation hall, Jason knew, was there any activity. The masters and tyros celebrated the end of the season with an all-night revelry that lasted until the award of the supreme accolade at Canthor's keep the next day. Even Farnel was attending the festivities. He would not sulk and planned to be as merry as the others to prove that he did not care. But he had sent Jason away. After a few bottles of ale, the sorcerer could no longer count on eyes sharp enough to keep his tyro from trouble with Erid and the others. After what had happened at the preliminary selection, it was doubtful that Jason could hold his own.

Jason inspected the beach at the base of the cliff. He had had no interest in watching the flurry of tent striking during the afternoon as the hawkers hurried to depart for the next market. With the sailing of the nobility, Morgana was transformed in a single day to a moribund isolation that would not be shaken until the beginning of the season the next year.

A spark of light below grabbed his attention. Drandor's oddly shaped tent was standing in almost perfect isolation on the sandy beach. Why was the trader still here?

A sudden movement focused his attention more. Drandor pulled the heavy roll of parchment from the opening of the tent and dragged it with short jerks across the sand to a scaffolding newly erected nearby. The trader grabbed it in the middle and hoisted it up into outstretched and curved retainers. He pulled on the roll and uncoiled what appeared to be a large image softly painted, almost transparent so that light could shine through. He wound the bottom edge reaching the ground onto a bare axle connected to a crank at the bottom of the frame.

A cloud dimmed the moon and a few warning drops started to fall. Jason pulled his cloak around him and started for cover. Then he stopped and wondered. A storm surely was coming. Why didn't Drandor seek shelter as well? What, in fact, was he doing instead?

Drandor pulled a large oil lamp, backed by a reflector, from the tent and struggled to get it lit. Finally, a circle of light beamed on the parchment flapping in the wind. The scene was an unfamiliar one, a rock-strewn foreground set against a reddish sky. Unfamiliar beasts grazed and hunted in splayed grasses and tangled briars.

Jason gawked. What strangeness was being displayed? Certainly nothing like an illustration in any of the scrolls in his library.

Just as the first sheet of heavy rain crashed from the sky, Drandor knelt by the bottom of the scaffolding and started working the crank. The image disappeared onto the axle below and another appeared from the roll above in its place. The lamplight shone through the new image similar to the first but with the nose of another beast appeared on one side, Drandor continued cranking and a third image appeared and then a fourth. The same beast was projected again, although with slightly more showing than before. Rapidly, the trader ran through a fifth, a sixth, and then many more. The set of figures was in a sequence, each one showing the next posture as the animal extended his neck to reach for a fruit dangling from a low branch.

Jason felt the numbness of the past week dissolve away like muscles uncramping in a steaming bath. The trader's actions were somehow producing a tantalizing fascination that kept him watching, even though he was getting soaked to the skin. He listened harder at the wind whistling past his ears, ran his tongue over his lips to taste drops of rain, and rubbed the cool wetness of the coin about his neck, using all his senses to experience what was happening. What Drandor was performing was some sort of a puzzle, one , that he had never seen before.

As the scenario unfolded, more figures came into view. Meteor-like rocks streaked across the sky. One swooped low, almost touching the plant tops, and men with grayish skin and wearing loincloths descended among the beasts. While some stalked the animals with nets, others used picks and shovels to pry into the boulder-strewn ground. The soaring stone that had dropped them to the surface reappeared over the horizon. Pieces of discovered crystal were dumped onto the net-ensnarled beasts, and then the tangles of rock, animals, men, and nets lifted back into the sky. Like nickel drawn to a lodestone, they were attracted to the flying monolith as it sped away. It was almost as if he was not seeing a sequence of individual images but a single animation of movement. Jason had not counted, but there were hundreds of similar images flashing past, each a little different from the one before.

Jason shook his head. He could make no sense of any of it. Then a movement on the path that led up the face of the cliff pulled him out of his contemplation. Golden curls, plastered down by the rain, bobbed above the edge. He recognized Delia struggling upward on the slippery stones, tripping over the tatters of her soaked gown.

"Jason!" she cried. "A stroke of luck in my favor! You must help me. Drandor is distracted, and now is my chance."

She ran forward and grabbed his arm. "Quickly, before he releases it to come after. I must get to the harbor. I plan to sail with the flotilla of the high prince back to Pluton."

Jason thought about what he should do. She was indentured. Drandor probably could produce some document of sale. And Canthor would not care about the apprehension in her eyes. Maintaining the reputation of Morgana to the traveler would be his only concern. To get involved would mean risking expulsion, being forced to leave before Farnel could teach a single thing more.

"The high prince has already sailed," Jason stalled. "And to gamble in the token markets of Pluton is foolish."

"Yes, I admit it," Delia answered. "But many others have I seen rise from the streets to manor houses on the sea cliffs. In addition, even those who lost and had to sell their freedom to pay their debts did not fare so badly, if their masters were kind.

She lowered her eyes. "My first acted with discreetness. And the whip of the second was easy enough to avoid if you made no errors in totaling the sums in his counting house. However, when his own fortunes crashed and he could not choose to whom his properties would go, Drandor carried me away.

Delia's face clouded with the painful memories. "And from the first, he has licked his lips in anticipation. Every night he heats his tongs and pinchers and oils his chains. He leaves crude sketches of my scarred face and maimed limbs for me to find in the morning.

"With him, it is a game. Evidently, his partner, Melibar, prevents him from acting too rash with their joint property without due cause. And so, he hints, threatens, and tells me his fantasy a bit at a time. Then he waits, waits for my reaction, for some protest, a falter in carrying out a command, any shadow of an excuse for him to justify feeding his desires."

Delia stopped and shuddered. "And by the laws, it has worked. I can stand it no longer. I must be away."

Jason hesitated a moment more, but then, this time, the reasoning became immediately clear. He had already made the decision to aid her when he bought the puzzle in Drandor's tent for a coin of copper. There was no reason to change his mind now.

He reached for Delia's hand, then dropped it as his thoughts returned to a jumble. *How* could he help? Except for the harbor area, he was as defenseless on Morgana as she. To whom else could they turn? Farnel would not want to get involved with a complication that had nothing to do with his art. And any other master or tyro would be interested in them only as the recipients of some degrading spell.

Suddenly, a deep growl rumbled through the air, dark and menacing, powerful like rolling thunder that could not be deflected aside.

"It is free for the hunt!" Delia exclaimed. "Drandor has discovered my absence far sooner than I thought."

The short hairs on Jason's neck bristled. It was clear that something had to be done now. In indecision, he took a tentative step backwards.

Storm-flight

"WAIT, THERE is more." Delia did not pause to thank Jason for his aid. Instead, she ran to the cliff edge and dipped back over the rim. She returned, struggling with one of the lattices and the imp bottle that Jason had seen in the tent a few days before. "My passage from the island. Any captain will trade a berth for items that can fetch a goodly sum elsewhere."

"They will slow you down," Jason said.

"I can manage." Delia juggled the bottle under one arm and tried to swing the lattice across her shoulder. "If Drandor must face his partner's wrath for their loss, then so much the better."

A second growl rolled through the air and then another.

"I have agreed to aid," Jason muttered. He rushed to the lattice, flung it across his back, grabbed Delia's hand and jerked her about to follow him across the cliff top. She took a cautious step, and immediately they both fell in a splatter. The rain had given the granite a treacherous slickness.

"The imp!" Delia shouted. "His light will help guide the way."

She rattled the jar, and a weak flickering pulsed from its interior. "Patience, Master," a thin voice called. "In an instant, I will be ready to do your bidding."

Jason ignored the imp's babbling and peered into the darkness. Like the bow of a great ship, the monolithic plug of granite on which they stood pushed defiantly into the sea. On the side adjacent to the bazaar, the wall was steep, although generations of patient hammering had pounded a path to the broad and rolling top. The other side was more sheer still, and a descent at night carried too much risk.

"Which way?" Delia shouted.

"I, I do not know," Jason replied. "It will take some thought."

"There is no time for that," Delia protested. "You must have come from somewhere. Where is your shelter?"

"Yes, the way I came," Jason jolted to a conclusion. "The cliff top slopes back into the interior of the island. We will pass close to the dwellings of many of the masters and tyros, but with all of them at the presentation hall, we will have many choices."

Jason climbed to his feet and started out at a fast walk, one arm shouldering the lattice and the other guiding Delia to follow. Barks of excitement sounded closer than before. He began to trot and then, jumping over a large crack, broke into a run. Soon, they were racing down the slope, dodging jagged ledges as best as they could and skirting boulders too large to vault.

The wind tore at Jason's cloak, and the cold chill of the water soaked through. He squinted away the rain as best he could. Delia gasped for breath as she struggled to keep pace when she tripped and scrambled for balance.

The time ticked away. It had taken a small part of an hour for Jason's leisurely ascent, but the return seemed far longer. He wanted to charge forward even faster, to sprint at top speed until they could reach some cover. But the small slips and stumbles impeded their progress. The race through the blowing rain progressed in agonizing slowness.

Finally, the way leveled off, and the soggy crunch of pebbles underfoot indicated that they had intersected a path used by the sorcerers. Jason slowed, but Delia plunged onward, the change in terrain catching her by surprise. Her feet skittered on the wet stones, and she fell again, pulling Jason with her. They collapsed in a tumble of arms and legs. The lattice clanged loose, and the imp bottle squirted free to roll down the trail.

The rain diminished. The full moon shone through. Arms around each other, the two panted deeply, trying to regain their breath. Jason glanced back to the cliff top and choked in surprise. There, framed in the moonlight, were two silhouettes. If he had not recognized one as a man, he would not have believed the scale. Drandor had been small, but even so, a dog on all fours should come no higher than his waist, not halfway to his shoulder. The mastiff's limbs were not long and spindly like a racing hound's, but muscled and full. Its head was all snout beneath slight ridges that marked the eyes and ears. The trader pointed at the imp light, and then let go of the leash. The hound howled. With a surge of strength, it jerked its huge body to charge down the hill.

Jason pulled Delia to her feet. Now, which way to go, he thought.

Delia sensed his hesitation and randomly selected which direction to flee down the trail. They sprinted by the lattice, and she bent to scoop up the imp bottle as they passed.

"Not that!" Jason shouted. "The rain is washing away all of the scent. When the moon clouds over again, that light is all it will have to track us by."

He stared back over his shoulder to gauge how much time they had to find a place to hide, and his heart sank. The dog seemed to skim down the slope in great bounding strides. It had already covered half the distance between them while he and Delia had moved hardly at all. Jason ran for another few steps and then halted, shaking his head.

"It will be of no use," he gasped. "It will run us to ground in the end. Whatever we do, it may as well be here. "

"But what?" Delia's eyes widened. "I have seen what has been left of the carcasses from the times before. " She pointed back to the cliff top. "See, Drandor is following so that he can savor what will happen."

She looked at Jason. He was transfixed with indecision. He did not know what to do. "Think of it as a puzzle," she cried with sudden inspiration. "You bragged at your prowess with them. Put it to practical use."

Jason watched the rushing hound and the trader moving more slowly behind. For a moment, they disappeared into blackness as the moon again winked out. What had she just said — a puzzle? Yes, that was the way to think of it — nothing colored by the emotion of the moment, but abstract and impersonal — how does one defend against an attacking dog? His library. Didn't he have a scroll on that very subject? Yes, he did.

Jason shook himself into action and ripped off his cloak. He began to wrap it in a thick bundle about his left forearm and as he did so, he felt a small, hard lump in one of the pockets. With a grunt of recognition, he removed the metal puzzle he had purchased from Delia a few days before.

"Your hem," he said. "Tear me a strip and then get low to the ground."

Delia opened her mouth to speak, but Jason motioned her to silence as the hound came rushing up to the bottle, howling at its discovery.

The sky was now completely black. Only the glow of the imp cast any light. The chorus of clicks and pops of the rain against the pebbles of the path masked the noise as Delia ripped her gown. Together, she and Jason crouched to the earth and held their breath, watching.

The dog circled the bottle and gave it a push with its snout. The imp's incandescence flickered brighter, bathing the head of the hound in a ruddy glow. Lips pulled back to expose long rows of ghost-white teeth, the cuspids slender and pointed, extending to the chin. Tiny eyes darted, cruel searchlights scanning for their prey. Clouds of steamy breath pumped from its nostrils into the humid air, a smoldering fire not quite extinguished. The mastiff growled in frustration. It pushed at the imp bottle a second time and then put its nose to the ground, sniffing the trail.

Jason and Delia lay perfectly still, huddled behind a low rock beside the path. Scarcely breathing, they watched the hound circle the bottle and shake its coat, holding its head high, testing the wind. It hesitated a few moments longer and then turned to where Jason and Delia were hidden.

With a slow, deliberate step, one paw at a time, like a skilled man-at-arms, the hound walked down the trail, eyes scanning and ears cocked for any suspicious sound. Delia's hand tightened on Jason's forearm as the dog drew closer. He touched her hand in reassurance and then began to wind the strip of cloth around the clump of metal. The hound drew abreast of the rock, just as Jason finished and ceased all his motion. He gripped the small wad in his fist and tensed the muscles in his legs. If he could lodge the missile in the dog's throat, it would stop its charge. It would be petrified, trying to suck in sweet air and no longer concerned about any prey. But he would have only one chance. If he missed, there would not be another.

The hound stopped and growled. It was a low and nearly subsonic, seeming to vibrate even the boulder behind which they crouched. Cautiously, Jason rocked himself forward and raised his head. With a barely perceptible motion, his eyes cleared the horizon of the granite, and he peered out onto the path.

The hound was looking the other way in a sweeping scan of the darkness, its ears still erect. Gradually it turned back full circle to stare in Jason's direction.

For a while, nothing happened. Jason and the dog stood frozen like garden statues, separated by obscuring rain. Then, in a sudden blur, the mastiff leaped forward. With a roaring growl, it vaulted the rock, jaws wide and front legs extended. Jason stood up to meet the onslaught. He took aim through the opaqueness and at the last possible instant hurled the cloth-wrapped weight at the gaping mouth.

The aim was true but the missile bounced off the beast's tongue and fell to the ground. The mastiff plunged onward not deterred in the slightest, grabbing Jason about the shoulder and tumbling them both to the ground. Jason reached up with his free hand, but his shoulder was already starting to stiffen. His blow stopped short in a stab of pain.

This cannot be happening, Jason thought. He was a wordsmith, one who put this kind of stuff down on vellum, not one who lived it

He locked his legs around the dog's barrel chest and tried to tip the mastiff to the side. In response, the beast spread its front legs in a wide vee and settled its rear to form a stable tripod and Jason's legs fell away. Even through the protection of his cloak, he felt the pressure of the teeth and the spasm of the jaw muscles as they gritted down harder on the cloth. The hound jerked Jason's arm from side to side, with each tug pushing it backward and up over his head.

Jason ignored the tactic. He concentrated on twisting his arm as much as he could in order to pry it from the viselike jaws. But the hound's grip was too firm. In a moment, his limb was well extended above his brow. The dog then suddenly let go and dove for his exposed throat. Instinctively Jason brought his arm flying back down across his face. In the last instant, he managed to interpose it as a barrier to the gnashing teeth.

The mastiff began to work Jason's arm aside. This time, Jason clenched his muscles tight and tried to keep his arm between the foam-flecked mouth and the arteries pulsing in his neck. The beast growled at the resistance. It stopped the jerking back and forth and clamped its grip tighter. The sinews in its neck and shoulders knotted. Then, with a mighty heave, it flung Jason's arm aside like a discarded bone.

Jason pulled his arm back, but a massive paw stomped on his elbow, pinning it to the ground. He twisted to the opposite side, but he could not break free. He tugged and pulled, but he was held fast. The hound saw the end of resistance and howled with success. In desperation, Jason flung his other hand palm upward across his throat. The mastiff stared down at Jason, clicking its teeth in anticipation. Jason closed his eyes for what would happen next.

Suddenly, the hound barked with pain. It lurched backward and turned its head to snap at what had dropped onto its back. Jason opened his eyes to see Delia astride the huge beast, clutching a small, bloody dagger. The hound's motion threw her to the side, but as she fell, she slashed again between the ribs. The thrust plunged true and stuck. In a burst of gore, the mastiff staggered and fell to the ground.

Jason rose to his feet. He pointed at the blade dangling from Delia's side.

"It was to be my last resort if Drandor had his way," she said vacantly, still not comprehending what she had done.

Jason nodded. He studied the dead hound at his feet and opened its jaws. "More than fifty teeth. No wonder they looked so savage." He dropped the head and frowned in thought. "A latticework can be from any smith's shop and an imp from across the sea, if from nowhere else. But there is no breed from which could come such as this."

Jason stared back into the blackness. "Drandor," he said. "We still must flee. He cannot be far behind."

"And the lattice and the bottle," Delia answered.

Jason grunted and gathered his remaining energy. He ran to fetch the array of wires and colored nodes.

"Wrap the imp in what remains of my cloak," he called back. "The trader probably knows these trails less well than I."

"Where do we go now?"

Jason began a shrug and then stopped with the reminder of pain. The cuts in his shoulder were not deep, but they would have to be attended to. The fight with the hound had been exhausting. He had no more energy with which to think deliberately. "To the hut of Farnel the Sorcerer. It is the only thing that comes to mind."

A Well-cast Charm

JASON POUNDED with the last of his strength on the rough-hewn door. The rain had stopped. Dawn was breaking over the high hills to the east. Now, with the light, they needed a shelter in which to hide. Because of Jason's injury, they had had to move slowly, and Drandor had remained fairly close behind.

"Away with the summons," Farnel growl from behind the door. The sorcerer had already returned. "The presentation is not until noon. And I need not rush. The loose tongues of the other masters made clear how their votes would be cast. I have seen enough tokens bestowed on Gerilac. One more time will hardly matter."

"It is your tyro!" Jason shouted. "And I have a problem — something that your experience with the ways of the island may be able to resolve!"

The door creaked open. A bleary-eyed Farnel in a rumpled nightshirt squinted out into the growing brightness. He grunted recognition and motioned Jason inside. With a second wave, he indicated the fruit on a side table and lumbered back toward the bed.

"Jason offered me aid when I was most needy," Delia said without moving. "I hope the kindness of a master will be even greater."

Farnel turned back, rubbed his eyes, and looked closer at Delia. He shook himself awake. "Speak again," he said.

"I ask for your help," Delia replied.

"And more, something that gives difficulty to the tongue." A hint of excitement crept into Farnel's voice. In an instant, he was transformed from a groggy-headed old man into a straight-backed master of sorcery, dancing eyes hinting at the dart of thought suddenly alive within.

Delia spoke again, perplexed. "Do you mean things like 'fresh cheese' or 'six sick sheep'?"

"The voice is a pure one." Farnel looked at Jason, rubbing his hands in satisfaction. "Perhaps you have been of some value after all."

"Her delights do not matter," Jason said. "That is not why I have brought her here." He was still exhausted from the struggle. The pain in his arm was now a constant throb.

"Nor are they my interest either," Farnel snapped. "Can you not hear how she speaks? Are you so intertwined with puzzles that practicalities of the art completely escape you? That voice! No one on the island, tyro or master, has one that comes close to its purity. Wrapped around a charm, it would be perfection. My peers would offer much of their learning in order to cast a cantrip or glamour with such clarity."

He stopped and thought. "Yes, we must try it. It is worth the effort. Far better than debating the virtues of Gerilac's style or struggling with meaningless competitions. If the others hear the value of faultless words, then convincing them of the purity of my art will follow easily. How could anyone resist the truth of what I always have maintained if it is so perfectly spoken?"

Farnel glanced around his hut and scowled in annoyance at the disarray. "Come in. Come in and make yourself comfortable, lass. I am most curious as to how you will repeat what I will tell you."

"But that is not why we are here," Delia said as she and Jason passed through the doorway. She looked around the rough furnishings and eventually sat in the only uncluttered chair. "Drandor may have been close enough to see us enter. I do not care to confront unprepared anything else he might fetch from his tent."

"To aid in some petty squabble is not why I have asked you in." Farnel waved away the words. "We will select the charm before anything else."

"Then make it a *Wall of Impedance*." Jason grimaced as he lowered the lattice to the floor. Farnel's flying off on some diversion of the art was not something he wished even to contemplate. And he was annoyed with himself for not recognizing the potential of Delia's voice, as had the master. "*A Wall of Impedance*, some sort of chant to block the hurt."

Farnel noted Jason's pained expression, and then his eyebrows rose in question marks as he saw the bloodstained sleeve. "Erid?" he asked.

"Later." Jason shook his head. "After I have some rest."

Farnel frowned like a spinster who had forgotten someone's name. "I have some sweetbalm here somewhere. Payment by an alchemist who wanted a private cantrip two seasons back. It is old and stale and, as a side effect, it sometimes produces a great desire to sleep. But it might aid until a charm is cast."

He rummaged through a box at the foot of his bed and then tossed

Jason a small tube of salve. Jason grunted thanks, removed his tunic, and applied the balm to the cuts on his shoulder. Almost at once, the throb diminished and the swelling began to subside.

The master watched the red begin to fade from the wounds. "Each of the other arts has its place, I suppose." He turned his attention back to Delia. "Now the *Wall of Impedance*. Yes, just the thing to teach the lass. Simple enough that it is one of the first instructed to the tyro, but with enough potency that the enunciation must be exact."

The sorcerer took the imp bottle from Delia and set it on a table. "Pay attention to the beginning," he commanded. "The last few syllables are not quite the same, and that makes all the difference."

"The help I seek is not one of instruction." Delia shook her head and looked out a small window facing the trail. "But if I can remain hidden long enough, perhaps the trader will give up the search and sail on to Pluton, as he had planned before I fled."

"Pluton," Farnel shook his head. "A trader will find little to barter there. Fortunes are measured by sums and abstractions on paper, not by trinkets from faraway lands. Why, even the common gossip of the day must be bought, rather than freely received."

Delia ignored the comment. "Will you provide the shelter and more active aid, if that is what I need?"

"Will you attempt the charm?"

Delia looked once more out the window. She touched the iron around her wrist, and her shoulders sagged. "Oh, if you must, tell me the beginning. It is far less than what I would otherwise have to pay."

Farnel rubbed his hands together like a small boy anticipating a new toy. Jason settled down onto the floor beside the lattice and tried to make himself comfortable. He was still aware of the wound in his shoulder, although the pain was much reduced. For the *Wall of Impedance*, he had required more than two hours, practicing each syllable over and over until it was spoken without flaw.

The effort had been such a drudgery that he had not even bothered to string them together and try the complete charm when he was done. None of them had he practiced. Once one was explained to the end, his interest had waned. Far more intriguing would be when he finally began to learn about self-enchantment.

As Farnel droned on, and Delia echoed, Jason idly fingered the coin about his neck and tried to recapture his feelings when Drandor had projected his images on the beach. He frowned at the lattice as he struggled to understand its structure.

All the vertices were colored differently, yes. But they were not completely random. There was a pattern nonetheless. Starting from one that was red, blue, and yellow and moving one vertex to the left, the red was changed to purple, but the blue and yellow remained the same. Two vertices to the left the purple was replaced by a maroon and still the blue and yellow were there. All the way across the lattice in this one row, blue and yellow were always present.

Proceeding upward from the same starting vertex of red, blue and yellow to the next higher, the colors were red, green, and yellow. On all the vertices in the column, red and yellow were the unchanging ones. It was the blue that was different. Traveling into the depth, red and blue were constant. It was the yellow that was replaced.

"Why did each of the three directions change just a single color?" Jason mused aloud as he reached for the golden loop around one of the vertices. "Why is no combination of three ever repeated?"

"The Postulate of Invariance." The imp in the bottle sprang to life. "The Postulate of Invariance. Seven exactly. There can be no less or no more. It is Melibar's, and you must not touch."

"Quiet," Farnel snapped. "I am in the midst of instruction."

"Seven exactly." The imp's eyes gyrated in uncoordinated circles. "Nor can one force there to be any more or less."

"Cease the provocation so it will be silent." Farnel scowled at Jason. "At the very least, you understand how important it is that I not be misheard."

"As you said, the sweetbalm is old," Jason answered. "The pain is not completely gone. And an idle wait for several hours to hear over and over again parts of a spell I already know is not something I would freely choose."

"An example recital of the completed charm would speed the process, I admit," Farnel said, "but the ale from last night makes me slow enough that I dare not try it myself." He watched Jason cautiously test the mobility of his arm. "But perhaps necessity will be a better motivation," he rubbed his chin as if he was trying access the progress of a new beard. "Show us what you have learned, Jason. Speak the charm for yourself."

Surprisingly, Jason felt a small spark of excitement through his fatigue. There was no confusion, no doubt that he might fail. Instead, it was an opportunity to redeem himself in Farnel's eyes. He glanced at Delia, who was looking at him expectantly. He searched through his memory to see if he still could recall the beginning and found that the first words were there, sharp and firm. He rose on shaky feet and walked to the mirror.

Jason licked his lips and rattled through the first few syllables in a rush. He expected the nauseating backlash of a miscast charm, but he felt none. Farnel's reflection nodded approval. Encouraged, he concentrated on the next grouping.

Again the words sprang from his lips with crispness. He caught the cadence of the chant and, with rising confidence, completed the first recital. Jason smiled as he began the repetition. Each charm had to be spoken three times to be enacted, and the difficulty increased with each enunciation. But his words remained clean, projecting forth without effort as if he had cast them a thousand times before.

He raced into the final recital like a boulder crashing downhill. The words tripped from his tongue, every one perfect and without fault. His voice rose from a whisper to a booming shout. Hands on hips like a great orator, he mouthed the last phrases and with a flashy bow surprising for his exhaustion, he concluded the charm and turned to receive Farnel's reaction.

"It all came easy, both the recall and the casting," Jason smiled.

"A bit too dramatic, but well-spoken nonetheless," Farnel said. "It is a pity that you could not have done as well for the other masters."

"But at least it is a better promise of what is to come from your instruction." Jason started to wave the thought of his previous failure aside but winced at a sharpness in his shoulder. "How soon until the pain is completely blocked? It feels no better than before."

"You should be numbed upon completion of the last syllable," Farnel frowned. "There is no delay in sorcery."

"But my arm!"

Farnel studied Jason's still pained expression and shook his head. "Then, it is another miscasting. Somehow, with your dramatic flourishes, you garbled the charm."

"I feel no other ill effect, and you heard it all the way through without pointing out any error."

"Probably it occurred in the leading phrase of the first recital, just as the charm was beginning. An error there would render the rest a mumble of nonsense without power or meaning. Yes, that must be the reason. It was indeed too much to expect for you to get through it all so easily."

Jason opened his mouth to frame some sort of a reply, but before he could, a heavy pounding shook the door. With a crash, it flew open and banged against the wall. Canthor and four men-at-arms entered the hut. One pointed to Delia and the bottle beside her. Canthor nodded and looked back to Farnel, shaking his head.

"To the keep, old friend," Canthor commanded. "The trader Drandor has charged that you have possession of three of his properties and demands their restitution."

Sorcerer's Gambit

"THIS IS not a matter of harmless bickering, to be forgotten after a night in the keep." Canthor tried to scowl at Farnel, who sat at the other end of the table. "Morgana must show to everyone that its justice applies to master and bondsman alike."

The council room of the keep was seldom used in Canthor's administration of the island. From two small slit windows, the morning light stabbed into the shadows. Jason and Delia stood between two men-at-arms behind Farnel's chair. Up and down the length of the table sat the other sorcerers of the island, all puffy-eyed and slack-jawed from the night before. When a charge was brought against one, then all had to be present to hear the evidence and decide what must be done.

Drandor paced behind Canthor's high chair, his footfalls echoing off the round walls. A faded banner hung behind the trader, splotches of mildew mingling with tattered threads. Spiders scampered across the fitted stone and into niches in the crumbling mortar. Recently broken webs hung in the doorway like discarded dreams.

Even though it was a bracingly cool morning, Jason felt disheartened. He had been up all night and dosed with sweetbalm besides. Again he had miscast a spell in front of Farnel, and now there were additional complications, additional obstacles between him and getting rid of what blocked his inspiration. He gripped the back of the chair tightly to stand erect and forced his sluggish attention to follow what was happening. There are too many, he thought as he studied the row of masters facing him, but the sweetbalm dulled his senses enough that this time it did not seem much to matter.

"Justice I expect," Drandor said. "Of the evidence, there can be no denial. The imp bottle, the lattice, the girl, all belong to me and my partner, Melibar. I have the bills of possession here for you to examine."

"But it is so unlike a master to bother with material objects," the tall sorcerer on Canthor's right replied. "Our work is what we can shape with the mind. And to summon the full council for what surely must be a private matter is most unwarranted. Did you not deal directly with Master Farnel? Despite his antiquated techniques, he is most honest and reasonable."

"I did try my own negotiations." Drandor shot Jason a glance. "But they met with mishap at the base of the granite cliff. Prudence directed that I appeal to a higher authority, rather than attempt more on my own."

"Trader, justice you shall have." Gerilac rubbed his forehead in irritation. "And the quicker you are quiet, the quicker it will be meted." He scanned around the table through eyes bloodshot and like beacons with only weak flames behind. "After last night, I am sure we all wish to move quickly to settle this matter. And since we are all here, we also can cast the final vote and present the supreme accolade. Let us be done with everything so that we can return to much-needed rest."

"You need not show such haste," Farnel growled. "We all filled our cups as many times as you. And the tokens from previous years are keeping you in a pampered style. The five hundred from this season probably will add little difference."

"Five hundred tokens?" Drandor asked. "This sculpting of phantoms brings so much to the one who performs it best?"

"That concerns only the masters," Canthor said. "We are here at your behest, trader. And when the complaint has been settled, you will be dismissed before we proceed to the other."

"But five hundred!" Drandor persisted. "It is a very large sum."

"Much more than the objects you are making such a clamor about," Canthor answered. "You have disturbed my sleep and that of a good many others. Isn't it sufficient to return them to you and let the matter drop?"

"The lattice and bottle are the trader's," Jason blurted. "Take them and be gone." He tried to stand more erect and face the line of sorcerers. "But surely someone here can meet the price for the girl. Pay what is required so that Delia need not accompany the trader as well."

"Five hundred tokens." Drandor ignored Jason's interruption. "And I infer that the selection of the winner has not yet been made." His eyes narrowed, and he showed his teeth in a crooked smile. "I, too, deal in trinkets for the mind. And if I may be so bold, I wager that what I can create has greater merit than the best you have to offer."

"You are no sorcerer," Gerilac said. "You deal no more than the imitations of the bazaar."

"That is not so." Drandor's smile broadened. "My charms are far more powerful than any you can muster."

"Tradesmen's banter." Gerilac massaged his furrowed brow and slumped his elbow to the table. "Anyone trained in the art can tell the difference."

"Then put it to the test," Drandor challenged. "I spoke of a true wager, not just a simple prize. Perform your best sorcery before the masters as judges, and I will invoke mine. If I win the accolade then, of course, I garner the high prince's tokens as well. And —"

"And what?" Gerilac snapped.

"And If I do not," Drandor continued, "then you can add to the prize that goes to your winner an additional five hundred tokens that I will secure from my partner, Melibar."

"Why this sudden interest in our art?" Canthor asked. "You have camped in the harbor bazaar for many days, but never ventured forth before."

"Before, I did not know this recognition carried with it such tangible worth," Drandor said. "A large cache of tokens I must assemble. Melibar wishes it so." He turned and smiled at Canthor. "Besides, I cannot pass an opportunity that is now such a sure proposition."

"All of this is irrelevant." Gerilac deepened his frown. "We are not here to ponder the empty words of someone who is not even a member of our council. Let us be done with his business and proceed with our traditions."

"Our tradition is one of openness to all forms of expression and judgment on merit alone." Farnel rose suddenly to his feet. "Something we masters seem to have a hard time remembering," he rasped with his still-hoarse voice.

He pointed across the table to Gerilac. "Are your simple wishes the molds in which we shape the thoughts of our tyros who will someday follow? Are they to emulate a sorcerer who fears the challenge of one who is not even a master?"

"I do not fear this tradesman," Gerilac growled. "His spinning mirrors or whatever would bore us all. It is an idle exercise not worthy of any of our time."

"Not even worth an additional five hundred tokens?" Farnel asked. He looked around the council room. "It is true that my reaction is one of principle. But additional tokens brought to the island from the outside are eventually of benefit to us all, no matter who is the first recipient."

A few of the masters nodded and then the one nearest Canthor turn

59

his palm upward in agreement with the trader's offer. "Five hundred tokens more," he said. "As if the high prince visited not once this year but twice instead."

Like a rippling wave, the others around the table agreed, one after another, until only Gerilac remained. All eyes turned to him, and there was silence. Gerilac looked around the chamber and finally stared at Farnel.

"You do this just for spite," he spat. "But very well. It appears we choose to defend the accolade against this preposterous challenge. Let it be tomorrow morning in the hall. There is no need to wait any longer."

Jason struggled to think through his weariness. Dimly he realized that another presentation in the hall, and open to an outsider at that, was a chance to remind Farnel of their own bargain. He was sure that now he could cast a *Power of Suggestion*. He still was too spent to reason through all of the consequences but felt he had to act.

"If there is to be another competition," he said, "then it need not be limited to two. The other masters should have their chance as well."

"What is the point?" Gerilac asked. "The competition among the masters has already been held. Only the best need perform again."

"You have not seen the work of Master Farnel," Jason answered. "This gives him the chance to compete when he is not ill-disposed."

"Enough!" Farnel rose and pushed Jason back, his eyes wide at what his tyro had proposed. "One day is insufficient time. My cause cannot be aided by another hasty preparation. I will not suffer the embarrassment again."

Gerilac watched Farnel's reaction, and then the deep furrows in his forehead relaxed. "Insufficient preparation, did I hear you say, Farnel? How could that be if your theories are correct?" He shrugged and beamed a broad smile, his discomfort now completely gone.

"I am a fair man, even though you perpetrate these petty spites. If you wish to present an example of what you define as art with only a day of thought, then let it be so. It is not my intent to bar any glamour so vigorously extolled by its creator. And since it is not a real secret that my production will be the other one the masters will be seeing, perhaps the contrast will be amusing."

"I do not wish to present." Farnel slammed his fist on the table and croaked, "For no such permission did I ask."

"If I am to dance to your manipulations," Gerilac said, "then so should you to mine. Present your art in the hall tomorrow. Present it so the rest can compare and then judge the relative merit for themselves.

Perhaps when it is all over, you will be silent at last."

Gerilac did not wait for Farnel's reply but turned to the other masters for their agreement. Farnel started to say more, then clamped shut his mouth as the first few indicated agreement with Gerilac's words. The master watched silently as, one by one, the others nodded. With a deep scowl, he slumped back in his chair.

"Wait, there is no call for any other," Drandor protested. "We already have agreed on the elements of the wager."

Gerilac frowned at the trader. He studied the imp bottle and lattice and then finally he ran his eyes over Delia's gown and at the iron bracelet about her wrist.

"Make her part of the prize," he demanded. "As long as you inconvenience the masters of Morgana, you must offer more as your share."

"It is not a contest of equal risks," Drandor protested. For a moment, he was silent, and then he smiled. "But neither is it one of equal chance. Very well, the girl is part of the final award."

He looked at Jason. "But to be fair, if I win, then the tyro is mine as well. Melibar will replace my pet with another. It, too, will need amusements."

"But he is a free man," Farnel protested.

"Your other master was the one who asked to raise the stakes," Drandor shrugged.

Farnel looked around the room. None of the masters objected.

Jason slumped back against the wall. What was transpiring about his fate did not sink in. Instead, his thoughts lumbered off in a different direction. Now that Farnel was back in the competition, he had somehow to figure a way for them to win and for him to show his merit as a spell caster. But the sweetbalm was taking its toll. Jason's consciousness was dissolving in a muddle. Fatigue pressed down on him like a heavy stone. He needed sleep before he could be of much use to anyone

"Then it is settled." Canthor slapped the table for attention. "These two properties to the trader at once, for which he agrees to mention the incident no further. And all the rest to be decided after a meal or two to repair yesterday's excesses."

Farnel looked at each of the other masters, but no one protested. With a nod to his men, he left. One by one, the others silently followed. Only he, Jason, and Delia remained in the chamber.

"And what is the rest of your plan, quick-witted one?" Farnel growled. "We have done nothing on the battle scene since we abandoned it. There is hardly time to pull it together now."

Jason opened his mouth to speak, but no words came. It was best if he said no more. In a groggy haze, he followed Farnel and Delia back to the hut.

Delia's Talent

JASON BLINKED open his eyes. It was evening. He had struggled to keep alert and be of some help when they reached the sorcerer's lair but finally had succumbed to a deep sleep that had lasted for hours. He stretched tentatively and then with greater force, still felt somewhat groggy, but better than before. He rose to sitting and readjusted the tatters of his tunic over his shoulder. He centered the brandel on his chest and pushed aside his torn cloak, which had been balled into a pillow in the corner of the littered floor. Delia saw him stir and stepped between the helmets and maces to his side. She touched his shoulder, radiating concern.

"The swelling is much less," she called out to Farnel, who sat atop a stool on the other side of the hut. "The sweetbalm, despite its age, has done well."

Jason reached for Delia's softness, but she pushed him away. "There is little time. Even if master Farnel instructs me through the night, we may not be ready." She smiled and slid away. "But he says that I am an attentive pupil, and I think even his spirits rise as we progress."

"Attentiveness is only a part of it," Farnel said. "She has a natural aptitude — an ability for recall as well as enunciation. I have heard of other instances, but never met such a talent before."

Jason struggled to his feet and tried to shake the last bit of fuzziness out of his head. As the very last of the fog cleared, the terms agreed to with Drandor came into sharp focus. What would happen to him and Delia if Farnel's presentation was not judged the best? Tendrils of fear started to bubble within. Now there was more at stake here, more than just getting Farnel to teach him the self-enchanting charm.

"Just a few moments more," he blurted. "A few moments more, and I will be able to assist. Let me cast the charm."

"No, it is to be Delia." Farnel's voice was as firm as a sergeant's. "With her, we just might have a chance after all. Oh, to be ten years younger, lass, with a tyro such as you." He beamed as Delia positioned herself back in the middle of the room. "Gerilac and his followers never would have a chance. Now quickly, the next phrase is but a copy of the previous one with the middle syllables borrowed from the very beginning. Can you feel how it goes?"

Jason frowned and tried to figure out how to protest the decision. While he pondered, Delia began to rattle off a long string of melody, her voice crisp and purse like the notes of a golden harp. He listened only half-attentively at first, then, as she continued, he sagged back to the ground, surprised by what he had heard. Most of the charm fragment was familiar, but other parts were new, completely new, phrase that he had never learned in all of the months he had studied. Wide-eyed, he looked with respect at the slender form in the center of the room.

"Perfect, perfect," Farnel beamed. "You know all of the parts. Now we can begin the practice of the complete glamour. Start with *Dark Clouds* and then slide into Clinton's *Granite Spires.*"

He looked at Jason. "She even handles the transition without a flaw. It is a rare talent indeed."

Farnel had given him no such praise, Jason realized, even after the best of his training sessions. "Why spend time now in instruction?" Jason asked. "Should not the master be the one to rehearse for the final performance?"

"My head and stomach are not yet completely clear," Farnel said. "And it does not matter. With Delia's talent, I am sure she will be able to conduct a winning presentation. And enough of interruptions. Tend to your mending, and *we* will pay attention to the sorcery."

Jason started to reply, but before he could, Delia began the charm. Almost involuntarily, he closed his eyes and concentrated on her voice, following the flow, hearing the firm command she gave to the words and phrases. "Octavo, volustram, pentatamin, ..."

His own chanting, the little vocalizing of fragments he had done, was technically correct, but it was the drone of a scribe compared with the beauty of her song. Even though his eyes were shut, Jason felt himself being drawn into the enticing web that she wove with her words. Farnel was right. She was the one who had the talent to achieve their goal. Even if he could perform all that he knew with confidence, his glamours would be pale shadows next to the richness that sprang from Delia's lips.

"How is the effect?" Delia asked when she finished. "I felt none of the increasing of resistance."

"You must have made some small error, as Jason did this morning."

Farnel frowned. "I detected no fault, but I see no clouds and mountains." He rubbed his chin. "Perhaps we have proceeded with a bit too much haste. Let me cast the beginning. I think that my stomach distress can take on something as simple as that. Listen for a difference, and when I am done, you can continue with the rest."

Farnel climbed down from the stool, Delia replaced him, and the glamour was begun again. The same words rumbled from Farnel's throat, heavy with the assurance of a master. But the sorcerer took twice as long to complete the charm, slowing the tempo near the end rather than finishing with a burst of speed. As he said the concluding syllable, a look of befuddlement started to grow on his face.

"Strange, I would have expected more retardation," the master muttered, "especially with the way I feel." He waved his arm at the far wall. "But at any rate, that is the way the scene opens, and you have heard how it is done. Now, with the setting in place, you can begin to bring in the characters and their emotions."

"I am supposed to see a background on the wall?" Delia asked. "It is the same clutter as before."

"What?" Farnel exclaimed. "Impossible. I have not miscast since I was a tyro. One does not become a master with sloppy technique."

"I see nothing," Delia repeated. "If I squint, then some of Jason's scrawls resemble a small ship, but that is all."

"It is the joining." Farnel turned to Jason. "Your little theory of patching together the charmlets has a flaw. We must go back to Alaraic's *Foreboding* and Magneton's *Walls of Closure*, as I first suggested."

"There is no flaw," Jason said. "My analogy with the word ladder was only a means to see which charmlets to couple together. Once that is determined, the transition proceeds in a standard fashion."

"Then the casting, after all," Farnel waved away Jason's words. "The ale has addled my senses more than I thought. I have misremembered some syllable and taught it incorrectly to Delia as well."

"The charm I tried in the morning was a different one," Jason said. "Yet it did not complete either." He frowned and rose to standing and reached for tendrils of thought that danced just beyond his grasp. "Try the first charmlet without the connection. See if it works by itself."

Farnel scowled, and then shrugged. He turned to face Delia and ran through *Dark Clouds*. "Well," he said when he was done. "Surely, there was no mistake in such a short glamour. Even a beginning tyro can do it."

"Nothing still," Delia replied.

"We must try again, "Farnel said. "Too much is at stake. Slower and more carefully, this time, much more carefully."

"How often does a miscasting occur," Jason asked." What are the odds?"

"Who can say," Farnel shrugged. "Perhaps one in a thousand — maybe ten thousand. I do not know. It does not matter."

"Suppose it were one in a hundred," Jason continued. "I miscast in the presentation hall, and today there were four more. Then, let's see — then five in a row would occur only once in every ten billion times!" Suddenly, there was a puzzle here, he thought. Like incessant knocking on the door, it could not be ignored.

"We must continue as I direct," Farnel scowled. "There is no time for your amusements."

Jason shook his head and marched to the door. Something was wrong, terribly wrong. And Delia and his fate were intertwined with whatever was happening. "I must think!" he called back as he stepped outside.

JASON CLIMBED onto the granite cliff far from the hut, away from any distractions. He had to focus. Too much was at stake. He started his thoughts down a long familiar pathway. He mentally recited the drill: review the observations, marshal alternative possibilities, test them one by one, and then iterate until the correct solution to the puzzle is obtained.

Start with the observations. He had miscast the simple Power of Suggestion in the presentation hall, he thought as he paced. But that was reasonable. He had been insufficiently calm. That easily can be dismissed. But then four times in Farnel's hut, four times charms went awry.

Next, the possibilities. The observations could be by chance. After all, although unlikely, it was not impossible. Or perhaps, somehow Gerilac had enchanted the three of us so that we just thought we were not casting properly. Some subtle change so that our minds were tricked into not noticing. Or maybe some other of the crafts were involved. A magic sphere, perhaps, that enclosed Farnel's hut and prevented the charms from working. Or …

Jason stopped. His thinking was leading into the absurd. He had such little experience in sorcery. How could he possibly figure this out? But he had felt the same frustration many times before and ultimately was able to succeed.

Stick to the drill. Proceed to the test. Let his unconscious help him along the way.

Then the tests. For the first possibility, one chance in one hundred million, not ten billion as he had first calculated. It still was exceedingly small, but sometimes what seemed like rare occurrences turned out to be quite common. Jason thought and thought, but he could come up with nothing that would change the odds. Possibility one was not the answer.

For the second, perhaps when he and Farnel were first in the presentation hall, Gerilac did indeed perform a light enchantment on them. But, Delia was not there then. The other master did not know about her at all. How could it be that she could not cast spells as well? Possibility two was not the answer either.

For the third, Jason mentally scanned through the scrolls he had in his library. Magic spheres were mentioned, but none that prevented successful casting of charms. And even if unrecorded, if such a magic sphere did exist and had surrounded Farnel's hut, its extent could not be very large. As a test, Jason recited a *Power of Suggestion* from where he stood, now far away from the hut. The words came smoothly to him as they had done before, but there was no result from the casting. Possibility three also was not the answer as well.

So he would have to venture into the absurd, down the tendril that had briefly presented itself when he had first started. But then he immediately stopped. He had formulated the puzzle incorrectly, he decided. It was not 'why had there been four miscast charms in a row?' The problem was 'how was Farnel's presentation to be pulled off — using sorcery or no?"

Jason resumed his pacing. Yes, this was a puzzle that perhaps he could solve.

JASON SLAMMED open the door to the hut. "We have a compact," he said. "I stand by my part of the agreement still. I will help to win the competition, and you will instruct me in sorcery in return. And Delia will be free."

For a heartbeat, no one moved. Then, Farnel turned his glance away, flinging out his arms in despair. "We accomplished nothing by more blind thrashing,"

Jason guessed what had not happened in his absence. "If we cannot depend on our charms working, then we must conceive a production that does not use them. We have no choice but to work with what we have."

"A production with no glamours? Impossible!" Farnel snorted.

Jason did not reply. His spirits had lifted. He was back in the center of things, part of the solution rather than a hapless bystander, watching others try to unravel problems he had created. If they were to win the competition and save themselves from Drandor and Gerilac, if Farnel were to gain his measure of respect at last, it would be because Jason found the key to the puzzle, the means to the end, the plan for their salvation. He was in his element, as comfortable as if he were back in his own cozy den.

Pikes and long swords were still stacked in the corner. Delia sat on the stool in the middle of the room, and, behind her, the walls were covered with the outline of their original design. "You said my writing reminded you of a ship."

"Over there." Delia pointed. "The one on the left."

"So it does," Jason agreed. "But it is quite out of place with the effect we are trying to achieve."

"And an accidental sketch is hardly of sufficient quality for a presentation designed for a high prince," Farnel muttered.

"Seascapes, castles, interiors of a palace." He whirled toward Farnel. "Other settings. Can we quickly assemble such properties as well?"

"I have a few stored at the hall from previous years." Farnel shrugged. "And so do my peers. We trade them back and forth as we have need."

"Then let us go and select the best." Jason waved at the outline on the walls. "We have until morning to find a substitute for them all."

"But there is no time for me to learn a whole new set of charms," Delia protested. "And they might fail just as surely as the few that I know."

"Practice only what Farnel has taught you," Jason said. "You need worry about any more. Your performance tomorrow still must be flawless. It remains our hope for winning the prize and keeping our freedom."

The Wordsmith's Reward

JASON FLUNG open the door to Farnel's hut. It crashed into the wall, sounding like the crack of a siegestone hurled against a keep. Even though he had not stopped to rest since his suggestion to Delia for her to get some sleep, everything still was not ready. The sky was brightening anxiously as hurried through the debris littered floor between him and the master's bed. Gently he shook Delia awake.

"It took longer than we thought," he said. "Some of the other sorcerers did not take kindly to Farnel's requests in the middle of the night. He is at the hall trying to put into order what we have already collected."

Delia rose and stretched. "The list I made for Master Farnel before you left," she asked. "Did you use it to ensure that a scene was found for each charmlet?"

"Yes. I was most deliberate."

"Without a plan and attention as things progress, the most brilliant insight produces nothing." Delia agreed. "My fear of Drandor was overwhelming, yet I did not attempt to flee until I had decided exactly what I would take and knew when he would be preoccupied."

"But despite that, if I had not been on the cliff, you would not have the chance you do now."

"If not you, then I would have found some other." Delia laughed as his face clouded over. She stood and smiled. "Indeed, you were the one. And please do not think me ungrateful."

With a fluid motion, she suddenly clasped her arms around his neck and pulled his lips to hers. Jason blinked in surprise but then felt his pulse quicken. He stepped forward and drew her close. For a few heartbeats, they embraced. Jason's thoughts of sorcery faded away. Bodies pressed together, he pushed her toward the bed.

Delia teetered for half a step and then stiffened. "No," she whispered, "that is not what I meant."

Jason stroked his hand down her back, pressing her tighter. He thrust his thighs against hers, forcing her another step backward.

"No!" She wrenched her face away and pushed down on his entwining arm. "I have given you all I meant to offer."

Jason stopped. He backed away as she smoothed the front of her gown. Hard lines had replaced her smile, and he shook his head. "With the bracelet of iron, surely there have been many. And after your invitation, what was I to think?"

Delia opened her mouth to speak and then snapped it shut. Anger flared out of her eyes and twitched the muscles in her cheeks.

"Gambling in the token markets was a choice I made freely," she sputtered at last. "And I admit that I knew what the consequences could be." She waved her arm with the bracelet in Jason's face. "But despite this, I am still more than a toy to be pawed by an owner and then passed to another when he grows tired. That is my past, not what I will be."

"I understand I have no *legal* claim over you," Jason protested.

"Nor am I some doxy from the sagas who swoons to do every bidding of her rescuer in boundless gratitude," Delia rushed on. "I am free-willed as much as you. I asked for your help. You gave it without qualification. And I have thanked you. My obligation goes no further."

"A weakness of the moment," Jason turned away his eyes. He felt foolish that he had misjudged her intent and relied too strongly on some ill-defined feeling that now he could not quite describe. And what would she think of him? Probably as a bumbling tyro from the Wheatlands, who thought with his loins rather than his head, or an apprentice puffed with vanity, so sure of his attractiveness that he did not bother to ask.

Jason frowned at the direction of his thoughts. And if she did think that, why was it so important? If Farnel's production won the competition, she would be free to go her own way. After that, could it any longer matter?

There was a heavy silence. "Perhaps if I did not wear the bracelet," Delia said at last, "then the feelings molding me might be different. But the ring of iron is the reality. I cannot deny all the rest that has happened because of it. I feel a bonding to you, Jason, but not like that."

"We still have business together." Jason tried to speak as if nothing had happened. "For now, our fates are intertwined. And we must rush. Gerilac has already started. Drandor is ready to be second. And the other masters have made it quite clear: if we are not prepared in time, our chance will be forfeited."

"Then let us be off."

Jason started to reply, but hesitated. The moment had passed. There was too much yet to be done. Without speaking, he turned for the door. In a short while, they were on the path of crushed white stones, walking swiftly to the presentation hall.

Into the Hall

ROSE-TINTED CLOUDS hung low over the hilltops in the center of the island while the sky above the harbor was just beginning to show glorious blue. Canthor's banners hung limply from his keep like deflated balloons, and the details of the hall were muted in shadow. The faint groan of rigging in the harbor mixed with the crunch of Jason and Delia's rapid footsteps on the rock, but otherwise the air hung heavy with the morning silence.

"They expect Drandor to be finished when the sun tops that ridge." Jason nodded to the east. "There barely will be enough time to get you in the well. But with my transporting the scenery, I could come for you no sooner."

"I still do not understand," Delia said as they hurried along. "The scenery is supposed to be an aid to help the sorcerer cast his spell. An aid to put the watcher in the proper frame of mind. We were working with helmets and pikes, swords and battleaxes, to suggest battle scenes. Now you have replaced them with wave caps and fogs. They are not related at all to what I will chant."

"Precisely," Jason replied. "The more divergence, the better our chances will be. You'll see —"

He halted and pointed ahead to the hall. Erid and the other tyros were standing with studied nonchalance in the frame of the stage doorway. Jason's heart started to race, and his breathing became more labored. "Look, robes of gray. We can ill afford the delay of dealing with Gerilac's tyros."

"Then let us hasten," Delia pulled Jason's hand to get him moving again.

"Faster, faster," Erid shouted when he spotted them as they resumed running. "I want to see your expressions when your entry is barred."

.Jason managed a deep breath and, with Delia's helping tug, willed his feet forward. But as he tried to gain control of his feelings, his pace was as slow as an old man's shuffle.

Erid and the others watched until they had almost arrived, then sprang back into the hall and slammed the door. The bar dropped with a heavy thud. Jason tugged once on the door handle and then froze. Even if he could get the entrance open, Erid and the others might be waiting on the other side.

"It's just another puzzle," Delia said after a moment when he still did not move. "Just like with the mastiff."

"I have no scroll in my library that deals with getting past hostile tyros waiting behind a door."

"Then surely you have some general techniques that you use for your puzzle solving. Not every possible solution is described somewhere in your archive."

Jason took another deep breath. Yes, he did have triggers, a whole list of them. It was worth a try to see what might apply. With the tyro's out of sight, his composure started to return.

"You are right, Delia, just another puzzle," he replied after some thought. He cocked his head to the side and smiled. "It is quite fundamental, really. One on the list of triggers that I use to jog me out of inaction when I am frustrated and cannot proceed to a solution. 'If the possibility does not work, try another'. That one is at the top of the list."

"How can something as simple as —"

"Maybe the patron's entrance before they can secure it as well," Jason said. "Somehow, we will work our way back from it to the stage."

Delia frowned at being interrupted but then agreed. With no more words between them, the pair circled the hall and approached the entrance. Seen from the front, wings of unlike design jogged away from the central structure, one sprouting twin towers at its far end, the other a staggered tier of small boxes like bird nests on a cliff. Four doors cut the façade, each one grander than the one adjacent, the last filling an archway twice the height of a man.

They hesitated for a moment. "'When in doubt, move in the direction of the goal'," Jason said. "Another of my triggers." Together, they bounded from the rock path and through the largest entryway into the hall.

Immediately they plunged into murkiness. Two candles in a wall sconce illuminated three identical doors and a single staircase leading off to the right. Jason ran forward to try one of the latches, but it did not yield. "These probably all lead into the Maze of Partitions on the first floor. It would take who knows how long to work our way through to the stage."

They raced upstairs and found a long corridor snaking off to the left. The wall nearest the stage was lined with doorways and elaborate portals that opened onto boxes beyond. Jason poked her head in one. It was empty, the far wall hung with shutters that had been pulled firmly closed. In the next were lavish furnishings, couches with gilded frameworks, and deep floor cushions of shiny silk.

"Come along," he shouted as he withdrew. "These probably all open onto a balcony above the Maze. Let's follow the corridor to the end. There should be another stairway there."

Running faster on the smooth floors than they had been able to outside, they traversed the straight runs of the passageway and followed the bends that wound about the outer wall of the hall. Finally, they reached a barrier of brick and stone that blocked them from going farther. They searched for another exit, either up or down, but found none.

"It is too late to retrace our steps back to the entrance and try again," Jason said. He grabbed at the closed door on the last box in line and tried to wrench it open. The thin wood creaked, bowing from the jamb, but bolts at the top and bottom set from the inside held it in place. Tendrils of cold air whiffed from the crack as the door sprang back. The only feeling like it had been when he had been in the trader's tent.

"Someone is in there!" Jason exclaimed. "Who could it be? All of the masters will be in a compartment in the first row, and these presentations are for no others."

"Does it matter?" Delia asked. I thought our goal was to get me into the well."

Jason grunted and tried the door on the next box adjacent to the one that was sealed. It flew open. He entered and motioned Delia to follow.

The interior was more luxuriously than most, with patterned draperies hanging on three sides and even a painting on the closed shutters facing the stage. Lighted cressets brimmed with scented oil, and additional bottles stood amidst sand buckets underneath.

Jason climbed over a down-filled bed in the middle of the room and flicked at the latches on the shutters, pushing them open to look out onto the lower floor of the hall. His eyes swept the stage, and he suddenly stopped in mid-glance. "It is like what I saw the night of the storm. But this time, Drandor has made it much more real."

The trader had tilted a mirror over the chanting well. The light that arched upward did not disseminate throughout the hall but instead

74

reflected horizontally onto a curtain that hung from the stage. On its surface, the projected scene moved and changed. From some impossibly high vantage point, one saw the offshore islands of Arcadia, sparkling in the sea like diamonds on a tiara.

Then, in a breathtaking dive, the islands grew and moved from the center of focus to vanish off the edges of the curtain. Morgana remained in view, swelling larger with each instant. The hills, the harbor, and the individual buildings resolved into recognition. The detail was not that of a sorcerer's illusion or even of a good painting, but somehow the production was compelling, drawing Jason in so that he could not turn aside. He felt like a hawk swooping on its prey, expecting any minute to see a small rodent scamper among individual tufts of grass.

With a stomach-retching turn, Jason felt himself stop the plummet and reverse direction above the highest tower of the presentation hall. He raced over the peak with only inches to spare. He banked to the side and glided for a pass over the harbor. With a final turn away from a setting sun, he sailed from the island in a growing twilight.

The masters sat in the first row of the lower level. They burst into an incoherent babble at what they had just seen. Jason hesitated. They were so far away that it should not matter, he told himself. He wrestled his feelings back to normal as Drandor emerged from the well with his smile at its widest.

"Most interesting." The sorcerer on the right arose to greet the trader. He stepped past the small table with the open scrolls and bulging bag of coins. "These glamours do not have the detail, but if I had to decide between yours and what I saw of Gerilac's today, my choice would be clear."

"Intriguing, I agree," the next in line said, "but should not Master Gerilac be given the benefit of the doubt? We all have seen his *Women of the Slave Quarter* before. The high prince himself whispered that he enjoyed it well."

"You are to judge only what you see now." Drandor's smile melted away. "Past performances were not to be a factor."

"But it is so little time from our celebration," the second sorcerer whined. "Like us all, Master Gerilac is not fully rested. It is no wonder he was unable to weave again the glamour that we enjoyed when the prince was here."

"You have seen my performance," Drandor insisted. "It is no concern of mine that the other cannot not be given." The trader looked about the hall. "And if the last does not start at once, then we should waste no more time and proceed to your vote."

"A few minutes more," Farnel called out from backstage. "My tyros will arrive shortly."

"The vote," Drandor demanded. "You have seen enough. Gerilac has foundered, and I have produced as promised. Give me the tokens, the girl, and her companion: all as agreed."

The words stunned Jason. Like images brought into focus by the turn of a microscope's screw, the foggy memories in Canthor's keep suddenly cleared. Yes, the agreement with the trader! There was more at stake here than just a five hundred token prize. He and Delia had killed Drandor's mastiff. What would the dealer do with them once back in his tent? With all the drawings of cruel tortures? And if Farnel's enchantment was not presented, there was no way that the master could win.

Jason tore his eyes away from the stage and scanned down to the floor. "There!" he exclaimed, "From our vantage point, we can see a path below the long tapestry on the left, a narrow walkway that winds to the stage."

He turned back into the box and grabbed the nearest draperies from their hangings. While the masters argued, he tied several together and threw one end of a makeshift rope over the shutter rail. Delia nodded understanding. With Jason bracing against her weight, she shimmied down its length to land on the floor below. She then looked up expectantly, but he waved her on, holding up the free end of the drapery still in his hands. As she sped onto the walkway, he glanced back into the box, looking for a means to anchor his own way down.

While he tested the weight of the bed and tried to maneuver it into a position so that it would not slide, the agitation of the masters increased as more joined in the debate.

"But we agreed to three," one shouted above the rest. "It does not matter," another answered. "Farnel has not yet started and has forfeited his chance. Let us vote and then be done."

The Purging Flame

OTHER VOICES blurred the argument into indistinctness, but then suddenly Delia's clear tones cut through them all. Her words pulsed with energy, crystal sharp and demanding attention, filling the expanse of the hall. Not strained or forced, they carried rich harmonics of mystery and allure. "Oragamadon, thysph, mentos, akador, ..."

For a while, the babble rumbled onward. Then, one by one, the masters stopped to listen, their own voices hushed when they became aware of what they were hearing. Like enraptured children, they settled back into their seats, concentrating on the charm.

Delia ran through the first glamour with the same skill she had exhibited in Farnel's hut. The spell for *Dark Clouds* blended into that for Clinton's *Granite Spires*. As she reached the last syllables, the stage curtains parted in darkness. Then, with the final word, the scene behind sprang to life. Jason dropped the drapery and returned to the open shutters to watch what the reaction would be.

On the stage, a two-masted sloop, its sails billowing from offstage fans, frothed in a shallow sea. Bellow-driven sprays dashed against canvas boulders. The largest rock was topped by a light that swept in slow circles and caught the dust that churned in the main vault of the hall.

Then, as rapidly as the scene had appeared, the stage returned to blackness and Delia started the next portion of the charm. An excited murmur started to swell along the masters' row. Jason smiled. It was working as he had thought.

The sorcerers could not have doubted that Delia's words would produce images of the mountains surrounded by high clouds. Her voice was too pure. To see scenes of the ocean instead had to be an intriguing surprise.

"But that is no sorcery," Drandor shouted. "I have made sure that there is none. I am the one who must win. By logic's laws, there can be no other way!'"

Louder hisses for silence drowned out the trader. Except for Delia's voice, the hall quieted like a wizard's tomb. The masters sat attentively now, anxious to see what the next images would be. Drandor stomped his foot in frustration and looked up in Jason's direction to the box on his left.

Nothing happened in response. Only Delia's voice filled the expanses of the hall. Then, as the curtains began to part for the second time, the shutters on the next box banged open and a bottle of oil sailed out to crash onto the walkway below. A lighted torch followed and, in a flash, the long wall tapestry burst into flame.

Two more bottles hurtled from the opening and shattered like the first. A brace of torches scattered over a wide arc. In two heartbeats, the first level was ablaze with half a dozen fires.

Jason glanced back at the doorway of the box he stood in and then to Delia, still chanting in the well below. The decision to give her aid has not yet run its course, he thought, and then 'move in the direction of the goal'. He threw the drapery aside, climbed up onto the ledge and vaulted from his perch.

The momentum of his kick carried him past the walkway below. He crashed through a thin panel canopy, hit a pillowed divan, and tumbled to the floor. He staggered to his feet and tried to catch his bearings. The sorcerers were aflutter. They had seen the fire, and Delia's voice no longer held them in thrall. Like huge gray birds, they ran in all directions, tripping over buckets and shouting commands.

But the frenzy of the fires was already greater. Licks of flame touched oiled paneling, bursting the wood into glowing splinters that started dozens of additional blazes where they landed. A storeroom of paints and canvas exploded, sending globs of incandescence throughout the interior. Far faster than one could believe possible, the entire hall was embraced in hellfire.

The mirror that projected images from the well reflected Delia's apprehension as she debated what to do. She might remain, struggling to continue until it was too late. Jason had to get to the well and help her escape. The walkway she had taken was now engulfed in flame. 'If a possibility does not work, try another', he remembered. He glanced to the side and dove through a low doorway as the expanding fire caught another tapestry that billowed in yellow and orange.

Jason raced along the snaky corridor, trying to move in the direction of the stage, ducking at intervals into the boxes to see if they had another exit to shorten his path. A rush of hot air like that from an alchemist's athanor brushed his cheek, but he ignored it and climbed a small ladder to peer over a wall. Waves of fire raced down both sides of the hall, exploding the tapestries along the way into blazing columns. The stage curtain caught. To the rear, a massive bean groaned, sagging as its supports began to burn.

Delia! She could be confused, not able to find a way out. Could he reach her in time? Delia, where was she? He could not tell.

Drandor appeared from an aisle to the side, the imp buzzing free around his head. The trader swiped at the small table near the front of the stage and scooped up the bag of tokens as he ran.

"It is all rightfully mine!" the trader shouted. He looked around once before plunging down the stairs that led to the well. Delia screamed, and then Jason could hear only the roar of the fire.

Blistering air rolled past Jason's face, forcing him below. He peered back the way he had come. It was blocked. He touched the wall at his side, and it was hot to the touch. Acrid smoke billowed overhead, stinging his eyes and forcing him to his knees.

'Moving in the direction of the goal' would no longer work. There was no solution to reaching the stage and Delia. Now, he would have to get out as best he could and hope for the best. The technique was still 'move in the direction of the goal', but there was a new goal — the entrance to the hall.

He closed his eyes to block the sting and began to grope along the floor. He felt the cold metal of a water pail and doused it over his head. Pushing along the baseboard, he grasped the hinge of a door. But the metal was hot, burning his hand, and he crawled further down the aisle.

He detected an opening to the left and scrambled into it, only to crack his head against a panel a few feet beyond. He flung his hand about and felt a wall on one side and open space on the other. The smoky air pushed lower. He choked as he gasped for breath. Flinging himself to the side, he proceeded another few feet before again bouncing off a wall ahead.

Jason opened his eyes. The haze of gray and black was worse than before. High wooden panels of slick veneers blocked his view. Like the first story of a house of cards, the wooden walls zigged and zagged off into an unfathomable distance.

He recognized where he was. The Maze of Partitions. The terror of it began to boil. A maze! He was in a maze. He could flounder around within it aimlessly until it was too late. He needed a better idea. A better solution to the puzzle in order to survive. He pondered for only a few moments more. A maze. It is just a maze. It eventually leads to another entrance at the front of the hall. If the passages are simply connected, then he may have a chance.

He squinted his eyes shut and placed the palm of his left hand on the panel. Moving slower than he had done before, he crawled on his knees along the boundary and into the maze. The panel ran for a good distance before it ended, abutting another wall at a square angle, barring the way. Jason turned to the right with his hand still in front, guiding his movements, and continued in the new direction.

The air grew hotter. It hurt to take a deep breath. The crackle of the fire funneled down the narrow passageway. With a burst of effort, he tried to crawl even faster.

Time dissolved into a meaningless agony. Onward he crawled mindlessly, moving to the right when he ran into a barrier directly ahead, in the other direction when he felt his fingertips curve around a corner to a panel going to the left. He snaked into a spiral, back out again, and then along a narrow straightaway. He scrambled through a long traverse and then a set of convoluted aisles.

For what seemed like the thousandth time, Jason reached the end of a panel. He slid his hand across rougher wood in front of him and then felt smoothness projecting back along the other side.

"Another dead end," he mumbled as he turned around and continued back in the direction he had come. He winced at the intensity of the heat and coughed with the choking smoke that now filled every breath. Faltering, he pushed himself another step onward.

Jason opened his mouth to lick his lips and then snapped it shut again. He steeled himself to slide another half step into the heat, but he could not find the strength. He had to follow the left-hand wall all around the maze. It was like solving a complex puzzle on paper, horribly inefficient but the only way that was sure. Only then could he be certain of finding the doorway that led back out to the front of the hall.

Doorway, his thoughts dimly lumbered as he laid his head down on the ground. Doorway to the outside. Visions of the maze, the presentation hall, and the swirling smoke tumbled in his head.

Jason felt a blistering pulse of heat course across his hand and he pulled it back. The fire now danced on his clothes. He sprang to his feet and whirled in desperation in the other direction. He clawed at the wall until he felt the wood of the door. The door! It was a door! With a last effort, he pulled it open. Daylight was ten paces away. He tumbled forward into the brightness, trying to snuff out the flames as he rolled.

16

Inconceivable

JASON STRETCHED himself awake and took a deep breath. He felt flagstones still warm beneath his back. Acrid smoke from the remains of the presentation hall only yards away stung his eyes. Vaguely he remembered the helping hands that smothered the fire and then the application of the sleep-inducing salve. Its caressing aroma still lingered. With surprising ease, he managed to sit up and look about.

Only a few charred timbers still stood. The rest smoldered under the collapsed roof and piles of charcoal debris like the remains of a castle that fell to a successful siege. The onshore breeze had not yet blown away all the smoke and haze. A few of the masters directed their tyros to douse the remaining spots of fire. Others wandered aimlessly around the perimeter, eyes clouded in a daze as if they were looking for the words to forgotten charms in the rubble. A shadow blocked out the sun, now low in the western sky.

Jason struggled to his feet. "What about Delia?" he asked.

"The curtain was in flames before I was able to come to her aid," Farnel shook his head. "And I talked to other masters who were closer, They babble about the imp shielding the trader from the heat as he dragged her away and of something else that met them at the rear door, dark and shadowy — a presence black and cold that directed both Drandor and the imp."

"Where are they now?" Jason asked.

"A harbor pilot says that Drandor sailed on the tide for Pluton even before the blaze was fully controlled."

"And the one who hurled torches and oil from the second-level box, starting the fire?"

"No trace, either. Perhaps whoever it was worked with Drandor as well, creating a distraction when it appeared that the trader might lose the competition. But that is all speculation. We cannot be sure."

"Then I must —" Jason began.

"The spell worked," Farnel cut him off, "Better than the others."

"Yes, better than the others," Another master approached and solemnly gripped Farnel's arm. "With what we saw, there was no other choice. Gerilac failed completely. Not one image came to my mind when he was done"

The trader's technique was amusing, the master shrugged, "but nothing compared with the shock that you produced, Farnel. The effect caught me by surprise. I expected mountaintops and clouds. With the words I heard, there could be no other. And then to view the sea — a masterstroke. The image was not strong. It remained entirely on the stage, rather than surrounding my senses as any good illusion should.

"But such difficulty you must have had to make the charm sound so like the other! A little weakness in execution can easily be overlooked. Something only a master could appreciate, it is true. But within our craft, it is a spell that will become a classic. A pity that we were interrupted before you proceeded further."

The sorcerer looked over his shoulder at the ruins and then shook his head. "No, not a new technique from which to build next year's productions to the high prince. But with the work of a dozen generations burned away in a morning, it is unclear that that is very important."

"We must proceed." Farnel straightened to his ramrod stiffness. "For the next year, we must start the construction of a new hall and a new direction in our craft as well — charms that challenge the mind, rather than cater to its weakest desires."

"Yes, to plunge onward is best." The other sorcerer managed a weak smile. "That is why we went ahead with the vote, to salvage as much as we could of our tradition. By eight to three to one, Farnel, you are the winner of the supreme accolade. And perhaps there is even something of value in what you have wrought. You must teach me the technique when I feel I am able."

"Instructing you might prove to be a disappointment." Farnel coughed. "It is perhaps best to wait until the shock of the loss of the hall is forgotten. And besides, I have my part of a bargain to honor first. A just payment for favors rendered." He looked at Jason and smiled. "No small part of my success today is due to my tyro here. He has helped me to the prize, and in return, I must give him the knowledge that he seeks."

Jason smiled back. His plan had worked as he had hoped. There had been no sorcery involved at all. Delia had failed, just as she had the night before. But her words were so perfectly uttered that the masters could not bring themselves to believe that a charm was not cast. And so, guided by the stage props Jason had designed, they saw a sea scene, somehow formed with the words that should dictate mountains and clouds. Of course, it had been weak. But they would have reasoned, what more could one expect with a charm so inappropriate for what was produced?

From here on, there would be no more stumbles. Despite how it was accomplished, Farnel had achieved what he wanted. Now the others would listen to the sorcerer with more respect. This time, Jason thought, he would study diligently and master each charm along the way before he proceeded to the next. This time, he would learn the Power of Suggestion so that it would never be forgotten.

This time … His thoughts faltered and then stopped. He already knew the *Power of Suggestion*. Effortlessly, he could recall the simple glamour and many more. That was not the problem. The puzzle of the miscast charms remained. Now, there was even one more. He ticked off his own failures, Delia's, and Farnel's — and now even Gerilac's.

The possibility that he did not pursue while pacing along the cliffs roared back into his mind. It was preposterous, it was inconceivable — and yet it had to be tested. "Has anyone of you tried to cast a charm since your celebration after the high prince left?" Jason asked.

"We were all too indisposed from the revelry," the master answered with a blush, "although several did attempt something simple to steady themselves after the fire."

"And the result?"

"Miscast, everyone." The sorcerer shrugged. "It is still too soon, and the events of this morning could only make one more upset. And whatever the disturbance is, it will wear off soon enough. We often rest for a month after a season to recuperate our powers. When it comes time to prepare for the next, we will all be ready."

"But if the charms continue not to work, what then?" Jason persisted.

The sorcerer cast a worried look at the remains of the hall and ran a hand across the nape of his neck. "Then we will be forced to act like all the others. Deep enchantments, cantrips for far into the future, curses, and ensorcellments. All life-draining and making us feared by everyone."

"And if they too have lost their power? If the basic law of sorcery, 'thrice spoken, once fulfilled,' is now no more than a rhyme of nonsense?"

"A law no more? Impossible!" Farnel scoffed. "A charm is sometimes misremembered or forgotten; that has happened. Or even a master discovers that he can cast no more. But the law applies to all charms and all men, on Procolon as well as Morgana, on the seas, under the ground, and on the stars at the very limits of the sky. Stopping the law from working is the same as suddenly preventing every tossed rock from returning to earth. What mechanism could cause such to happen? How could you even conceive of such an absurd thing?"

"For me, nothing else explains all of the observations," Jason insisted. Since the night of the presentation to the high prince, there is not a single charm that has been completed successfully. The simple and the complex, joined or unrelated, they all do not work. What else can it mean but that the law no longer functions? Sorcery is no more!"

A New Direction

JASON KICKED at some of the rubble at his feet from the ruin of the presentation hall. All of the sorcerers were forming a ring around him, all jabbering like angry jays about the impossibility of what he had said. He covered his ears and closed his eyes. Even with the sweetbalm, the cacophony was too much. He could not think, but he knew he had to.

Yes, he could resume studying with Farnel, but, with sorcery gone, there was no point. He was no closer to removing his mental block than when he first arrived on the island.

"But there was Farnel's charm this morning," one sorcerer's protest filtered into Jason's head. "And even, in a peculiar way, the moving illusions on the trader's screen."

The trader, Jason thought. When there is a strange observation, link it with other unusual happenings. 'Consider the possibility that the peculiar are related.' It was only after Drandor's ritual on the night of the celebration that there were no more working charms. Yes, somehow the trader was connected!

"In any event, Jason, forget all this irrelevant thinking." Farnel spoke close to Jason's ear. "Don't you understand? I offer you instruction, freely given and as long as it takes so that you may learn the spell that you desire. The important thing is the rebuilding of our craft. If there is some sort of blockage in our chanting abilities, it will pass with time. We will be back at full strength well before the next season." He stopped and looked at the ruins. "We must. There is no other way."

Would the powers return unbidden? Jason thought. If Drandor's rituals were involved, was there not forethought behind what had happened, forethought coupled with some mechanism that shifted the very fabric of existence, as Farnel had said, throughout the world and encompassing the stars beyond? Was there possibly another of the trader's rituals that would turn the law of sorcery back on?

If the law were restored, then after that, it would make sense to study with Farnel. Then he could then be made ready with a full arsenal of glamours — enough to hold his own with Erid and advance to learn knowledge of the spell that he desired.

That is the path that the sorcerers should pursue first, not rebuilding a presentation hall that might never be needed again. With his eyes still closed, Jason shook his head. No, that was not going to happen. They were all too old, deep ruts in the road of tradition. If sorcery was going to be restored, then he was going to have to be the one to do it, the one to solve the puzzle of how the art so easily could be vanished.

Like a massive flywheel giving up the last of its energy, Jason line of reasoning ground to a halt. Pluton! Drandor had gone to Pluton. To track him down, he would have to follow. That would mean new and even more uncomfortable places. Many bustling bazaars and each with not hundreds but perhaps thousands of people. More churning inside, more shortness of breath.

Jason felt the purse at his side. It had been light enough when he had come to Morgana. Now even fewer coins remained. He needed new clothing to replace the ones on his back that reeked of smoke. Then there was the boat fare to travel. And Pluton was the most costly of the islands. After the expenses at the outset, there, he would have only money enough for a few days at most. After that ran out, he would be reduced to begging on the street for crusts of bread — still blocked and even further from a solution.

Find Drandor and deduce how to reverse what he had done. Do it in a matter of just a few days. And in a crowded metropolis that could drive him into catatonia. It was a staggering challenge with only a small chance of being overcome.

But what was the alternative? Yes, Farnel would share his meager meals with him for a while, but eventually, even the sorcerer's resources would be consumed. The master would have no means of livelihood either. The end would be the same.

The others standing about did not matter. He had to think some more.

HOW LONG he pondered he did not reckon, but Jason did not care. Finally, he had decided. There was no alternative. He had concluded what he must do — track Drandor and unravel his mysteries. Despite everything else that would happen to him along the way, solve the puzzle of why sorcery has stopped working and how to get it restored. There was no alternative, and so it must be.

And who knew? Perhaps, he might also be able to free Delia from the trader's grip as well. And the second time, her gratitude might be worth more than a kiss. Or better yet, he could turn his back and walk away when it was done so that she would know he was made of finer clay. He remembered their last time together. How did he feel about her anyhow?

He stopped the line of thought. That he could not resolve now. Something to be pondered later — later, after he had accomplished his new goal.

"Yes, I must go to the harbor," he opened his eyes and uncovered his ears. He pushed through the ring of sorcerers as if they were not there. "I must book passage and sail for Pluton with the next tide"

"Wait," Farnel said. "Didn't you hear what I told you?"

Jason did not answer. He started down the path of crushed stone. "When I return, Master, it will be with sorcery restored. Then, will I take you up on your generous offer."

"But how?" Farnel yelled after.

"I must find Drandor on Pluton and learn what he knows. Examine the contents of his tent. Listen to the imp when he babbles about the lattices and his partner, Melibar. Yes, the lattices, Melibar, and the Postulate of Invariance."

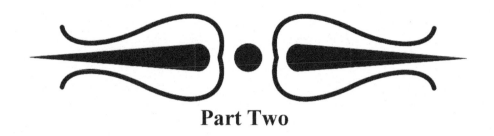

Part Two

The Postulate of Invariance

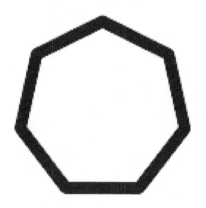

Whispers of Memory

THE PASSAGE from Morgana had been uneventful and the contrast between the two islands was more or less what Jason had expected. The population of Morgana was small, barely enough for a viable community to support a dozen masters and cater to the lords when they came once a year. Pluton, on the other hand, was an active trading and financial center, a stopping point for the traffic between mainland Arcadia and Procolon across the great ocean, and the nexus for the island traders that flitted up and down the archipelago like fleas hopping from dog to dog.

The journey from the harbor had taken him the better part of a day — ducking into deserted alleys when he was unable to stand any more, closing his ears and rubbing his coin, and then venturing farther when he felt well enough to continue. Now, up on the slope, the crowds were less. He took a moment's rest to get a better feel for his surroundings.

In Pluton's crowded harbor, several large ships lay at anchor in mid-bay, awaiting their turn for a berth. The piers jutted into the dirty water with regular spaced precision from two arms of land that gently curved into an enclosing circle. A small opening led to the unprotected sea outside the bay. Through the gap, one could follow the shipping lanes to the heartland of Arcadia, which lay beyond the horizon.

A narrow road that ringed the shoreline was a tumult of wagons, dust, and shouting drivers. Small boats pulled by oars and even a few biremes slid over the glassy water, dashing between the waiting ships, moving people and messages too important to delay onto the crowded shore.

Two smaller islands poked above the bay's surface, one covered with trees except where it had been cleared for an elegant estate, and the other rocky and bare, pockmarked with the dark entrances to deep caves that came to the water's edge.

All around the ring of shore, the land sloped abruptly upward to a circle of hills. Rough planked shacks stood adjacent to a wagon road. In the tier behind, single story mudbrick boxes painted white crowded together. Above them, the larger structures of brick and iron marked the exchanges and counting houses that distinguished Pluton from all the other islands in the chain. On the topmost slopes leading to the hillcrests were the manor houses of the wealthy — polished stone, fine-grained woods, and patches of cultivated greens, towering exquisite jewels over all the rest.

But his search would not take him all the way to the hilltops, Jason thought, at least not initially. It took a while to cubbyhole the other passengers when they were alone during the voyage, but the advice of all of them was to seek out a divulgent when he first came ashore. Information was a commodity on Pluton like everything else. Whatever he wanted was available if he had enough for its price.

Jason paused before he entered the courtyard gate before him. He patted his now much lighter purse and frowned. If he did not have the needed sum, he would have to find an old acquaintance — one perhaps disposed to offer him aid.

Augusta! How did she remember him? One of the merchants on shipboard had mentioned the name in connection with something called the Vault in the Grotto. Was she the same? Unbidden, the whispers of memories flooded back.

"But I can wait no longer, Jason. Please try to understand," he heard the voice from the past say.

"We have forsworn all others, Augusta," Jason remembered his reply. "You do not care for this Rosimar's rough manner. I can see it in your eyes."

"But he is already an acolyte, Jason. The guild on Pluton has offered to teach him the mastery of magic there. And he has asked me to go with him. Pluton, Jason, Pluton! Center of the islands and focus for trade. Why, in a single day there will be more excitement than this outland has in a year."

"And is that so important?" Jason asked softly. "When I am with you, the rest does not matter to me."

"Ah, Jason." Augusta smiled, placing her hand lightly on his. "Your sweet words are always a delight. But one must be practical as well. You are only an aspiring wordsmith. It is a meager existence at best. I know that within a year I would be longing for the silks, cold fruits, and prestige that the woman of a master magician is able to command. Rosimar gives me that promise. From you, I can see nothing for a long time to come …

Enough, Jason growled at himself. He covered the old hurt and pushed it away. No good came from dwelling on opportunities already lost. His goal now was tracking down a mysterious trader. Only as a last resort, would he determine if Augusta of the Vault in the Grotto was the one he previously knew.

He wrenched his attention back to the courtyard in front of him and scanned its interior. It was large and noisy, crammed with stalls and partitions around the periphery. The scene reminded him of the bazaar that had flourished on Morgana a fortnight ago, but here the structures were more permanent, made of stone and wood rather than canvas and paper. Each was decorated in gaudy colors spilled from a maniac's easel. Hawkers at the entrances called out what could be exchanged inside. With long ceremonial daggers, they pointed to hastily chalked lists on panels that swung out over the milling throng. From time to time, scurrying messengers flitted through the crowd to erase an entry or change a price.

"For the name of Lady Magma's lover," one called, "I have been offered three tokens. Does anyone on Pluton desire to know it more?"

"Gold from the west in exchange for grain," another shouted. "Two brandels per bushel. Trade now while my purse is still full."

"A barge for the southern kingdoms will sail on the tide," a third said. "How much for a one-hundredth share?"

At the far end of the court, on a board flanked by pages in silken hose, were listed the trading rates for metals and staples around the world. Gold, silver, wheat, stone, spices, and slaves all had entries scripted in bold black numerals. Below the board sat the changers, huddled between their huge scales and weights. Next to them were the assayers, with rows of reagent bottles and shelves crammed with specimens. A richly dressed merchant exited from the freshly painted cubicle directly ahead, and perfumed ladies ducked to enter an equally elaborate façade to the left.

Jason waited for a break in the human traffic and walked toward an entrance smaller than the rest. It had no hawkers outside, but the faded panel of fare was crammed with entries in a small, nervous script. "Tomorrow's departures," the first read. "The true age of the high prince," was the second. "The size of Procolon's fleet," proclaimed the third.

He ducked through the low opening into a room crammed with furnishings. Stools short and tall were pushed against shelves sagging from the weight of leather bound books. Scrolls of parchment lay unwound on the floor, weaving a coarse tapestry between small chests and smooth boxes bolted shut with massive locks. Two oil lamps on the far wall shone above a high table with chairs on either side. Hunched over a ledger like a mantis watching its prey, a thin and gangly figure mumbled as he scanned entries and made small notes with a quill.

"Tomorrow Gandis will pay twenty tokens for the name of Trocolar's latest partner. And since I bought it from Brason for sixteen, that is a profit of four. Sixty-seven tokens for the week. Two thousand eight hundred and twelve in all. Ah, if only the election were another month away. Cumbrist would not have a chance. Three thousand at the most — not a brandel more."

"I seek information," Jason said when the other did not look up. "And I think I will not be able to afford the surroundings that the other divulgents seem to offer."

The man behind the table jerked to attention. His elbow bumped the bowl of ink onto the sawdust floor. "Calm yourself, Benedict, calm yourself, or it will be Cumbrist for sure."

The divulgent breathed deeply as he watched the ink sink into the ground. Then, focusing on Jason, he motioned to the empty chair. "I am Benedict, pansophical divulgent. Ask me anything and I will know. Gossips of the guilds are a specialty. Futures of the exchanges with generous guarantees. For a copper, the use of the seat is yours."

Jason halted just as he was lowering himself into the chair. He pushed it aside in irritation. Spending the morning dodging the hordes had left him with little civility. "An unthinking way to treat a potential customer," he growled. "It makes one want to try somewhere else."

"You will find none charge less than a copper. *Everything* on Pluton has a price. And besides, you need to look no further. Anything you wish to know, I will tell."

"Then what of a trader called Drandor? How much for where he is now?"

"For two coppers I will speak my fee." Benedict centered the ledger on the table. "How soon do you wish to know?"

"You have heard of Drandor?" Jason exclaimed. "What luck on my first try! Then what of Delia, the slave girl with the golden curls? Is she still safe? Who is the partner, Melibar? Has he interceded on her behalf?"

"One at a time! For someone who begrudges the copper for a chair, you talk as if your purse were full. Show me your assay so that I will know you are worth my time."

"Assay?" Jason shook his head. "I have come to this exchange directly from the harbor." He furled his brow. "And even that cost two coppers for the directions."

"What, no writ certifying your worth?" Benedict asked. "Not a single token in any of the vaults? Then why are you here? It cannot mean you seriously intend to trade."

Benedict stopped, and his eyes widened. "A thief!" he exclaimed. "A thief. You are not here to pay for information, but want to wrest it away for free."

He snatched the ledger from the table and raced to the wall. The divulgent stuffed the book into a large box on the floor and slammed shut the lid. A flash of painful blue light sparked from the container as it closed. The air crackled and hissed like that around a lightning rod in a storm. Jason caught the pungent smell that came with it.

"Forever protected, save by my command." Benedict shot back a triumphant look. "No hammer can dent the walls, nor can the box be moved from where it sits on the floor. And unless I am calm, even my words will have no effect. A knife at my throat will not force entry if I do not wish it so. A small strongbox as those of magic go, but effective nonetheless. You will have to try your thievery on one who is not so fortunately secured."

"I will take nothing here that you do not freely give," Jason growled. "And if I must have some piece of paper before we can talk, then tell me how one is obtained, and I will be back."

Benedict eyed Jason critically, but a roll of drums outside in the court stopped him from speaking. He hurried back to the high table and grabbed a belt from a shelf. It was plain leather and buckled on the side. In the very front, it looped through a row of small columns that butted together and protruded with thumb levers. Buckling the belt around his narrow hips, the divulgent dashed past Jason and through the opening.

"No more time to weigh your merits," the divulgent called. "The court is full, and many will want to wager on the outcome with less than a full token."

Reluctantly Jason followed Benedict outside.

The Contracting Cube

JASON FOLLOWED Benedict, his annoyance growing with each step. He flung aside the curtain, but then stopped. A throng had assembled in the courtyard. His heart started to race. He did not want to be there, mingling in the chaos, hearing the babble that pounded his ears with incoherence.

But as he turned to reenter the safety of Benedict's tent, the jostle of bodies in front of him ceased and all eyes were on the center of the court. A pathway had cleared itself back to the rate board. From behind the changers marched a small troop of men-at-arms. The first two pushed the crowd farther back on either side. Behind them came two lines of three, supporting a huge gleaming box on their shoulders.

Jason stepped back a few more steps until no one else was near. Clearly, no one was paying him any heed. All eyes were focused on the men-at-arms and what they carried. He breathed deeply, once, and then twice more. His pulse rate slowed. He was able to stand his ground.

The coffer was a perfect cube of glistening metal, polished to such smoothness that the surrounding scene was reflected better than if by the finest mirror. Along the top edge, just below a row of hinges, was the arcane script that magicians had chiseled into the side as part of the ritual of construction. Near the bottom of the front, a small pipe protruded from the interior. Except for these, nothing else marred the clean, rigid, and flat surfaces.

A riot of anticipation started through the crowd as the next in the procession came into view. It was a man with eyes wild with fear, his hands secured behind his back, and his neck circled with iron. From the heavy black ring, a chain ran to a second prisoner, similarly bound, and then to a third. The last was a woman, clad only in a thin chemise, stumbling barefooted after the others.

As the procession stopped in the center of the court, the men-at-arms set the cube on the ground and flung open the top face with a crash. Two more guards struggled forward underneath the weight of a pair of huge containers of glass that billowed at the top and bottom, the lower portions filled almost full with sand. The last brought up a ladder, placing it against the side of the box. The top rung came to rest near the rim, well above Jason's head.

"Only the turn of a single glass and then it will be over," someone shouted.

"No, it will take more than two," another countered.

"A token and three that the first glass will be done before the first contraction," a woman in an embroidered gown at the rear of the crowd said to her companion. "A token and three coppers against your token plain."

Jason felt his chest start to tighten again as the noise grew louder. Two more steps back, and he was at the entrance to Benedict's tent.

The man accompanying the lady in the rear-most row signaled agreement and pulled a gleaming coin from a pouch. The woman produced hers and then frowned as she searched through her purse for the rest.

"Perhaps I can be of assistance to my lady." Benedict suddenly appeared and patted the mechanism strapped to his waist. "Brandeis for tokens, coppers for silver galleons, dranbots from the south, and regals of the inland. I can change them all. Only one extra for the fee and whatever you have can be transformed into another."

The woman nodded and reached a final time into her purse. "All copper and silver." She dumped a pile of brass and tin into Benedict's palm. "I expect to wager more before it is done."

With a speed that Jason could hardly follow, Benedict inserted the coins into the slits in the top of the device at his waist. As the metal clattered downward, he tripped the levers near the bottom and his palm filled with another collection, different from the first.

"May your wagers be perfection," Benedict handed the money back to the woman. With a slight bow, he darted away into the crowd.

Jason steeled himself to retreat no further and turned his attention back to the center of the court. The tallest of the men-at-arms paced around the cube, shouting to the crowd. "Eighteen has been bid, but the debt is thirty-five. Expert trader Trocolar's due is thirty-five, and he will accept no less. Speak now, else the justice of Pluton will run its course."

No one shouted an offer of payment as the guard made a final circuit of the metal box. He jerked his thumb upward and the prisoners were goaded onto the ladder at spear point. The first reached the top and hesitated, and one of the guards prodded him over the side. There was a muffled thud as he hit the bottom and the chain pull tight on the one who followed. When the woman reached the top, she turned and looked out over the throng.

"Trocolar," she shouted hoarsely, "Trocolar. I cannot pay him; it is true, but my spirit will not rest until he suffers the same. If ever he becomes short even by one token only, then I charge your judgment to be no less than what you have prescribed for me."

With her chin thrust out defiantly, she turned and leaped in after the others. Two of the men-at-arms grabbed the lid of the cube and arched it up over the hinges to clang shut. A blue flash like the one from Benedict's strongbox cut through the air overhead. Low-hanging banners about the court seared and smoldered, turning black along a thin horizontal line at precisely the height of the top of the coffer. One of the glasses was tipped over. As the sand began to fall, the crowd broke into another round of spirited betting.

Jason looked about, not understanding what was happening. The crowd continued the offer and acceptance of bets, but no shouts could be heard coming from the cube, nor any pounding on the walls. In perfect silence, it stood gleaming in the high morning sun. The sand drained from the glass and, just as the last grains emptied, the second one was started.

'There are three this time, rather than the usual pair," someone said. "That is the reason. Without her, it would have long since been over."

"But the pressure does not relent," another replied.

"Three coppers that we will not see the turning of another glass," offered a third.

A sudden shimmer caught Jason's eye, and he glanced back at the cube. The walls vibrated as if struck by a hammer and then with a sudden jerking movement they simultaneously contracted like a fist securing a golden coin. Jason blinked at what he had seen. He climbed on a nearby chair to look over the heads in front of him to be sure. The cube was perfectly formed as before, the length, width and height still measured the same. But with no excess material or visible seams, it had shrunk to half its former size.

With a sickening feeling, Jason realized what was going to happen. Before he could turn away, the metal box jerked a second time and then again. With each movement, it continued to halve its dimensions, height, width and depth still the same but a fraction of what it had been before and confining its contents closer together in smaller and smaller volumes.

The vibrations of the walls intensified, so that a low-pitched hum filled the air of the courtyard like a swarm of bees descending on a new home. After a half dozen contractions, it was no bigger than a large man's fist, and Jason could see drops of reddish pulp appear at the end of the pipe at the bottom. With the next constriction, it gushed in a steady flow, Bits of cloth and shattered bone swirled out onto the courtyard, and one of the men-at-arms swept it into a drain. What remained added its stain to the sun-bleached blotch that was already there.

"Less than two full glasses after all," someone shouted above the groans of the losers, "Pay up, pay up, to the ones who wagered correctly and won."

Jason turned away and staggered back through the entrance to Benedict's cubicle. On Pluton for less than an hour, and already he wanted to be away. He thought of the tangle of three bodies as they cramped together and the woman's face that he had seen just moments before. He sagged into a chair, shook his head to clear the images away, and tried to focus on why he had come.

After a hundred heartbeats or so, he heard the slide of the curtain, thankful for the distraction as Benedict entered.

"Still here?" the divulgent asked. "If you stay, the chair rent remains one copper."

Jason started to rise, but then slowly settled back into the chair. Disgusted, he threw a coin on the table and placed his arms around his stomach. It would be worth the cost for a few more minutes to allow his insides to settle.

Benedict circled to the other side of the table and scooped up the copper. With a laugh, he slid it into the changer at his waist and patted it with affection. "Faster than any of the rest, and they know I am accurate as well. It garnishes little profit, even when the courtyard is full, but each token I accumulate brings me closer to Cumbrist's total." With the practiced motion of a gambler about to leave the table, he levered a half dozen coins into his palm and then recycled them through the top.

"A curious device," Jason said, reaching for any distraction to blur the memories of outside. "It seems to be a collection of distinct columns fused together. The type of coins that come out the bottom of a particular shaft are all the same, even though a mixture is inserted in the single slit at the top. Somehow, internally they are permuted about."

"A minor magic." Benedict shrugged. "Necessary to make the thing invulnerable. More of a puzzle than anything else."

"A puzzle? Do it again, but more slowly so that I can watch."

"Another copper," Benedict replied. "I am no practiced performer, but it would be folly to give away my skill when fetching a price would be better."

Jason scowled and waved the thought aside. "Never mind, then. Let us return to why I am here. Where do I get this assay? Or must I pay for that information as well?"

Benedict pursed his lips. "Everyone on Pluton would know. The value of the knowledge is worth far less than the smallest coin we could exchange."

"Then answer more questions until I have received full value," Jason bounced a second coin on the table.

"Well enough." Benedict nodded in agreement, as he grabbed the copper. "As for the first, any vault will perform the service for a small fee — even certify what is deposited in accounts other than their own."

"Another small fee," Jason growled, "given to a vault which also will probably charge for me to sit while I explain what I want." He paused as another idea popped into his head. For an instant, he turned it over, then shrugged and made up his mind. The decision was a small enough one. "And the Vault in the Grotto. Will that serve as well as any other?"

Benedict ran his fingers over the small, weathered disk.

"I owe you still, and so I will answer fairly. Of all the vaults on the island, that is the last with which I would entrust my wealth. The others have protection that is true magic, strongholds like mine, but larger — large enough to hold the fortunes of many. The one in the grotto, however ..."

He shook his head. "It depends on the tide to protect it. I would not take the risk. No matter that the fees are smaller. Cumbrist does not choose such folly, and neither do I."

"I have no fortune to be so concerned," Jason said, "and on the sloop from Morgana, I heard that an Augusta earns her livelihood there. Perhaps she is none other than an old friend and will be less eager to demand a fee at every turn. Give me the directions to where she is, and then we will be done."

"In the end, you will receive what you pay for." Benedict shrugged. "The difference is the degree of risk. And as for the consequences, think again of the exhibition we just saw in the court."

Augusta

"THE LEDGER does not indicate that you are expected."

Like a guard at portside, the clerk on the left looked up suspiciously from the paper-strewn desk. "Surely, one of us can handle your needs just as well."

Jason glanced around the small room. The sign hanging from the far wall simply stated "Vault in the Grotto" and nothing else. Neither of the two women could be Augusta, despite the number of years since he had seen her last. And the drab decor was not what he had expected. Simple curtains of cloth hung from the walls to hide the rough wood planking underneath. Candles from a single chandelier overhead added their feeble glow to the filtered sunlight from the windows facing the street on the east. Missing were the fancy divans and tables heaped with fruits and drink. Unlike the other vaults he had passed, there were no laughing women in low-cut gowns to entertain the traders while they waited.

"Tally the account as of the moment." A door to the rear swung open, and a woman with an armful of scrolls bustled through. "Trocolar will be here within the hour, and I do not want him to find some petty excuse to move his funds."

"Augusta?" Jason blinked in recognition. She was full figured, perhaps a trifle heavier than he remembered her. Her face was broad, and her eyes twinkled. None would call her a beauty, but few men would ignore her smile. Her hair was clipped short, combed straight back with no frilly nonsense and held in place by tiny combs. She was a few years older than Jason at most, but already the hint of wrinkles had appeared in the smooth glow of youth.

Augusta frowned at Jason and then broke into a smile. "My somber wordsmith!" she exclaimed. "A happy event on an otherwise miserable day!" She dropped the pile of paper onto the nearest desk and circled around the side.

"Processed in less than an hour." She waved back her clerks. With a fluid motion, she slid her arm around Jason's back and pushed her cheek forward for a kiss. "You always were the dreamy one. To seek me out after all these years! It is good to think that at least one man is interested in something other than the number of tokens I hoard in the vault."

Jason started to speak and then thought better of it. He followed Augusta back through the doorway into a room scarcely larger than that occupied by the clerks. Slowly, he sat on the bench she had cleared with a swipe of her hand.

"Now, tell me everything that has happened since we went our separate ways," Augusta said. "Do not hold back any detail. I want to hear it all." She stopped and looked at a water clock dripping on a shelf. "I want to hear it all, that is, until Trocolar comes blustering forth with his accusations and threats."

Augusta breathed deeply. She settled in a chair opposite Jason and rubbed the frown on her forehead. After a minute, she looked back at him with a weak smile. Jason rose and circled behind her. More sleeping memories awoke as he placed his hands on the taut tendons of her neck.

"You are overwrought," he said as he began to massage the tightness.

Augusta let out a long sigh and patted Jason's hand on her shoulder. "It has been too long," she whispered. "Rosimar was the practical one, and his back rubs could never compare with yours."

"Rosimar!" Jason stopped. "Are the two of you still —"

"A child's entanglement, no more enduring than our own." Augusta laughed at the thought — a kite set free in the wind. She wiggled her shoulders for him to continue.

As simple as that, Jason thought as he resumed kneading. Rosimar was dismissed with a few words. He and Augusta were chatting and sharing pleasures together as if they had never been apart — as if there had been no deep hurt, no searing wound that left him so disillusioned. He pushed his thumbs along her spine and arched her shoulders back, digging for the feelings of what had been.

The frustration, the despair, the helplessness had brought him to tears, he remembered them, yes, but now only as abstractions, merely faded labels for an event which marked his passage into manhood. The fire, the intensity, the overwhelming flood of emotion that had consumed his thoughts — those were hollow voices that spoke no more. Beneath them, the delicate whispers of his first love and the unfolding of his innermost self to share with another were trampled and torn gossamers hidden away in a box as strong as Benedict's. Could he dare to open it again, to hear the broken murmurs and try to make them whole?

Jason flexed Augusta's shoulders in larger oscillations, watching her gown fall slack and then pull tight across her chest. And yes, the passion, could that again be as sweet?

"You were going to tell me of your adventures." Augusta cut through Jason's reverie. "What made you decide to seek me out at last?"

Jason hesitated. He was on Pluton for a different reason entirely. Seeing Augusta was only a means to an end. He wrenched his mind back to why he had come. "I need an assay, an assay so that I can barter with a divulgent. I had hoped that you might help me for less than others would charge."

Augusta stiffened as if she were a sapling left too long in the sun. For a long while, she was silent, finally standing to face Jason. "So practical. Now so practical and blunt. You have changed, my dreaming one, you have changed indeed." She looked at him intently and sighed. "No matter, do not apologize." She laughed at last. "My vanity has withstood stronger affronts. Besides, there is no reason to rush. I am in such a position now that I do not need to seize the first opportunity that presents itself."

"About your position. The Vault in the Grotto — what role do you play?"

"I own it with no other shareholder," Augusta answered. "All decisions are made by me alone. I *am* the vault. Those who held it previously were foolish where I was wise. Or perhaps it was the luck in speculating in the exchanges. It does not matter. In the end, their choice was to surrender title to me or accompany the mercenaries and their contracting cube. It is not a bad result for one who once thought trailing the robe hem of a master magician would be enough."

"I saw the cube in the courtyard today," Jason said. "For what sort of crime would something such as that be used?"

"For debt," Augusta replied. "For inability to pay. On Pluton, tokens and life are the same. Without one, you cannot have the other."

"But why the obsession?" Jason asked. "On none of the other islands is there so much focus on one's wealth."

"Because here it truly can be measured. There are no ambiguities or changes other than those of your own making."

Jason frowned. Augusta smiled and reached for a small bag piled with many others on a cluttered desk. "It is because of the token," she said, flinging him the sack. "You are a wordsmith. You should know the properties of something created by the craft of magic."

Jason nodded as he reached into the pouch and extracted one of the shiny disks. He held it in his palm and felt the tingling that coursed up his arm. Mirror flat and unblemished by a single scratch, it vibrated with the magical forces that gave it life, a quivering existence more real than flesh and blood. The coin was a geometric perfection that would last forever, long after all around it had returned to dust.

"Yes, 'perfection is eternal'." Augusta watched his eyes as he fondled the cold smoothness. "A token illustrates so well the Maxim of Persistence upon which all magic is based. At first, the small guild on the island made them as curiosities, a training ritual for the initiates and nothing more. They were sold as souvenirs to the traders who stopped on their journeys to the other isles and the mainland.

"But the tingle is addictive. Gradually, as more and more people coveted them, the token's true value came to be realized. They are small, lightweight, indestructible, and impossible to counterfeit. The flutter in your palm is unmistakable. Once you have handled a token, nothing else can ever be mistaken for one. And since Pluton saw goods and moneys from many lands, tokens became the standard by which all else was measured. Even more reliable than gold, they are the medium of exchange. With them are balanced the transactions between Arcadia, Procolon, and the other kingdoms. Why, it is said that there are no more magical items in the world than those in the stores of tokens here in Pluton!"

Jason replaced the coin in the sack and tossed it back on the desk. "Brandels or brass, it is all the same. The cutpurse or the marauder can take away in a trice what a lifetime has carefully built."

"And so it was on Pluton," Augusta agreed, "until the guilds again exercised their arts, building strongholds both large and small, impregnable havens for the coveted tokens that only the true owner could unlock. With a standard that was unimpeachable and a mechanism that made the possession of wealth secure, Pluton blossomed as a trading center. There is none like it anywhere on all the shores of the great ocean."

"And the obsession?" Jason asked.

"As in any land, wealth is a measure of power." Augusta shrugged. "But, unlike elsewhere, on Pluton there is nothing else. The stacks of coins hidden away in the vaults are true treasures and forever secure. No force can take that basis of power away. The measure of a man is the size of his assay, not the circumference of his bicep."

"And hence the price on everything?"

104

"And hence the price. We have no hereditary rulers in any of our guilds. All is decided by election, with each one's vote proportional to the tokens he has on account, even for the ruling council. In a few days, we will determine who is to lead us for the next three years. And hence, everyone strives to increase his assay by whatever means he can. Why every piece of information brings a fee. The divulgents scramble to accumulate wealth the same as anyone else. And for those already owning treasures, there are the gambles of the exchange by which they trade back and forth their riches."

"I need to find a trader who has come to Pluton," Jason said. "How much will it cost?"

"If you must know as soon as possible, prepare to pay a full token," Augusta replied. "All divulgents will profess already to know, but they must spend large sums to ferret out the facts."

"A full token!" Jason repeated. "I know that even a slave girl can be purchased for fifteen. My purse is not completely flat, but — but I do not have anywhere near enough for that."

"That is the rate, nonetheless," Augusta nodded. "The divulgents are skilled in their trade and will learn far quicker than you would yourself. But without a purse that gleams, then from them you will gain little —"

"A full token," Jason protested. "And that fee might be the first of many."

Augusta ran her tongue over her lips. Tilting her head to one side, she smiled and motioned him to sit again.

"Jason," she said softly. "I can better help you with your needs. My vault will offer you four tokens in exchange for — for a week's indenture to my service."

Jason frowned at the sudden change in her tone. "What tasks would I be called on to perform?"

"You would be an aide, a messenger, whatever I decide needs to be done," Augusta answered. "For example, I wish an offer taken to Rosimar's guild. I know that he is close to perfecting a new ritual but does not have the resources to investigate the final steps. He will give a generous share to an investor who provides the wherewithal to see it finished."

"But why four tokens for a week's labor?" Jason asked. "The rate seems far too sweet."

"It is better than you will find anywhere else," Augusta agreed. "And as to why ..." She shrugged and laughed again. "I spoke earlier of opportunity. It is an opportunity for us both. I now can afford to indulge in dreamers."

"I do not like the idea of the indenture. I have seen enough already of what the consequences could be."

"In one week you will have the means to locate this trader, and I will have ample chance to convince you, perhaps, to stay for another. If what you seek is so important, you must risk what you have, in any event. Do you not think it better with me than with some other?"

Jason scowled at the rush of ideas. His instincts told him to proceed with caution. To think things through carefully before deciding. His quest was to find Drandor and solve the puzzle of sorcery. But as he gazed at Augusta's smile, he felt the confusion of his old longings. Her offer was attractive. On his own, could he proceed as quickly? Was not his striving now for deeper-seated reasons as well? Was it not to see the respect in her eyes, finally to be regarded as more than a comfortable dreamer with nimble fingers, to savor her words when she apologized for the hurt?

He puffed his cheeks and let out a sigh. "A place to stay and ..."

"One of my clerks will arrange all of that." Augusta smiled again. "Room and board are part of the deal."

A week delay, Jason thought. But in exchange, Drandor located and his purse would be no lighter. "Then prepare the papers, and instruct me to the guild that is to receive this offer of your assets," he said.

The Vault in the Grotto

JASON RETURNED to the drab building at the foot of the Street of Vaults. He pushed aside the thought that at the end of his week of indenture and with Drandor's location then known, he still would have only a few days to solve the puzzle of sorcery and get it restored before his money ran out. Instead, he tried to concentrate on more positive things.

Even with detailed directions, his frequent stops to compose himself had taken him more than two hours to travel to the magician's guild and back. But he was satisfied with what he had accomplished. Augusta's offer had been readily accepted by Rosimar, just as she had said. He was even invited back in four days to monitor the next steps in the experimental ritual. If, eventually, the whole sequence worked, then tokens could be produced at a fifth the traditional effort. Augusta's investment would be returned twofold. She could expect an additional ten tokens every month after that.

"On this evening's tide. Another day I will not wait," a heavy voice boomed from the back room as Jason approached. "And if you do not comply, I will tell the others that you cannot because they are gone."

"I only point out that the hour is already late, and the level is rising," Augusta shouted back. "You speak of risk, but choose to ignore the true threat for the insignificant."

Jason passed through the doorway. Augusta was scowling at the heavy-set man slumped in the chair. His sagging jowls gave him a bulldog look that the fine tailoring of his cape and collars could not hide. With watery, pale eyes, he returned Augusta's stare.

"Tonight," he repeated. "You can have an oarsman light the way. After all, I would have no such trouble with any other vault along the street."

"Any other along the street would charge three times the fee to hold

107

your tokens secure," Augusta replied. "Their precious magic boxes do not come cheap." She stopped and looked in Jason's direction. "My new indentured servant," she said. "And this is Trocolar, elected leader of the tradesmen."

"After the next polling, leader of the council as well," Trocolar said. He ran his eyes up and down Jason's frame. "Stocky enough, but I doubt he would last more than a day at the oars. No, tokens are my concern, Augusta, not flesh of questionable value. My tokens are what I want, and I want them now."

Jason bristled at Trocolar's rude manner, but he held his tongue. Instead, he watched Augusta for the key to how he should behave.

Augusta worked her lips, but no words came. After a moment, she sighed and slapped her hands to her sides. "Then let us get to the skiff at once. Because of the hour, you will have to pay my rowers double as it is. And you should accompany us, Jason. One more will make the loading proceed quicker."

Trocolar stood with majestic slowness, his face drawn in a slight smile. With a perfunctory nod as she passed, he followed Augusta through the front room and out onto the street. Jason came last. In a silent single file, they made their way down the slope to the harbor's edge.

Soon they were gliding across the water in a narrow boat. Oarsmen front and back propelled them toward the smaller of the two islands in the center off the bay, the one of gnarled rock that looked devoid of life.

The weather-beaten hill loomed larger and larger with each stroke. The sun, low in the west, hid most of one side in soft shadow, the deeper blacks marking the entrances to the caves. The boat headed for one opening larger than the rest. Like the mouth of a large serpent feasting on krill from the sea, it sucked in each lapping wave and expelled it with the next breath.

The oarsmen maneuvered the boat into the entrance and paddled into the dark tunnel. The oars were secured in an eerie quietness, and the skiff coasted forward on the still water.

After a while, they halted with a gentle bump. There was a fumbling in the bow, the scrape of flint on steel, and finally a gentle whoosh as an oil cresset chiseled into the rock sprang to life. Their way was barred by a heavy iron grating that protruded from the ceiling above and disappeared into the dark water below.

Augusta placed her palm on a small box next to the burning light. After it opened, she extracted a large brass key. "You see, there *is* magic protecting the vault that resides in the grotto." She worked the lock on the grating. "But only what is necessary to complete the security. For the large containers, we never had to pay."

"Holgon, my magician, would not be impressed by such items," Trocolar rebutted. "And guarding a single entrance does not guarantee that others do not exist."

"Yet you have seen fit to leave a considerable treasure here," Augusta said. She motioned to the oarsmen. The one in front grabbed the protruding handle of a bolt and pulled it free. The other tugged at a circular chain draped nearby. With a rusty creaking as if it were an old skeleton being brought back to life, the grating began to rise.

"A considerable treasure," she continued. "And none of your reasons for withdrawal carry much persuasion."

Trocolar grunted, but did not answer. Instead, he pointed to the red horizontal line painted on the wall.

"Yes." Augusta nodded. "In less than an hour, the tide will be too high. I warned you before we came. All your tokens will not save us if we are caught in the passage between the two pools."

The grating clanged against its upper stops. The two oarsmen hurried to get the skiff back into motion, while Augusta lighted a torch from the cresset. In its flickering light, Jason and the others glided deeper into the cave.

Immediately behind the grating, the ceiling and walls receded from view. As if traveling on calm seas under a starless night sky, the small boat slid through the water. Jason breathed still and fungal air, the only clue to his true surroundings. He tried to pierce the gloom, but there was nothing to aid in orientation. The rhythmic splash of the paddles wove complicated patterns with the rustle of Augusta's smoking flame. No one spoke. The feeling was oppressive, but Jason felt no panic. There were only the people in the boat, not great numbers, no senseless confusion and noise.

After several minutes, the pace of the paddling quickened as did the tenseness in the oarsmen. The walls again came into view. Like a crumpled funnel, they converged on the skiff, defining a narrow passage where none had been seen before. The undulating surfaces resolved into distinguishable textures, dry swaths with large crystals of pegmatite, glistening walls of fine-grained granite, areas of gas-smoothed slickness, and jagged fissures that trickled with rainwater seeping from above. Closer and closer converged the walls. A boat length away and then barely two arm lengths apart, the rock pushed in from either side.

Augusta lowered her torch. The ceiling crushed inward like the walls.

The oarsman in front ducked to the side to avoid a low-hanging projection, and it whizzed past Jason's ear. Augusta set the base of the torch on the keel board and experimented with huddling low at its side. "We probably will have to extinguish our light on the way back. There will be just enough clearance for the skiff itself to squeeze by."

"How high does the tide rise?" Jason asked.

"Above the ceiling at the narrowest point," Augusta answered. "The vault is shaped like a carnival-man's barbell, with this passage the only connection between two large chambers on either end. And for most of the day, the inner chamber is sealed off. There is no way to get through. Only at lowest tides, when the water level is under the red line, can one attempt a passage. And even then, the margin of safety is none too great."

Jason copied the others, hunching over and then squirming even lower when a sharp outcrop skittered across the top of his head. The rower behind gave up trying to paddle the water. Instead, he began pushing his oar against the sides of the passage to propel them along. The skiff scraped and splintered as it rubbed against one wall and then bounced off to grate against the other. The unyielding rock pressed Jason still lower and then with a sickening groan on both sides, the boat halted, jammed against the walls. For a few moments, they did not move, but the oarsmen rocked back and forth, and the inflowing tide pushed them free.

Jason waited for the next constriction, but instead, the pressure on his back gradually lessened and then abruptly fell away. He watched Augusta stretch and extend the torch as she had done before. Once again, the walls receded to provide an easy passage. The confinement had vanished like an oppressive dream.

"We are in the inner chamber," Augusta said. "And now to the vault itself. A small, separate cavity that took some fifteen years to suck dry, even with pumps of magic. The ledge above it does not provide enough space for the treasures."

As she pointed out the direction, the skiff sailed across the bowl of water. When they reached the wall, one oarsman secured the boat to some iron rings. The second rower sprang onto a rope ladder suspended from above.

Jason and the others followed, climbing onto a wide ledge above the level of the water. Augusta's torch lighted several cressets, and Jason blinked at the sudden increase in light.

The shelf cut back into the overhanging rock for a sizable distance, creating a pocket far larger than the size of Augusta's rooms back on shore. Sand and planking made the irregular floor more or less level. A single table supported heavy ledgers, and a collection of scrolls was crammed into the cracks and crevices in the walls. Blooms of mold followed the trickle of water down the sloping surfaces. Splotches of growth peppered the more exposed vellums. Billowed soot covered one portion of the low-hanging roof where a fire had been tried long ago. Ash mingled with small bones and discarded refuse on the floor. Two spots of blackness led off further into the interior. A heavy cauldron lid covered a jagged hole in the rear from which dank smells rose to taint the air.

"The two side tunnels lead back to smaller caverns," Augusta explained to Jason. "And the lid covers a shaft that goes down to the vault itself. All of it is natural. The magic pumps and the lock on the entrance grating are my only indebtedness to the guilds."

An oarsman pushed the lid aside and threw a ladder down the tube. He climbed onto it and disappeared from view. Augusta motioned for everyone else to follow. Jason descended into the vertical tunnel, knobby and twisted, about five times the height of a man. The shuffle of hands and feet echoing along the shaft made conversation impossible as he descended, and as he went lower, the air was filled with the drips and gurgles of running water and then the suck and push of throbbing pumps.

His foot hit bottom, splashing in a small, stagnant pool. A glow of imp light caught his attention on the right. From bottles fastened to a semicircular wall, the dim, blue glow bathed complexes of wheels and levers that pushed water up a tube and out of sight. Behind them was an array of chests, ordered in precise rows and columns into a great square. Splashes of soft greens and yellows covered the tops and side planking. Long tendrils of oozing growth stretched to the wet and rocky floor. The far walls could barely be seen.

The volume was larger than the hold of Arcadia's biggest grain ship, Jason calculated as he made room for the others following. Yes, bigger than a galleon's hold and three man heights beneath the level of the sea.

"What miserable storage," Trocolar sneered as he followed Augusta back to the chests. "Look at this dampness, the cracks in the walls. Even a gentle shift in the earth would cause the trickle to become a flood. It is worth the fee to have my tokens reside in a dry, clean vault, rather than in this slimy mess."

"The cloth and oak may rot," Augusta said, "but for tokens, it does not matter. Never will they alter."

"Nonetheless, mine will be gone," Trocolar replied. His eyes glistened as a chest lid was flung back and the subtle glow of the tokens added to the imp light. The trader turned to Augusta and pulled his jowls into a slight smile. "And do not profess that it is of no concern. The loss of my fees just before the election will give you a smaller vote. I plan to persuade other traders to withdraw their holdings as well. Altogether, it will make a considerable difference."

"The issue is in doubt." Augusta shrugged. "Neither your faction nor mine has sufficient wealth to win on the first round."

"But there will be the subsequent ones," Trocolar said. "And, in a contest between the vault holders and the traders, what do you think the outcome will be?"

"The vault holders have governed Pluton fair and well for two decades," Augusta replied. "Your trading has never prospered better."

"But not as well as it might," Trocolar snapped as he waved his arm over the chests. "I have not forgotten the innocent-faced girl who charmed a debt holding from me all those years ago."

"I paid you a premium for the writ," Augusta's voice hardened. "You received more than you were due and a year early besides. You have no cause for complaint."

"No, no cause for complaint," Trocolar spat. "No cause for complaint. I am reminded of it each time the others ask me again to tell the tale. No cause for complaint, because I did not ask why you wanted the writ. This vault should have been mine, Augusta, not the prize of some barefoot mainland girl who chanced upon it first!"

"You were greedy enough for immediate gain," Augusta shot back. "I took the gamble that months later the vault holders would not be able to pay. And we have been over the same story many times before. You keep your treasures here for the same reasons as the others. Despite how you feel about who earns the fees, you are eager enough to take advantage of the fact that they are less."

"This time, there is a difference," Trocolar said. "This time, I am close enough that my faction may win." The trader stopped and grabbed Augusta by the shoulders. "I have paid the divulgents, and they have told me what I needed to know, Augusta. I have learned from what you taught me as well. Your only indebtedness is for the pumps that keep this pit from washing away. Periodic payments to the guild that made them will continue for many years. But you are aggressive, Augusta, always hungry for more, speculating to the limit and holding back barely enough to transfer the sums when they are due."

Trocolar sucked in his breath and raced on. "Understand that I am your new debtholder, Augusta. I paid a premium for the writ, just as you had done with me. And if I win control of the council, their first act will be to change the laws governing magical items procured by the vaults. Those are too precious to be so capriciously obtained from the guilds. A proper vault should have title to its items of security free and clear. Someone who places his treasures for safekeeping should expect no less. Yes, there will be a change to the laws so that such liens immediately will be due and payable.

"Think of it, Augusta. In a few days, it might all be over. In less than a week, you may be a true debtor, unable to pay. Everything you have, including your life, could be mine to do with as I will."

Trocolar tilted back his head and laughed, his voice bouncing off the walls in booming echoes. Then, with a swirl of his cape, he turned and headed back for the ladder. "I will count them in the skiff after they are loaded," he called back. "Holgon, my magician, has found a potential partner who thinks a few hundred is an impressive sum. Wait until he sees me with some eight thousand more."

In the gloom, Augusta's shoulders sagged and Jason ran to her side. "How serious is his threat?" he asked. "Can you not pay him from one of the other chests that are here?"

"The total number of tokens on Pluton is known." Augusta shook her head. "And for every credit to an account, there must be a debit elsewhere. These chests are not mine to do with as I please. They belong to many others. And Trocolar's knowledge is accurate. The total of what I owe on the pumps exceeds all that I personally have on account."

"Then a new partner. A share in future profits for someone to pay what will be due."

"If Trocolar controls the council, none would dare thwart his intent." Augusta shook her head again. "No, now my hope will have to be that Rosimar succeeds sooner than expected. When we return to shore, you must go to him immediately and tell him the increased importance of his endeavors."

Augusta started to smile bravely at Jason, but then stopped. For a moment, she looked away. Finally, she turned back and placed her hand lightly on his arm. "I am sorry," she said, almost in a whisper. "You should not be involved. For a single token, it is too much to risk."

"I will help you if I can," Jason said, "although my knowledge probably will be of little value."

"It is more than your knowledge that is bound in my plight," Augusta replied. "Your writ of indenture was recorded with the rest of the transactions of the day. And such bindings cannot be revoked, regardless of the sum. For the next week, you are one of my assets, Jason, part of what I must surrender to a creditor if I cannot pay." She stroked his arm and finally completed her smile. "You see, I will have company if Trocolar manages to send me to the cube. It is to your benefit as well as mine to speed Rosimar along the way."

A Matter of Scale

JASON'S LATE evening message to the guild had first been met with resistance. Rosimar had wanted to proceed at his own cautious and methodical pace. But the threat to Augusta had eventually won him over. The preparations for the next phase of the ritual were ready in three days, rather than four.

It was a small victory, Jason thought. It felt that he was sinking into a sandy pit with no bottom. First, his scheme to learn a spell of enchantment was thwarted. Then forced on a mission to decipher what was wrong with sorcery in a span of only a few days. And now, even more urgently, to help restore Augusta's fortunes before he could even attempt that.

When Jason returned on the third day to monitor the progress, he did so with keen interest. If the remaining errors in the new ritual could be corrected soon enough, Augusta's fortunes would receive a much-needed boost. A hundred tokens returned with another hundred as well would more than compensate for Trocolar's missing fees.

Jason gazed up and down the length of the huge rectangular hall called the ceremonium that dominated the grounds of the guild. Scattered everywhere was a clutter of apparatus large and small: giant presses, arrays of pulleys and cogs, cascades of vats and piping, cages of exotic beasts, clockworks, balances, and beams. The roof of the structure arched to a giddy height. Through carefully fitted isinglass panels, the morning sunlight flooded the parqueted floor.

Directly in front of where Jason stood, the neophytes strained against the huge lever of a ballista and the ratchet clicked another notch. The twisted leather rope groaned from the effort. At the far end of the ceremonium was the target, a row of whirling saw blades with teeth sparkling from the diamond dust freshly applied. Behind them stood the grindstones, each the width of a barrel and twice the height of a man.

"Much more impressive than delicate tongs and tinkling finger cymbals, is it not?" The lean man next to Jason waved at the equipment while the final adjustments were being made. His nose was pinched between tiny rat-like eyes. Bony forearms dangled from a robe two sizes too small. Although his face was smooth, his shoulders slumped forward with the posture of an older man. "The larger guilds boast of innovation, but none of them have dared to take the chance."

"And if the plate of steel can be split into strips by hurling it against the blades, what then, Rosimar?" Jason asked. "How soon until Augusta receives her return?"

"The mistress of the grotto." Rosimar's eyes narrowed. "I am surprised that you would bother again to curry her favor. She uses men like honey pods, discarding the husk after she has sucked them dry."

"My fate is intertwined with hers," Jason tried to say casually. "The more that her wealth increases, then the greater is the chance that she will be able to pay me my wage when it is due."

"One does not have to be a divulgent to know what is at stake," Rosimar said. "She needs the aid of a master magician, not one who failed to win her fancy in the past. Many saw Trocolar march off under guard to another vault yesterday evening. The trader's factors align. He has her positioned where she has never been before."

Rosimar stared at Jason. "Understand that that is the only reason. Understand it well. If Augusta asks for help, I will give my consent. Even if it means a trip through that tiny hellhole to the vault itself. If it is for our future business together, to influence the tally when the leading factions gather for the vote, not to recapture what has gone before." Rosimar hesitated a second time. "Besides, she can have no more than a passing interest in you, in any event."

Jason blinked at the sudden tension hiding behind the precisely enunciated words. Evidently, Rosimar's feelings for Augusta were still strong. He grimaced as he tried to sort out his thoughts. Augusta and Rosimar. Did that matter? What of Delia, who still was not free? He felt guilty that the image of her golden curls, the sound of her voice, the sense of her brave spirit, all were fading next to the urgency he now felt next to the sharpness of Augusta's attractive presence. In the end, which did he want? It was a tangle he could not resolve.

"Augusta has mentioned that this time the polling will be in the grotto," Jason said. "On the ledge above the vault. Why not have it instead in some neutral place?"

"No place is neutral on Pluton," Rosimar answered. "Each is owned by someone who charges for its use. By tradition, the site is rotated among the leading factions, those strong enough to ensure there is no interruption while the counting is going on."

The magician looked off into the distance, and then shook his head from side to side. Exhaling deeply, he turned to direct two initiates entering the ceremonium, tugging at the end of a large, woven hose. "Attach it to the flute at the left," he said. "The rest are already connected to the bellows in the outer chamber."

The initiates screwed tight the flange that bound the hose to the large, hollowed log running by Jason's feet. The whole end of the room was crowded with giant caricatures of musical instruments, triangles thrice the height of a man, harps with strings like hawsers, and double reeds as thick as tabletops. From each device that was powered by air snaked a hose through a doorway to the rear.

"It is a matter of scale." Rosimar followed Jason's gaze. "The casual travelers think that the magic guilds must be the focus of Pluton's power, because from them come the tokens upon which all else is based. But they do not know the number of steps it takes to make even a single perfect disk, an intricate ritual requiring months and consuming exotic ingredients besides. And with the competition from all who know the secret, and the many mouths to feed between the steps, the profit is small, barely enough to make the whole effort worthwhile. When considered from the standpoint of outlay and return, the boxes and vaults are far more efficient in producing wealth. It is better to receive tokens already made than to struggle to form more with the painstaking steps of our art."

"And yet you experiment with the giant apparatus here," Jason said, "and have taken Augusta's writ to buy all these hoses, saws, and weapons of war."

"It is a matter of scale," Rosimar repeated. "Why labor to produce a single disk when hundreds can be made with the same steps? Why gong a petite triangle to fill a small volume with sound when the entire hall can resonate from one a hundred times as large? Instead of cutting each sheet of steel into strips one careful stroke at a time, we will attempt to cleave many at once by firing the plate at the whirling saws and playing the music at a tempo to keep in step.

"The grinding will be done by the big wheels rather than by hand-held files," the magician continued. "And all the rest has been proved. If today the cleaving can be made to proceed in concert with what the ritual demands for perfection, then the entire process will work without a doubt."

Jason eyed the whirling row of saw blades and the ballista as the neophytes lined up the sheet of gleaming steel in the carriage that would hurl it forward. "And yet the scale and weights standing next to the ballista are normal-sized," he said.

"They control the timing," Rosimar answered. "Now, the scale is balanced with seven lead weights on either side. When one is removed from the left, the right pan swings to the ground and signals the ritual to start. After the triangle sounds, two are removed from the right, and the scale will move in the opposite direction to pace the next step. Alternately, the balance pans will be unloaded. The rigor of the ritual demands it to be so. And when the last is removed, and the scale returns to level, the ballista will be fired. The plate will be ripped into nine strips, each one ready to be stamped with the outline of a row of disks."

Rosimar looked around the ceremonium and smiled. "In fact, all is in readiness, and we will soon know the result. You there, Grogan, I want you to remove the weights while the other masters and I attend to the bellows in the antechamber."

The neophyte sprang to his feet and clutched his hands together. "Not me, Master. The whirling blades and creaking wheels give me a fright. My ears ached last night when the flutes were sounded in the seventh step."

"Your hand is steady," Rosimar replied. "It is an opportunity to show what you have learned while all the masters are watching."

The neophyte extended his hands palms upward. Rosimar scowled at the blur they made with their shaking. "Crandall, then," he said. "You probably can do it as well!"

The second neophyte did not respond. Together, the two of them raced from the hall without looking back.

"A moment." Rosimar's scowl deepened. "They are young, and the task is unexpected. I will have to go to the headmaster and get permission to use one of the initiates. And if it is not granted, then we will have to wait until tomorrow."

"But if the process is proven, can we have new tokens today?" Jason asked.

"Within the hour," Rosimar said. "We could use the very strips produced by the test."

"Can *you* not perform what is to be done?"

Rosimar looked at the still swinging doors through which the neophytes had departed. "Oh, very well. The task is simple enough. Come."

Without saying more, the two approached the scale. Besides the two pans, each carrying the ornate metal spheres was an array of springs and switches clustered around the balance arm. From them, ropes, pipes, and pulleys led to other apparatus in the ceremonium.

"How heavy is each lead sphere?" Jason reached an index finger out towards one.

"Do not touch!" Rosimar commanded. "Magic must be precise. Otherwise, it will not work."

"I did not touch anything," Jason said. "I was only indicating. And I would think that, for such grand equipment as this, little perturbations would be of no consequence. Are you saying that the ritual would not work if a gnat landed on one of the spheres before it was removed?"

Rosimar scowled and without further warning pulled at the top most sphere from the left arm of the balance. Surprised at its weight, it slipped from the magician's grasp like a ball of butter. He reached out to grab at it and crashed his arm into the scale. With a dull clatter, the weights bounced off onto the floor. The giant triangle gonged three times and then there was a sharp crack as the ballista released its charge. The sheet of metal arced across the room, tumbling while it sped, and struck the row of saws broadside rather than on end.

With an ear-piercing shriek, the plate exploded into shrapnel that flew back across the room. One piece bounded beside Jason's leg, and another grazed his ear, knocking him to the ground. The bellows started pumping, and the flutes and horns blasted monotones in a giant dissonance.

"A resonance!" Rosimar's shout mingle with the noise. "A resonance that feeds on itself. Stop the bellows and saws. Shut it all down!"

But the shrieking grew louder. Isinglass buckled from the ceiling and crashed to the floor. The bounding shrapnel continued to carom off the walls and equipment. A large chunk hit the nearest flute in midsection, smashing a hole in its side. The hot air blasting forth kept Jason pinned to the ground. In the confusion, one of the giant grindstones, freed from its mooring, lumbered by to collide into the opposite wall.

Jason held his breath. As the crash of breaking wood and the whiz of hurling projectiles continued unabated, he dug his fingers into the flooring and waited for the tumult to pass.

After a long while, like the debris settling after the passage of a cyclone, the hurling projectiles, the runaway equipment all came to rest. Cautiously, Jason rose to his feet and dusted himself off, blinking at what had happened.

The hall was in complete disarray. Two grindstones were tumbled among the wreckage of the musical instruments. One had plowed through to the chamber beyond. The complicated array of ropes and linkages was a tangle of broken beams and knotted loops like a huge version of Drandor's lattice dashed against a rock. The saws had stopped spinning; one end of the shaft was out of its bushing and leaning against the floor.

"You did touch the scale!" Rosimar shouted, "I know you did. And that ruined everything. You can tell your mistress that you have performed your mission well. It will not be from this guild that she will get the tokens to save her fair skin."

Jason started to rebut, but before he could one of the oarsmen from the day before raced into the room. "Master Rosimar," he cried, "Master Rosimar, come to my mistress' bidding! She will pay you ample fee!"

"What has happened?" Jason asked, trying to block out what he had just seen.

"Most unexpected," the oarsman replied, "and yet most welcome news indeed. Trocolar the trader has changed his mind! He will redeposit his holdings into the grotto and with even more tokens besides. Augusta will earn her fee and a larger one than before."

"She asks for me?" Rosimar shook himself away from surveying the wreckage. "Augusta asked specifically for me?"

"Trocolar brings with him his magician, Holgon, to ensure that all is secure. The mistress wants to be represented properly as well."

Rosimar straightened and pushed out his chest. He glared at Jason a final time. "An opportunity," he said. "An opportunity despite the hellhole. An opportunity for her to realize who is her better choice."

120

Sleight of Hand

"MY ORIGINAL treasure plus hundreds more," Trocolar said. "You may deduct the storage fee from what is there."

"Why the sudden reversal?" Augusta asked, suspicion lurking in her eyes.

They were all huddled together around the chests in the vault, their voices echoing from the walls above the beat of the pumps and the drip of seeping water. Trocolar had already been there when Jason and Rosimar had arrived. There had been no time to tell her what had happened at the guild.

"Why the reversal?" Trocolar shrugged. "It is because of my new partner, the one whom Holgon found. He has presented to me a plan that is greatly to my benefit. For my part of the bargain, all I have to do is carry out a few simple steps, like redepositing my tokens here, along with his more modest amount. He was furious when he learned that I had made a withdrawal. So many tokens in one spot, he said. Far more than he could quickly assemble himself, each the result of an independent act of ritual, none of them shielded by a magic vault. And the more there are, the easier is Holgon's task."

"What has Holgon to do with this?" Augusta asked."

"He arrives shortly," Trocolar said. "As long as he can perform his ritual of safekeeping, then these treasures are again yours to guard."

"Other than the pumps and the tokens themselves, there is no magic needed here," Augusta shook her head. "It is the tide alone that keeps the Vault in the Grotto secure. You know that as well as I."

"Nevertheless, my partner insists," Trocolar replied. "He has prescribed the ritual himself. And you can use your Rosimar here to ensure that nothing goes amiss."

"I am no bondsman to Augusta," Rosimar said weakly. He pushed himself from where he sagged against the slimy wall and tried to fill his lungs. The color returned to his cheeks.

"I serve her for a fee," the magician continued, "and because — because that is what I choose."

"Dear Rosimar." Augusta stroked the magician's arm. "Your fear of small places has not gotten any better. I would have asked another master, but you are the one I trust the most in such affairs as these."

Jason nodded to himself. He knew what the magician was feeling. A different trigger but very much the same reaction.

"No matter." Rosimar swallowed. "My strength is already returning. And I am as curious as the rest about what this ritual of safekeeping might be. At Cantor Guild, we have heard nothing like it."

"Nor has any other on the island," a voice rang out from the shaft leading to the landing above. A magician robed in deepest blue like Rosimar splashed down onto the vault floor. Heavy-framed and balding, his eyes burned with some hidden hunger. "It is an example of a new departure. Like none you have seen before."

"So say they all, Holgon, so say they all," Rosimar replied. "But somehow, on close examination, the new rituals turn out to be mere variations on what has worked before."

Holgon ignored the remark and turned to direct three neophytes struggling down the shaft with the magician's gear. "Your partner arrived with me, trader Trocolar," he called over his shoulder, "and he says that we may begin. He would join you down here in the vault, except that the air circulates too little for his needs. The landing above is as close as he chooses to come."

"But it was to be this very place," Trocolar protested. "He explained that no other would do."

"He assures that all is well," Holgon said. "Once the tokens are securely hidden in their chests, and the pumps are stopped, then I can proceed."

"Stop the pumps?" Augusta exclaimed. "But then the vault will begin to fill!"

"Only for the duration of my ritual so that there is no distraction," Holgon raised his palms in a gesture of reassurance. "It will be short enough so that little additional seepage will occur."

Augusta looked at Rosimar, and the magician shrugged indifference. She signaled an attendant by the pumps, and soon the deep, rhythmic throbbing stopped.

Holgon bowed to Augusta and moved to where his neophytes had erected two tripods in front of an uncluttered stretch of wall. On each was a small box, colored in bright blue with a red sash running around the edges and yellow, five-pointed stars in the middle of each face. Between the two had been placed a large chest with its lid closed.

Holgon pushed the tripods closer together until they touched the ends of the chest and then opened its top.

"Sand," he passed his arm over the opening. "Ordinary sand from the harbor, nothing more."

To emphasize what he had said, the magician dipped into the chest and scooped out a handful of its contents. He let the sand cascade back into the container from between his fingers like water in a rapids finding passage between interfering rocks. When the flow stopped, he brushed his hands of the few grains that remained and then closed the lid. Next, he directed attention to one of the tripods and lifted the tall box standing on it. With exaggerated flourishes, he unhinged each side from the top so that, hinged at the bottom, they flopped down below. Holding the structure in his hand, he displayed it from left to right. Then the master replaced it on its stand, closed it again and repeated the procedure with the other.

"Street conjuring," Rosimar snorted. "No ritual of true magic has such gaudy display."

Holgon ignored the comment. With his face frozen in a blank smile like that of a mime, he produced a small dove from the sleeve of his robe and pointed at a jeweled collar around its neck. "A bracelet of teleportation," he said. "Completed except for the final step."

Then he placed the dove in the box on the left from the top and snapped shut the lid. He showed the one on the right a second time to be empty and closed it up as well.

"And now we wait until the conditions are right," With another flourish, the magician drew his arms inside opposite sleeves and stood staring straight ahead.

Everyone was silent, and nothing happened. Jason smiled in amusement. As a small boy, he had seen traveling minstrels claiming to be magicians do much of the same. On one hand, he knew what was going to happen next, but then, perhaps, just perhaps, there would be a surprise instead.

"The journey begins." A muffled voice snaked down the shaft. "Set the example so that it can be properly completed."

Holgon grunted and resumed his ritual. He produced a small wand from his sleeve and sent it through a rapid series of gyrations like a windsock flapping in a light breeze. The magician tapped the box on the left, and the sides unlatched and fell open. It was empty, and the dove was gone. Then he put the wand away and cradled the box on the right to his chest. Opening the top, he reached inside and produced the bird wearing the collar. The magician waved the dove back and forth. With a small bow, he hid it back in the container.

Without waiting for comment, Holgon repeated the steps he had just performed. When he was done, he showed the right-hand box to be empty and the dove to reoccupy the left. A murmur of impatience ran through the watching assemblage, but Holgon paid no attention. Again he enacted the ritual and yet again.

"And thus it is finished," Holgon shouted out after the ninth performance. "The fortunes and futures of expert Trocolar are now well secured."

"That is no ritual of magic," Rosimar growled. "And the wand patterns were as ill-formed as those of a neophyte. No circles closed, and the cadence was off by at least half a beat. It takes perfection to perform magic, Holgon. I am surprised that your technique shows such a lack of grace. Is that what becomes of one who indentures himself to a trader instead of working in the security of a guild? Does he become a performer of street tricks that mimic magic and waste the watcher's time?"

"Then how do you explain this," Holgon replied. He opened the lid on the chest between the tripods and again reached for a handful of its contents. This time, before returning the sand to the box he opened his palm and held it out for inspection.

"Pyramids!" Jason exclaimed. "The grains of sand. They now are all perfect little pyramids, not angular and misshappened as one would expect."

"Precisely so," Holgon smiled as he returned the sand to the chest and reclosed the lid.

"And with that, the journey now ends," the muffled voice from above was heard again.

"I am still confused," Augusta said to Holgon. "You speak of fortunes and futures, but Trocolar's desires are not enhanced if I get a greater fee rather than none at all."

"Yes, it would seem to be a conundrum for you, Augusta," Trocolar agreed, "a conundrum to be explained in its own due time. But as for me, it is quite simple. If my partner speaks false, then his tokens are forfeited to me. If his words are truth, ah, then, my scheming one, you will have to worry about the shrinking cube."

Augusta's eyes widened, but Trocolar did not explain further. He motioned for Holgon to follow and pushed through the others to the ladder leading upward. The chest of sand was left behind.

"Send this one following after." Rosimar pointed at Jason after the trader's party had climbed to the top of the shaft. "He deliberately sabotaged what has taken us months to assemble. Your investment is jeopardized and also my guild's."

Augusta's face contorted in furrows seemingly as deep as a newly plowed field. She rubbed her forehead while squinting her eyes closed. "No, Rosimar, no more for today. Trocolar's threats are enough. For now, I wish only to think of the fact that his tokens are back and his fees as well. Perhaps this whole exercise is some elaborate charade just for my discomfort. Possibly his chance in the election is nothing but bluster, and he can do no more than torment me with his words."

"You need a steady hand and experience to guide you through the next few days," Rosimar said, "not an incompetent who interferes with magic."

"You stated yourself that the ritual had a flaw," Jason rebutted. "And your neophytes were none too eager to perform it."

Jason drew a deep breath to say more, but Augusta placed her fingers across his lips. "Hush, my dreamer. Do not bother to add your words to Rosimar's din. For now, let me be away so that I can rest. If you truly want to help, then try to understand what lies behind Trocolar's words. Does Holgon's pretty display have any real meaning, or is it merely a fantasy of the mind?"

She looked back at Rosimar. "And with Trocolar's fee, we are better positioned than before. There will be time enough to plan for additional funding for your guild, time enough after the elections are over, and we have won."

Without saying more, Augusta, like a princess sheltered from reality, glided past all who remained and began to climb the ladder.

Rosimar looked at Jason, grunted, and made his way to what Holgon had left behind. "If it provides her with reassurance, then it will be worth the effort," he said.

Jason joined the magician in taking apart the tripods. For over two hours, they examined the two boxes and their stands, looking for some trace of true magic, but finding only hidden latches and sliding panels. Finally, they opened the lid to the chest.

Inside there were no perfect little pyramids, just ordinary sand like that on any beach. The two spent another hour running their hands through it but found that the chest contained nothing else.

"You were right," Jason admitted at last. "It is no more than a conjuring trick from the mainland."

Rosimar started to reply, but the pump attendant approached and pulled at his sleeve. "Master, I need assistance. I have tried all the variations that I know. The pumps! I cannot get them to restart!"

JASON WAITED while Rosimar struggled up the rope ladder.

The magician shook his head, perplexed. "I thought I knew all the major rituals of perpetual motion. But apparently, the inner mechanism of the pumps is one that I do not understand. And the casings were very strange to the touch, like ordinary metal with no aura of magic about them."

No aura of magic. The words hit Jason like a thunderbolt. Could it be? Could it possibly be?

"'If a solution works on a similar puzzle, try it on the one at hand'", he mumbled aloud.

"Can you fetch me a token from the chests?" he asked the oarsman who had ferried them into the grotto.

"They cannot be removed once the ledgers are marked. Only on Augusta's orders are the transfers made."

"A single coin," Jason insisted. "What the test reveals could be very important."

The oarsman hesitated, but finally turned and descended the passageway. In a moment, he returned with a small bag of jingling metal. "From Trocolar's deposit, the one most recent."

Jason nodded, plunged his hand into the sack and plucked out one of the smooth disks. "Cold," he muttered, "stone-cold. No doubt it will be the same with the rest."

"Put away the distraction," Rosimar said. "The riddle is the failure of the pumps."

"The problem is far more basic." Jason shook his head. "Look at what has happened to your craft."

Before Rosimar could reply, Jason placed the disk against the wall and pushed it across the wet surface. He grunted at the result and tossed the coin to Rosimar.

The magician grabbed the token and examined it in his hand. His eyes widened, and his mouth dropped open in surprise. "Scratched!" he exclaimed. "Somehow, Trocolar managed to slip in a counterfeit among the rest."

"Check the others if you want," Jason said, "but, like the pumps, they pulse with magic no more."

"I do not know what you mean. Magic items last for eternity. They are perfect. There can be no other way."

Jason ignored the protest. He closed his mind to the magician's confusion and thought through the consequences.

"Augusta!" he shouted after a moment. "Don't you see? She must be warned. Quickly, let us speed to her aid."

"But the pumps! And the rest of the tokens! Yes, we should examine them all and see how many are bad."

"There will be no time," Jason insisted. "To the skiff. I will explain as we go."

Scentstones

JASON WATCHED Rosimar disappear in the other direction through the waterfront crowd. There was no time to try to make the magician understand further. The master would be convinced soon enough after he had tried some simple rituals with his guild.

First sorcery and now magic had been struck down! And it would not be like Morgana with only a dozen sorcerers. Already shouts about worthless counterfeits rang from a stall down the way.

He looked about. In his haste to follow Rosimar up the rise from the harbor, he was not at the foot of the Street of the Vaults, but one or two lanes over. He sucked in a deep breath. New unfamiliar territory. His stomach burbled with its first protest.

Jason rubbed his brandel. There was no time for this. He could not be stopping every few minutes along the way. After a minute, the feeling subsided enough, and he opened his eyes to look up the street. A flash of motion caught his eye. A spicy odor filled his lungs like that from an orchard of newly ripened fruit. To the side of the street, a sheet of white linen stretched taut over a frame in front of a trader's stall.

Painted on the cloth in lush reds and browns was a richly decorated leather sack. Small, translucent stones spilled out to sparkle into outstretched palms. No, it was not a painting, Jason decided as he stepped forward to look closer. The scene flickered. The hands seemed to move and clutch the sparkling pebbles in a sequence that repeated over and over.

Jason breathed the aroma and felt a rush of pleasure fill his lungs. What did the sign say? Only two coppers for a small stone, three for a larger one. He blinked in surprise at the direction of his thoughts.

Nearby, a second sign pointed to an adjacent alley — a big blue arrow that grew from a short stub to an elongated shaft vibrating with energy and somehow promising excitement down the path.

He sucked in his breath, reaching to savor the hint of spice that still remained in the air. Then he took a reluctant step towards the alley. As he did, two others rushed past to join a line forming down the way. Jason shrugged and ran to join the queue as well.

Crammed stomach to back in a single file, Jason waited his turn, his mouth watering. It was an orderly line, he thought. So many people, so close, but orderly enough that it did not matter. With a hand damp with anticipation, he fumbled in his pouch to see what coins were there. As he got closer to the counter, he saw above it another animation. Small stones poured in a rushing stream and fell onto a woman's thinly veiled chest. Pale eyes under silky, auburn hair seemed to look directly at him. Pouting lips beckoned with promises of more delights to come.

When he reached the counter, Jason emptied his pouch. "As much as this will buy," he said. "I have no tokens, else I would take even more."

"Your metal is good," the man behind the partition smiled as he scooped some coins from a large sack. "Or even items in trade. Collecting tokens is not my master's desire. And you are fortunate. These are the first scentstones to go on sale."

Jason waved aside the words as a half-dozen small smooth stones were placed in his outstretched hand. He spun around and shouldered his way back toward the street, clasping his purchase. With a glimmer of recognition, he noticed that the divulgent, Benedict, was in the queue, eagerly pressing forward with the rest.

But Jason had no time for such irrelevancies now. He ran out onto the street and then into the next passageway on the right. Hands clutched together and like a victim being hotly pursued, he traced a zigzag path through the alleys and lanes of Pluton, making it impossible for any would-be thief to follow, searching for the perfect hiding place in which to examine his treasure.

Almost an hour later, his energy spent, he ducked into a dim alleyway and pulled to a halt. He brought his fist to his face and cracked open his grip to savor again the encompassing euphoria. With the first whiff, his fingers relaxed. Slipping into a daze, he contemplated the pebbles in his palm.

"I must withdraw my vault holdings!" a voice shouted behind his back. "The rumors grow more persistent, and I must make sure!"

Vault holdings, Jason thought dimly as he inhaled. Augusta and the grotto. There is something that I must tell her, something about the ...

Suddenly, two merchants bumped past, knocking Jason to the wall and scattering the scentstones to the ground. A flash of anger burned away his inattention, and he swung at a flowing robe as it raced by. He took one step after, but then halted and dropped to his knees. With a frantic pawing, he ran his hands over the rock-strewn path, searching for his treasure. A hint of purple translucence caught his eye and then a small sparkle of orange.

He scooped up two stones and ran back onto the wider street. In the full glare of the sun, he opened his fist to verify that he had recovered what had been dropped. In disbelief, he realized that he held only smoky quartz weakly tinted with color. A hint of cinnamon drifted upward. The exotic aroma was no more.

Jason scrambled back to the alleyway to search the ground more methodically, but after several minutes, he found no pebbles more precious than what he held in his hand. He examined his palm again, but the compulsion was gone.

He shook his head at what he had done. He held common rock, inexpertly sprayed with a cheap scent. If they were more clear, the stones might pass for semiprecious citrine and amethyst, rare enough in the islands. But as they were, they should have been no more than an idle curiosity, not worth his time. What gave them such an allure? How could such commonplace trinkets evoke such a desire?

Sorcery had not returned had it? There was no charm he had heard, no looking a sorcerer in the eye. Just to be sure, he ran through *Power of Suggestion* but as before, there was no resistance and no change. Not sorcery then, but yet somehow in some way disturbingly similar in effect.

Panic in the Market

ENOUGH! THE puzzles were piling up too fast, Jason thought. Sorcery, magic, and now plain pebbles with an almost irresistible attraction that vanishes after an hour! There was no time to think about them further. First, he must help Augusta and secure his own freedom before investigating additional enigmas. He brushed his palms. Locking his eyes straight down the path, he proceeded as fast as he could the rest of the way to the Street of the Vaults.

When he arrived, the hint of something amiss had already begun to spread along the street. Every vault was busy with at least two or three customers. Long queues snaked out of some down the way.

Jason stopped at the entrance to Augusta's offices and composed himself. He kept his eyes lowered to the ground and tried to ignore the angry glances as he pushed his way through to the anteroom.

"I am not making a formal withdrawal." One of two heavy-set men pressing against the partition waved his arms at the clerk. "I still intend to pay the full fee. I merely wish to examine my cache of tokens to ensure that all is well. They will be returned within the hour."

"We keep only a small quantity here to handle the usual transactions," the clerk said. "Your deposit is too large, and we must wait for the next tide to bring back more from the grotto."

"The agreement is for full surrender on demand for any sum less than forty tokens," the second customer insisted. "Any other vault on the street would not try to delay."

"Our service is as good as any other." Augusta pushed open the door from the back. "It is just that you are the fifth in a row to ask for a large withdrawal with only one depositing in between."

She handed a writ to the clerk and then forced a smile back to the customer. "And with a moment's patience, your treasure will be secure.

131

My aide will find a vault that temporarily overflows. I will arrange a loan for the rest of the day and then repay it when the fluctuations balance out."

The clerk ducked under the table and headed for the street, squeezing between three more customers who had entered and crowded behind the two in front.

"Any more withdrawals?" Augusta asked. "Step forward. Sums less than — less than three tokens can be honored at once. Larger treasures will take a few minutes more. And, of course, deposits of all sizes are readily accepted. There is still time to get them recorded so that your vote in the election will be more."

Before anyone could reply, agitated voices suddenly erupted in the street. Five or six more people surged into the anteroom, jamming the doorway. Outside a large crowd gathered.

"Ah, Trader Andor," Augusta called over the noise. "You were here but minutes ago with your withdrawal of twenty-five. No doubt all is well, and you wish to return your deposit to the vault's safekeeping."

"I want my wealth!" the short, balding man in front of the new arrivals shouted back. "This time, tokens of magic, not simple disks of cold steel!"

The crowd strained forward in a chorus of apprehension, pushing Jason to the wall and filling the small room. Augusta looked about in worry and ran her tongue over her lips.

"But they are true tokens," she protested. "Yesterday evening I counted them into the very sack you hold in your hand. Twenty-five exactly, there is no doubt."

"Twenty-five indeed," Andor snarled. "Twenty-five pieces of worthless metal!" He flipped the sack open and hurled a handful of coins to spatter against the wall at Augusta's back.

"They are no different from the ones securely held in the grotto," Augusta persisted. "One magic token is the same as another."

"Then the ones in the vault are worthless as well!" someone else shouted. "We have been swindled. Our fortunes are gone!"

"Gold or silver," another said. "If she cannot pay in tokens, let it be their equivalent, and we can exchange them elsewhere."

"If you desire another metal," Augusta replied hurriedly, "I will do what I can. But, like the tokens, my holdings here are small. The first in line and perhaps one or two more.

"The vault has no more tokens! Only gold for some in the back room. Get what you can! The rest she cannot pay." With a sudden push, those in front slammed aside the table and poured through the opening. They knocked Augusta to the floor and pounded into the other room. With raised fists and incoherent shouts, the rest of the crowd cascaded after.

Jason was not functioning well. There were too many people and all of them angry and shouting. Without resisting, he was pushed forward with the others. He reached Augusta where she had crumpled and somehow found the wits to elbow one of the depositors away. A fist slammed into Jason's back, staggering him to his knees. He twisted to the side and winced in pain as heavy boots trampled his legs. Scooping his arms around Augusta, he rolled to the left under the table, which had been banged against the outer wall. He reached out between the impatient feet that were stomping and kicking to get ahead and pulled in her under. Together, they huddled in a tight ball.

The press of the crowd funneling through the doorway strained against their shelter. Someone fell next to the table and then another went down. Like building blocks toppled by a single swat of the hand, a whole row staggered to its knees. The ones behind pushed these closer to the floor and scrambled over their backs. The doorway jammed in a squirming mass of entangled arms and legs like the tentacles of a hideous monster from the sagas. Cries of pain and panic began to mingle with the shouts of anger. The table planking groaned from the pressure, and then one pair of legs collapsed, confining Jason and Augusta to a small triangle of vertical space.

Think of it as a puzzle, think of it as a puzzle, Jason thought savagely to himself, but no possibilities came. It was worse than what had happened on Morgana, trying to get to Delia before the fire …

"Fire!" Jason yelled at the top of his lungs without thinking further. "Fire! Fire!"

JASON CLIMBED out from the small volume of safety. He did not feel proud about what he had done, but at least there were no bodies scattered about the floor. Enough people had emptied out so that the remaining could loot in relative peace. The door to the office behind hung lopsided from a single hinge. Scrolls and loose pages of parchment were scattered about like the first leaves of autumn. Everything was gutted. Even the candlesticks were gone. There was no one else there.

"Safe," he said. "It is safe to come out, Augusta." He helped her to stand. "I did not reach you any too soon. A run on the vaults was the logical consequence, once it was learned that tokens no longer hold special value."

He regarded Augusta, expecting her to reply, but found her staring at the street and the vault offices across the way. Everywhere the scene was the same. Crazed crowds carried out what small stores of wealth they could find. In frenzied fighting, they squabbled over what little there was.

"Safe," she echoed vacantly. "Safe. What has happened, Jason? I do not understand."

"It is the same for all the vaults, Augusta. All across the island, Arcadia, and Procolon. Magic is no more."

"All the vaults?" Augusta asked, shaking herself out of a daze. "Then none of the holders will have a basis for any votes. Those who have deposited will all demand their due. We are debtors one and all."

She looked at Jason, her eyes growing wide. "Yes, we are safe — safe until the election. Until Trocolar has his way."

"His fortune is based the same as yours," Jason said. "And so is that of everyone else. It is unclear who will be judged the richest, if tokens no longer matter."

"Not all his wealth is in the vaults," Augusta shook her head. "He owns ships, men, and warehouses full of goods: bolts of silk, barrel staves, links of heavy chain, seed corn, and flour. A thousand items that he can barter for advantage. He is well prepared to make profit on whatever strikes the speculator's fancy. Why, on the way back from the grotto, he bragged that he even had acquired a boatload of citrine and amethyst to add to his holdings."

"But at least his threat cannot be the shrinking cube," Jason said. "That device now functions no better than the rest."

"Then chains and hot needles." Augusta shrugged. "He will think of something else to —"

"Citrine and amethyst," Jason interrupted. "You say that Trocolar is the one with the gems?"

"Jason, they cannot matter. Trocolar showed me some samples. At most, they can be made into inexpensive baubles for the wide-eyed visitors from the mainland. He would need a powerful glamour to entice one with any knowledge to pay more than a copper for a barrelful."

"But, like magic, sorcery is no more. No one can mouth a working charm. The words have no resistance," Jason shook his head. "And yet, if not an enchantment, then what compelled me on the way here? Yes, now that I think about it, the displays on the street were like the projections on the cliff and the presentation hall, moving images on a screen that somehow shaped one's thoughts. Drandor! His strange animations. The smiling trader *and* Trocolar. There is a connection!"

He closed his eyes and plowed into deep thought. For a long while, he was silent. Then he turned and headed for the street.

"Wait, where are you going?" Augusta cried.

"I came to Pluton from Morgana with a puzzle to solve," Jason said. "But I have made no progress at all since I have been here. And now, there is the disappearance of magic and a new strangeness that cannot be explained. If anything, the mystery has deepened.

"Come. I will take you to Rosimar's guild for safety," he motioned her to him. "And then I will see Benedict, the divulgent to ask him how he fared with his purchase of the stones. It is the logical place to start. And this time I will not leave until I have negotiated the exchange of information."

The Three Adventurers

"MY BLADE is small, but I warn you, it bites deep, nonetheless."

"As before, I am here to trade." Jason glared at Benedict, who was huddled in the far corner of his cubicle, holding his strongbox with both arms to his chest like a small girl clutching her doll in a storm. Jason's sense of urgency had been growing ever since Augusta had been left at the guild. The cries in the street made it clear that little time remained before a complete collapse of order.

But the divulgent could prove to be of value. He would have to act in a role that made Benedict do what he wanted, Jason had decided, as uncomfortable as it might be — one from his fancies, that of the no-nonsense hero that filled the sagas. He willed himself into the appearance of competent calm and motioned Rosimar to enter behind him as he sat on one of the stools.

"A copper," Benedict said. "And two more for a guest."

"What I have for you is worth far more than three coppers," Jason replied. "Even more than the tokens you would charge for the contents of that now-worthless box."

"'Perfection is eternal', indeed!" the divulgent spat. "A stronghold impervious to the dent of the mightiest hammer, so I was told. Look at it now. No more than a tray with a well-hinged lid. And no hasp for an ordinary lock, at that. Even a child could flip it open and seize the contents if I did not stand on guard. It is as worthless as the tokens that you offer to pay."

"Let's go," Rosimar growled behind Jason's back. "This is an affair of magic, not gossip of the harbor. If Augusta had not wished that I come along, I would be elsewhere, employing my skills as a master."

"There is no time to learn everything that we must know," Jason said. "The knowledge of a divulgent may save us many a step."

"His brain is addled." Rosimar moved to Jason's side and waved across the high table. "He can only impede what I must do."

"I plan to convince him that our goal is the same," Jason replied. "That we can work to the benefit of us all."

"No, not of us all!" Rosimar thundered. "By no means will *we* achieve what *I* seek."

The magician's face flushed. With a deep glower, he raised his fist in the air. "This time, I will not be haunted by your memory, Jason. This time, there can be no doubt about the value of what I provide. This time there will be gratitude without reservation. This time, Augusta will not whine and complain about the love she left behind, about how slowly I advanced in the hierarchy of the guild, about how few were the gowns of silk that I could afford. When I snatch her away from Trocolar's certain torture, there will be no excuse to cast me aside and strike out on her own."

Rosimar's knuckles whitened like freshly popped corn. His hand shook as he continued. "And this time, I will make sure that the credit is properly placed. In the end, it will all be mine, not shared with a wanderer — one who curries favor by resurrecting the past, rather than with solid works expertly done."

Jason returned Rosimar's stare, looking for a spark of reason behind the emotion. In addition to everything else, he did not need the distraction. He pushed the confused tangle that defined his own feelings toward Augusta away and focused on why he was in the divulgent's cubicle. "There is no time for that now, Rosimar. Three working together will serve Augusta better than each laboring apart."

"If I will not share with one, then neither will I with two," Rosimar replied. "And I see no advantage in a timid divulgent who does not know even the value of pebbles I can fetch from an ore dump."

"Did you not see the exchange board as you passed?" Benedict said, oblivious to the other conversation. "It is empty, wiped clean in the past hour. No longer is value measured in tokens. Each commodity is bartered, and no standards prevail. And I know what will happen as a consequence. There is information from the past and other places that foreshadows the events here. Already I have learned of the effects on the shoreline. Ships have missed the tide because the fee for the crew's provisions could not be settled. Goods will remain to rot in storage because no one is sure of their true worth. Commerce will halt like a stepped upon snail. Many stomachs will be empty before a new order is established."

137

The divulgent's eyes took on a faraway look as he stroked the lid of the box in his lap. "But scentstones are different. They possess a spicy essence that men will fight for. They produce a thirst that cannot be slacked. And more importantly, there are not enough to satisfy the demand. Already a sack weighing three dranbots has been traded for a barrel of the purest oil. There is a rumor that my rival, Cumbrist, will offer the use of his cubicle for the next year for three handfuls.

"I desire them as the rest do," Benedict continued, "but I can see also a second purpose they serve as well. The price has doubled in the last hour. In the next, it probably will double again. With only two more days to the election, who knows what one's fortune might turn out to be?"

"I saw you in line to buy some of the first," Jason spoke directly to the divulgent. "Worthless pebbles with allure for minutes at most."

Benedict's eyes glazed over, and he did not acknowledge Jason's words. Looking past Rosimar's shoulder, he stared vacantly at the curtain behind. Jason stamped his foot and then clapped his hands, but Benedict did not move. With little spasms, the divulgent's fingers twitched on the lid of his strongbox.

"The scentstones," Jason said. "Benedict, pay attention. Do you have them here?"

"My dagger." Benedict shook out of his reverie and fumbled with a blade at his belt. "It will be my answer if you press too close."

"Yet, before today, did you care at all about such grit?" Jason continued. "Does it not strike you as odd? Yes, think of something else besides the tiny stones. Break the connection as I did on the street. What of the threat to whatever else you have in your arms in addition to the granules of rock? Jerk your attention away."

Benedict huddled in the corner and raised his dagger. Slowly, Jason slid from the stool and advanced. "All of your information," he said. "Is it worth sacrificing that to save what rattles in your little box?"

The divulgent's face froze in a mask of tension. He jabbed the blade forward as he watched Jason approach. He started to speak again, but then paused, squinting his eyes.

"Now the stones themselves," Jason came another step closer. "What allure can they truly have? Look at them. Make sure that they are worth the risk."

Benedict shook his head in denial. But as Jason moved forward again, the divulgent thrust his hand inside his box to withdraw one of the stones. He fingered it hurriedly and cast it aside. Throwing back the lid, he reached to the bottom and extracted a handful of pebbles the smaller ones slipping between his fingers to bounce on the floor.

"Cinnamon," the divulgent muttered. "Only cinnamon! By the looks, all murky stones with inclusions and flaws." Benedict looked back at Jason. "But how can that be? It is as I have told you. Some purchased after mine have traded hands many times, and each exchange has fetched a more princely sum."

"I think I might know who is responsible for the mysteries," Jason returned to his stool. "And I hope that you know how to gain entry into his keep by some stealth. If we exchange what we know, then perhaps in addition to who and where, we will be able to figure out how."

Benedict studied the pile of rocks as they dribbled out of his hand. He inverted his palm to let the last few drop away. "Penniless," he mumbled. "Everything I traded for worthless rock. And more I borrowed from others, besides."

He looked up at Jason. "You may have information of some value," he concluded. "And as things stand, I have few options other than to hear what you have to say. Perhaps the fee for the chairs can be waved."

Jason smiled and motioned Rosimar to the other stool. But before the magician moved, one of the pages thrust his head through the curtain leading to the court.

"The men-at-arms," the boy said. "They are searching each cubicle, one by one. It is to impound the assets. All property belonging to the vault holders is to be seized against payment of their debts."

"Another exit?" Jason asked. "We cannot exchange information if I am bound."

"The debts of the vault holders are no concern of mine." Benedict retreated to the far wall. "From the mercenaries I have nothing to hide."

"And neither will you learn about the scentstones," Jason said, "nor of what has happened to the tokens and sorcery. Without information, how can you hope to repay your newly acquired debts?"

Benedict bit his lip. His eyes darted around the small room. He looked from Jason to Rosimar and then at the pebbles at his feet. "Why did I care?"

He shook his head. "The allure was so real. And no doubt, Cumbrist pursues them still. The divulgent who first understands it all will have knowledge of great value, to be sure."

The divulgent looked at Jason a final time. "Quickly." He motioned to a hinged panel in the rear wall. "We will strike the bargain once we are away from the exchange."

Benedict ducked through the opening. Jason rounded the high table to follow. He turned to look at Rosimar, who was slowly descending from his stool.

"The two of us will proceed without you if we must," Jason called back, "but a master's knowledge of magic may be useful as well."

Rosimar hesitated and then frowned as he heard the clink of mail. "Until you are to be cast aside." He shrugged. "Until then, I will permit myself to follow."

Trocolar's Keep

IN THE moonlight filtering through the trees, Jason shifted position to get a better view. Down at the shoreline, their small skiff could be seen bobbing on the gentle waves. Farther back across the water were the lights of Pluton, some mere pinpoints, but others the flickering brightness of fires out of control.

The role of the saga hero had gone away. Jason could not maintain that and at the same time cope with the new strange edifice in front of them. Hopefully, Benedict's familiarity would be enough, and he would be able to remain in control.

At the rising slope of the island, trees blanketed the hillside toward the crest, except on the right, where they had been cleared away for a garishly decorated structure of stone and iron. Behind the crest and out of sight was the other island in the bay, the one that contained Augusta's vault. Jason had not guessed that the larger of the two was owned by Trocolar. The leader of the tradesmen had indicated nothing when Augusta ferried him to her vault three days before.

But Benedict had been insistent. The island and the estate were indeed the trader's. The divulgent had said that if there were more to be learned, it would most likely be there. And so, under the cover of nightfall, Jason, Rosimar, and he had rowed across the bay and landed unobserved where the green canopy came almost to the shore.

"I will have the correct amounts in a moment," Benedict whispered above the soft jingle of coins. "My sorting device barely functions. The output from a single column is more often a scramble than not."

"Why not carry a pouch the way everyone else does and dip into it, once the price has been settled?" Rosimar growled in irritation. "The guards on the wall or some patrol will soon find us if you continue to fumble."

"A full purse is no way to bargain for several favors," Benedict replied. "You will empty it for the first and get no other. I acknowledge your mastery of your craft, Rosimar; respect my skill in mine. A divulgent prepares his cloak with many pockets, each with but one coin or two."

Benedict fingered the levers of his changer and scowled at the results in his palm. The divulgent selected a single coin from the pile to put in a pocket and returned the rest to the top of the device. "I am ready at last. The guard at the postern gate has told me much before, but never have I convinced him to let me enter. What we learn in Trocolar's private estate had better be of supreme value to justify our risk."

"Then perhaps I should proceed alone," Rosimar said. "I would have expected something more from this skill of yours than a simple bribe."

"A secret passage, perhaps?" Benedict snapped back. "Or maybe a ring that levitates the bearer over walls? You are the magician. What do you bring to our agreement in addition to your razor-edged tongue?"

"Enough!" Jason waved his arms for silence. The muscles in his neck were knotted like anchoring hawsers from anticipation. Keeping the other two from spatting was an added distraction that he could well do without. "Just get us inside. The rest does not matter."

"You are the least qualified to speak," Rosimar replied. "Except in stealth, you cannot move about on Pluton at all. The mercenaries will make sure all frozen assets are impounded. Their annual fees depend on how well they perform."

"Our goal is to learn how the laws of magic and sorcery have been turned off," Jason said. "And, if the random factors align, how to reactivate them as well. With the tokens in Augusta's vault once more a well-regarded tender, she will be no debtor, and I can act as I choose."

"But if not within two days, the election will be over and Trocolar will prevail," Rosimar replied. "After that, it will not matter for you whether the craft is again operative or not."

"If you see all outcomes so bleak, then why continue?" Jason asked, anger starting to rise. "Return to your guild and wait out the storm. From the safety of your surrounding walls, try to convince Augusta of your aid on her behalf."

Rosimar glared at Jason, then at Benedict. Finally, he shrugged and folded his arms inside his robe. Benedict said no more. He nibbled on his lip and started to move farther into the shadows.

They traveled the rest of the way to the estate in silence, flitting among the trees like field mice trying to avoid a prowling owl. While Jason and Rosimar waited on the edge of the clearing, Benedict darted across to confer with the guard.

The moon was bright in the cloudless sky. Strong shadows of the roofline traced a jagged pattern across the naked landscape surrounding the keep. The structure was not large — two stories with perhaps a half-dozen rooms in each — but the facework resembled that of a large castle from the mainland of Arcadia or even Procolon across the ocean. Miniature bartizans budded from crenellated walls. Tiny loopholes dotted shallow bastions. Each row of square-cut stone was slightly smaller than the one upon which it rested, giving the illusion of greater height as one scanned upward.

While Jason watched, Benedict appeared out of the gloom of the small gatehouse, beckoning him and Rosimar to come forward. In a moment, all three were inside, examining the dim walls and a grim-faced guard still clutching a fist full of coins.

"He says that they all are at their evening meal," Benedict whispered. "Including Trocolar's new partner, who spends most of his time in the dampness below."

"Then to the dungeon," Jason whispered. "We may learn everything we need before they have finished their wine."

"The stair is on the south wall." Benedict motioned with his head. "But the guard will not escort us down. And the entry is barred and locked, besides."

"A simple lock will not stop us." Jason said. "It is only a puzzle of a special type."

Benedict led the way. The passage was narrow, dirty, and hung with cobwebs. Just enough light to guide their feet flickered down from torches set high in the wall. On the landing below, Jason paused for his eyes to adjust to the gloom. A single short passage led to heavy wooden doors barred by a single beam chained in place. From his cloak, he pulled a finger-length shaft of metal with a narrow flange on one end and inserted it into the lock. With his other hand, he slipped in another tool and gave it a gentle twisting tug. After a few experimental probes with the first, he rotated the second a quarter turn to the left, and the hasp snapped open. He pushed the bar aside, and they entered.

The doors opened onto a vast room, the view interrupted only by stout posts that supported the beams and planking of the ceiling above. In each corner, small alcoves projected off at odd angles, their entrances barred by grates of iron. Each was filled to overflowing with sacks, barrels, and wooden boxes. Stuffed in crannies were heaps of chain, shafts of steel, shields, pikes, and bowls of polished copper. More goods cluttered the main floor: piles of linen, bins of grain, huge leather volumes bound in groups of six, and rough tarpaulins covering stacked crates and lumpy mounds.

In the very center, barely separate from the piles that pushed in from all sides, stood a small athanor with its coals still smoldering. Next to it was an array of large sacks, one tipped to the floor, spilling hundreds of small, translucent stones. The smell of cinnamon mingled with the musty and humid air. Pokers and tongs lay scattered about. Pushed to one side were two large lattices of wire.

"Drandor!" Jason exclaimed, forgetting the hushed tones he had used before. "This time, we will examine his wares with far more care."

He eagerly moved across the room toward the lattices. He eyed one of the supporting beams. The familiar form of the guarding imp was asleep in its bottle. Staying far enough away not to excite the little demon, he began to examine the structures looking for any differences since he had seen it last.

"Why is it so important?" he muttered aloud. "So important to Drandor that Delia took one of them rather than anything else when she fled? If only she ..."

Jason stopped and surveyed the rest of the room. Except for Benedict peering into one of the alcoves and Rosimar standing in the entrance, there was no one else there.

He grimaced in disappointment. Although he had never expressed it consciously, he had envisioned Delia to be with the rest — a daring confrontation and final rescue. But no matter that now. He forced himself to examine the lattices, to focus on what was most important before being distracted by anything else.

He took another tentative step closer to the structures, but stopped in mid-step as a chorus of footfalls echoed down the passageway leading above. Benedict dropped the book he was examining, flung open the grating in front of him, and squirmed into the alcove behind. Jason glanced back at Rosimar. The master stood rigidly erect like a status in a courtyard, making no attempt to hide himself.

Jason hesitated, and then decided. Benedict's solution was good enough.

He ran back across the room. "Quickly, Rosimar! Run Into one of the side rooms. The iron grates must be unlocked."

"Too small," Rosimar moaned. "Too small. The gloom, the musty walls. I cannot. The room, it confines. I must be away."

Jason peered into the sweating face and dazed eyes. He had seen the

144

same expression when Rosimar had ventured into the grotto. The noises outside became louder. Jason stepped to the doors and pulled them shut. He turned back to Rosimar and grabbed him by the shoulders. "This way," he commanded. "Control your feelings. It can be done. We must hide without delay."

Rosimar started to protest as he was herded toward one of the alcoves, but Jason clamped his free hand over the magician's mouth as if he were a bandit's victim. He hooked the grating with his foot, swung it open, and pushed Rosimar inside. With a final swirl, he looped his foot behind the iron bars and pulled them shut. Just as the wooden doors to the room creaked open, he shoved Rosimar behind a crate and tumbled on top of him.

Perseverance and Threshold

"I WAS sure we secured the entrance as Trocolar had directed when we left." Jason heard a voice he recognized as that of Holgon the magician. "But it is no wonder. Nine passes with the dove were boring enough. Today's tedium dulls even the brightest mind."

"Continue as you have been told, and you will be rewarded well," another voice answered. "The Maxim of Perseverance, 'repetition unto success', may not be as precise as the one before, but the results are nearly the same."

Jason strained to hear the second speaker and frowned. The voice was not unfamiliar, but he could not place it for certain. Below him, Rosimar's knuckles pressed to his mouth as if he were trying to prevent his teeth from falling out. Jason released his grip and waited for a reaction. Rosimar remained still, rigidly stiff and unmoving. Jason paused a moment more and then, indicating silence, rose to peer through a crack between the stacked crates.

He peaked out to see Holgon, bundled in a heavy cloak and wearing woolen gloves. The magician huddled over the furnace. He was talking to someone just outside Jason's view. Two guardsmen with bored expressions lounged against supporting posts, ignoring the conversation. From the metallic rustle of mail, Jason could tell that there were more men-at-arms in the room as well.

"It will take at least a hundred times," the soft voice continued. There was a hint of some accent about it and a breathless quality, as if each word would be the last before a massive gulp of air. "But with each repetition of the ritual, the effect becomes more long lasting. You rushed the first load of pebbles to the marketplace, Holgon, with no more than a dozen complete enactments. Some of the purchasers were able to shake the illusion that compelled them to buy and saw what the little stones truly were. Only when you increased the repetition for the next batch did the images hold firm beyond the first hour. And without the subsequent trades, an increase in value would never have happened."

Jason nodded to himself. That explained why there had been no outcry about worthless stones as there was for the tokens. Except for himself, Benedict, and a few others, the illusion had held. After the glamour that compelled him had faded, something else convinced the owner that they were still very special. With growing excitement about what he was learning, Jason strained forward to catch more.

Holgon sighed like a young girl denied permission to venture outside at dusk. He dipped into a nearby sack for one of the small stones. The magician gripped it with tongs, inserted it into the furnace, and began to stomp his feet. The guard on the left unbuckled his sword and lowered it to the ground. He then joined Holgon's beat, clapping his hands to the rhythm while simultaneously banging together two cymbals strapped to the insides of his forearms. The other guard scooped some pieces of rope from the floor and tied them together in a series of intricate knots while puffing his cheeks with air and then swallowing in noisy gulps.

"The *Rhythm of Refraction*," Rosimar whispered in his daze. "Except for the use of cymbals instead of drums, it is the magic ritual for making a lens that focuses all of the colors to the same spot."

"They are not synchronized in what they do," Holgon complained. "This will all be a waste of time unless we start over."

"Continue!" the soft voice commanded. "It is the number of repetitions that count, not the perfection of each step as it is performed."

Holgon extracted the stone from the furnace. With his free hand, he flicked open a small vent above the coals. A brilliant yellow shaft of light shot out into the room. Holgon held the stone to intercept the beam, and one of the guards scurried to hold a scrap of cloth on the other side.

"This one looks the same" Holgon sighed. "It is no different from all the times before."

"Patience," the soft voice commanded. "I suffer without comment the heat of this room. Repeat the ritual as you have been told."

Holgon shrugged and began to move the stone back and forth across the beam, momentarily blotting it out and creating bursts of light that hit the cloth. Another guard extracted a poker from the coals and let it cool, angry red fading to dull black. Then with each pulse of light, he poked the cloth with the tip.

"Enough," the voice said. "After a dozen passes, the burning point grows too cold. Start from the beginning and proceed as before."

Everyone returned to his former position, and the sequence reinitiated. Holgon heated the rock in the furnace and stamped the ground while the others executed their parts of the ritual in step with the cadence.

"With each heating," the voice continued, "each bathing in the flow from the flame, each singeing of the cloth, the barrier to the light weakens. Eventually, it will suddenly shine through."

"But why not have the glamour carry it all?" Holgon asked. "If the owner believes, it does not matter whether the scentstones are of gem quality or not."

"As I have explained, both the glamour *and* the ritual must be performed. The glamour by itself cannot do it all. It is the Rule of the Threshold, or 'fleeting in sight, fixed in mind'. The subtle messages that flash on the screen cannot be too short, or they never would be noticed. But if they are presented too long, the mind becomes aware that they are there, and their power is lost. The glamours in the marketplace strain to the limit. They can convince no more than they do now."

"It still sounds better than this excuse for magic." Holgon extracted the tongs for the second time. "Perhaps I should become like the archimage and learn more than one art."

"Your archimage!" The voice tinkled in what Jason took to be a laugh. "Soon his skills will be no more. The imps twitter that he has heard of the strange failures of sorcery all around this globe; that he finds no explanation for this at home; that he plans even to strike across the seas in search for the cause. But by the time he gets to Arcadia, Trocolar's payment to me of Pluton's mercenary constabulary will have long since passed. And then for the rest, it will be too late."

Jason strained against the crates that defined his hiding place, trying to ferret out the true meaning of all the words. He shifted his position and then felt a sudden kick from Rosimar's legs. The magician exploded in a frenzy of motion, his eyes twitching in a wild panic like a cow being led to slaughter.

"Air, clear air! I can withstand no more!" the magician screamed. He bolted upright and shouldered against the crates in front, sending them in a crash to the floor and knocking open the grating to the larger room. Rosimar pulled at Jason's cloak, trying to claw past. Together, they clattered out onto the dusty stonework for all to see.

"Seize them," the voice commanded as the men-at-arms sprang to life. "This is not according to my plan."

Melibar

JASON STRUGGLED to his feet, but managed only half a step through the clutter before he was hit from the side and hurled back to the ground. He rose to one knee, but two more guards joined the first, pushing him prone. Another slapped the flat side of his sword against Rosimar's head, crumpling the magician in a heap. Benedict bolted from his hiding place and tried to rush past Holgon, but the master thrust his glowing poker between the divulgent's legs as he dashed by, crashing him to the ground, where he lay gasping in pain.

"Trocolar advised me well to keep his dungeon secured," the voice said with the same soft cadence that had come before. "Thieves are everywhere. When these are fettered, search the other alcoves. There may be more."

Jason wiggled to look in the direction of the athanor and, for the first time, spied Holgon's companion. The figure was tall and thin, a head taller than even Canthor, the bailiff on Morgana, and thinner than a brace of lances bound together. He was covered from head to toe with a dark brown great cloak and deep hood that shielded his face in shadow. Eyes glowing like cooling embers peered out from the darkness. No other features could be seen.

The cloth of the cloak hung heavy and limp like laundry wrung only once, water glistening among the coarse threads. A small pool had formed from what dripped from the low hem to the floor. A belt of gold braid cinched in a narrow waist, and a multicolored cube hung from the clasp. Tiny circles of imp light danced around the hood. Gently moving air hissed behind the soft tones of the accented voice.

The guards dragged Jason to his feet and, with his arms held behind, pushed him toward the stranger. As he drew closer, Jason caught his breath. Cold air rolled around his knees and swirled up to his chest. As if stepping out onto an arctic meadow from a well-insulated hut, he found himself shuddering and tried to turn away.

But as he did, he remembered the suggestion of coldness in Drandor's tent and the wisp of icy air behind the latched door in the presentation hall. They had been only hints before, but now, he was sure they were the same.

"Delia," he blurted. "What has become of her? Your presence is tied with that of the smiling trader. You must know where they are. Where is Drandor, and how did he cause the changes to come to pass?"

"Drandor?" the voice asked. "Drandor, the cause of the changes?" The soft burble of laughter continued for more than a minute. "He has served his purpose well, and now he sleeps with my manipulants."

A long, thin finger with smooth, unwrinkled skin poked out from one of the draping sleeves and touched Jason's chest with an icy coldness. "Understand Drandor for what he is. A minion. A minion like Holgon here and no more. A minion who has traded his talents for what he might have when I am done."

The finger retracted and touched the center of the great cloak. "It is I, Melibar, who is the master. Melibar, the first among the navigators."

Jason peered into the inky blackness of the hood, but only a hint of the dark features could be discerned. He tested the grip of the guard behind. The man was well trained and held him firm.

"But what of Delia?" Jason insisted. He found himself wanted to know that the most of all. "What has been done with her?"

"Drandor does not always show good judgment in the treatment of his property," Melibar said. "Especially when it is jointly owned. I have done what is necessary in her regard."

Jason's thoughts raced to frame another question, but before he could speak again, more footfalls sounded on the stone passageway outside the room. All turned to look as three more of Trocolar's men came through the doors.

"The stones, the scentstones! The trader needs more of them now."

"They are not ready," Melibar replied. "As they presently are endowed, too many purchasers can break out of their spell."

"The demand exceeds the supply," the first of the newcomers said. "Already a woman is the price for the smallest hand clutch. Not even a fine team of horses will serve for one bigger than a robin's egg. With the collapse of the token, it is the new fever of the hour. No one bothers to trade in anything else. Everyone scrambles to recover in a day the fortunes that have vanished.

"And the prescription is so simple. Buy in the morning and sell at noon for a return that nets you tenfold. One cannot fail. Why, Trocolar is the richest man on the island. He has been offered an estate on the crestline for a single sack full. Make haste with what is here. We have all to come as guards, the entire household. He has promised us each a dozen stones if we are prompt."

"It proceeds too quickly," Melibar said. "It is not according to my plan. The crowds may prove fickle without the full use of the arts."

"Our orders are to transport the stones now. Stand aside. Our own fortunes are at stake with the rest."

"It does not follow the dictates of my plan," Melibar repeated. "The stones are not properly prepared."

"All of us here serve Trocolar the trader first." The speaker's voice grew threatening. "The wishes of his partners, no matter how well reasoned, must come later."

"Wait!" Melibar suddenly waved his cloaked arm over his head. "Wait until I have calculated the consequences. Do not show such haste."

The gentle hiss of the imps' wings about Melibar's head increased to a roar. Their glow intensified into painful stabs of light. Frost began to form over Melibar's cloak as he drew his arms to his chest and slumped into a ball. The cold air billowed down his sides, and a wet fog rolled across the floor. Trocolar's men hesitated, stepping back from the dense air as it encircled their boots. They looked from one to another, trying to see who would take the lead on what to do next.

For several minutes, no one moved. The air in the room grew chillingly cold. Jason could tell which held their breath by the absence of cloudlets about their faces. Then, as quickly as they had intensified, the noise and lights began to fade. Melibar stood erect and unfolded his arms. Small shards of ice tinkled to the floor.

"Enough." Melibar waved his arms again. "Enough. I have thought through the pattern of events."

The imp light dimmed to almost nothing. The whistling sound receded to the distant murmur it was as it had been before. "The stones in the sack will last long enough for the voting. I will do as the trader suggests and let you transport them now. But I must go along to ensure that Trocolar does not act too precipitously or even forget all the conditions of our bargain."

The deep shadow turned back to face Jason. "And as for these, place them in one of the side rooms. They perhaps are the minions of a disgruntled vault holder. Or maybe even his assets. Yes, it will save Trocolar the trouble of searching. For their capture, I will ask an additional fee."

Jason and the other two were thrust into one of the alcoves and the lock snapped shut. Holgon removed a crucible of molten metal from the athanor and poured it into the keyhole as the rest of Trocolar's men prepared to leave.

"A more difficult challenge than the outer lock," the magician smiled. "I am sure that Trocolar would want you here when we return."

Melibar exited with the last, pausing as he left to examine the lattices beside the furnace. Slowly, he ran his slender hands along the wires.

"So close and yet so different," he touched one of the vertices and tapping it gently. "So unlike where we almost succeeded before."

He ran his finger down one of the wires to an adjacent vertex and then at right angles up to a third. "And yet, two steps already taken. The basis is set for one more. And three should be enough. Three changes to the unfamiliar, and then none here will be able to cope. The remaining two shifts will come with ease. Then I can traverse at will, move back and forth between what I know and the unexplored, and add new vertices with no threat of dissent."

Melibar sighted down at the structures. "I shall discover what lurks beyond the last node in the thaumaturgy line. Yes, the satisfaction will be great."

He turned back to look a final time into the cell that confined Jason. "Drandor, the causes of changes? Not in this place and time."

13

Seven Exactly

AS THE last footfalls of Melibar's departure faded, Jason shook the bars in frustration. He had learned much but was little closer to his goal than before. He had to escape soon, before the trail once again grew as cold as Melibar's cloak. He stared for a hundred heartbeats at the broken sword blades on the floor. Trying to pry back the bolt had served only to snap the finely wrought steel. The rest of the crates contained nothing of value to aid in their escape.

Benedict huddled on a small keg in the corner, wringing his hands and moaning about the bums on his legs. "I should not have been swayed by the value," the divulgent muttered. "The risk, the risk, it was too great."

A loud groan cut off Benedict's whispering as Rosimar flailed his arms through the air and pulled himself to sitting. The trickle of blood from his scalp had clotted in a stringy cake that ran over one eye and down his cheek. "Air," the magician croaked. "I must get out to the fresh air."

Jason rubbernecked from one to the other and sighed. He moved to allow Rosimar to stumble forward and rattle the grating.

"Air!" Rosimar shrieked again. "I cannot withstand it! "Give me air!"

"The magician awakes." Benedict rose to his feet. "It is his magic that is our hope." He climbed over the intervening boxes and grabbed the front of Rosimar's robe, twisting him around. "You boasted of your worth. Now is the time to prove your mettle. You must get us out before that cold one returns."

"Magic." Rosimar shook his head vacantly. "Magic, magic swords and rings of power. Magic to give me air. If I had but one such object, I could barter my way to freedom." He turned and stared at Jason, squinting through the clotted blood. "But this one says that magic is no more. AJI my craft is gone, vanished like a demon's wind." He sagged to the floor. "None of my rituals work as they should. Empty forms that might as well be abstract dances for entertaining a prince! My magic is gone, and I cannot get my air." Rosimar started to say more, but stopped and turned to the grating. He gripped the bars and tried to thrust his face between them, gasping for breath.

Benedict watched for a moment and then placed his hand on Rosimar's shoulder. The magician did not respond, but continued to stare out into the storeroom, eyes bulging and forehead glistening with sweat. The divulgent nibbled at his lip and scanned about the alcove. With a long sigh, he slumped and resumed wringing his hands.

"They left the equipment here untouched." Jason said. "'When a new possibility presents itself, try it'". He grabbed at Benedict, as the divulgent started back for the corner. "Look about, man. Maybe there is something we still can learn from observation or something that Melibar said that can key a discovery."

"So close and yet so different," Benedict replied. "So unlike where we almost succeeded before."

"Yes, that is the idea," Jason agreed. "Melibar's words when he touched the lattice. You remember them well."

"Those are his exact words. A divulgent must retain what he is told with no repetition. Otherwise, he will find he has paid for nothing."

"You remember all the conversation? Everything?"

"I was sure we secured the entrance —" Benedict nodded and began again, but Jason waved him to stop.

"Never mind about Holgon. Concentrate on Melibar. What did he say when they were heating the stones?"

"Eventually, they will be sufficiently transparent. Never as fine —"

"No, after that."

"The Rule of the Threshold, or 'fleeting in sight, fixed in mind'."

"And the Maxim of Perseverance," Jason added.

Jason began to pace within the small confines of their cell while fingering the old coin around his neck. He squeezed between two open crates and flexed his palm around the grip of one of the unbroken swords.

"Melibar spoke of laws. 'Repetition unto success,' he mused aloud. As if they guided his efforts like those that apply to the crafts. Is there a sixth magic, a secret that only he knows about?"

Jason's thoughts exploded. "The glamours of the marketplace," he said. "And a ritual almost the same as the *Rhythm of Refraction*. Sorcery is governed by the Rule of Three, and Melibar spoke of a Rule of the

Threshold. Magic obeys the Maxim of Persistence, and he talked of perseverance instead."

His slapped his thigh. "That's it, Benedict, don't you see? It is fundamental solving technique. 'Similarities are a clue.' Sorcery and magic are not merely inoperative. There are still *seven* laws, just as there were before. The laws have not simply vanished. They have been replaced, substituted by ones similar but not quite the same. Seven laws. Seven before and still seven after the transformation."

Jason peered out into the storeroom. The leap of intuition was based on nothing substantial, but somehow he knew he was right. He grabbed a piece of debris and threw it through the bars to strike the imp bottle attached to the overhead beam.

"The Postulate of Invariance." The imp fluttered to life. "Seven exactly. There can be no less and no more. The lattices, they are my master's. You cannot touch."

"Yes, the Postulate of Invariance!" Jason yelled, grabbing Benedict by the shoulders and shaking him back and forth like a rag doll. "Invariance. A constant. Seven laws. There can be no more or no less. Whenever one is turned off, another must take its place.

"It is a new law of the arts, Benedict! We have found another law! No, wait, not a law, but a metalaw. A law *about* the laws. A statement that there are many, but that only seven can be in effect at any one time. Different arts, many principles that guide them. And no one even suspected! Not even the archimage!

"It has been the same throughout history, from the very first sagas," Jason continued. "The seven that we know so well were painstakingly discovered, and then no more were found. For at least a thousand years and, who knows, maybe back to the beginning of time, there have been seven constant laws and no reason to suspect that there could be more."

"You gibber too fast for even a divulgent," Benedict said. "Laws or metalaws, such abstractions make little difference. There is more to be gleaned from the tangible. What of these lattices of which the imp speaks?"

"The lattice is the proof," Jason replied. "It is the — the road map by which one navigates through the realm of the laws. The first vertex Melibar touched on the bigger lattice represented three of laws as we know them. Move one node to the right and the Rule of Three was replaced by the Rule of the Threshold. Continuing in that direction would change sorcery to something more exotic still. Instead, the next change was in a different direction, changing the Maxim of Persistence to the

Maxim of Perseverance. One lattice was three dimensional with three distinct axes for three of the laws; the other was flat for two more —"

Jason stopped. "That accounts for only five of the laws, not seven. There is something more that we do not yet understand."

"I see no fivefold mapping throughout those structures." Benedict squinted at the frameworks like a mole in the sun. "Only in small sections and there for a few nodes at most."

"It represents what Melibar has explored," Jason said. "It is how he keeps track of where he has been. Yes, that is it. Melibar cannot turn off a law. He cannot create one. He can only replace one with another in the same line. At the edges, if he moves in a direction for which there is no node, a new law is invoked that must be found through experimentation, one that he does not know."

"Your thoughts gallop too fast for me to judge their significance," Benedict protested. "And they seem to infer too much from the small hints we have heard tonight. How can you construct such fanciful structures from so meager a basis?"

"I ... I do not know." Jason slowed his patter. "It just came to me in a rush. As it oftentimes does."

He stepped back from the grating and took a deep breath. His present danger, his link to Augusta's fate even if he could escape, and his longing to rid himself of his inspiration block all faded away in the seductive rush of a new discovery. He felt the exhilaration of solving a complex puzzle — well, at least a part of one anyway.

"In any event, the knowledge is of little value." Benedict jarred Jason's thoughts back to their plight. "Knowing all the secrets of the realm is of no help if we still must remain here to receive Trocolar's displeasure. If he is elected head of the council, he can make the penalty for trespassing what he will." The divulgent lowered his eyes. "Although, I doubt it will be as severe as what he would do with an impounded asset."

The Magic Sword

BENEDICT WAS right, Jason thought. The puzzle he had solved was of no value. No value unless …

He closed his eyes. "But there still is sorcery and magic," he said after a while, "or, at least, something very close to them. We can use them to find our way out."

"What do you mean?" Benedict asked.

"As for this new sorcery, or whatever it is called," Jason answered as he looked about their prison, "it involves animations on screens and messages flashed in the blink of an eye. There is nothing here that will aid us to construct a glamour.

"But the new magic gives us the Maxim of Perseverance," Jason continued, picking up the sword from the crate in front of him. "Perhaps we can use it to enhance this blade and make it strong enough to pick out the mortar between the bricks."

"A magic sword," Benedict scoffed. "You have read too many of the sagas. If there could be such a thing, the guild that could make it would charge two kingdoms' ransom. Producing such an object would require many lifetimes and the labor of hundreds."

"The Maxim of Persistence is no more," Jason said. "I am not talking about a blade that forever retains its sharpness. We are dealing now with perseverance instead." He glanced down to the magician at his feet. "Rosimar, what is the ritual for the hardening of the steel that was used in the manufacture of the tokens?"

"The *Aura of Adarnance*", Rosimar mumbled without looking up. "It is one that must be mastered before the robe of the initiate is received."

"And the equipment?" Jason asked. "What is needed to act out the steps?"

"Bells and candles," Rosimar answered, "magic hexagons drawn on the floor, chalk and pearl dust, and a bottle of ten-year-old wine."

"We will improvise the best we can." Jason began looking into the storage crates with a fresh perspective. "Explain the details so that we can begin."

"No, I am the master," Rosimar said weakly. "All credit for magic will be mine."

"You are indisposed. Rest. Benedict and I can do as you direct."

"No!" Rosimar struggled to his feet. "Magic may no longer work, but all rituals will be mine. You stand aside while I perform. I will get the credit. There will be no mistake about who performs with skill."

For a moment, Jason regarded Rosimar's glistening forehead, the whitened knuckles that gripped the bars, and the eyes that twitched in erratic patterns like tiny searchlights. "It is not that important, Rosimar," he said. "You perform the ritual if you wish, and I will watch. But be warned, it will not be a single time that we must see it through."

Rosimar stared at Jason for a moment, then, with a snarl, he staggered to look into the crates stacked against the wall. "Tin cups," he muttered, "and metal spoons. They will have to serve for the pealing of the bells."

All three turned to rummaging through the stored goods and shortly had assembled the required equipment as best they could. Rosimar directed Benedict in the striking of the bells and the drawing of the hexagon on the alcove floor. He selected the longest sword of the lot and placed it within the pattern. With trembling hands, the magician decanted vinegar over a sack of flour while stomping a complicated rhythm with his feet.

When he was done, Rosimar picked up the sword and pressed it against the wall. With a grating sound, it skittered along the stone, leaving a faint trail where it had scratched the rock.

"And so much for this nonsense." The magician slumped back to the ground. "Magic is no more. We will not free ourselves by such misplaced cunning, regardless of your theories of lattices and hopping between vertices in some realm that cannot be seen."

"Again," Jason insisted, pulling Rosimar back to his feet. "The Maxim of Perseverance works on repetition. We must try the ritual again."

"And if I do not?" Rosimar asked.

"Then I will continue with Benedict as I had originally planned."

Rosimar grumbled and reached for the bottle of vinegar. "It distracts my mind from the closeness of the walls, at the least. One more time probably will do no harm."

JASON CLUTCHED his hand to his stomach to stop the growling. It was not panic this time. It was hunger. He ran his tongue over the dry walls of his mouth and eyed what was left of the vinegar. Benedict slumped against the far wall, the makeshift string of bells dangling at his side, mouth open and eyes drooping with fatigue. Rosimar sat on one of the remaining unopened kegs, head bowed, and shoulders slumped.

"Enough of rest," Jason said. "We must keep trying until there is a change in the sword."

"Enough, indeed," Rosimar growled. "It is an insanity. We are like children repeating a mindless game. There is no magic. It is gone. How can a few words by a stranger make you so sure?"

The magician rose and lumbered to the wall. With the remains of the chalk, he added another stroke to the ones already there. "Five hundred and seventy-two times," he grumbled. "Over five hundred Auras of Alamance. More rituals than what is performed in a guild in a year."

"Once more," Jason insisted. "Once more and then we will reconsider what we must do."

"You said that the last time," Benedict whined. "For over two days, we have stomped and chanted to no avail. In a few hours at most, the election will be over, and Trocolar will return in triumph. We will not escape. To continue wasting his wares will only increase his displeasure."

"Once more," Jason repeated. "What other plan do you have to offer in its stead?"

Rosimar grumbled and kicked at the sword that lay in the center of the hexagon on the floor. Both edges of the blade were as dull as parchment. Dozens of nicks and gouges marred the sides. He stooped to thrust it out of the way and then stopped, his eyes opening wide through his exhaustion. "It feels different. Not the tingle of magic, but somehow different all the same."

Holding his breath, he clasped the hilt tighter and touched the blade tip to the wall. He started to scratch the dull point across in a great arc to match the other scars that crisscrossed the stone. "There is resistance," he muttered. "It seems to take a great deal of strength to move it to the side." He increased the pressure on the guard and then staggered forward mouth agape. The blade had slid a finger's length into the stone.

"A guild's endowing fortune," Rosimar said in wonder as Jason and

Benedict sprang forward. "A stone-cutting sword as true as any in the sagas."

"Let us be gone." Benedict tugged at Rosimar's sleeve. "Save the marveling for when we are free. Try the iron bars and see if it performs there as well."

Rosimar grunted and extracted the blade from the wall. He slashed across the grating with two swift strokes. Instantly, the central portion of the bars fell away. Rosimar blinked in disbelief at what he had so effortlessly done. Jason touched the freshly cleaved surfaces and felt a polish as smooth as if they had been ground by diamond dust. While Rosimar stood staring at the sword in his hand, Benedict pushed him aside and scrambled for the opening. He ran across the storeroom and tried the heavy wooden door. It swung open easily. There was no sound from above. The keep was deserted. Everyone had gone to the harbor with the scentstones.

"I will not wait at the skiff," Benedict called back as he ran for the stairs. "I have gathered enough information to last me a good while."

"But the lattice," Jason said. "It will do no good unless we learn how to restore things to the way they were."

"I doubt that you can add to your theories without more hints from this Melibar." Rosimar climbed through the hole and headed after Benedict. "And he no doubt will be with Trocolar in the grotto. It is there that I am headed, to help Augusta before it is too late."

Jason hesitated and then scrambled after. There was not enough time to think of a better possibility. As he ran past, he cast a last reluctant glance at the lattices.

A few minutes later, they were in the forest and running for the small boat that had brought them to the island.

"If this Melibar is in the grotto, we should head for the city instead," Benedict shouted as they reached the shore. "With what I know now, I see it is folly for the three of us to proceed unaided."

"The mercenaries will be in the grotto to preserve order for the final vote," Rosimar said, scrambling on board the skiff. "I will speak to them there. But with this blade, I will need little else. Benedict, you can row," he commanded as the divulgent sat down in the bow. "No wavering when it is time to press advantage. Direct to the grotto. The voting should soon begin, but I judge by the tide that there is still some time.

"And as for you," the magician continued, turning his attention to Jason, "not another step. You can stay here until Trocolar's men find you upon their return."

"Put away the sword," Jason stepped forward. "We are all in this together, and I have contributed my share. Without my insistence, the blade would not have been made."

"Your proper share is not of importance," Rosimar snarled. "I have what I need, and that is enough. Back from the skiff, or we will see how well I can cut through soft flesh."

Jason lunged to the left, but Rosimar swung the sword in a flat arc to cut off the advance.

"Be off, I say," the magician ordered Benedict, and the divulgent pushed against the beach with the oars. The skiff bounded away on a receding wave, while Jason stood helpless, watching the retreat.

"I may change nothing," Rosimar called back, "but at least Augusta will know who tried at the last."

Stuck in the Stone

JASON WATCHED the boat bob away and pounded his fist into his palm. How would Rosimar proceed once he gained access to the inner chamber of the grotto and climbed onto the ledge above the vault? Probably by whirling the sword over his head like a drunken hero from the sagas and challenging anyone to take Augusta from his side. There would be no careful confrontation with Melibar, no appeal to the confused voters to turn away from the stones. The magician was likely as not to fail. And if he did, the arts would remain lost. Trocolar would win the election, and all of Augusta's assets, would default to him.

Jason kicked at some driftwood washed up on the beach. Somehow, he must also get to the grotto and be part of the final confrontation, no matter which way it went. Success for Rosimar or a failure — neither augured well, but Jason could not wait on the periphery for the result. Even without a clever scheme, he had to be there.

He stopped his gestures of frustration, closed his eyes, and thought. He decided what he should do. He ran back to the deserted structure and down into the dungeon. In a rush, he grabbed one of the tarpaulins, the rope on the floor, and a halberd and sword. He staggered up the stairs and back outside with the load, dropping it onto the beach. With only the halberd, he sprinted into the forest and began to fell the smallest trees he could find.

Two hours later, he shoved a makeshift raft into the waves and hoisted the tarpaulin on a mast no higher than his head. Strapped on board were three of the remaining sacks of raw scentstones. Perhaps, if everyone could see what they truly were, the spell could be broken. Paddling with a stubby log, he cleared the island and set a course for the grotto.

Low tide had already been reached, and the water level was on the way up when Jason maneuvered into the opening from the sea. He struck his sail and released the guy-ropes that held the mast in place, letting the log topple over the side. The portcullis was drawn up and the wall cresset danced with beckoning flame.

He cut a square from the tarpaulin, wrapped it around a small branch, and dipped it into the burning oil. Resuming his paddling, he headed for the narrow opening that separated the two large chambers.

Jason's raft was narrow, and he navigated the tunnel with ease. On the other side, the ledge on the far wall was ablaze with light. Dozens of torches cut through the blackness from the opening in the rock. Others bobbed from the flotilla of small boats anchored below, many with oarsmen waiting in them. As Jason drew closer, he could see the cut in the cliff jammed with people to the very edge, shirts of mail, embroidered robes, and flowing capes crowding together shoulder to shoulder. The slurred mixture of many excited voices radiated out into the vastness of the cavern and echoed from the other walls.

Jason's stomach began to rumble, but he took a deep breath. "Take me above," he ordered one of the oarsmen when his raft finally bumped against the cliff. "There is much that I wish to relate." He reached for his sword and swung it upward.

An oarsman stepping from one skiff to the next suddenly stopped. "Watch out! It may be a blade like the other," he said.

Jason smiled at the rower's words. Perhaps Rosimar's interruption would give him the means. "Fetch these sacks of stone," he replied before any of the others could think. "And watch your backsides. Like that of Rosimar's, this broadsword slices through mail as if it were gossamer."

The oarsman closest to him jumped to the side as Jason stepped forward, waving his sword. "The sacks to the landing," he said. "Make haste before my patience is tried. You will be easy targets if you flee."

The oarsmen nodded and cautiously came forward to pick up the bags Jason indicated. With repeated glances over their shoulders, they preceded him up the rope ladder to the landing.

"Make room, make room," the rower in front directed as they reached the top. "Another of the devil shafts. Move aside so that he can pass."

A space opened up along one wall, and Jason crowded by. He gasped. He had not counted on there being so many. His heart began to flutter, his breaths just short gulps of air. Hang on, hang on, he told himself while he rubbed his coin with his free hand. This is not much different from the crowd that watched the shrinking cube. No one was paying him any attention — yet.

In the rear of the cavern, next to the hole that led down to the vault,

Rosimar stood with his back to the downward-sloping rock and waving the magic sword in jerky arcs like windmill vanes in a storm. Benedict huddled to one side, his arms intertwined around his chest and his teeth working furiously on his lower lip. On the other side of the magician was Augusta. Her eyes darted back and forth over the group that surrounded them in a wide semicircle. Some stood with swords drawn, and others waved at the men-at-arms, encouraging them forward. Behind the front row stood Trocolar and other influential voters. Melibar and Holgon conferred in soft tones near one of the other openings that led further into the interior. At Rosimar's feet, two bodies were piled, one missing a hand and the second the side of his face.

"You are no swordsman, magician, and eventually you must tire," the red-surcoated man Jason had seen at the ceremony with the shrinking cube called out. The constable's eyes flicked over to Jason and then back to the magician. "And even with three of you, you cannot manage to descend the rope to the boats and guard at the same time. Drop the broadsword, Rosimar, and save us all unnecessary grief."

"I am no part of this," Benedict whimpered. "He forced me to row into the grotto against my will. I am a captive, no more free than the rest of you."

"Silence, divulgent." Rosimar gasped for air and waved the sword to the side. "As for you and your men, Constable Nimrod, if I do tire, which of you will rush forward first to engage the cutting edge?"

"Nimrod, do your duty," Trocolar said. "That I will be the winner when this interruption is over there can be little doubt. And the bonuses that I would be inclined to bestow for the previous years' service will be greatly influenced by your actions here and now."

"You have not yet won, Trocolar," someone shouted from the crowd. "The final tally is still to be summed."

"I know very well how many bags of scentstones that have been sold from my stock these last few days," Trocolar turned and called back. "I have had my clerks keep careful count. Even if every one of you decided on someone else, the total would be less than what I have held for my own. You see the sum that shows for me already on the slate. Now it is just a formality, and we are done."

"But it is unfair," the voice persisted, and several others joined in the chorus. "Forget about the madman. The important thing is how we consider the stones. Of them, I have none. My ship docked after the price had become too dear. I possess only a cargo of leather leggings from the mainland and some curious, flexible pipes from the southern kingdoms across the great ocean. I have brought samples of each for assay. The entire lot would have fetched fifty tokens. Surely, they still have value against something else here in Pluton."

The hubbub of dissent rose in volume like the crashing waves of an approaching storm, but Trocolar waved his arms for silence. "We have insufficient time, Luthor. Insufficient time to bicker the proper balance for each commodity. We would be here from one election to the next, trying to redetermine the relative merit of each. But nearly everyone has some stones. I have released enough to make sure of that. In point of fact, they are the new foundation by which all else is to be judged."

The trader looked toward Augusta. "If you have none to assay, then the logic admits of no alternative, Luthor. Your vote is null. Just thank the random factors that you are not a debtor as well."

"Rosimar, the stones," Jason called out. "Did you explain how they came to be?"

Everyone turned and looked at Jason. His knees nearly buckled. The taste of stomach acid slammed into his senses. So many, so many. He had not completely thought this through.

Rosimar also turned in Jason's direction, and his eyes widened. "An impostor," he wheezed, wiping his forehead with his free hand. "I have the sword of power. I have the only one. Take him away. HIs fate is no concern of mine."

"Stand back," Jason managed to reply, trying to hold back the upwelling that was struggling to spew from his gut. "You have no need to put it to the test. Just listen for a moment. What I have to say concerns you all."

"Attack, Nimrod. Do your duty," Trocolar said. "Secure these malcontents before there are any more."

"Do not listen," Rosimar shouted as he moved out from the wall and flailed his weapon through the air. "*I* am the one who is rescuing the lady. She belongs to me. I am the master who has forged the sword. He had not enough time. The one he holds is only common steel and no more."

The man-at-arms at Jason's side looked at Rosimar, then to the scowling face of his constable, and finally back to Jason.

Jason hesitated, but then drew his own blade partway from its scabbard. "Back, I say!" he shouted. He wanted to run, run away as far as he could. But just this once, he pleaded with himself. Just a little longer until he could be done. He moved to the wall, and though his hand trembled, he held his sword menacingly outward. "I have no quarrel with you. I want only the freedom to have my say."

"Impostor, impostor!" Rosimar shrieked. "If it possesses true magic, have him show what it can do." With a sudden rush, he whirled to the wall and sliced off a knob of rock as if he were cutting cheese. The outcrop crashed to the ground, and the magician attacked it with a two-handed grip, thrashing the stone to jagged slivers and crumbling slices.

"And yours," Nimrod called out. "We have not seen you cut nearly so deep."

"I did not come for petty display," Jason began, but his hesitation was enough. The man on his left completed his draw and pushed to attack. Jason doubled over with nausea and the side slash sailed over his head.

He slid along the wall and kicked a stool out of the way. A low slash nicked his calf as he stumbled past. His leg buckled in pain. Down on one knee, he looked about frantically. The men-at-arms were still giving Rosimar a wide berth. With one leg dragging on the ground, he continued towards the magician. 'Move in the direction of the goal', he thought dully. 'Move in the direction of the goal'. If he could grab the real magic sword, he would have the means to make them listen.

As Jason approached, Rosimar turned and raised the blade up over his head. But as they closed, Benedict bolted from behind Rosimar's back and tumbled over a stack of scrolls towards Nimrod's side.

"It is the amount of space!" the divulgent shrieked. "The magician can barely cope as it is. Confine him! Restrict him! It is the only weakness, as long as he wields the weapon!"

Nimrod frowned in confusion, but Benedict did not wait. "It is information," he said while he ripped off his robe and thrust it into the constable's hands. "Use it. There will be no fee."

Nimrod nodded with understanding. While Rosimar tensed for Jason to come another foot closer, Nimrod circled behind the magician and flung a robe over his head. Where the material touched the blade, it immediately parted, but enough fell on Rosimar's face to prevent him from seeing. Dropping the sword, he grabbed for the robe with both hands. "Air!" he shouted. "Air! Give me room. Let me out. I must have more air so that I can breathe."

The sword spun to the ground point first. Silently, it slid into the stone halfway to the hilt. Jason shuffled forward as Nimrod wrapped his arms around Rosimar and hurled the magician down. The constable disengaged and prepared to lunge for the weapon, but Jason waved him away with the tip of his blade. Towards the goal, towards the goal, he told himself. As long as there was progress, always move towards the goal. Then, grasping the guard awkwardly with his left hand, he strained to pull the magic sword from the ground.

The grip was hot. Stabs of pain coursed through his palm. Jason flinched in surprise but tightened his fingers, ignoring the biting teeth that seemed to gnaw through his flesh.

He tugged gently and then with greater force, but the sword did not budge. A flick of motion out of the corner caught his eye, and he moved aside just in time to avoid a thrust from two men-at-arms who converged from the right. Positioning his back toward the wall, he swung his blade in a wide arc to keep all hands away from the sword in the stone. The guardsmen paused, and he had enough time to decide what he must try. With a blurring motion, he dropped his blade and placed both hands around the magic sword's grip. Rising from his knees and using all the strength in his back, he strained to pull it free.

But again, the sword did not move. Except for a slight quiver of the hilt in response to Jason's tugs, it remained frozen in the rock. In desperation, Jason jerked to both sides and tried to twist the shaft. For a moment, the men-at-arms stood motionless while he struggled, but at last, they saw he would remain unarmed and converged from all sides.

"You see, you see!" Rosimar yelled. "He is not worthy. I am the one. I am the one who is to save Augusta."

"No!" Augusta yelled. Jason turned just in time to see the stool she held descend toward his head. In an explosion of light, he fell forward, his grip on the magic broadsword sliding away.

Fleeting Treasure

THE SCENE blurred as if it were viewed through cloudy water. A ringing persisted in Jason's ears. His calf throbbed with a dull pain, and his arms were bound behind his back. He was propped against a wall, and Augusta huddled at his side. Evidently, she had somehow managed to bind the wound in his leg so that it no longer bled. Near her feet, Rosimar twitched in his bonds and stared vacantly into space.

Nimrod now sat at the small table in the rear of the chamber. Solemnly, he examined the outstretched palm offered by the first in a queue that ran along the wall to the right. Behind his chair stood the cloaked form of Melibar, and next to him, holding the magic sword gingerly at arm's length, was another man-at-arms. In the center of the first row of the encircling throng, Trocolar stroked the bulge of his stomach with a jeweled hand.

"Eight small stones and one twice the size," Nimrod boomed over the buzzing all around. "An equivalent of ten altogether. Very well, Cumbrist, how do you vote?"

"For the head of the council, it cannot matter." Cumbrist looked up at the chalked totals on the slates erected behind the table. "But for the record, let it show that I add my support to the trader."

"The divulgent is right," another voice rang out. "There are barely a dozen of us left. And the common street hawkers have less than anyone here. We waste our time for the sake of tradition. Let us declare the trader the leader by acclamation and be done. It is in all our best interests to return to the shoreline quickly to protect what remains from the looters."

Trocolar smiled and bowed to the speaker. "I am pleased that others also see the practicalities of the moment. Now, if no one objects, I am ready to assume the responsibility of restoring order and issue my first edicts." The murmuring stopped. Everyone present looked to his neighbor to see what he would say. For a full minute, no one spoke, and then Trocolar strode to the rear of the cavern where Rosimar had made his stand.

"Constable Nimrod, you are now mine to command," the trader said. "No one voices dissent. "And my first instruction is for you to seize the vault holder Augusta and transfer her writ of personal ownership to me. Her and her remaining assets. She is a debtor, and as senior lien holder, I have first rights to do with her what I will."

"It is the rule for the surrender of the body to come after transfer of the other assets has been recorded," Nimrod replied. "Three days' grace is given to settle one's personal affairs. That has been the custom for many years."

"My first instruction," Trocolar repeated. "Carry it out now, or a reprimand will be the second."

"Our charter is to enforce an equitable peace." Nimrod's tone hardened. "Not to serve as the instrument for some private intrigue." He waved at Jason and Rosimar. "It is for the likes of these that we administer swift justice. The fate of the vault holder should follow the due course of law."

"The intruders concern me less," Trocolar scowled. "They strove to disrupt the orderly transition of power. Every faction here supports the retribution that is its due. All would help to heat the shears and turn the cranks. But Augusta's crime might go unpunished were I not to exercise my responsibility as leader."

"Some inner desire warps your reason." Nimrod scowled. "The danger of the day is from the two who are bound. Indeed, it is well that the younger was unable to remove the sword from the rocky floor before he was felled. He was no stiff-armed magician. With the blade in his hand, it is uncertain what the outcome would have been."

Jason frowned and tried to reason through the implications of what was being said, but his thoughts were slowed. He had been unable to budge the sword, even though he had strained with all his might. Yet now the constable held it free and clear of surrounding rock. Rosimar had called him unworthy. But surely he was a better man that the magician. He did not lie and twist the facts. He had been honorable in everything that ...

He remembered what had happened in Augusta's anteroom. He had yelled 'Fire!' when there was none. No one was hurt, but there could have been. How this new magic was bound up with such a thing, Jason could not fathom, but Rosimar had been right. His action was not that of someone who was worthy of wielding a magic sword.

"As you say, they are bound." Trocolar said. "But as yet the vault holder is not. Seize —"

"Your petty vendettas can be no more than second priority, Trocolar," Melibar interrupted. "Foremost, you must honor the terms of our agreement that made your victory possible. You now lead the council. My skills put you there. In payment, you are to provide me a year's service of your constabulary to follow my instructions and not your own."

Trocolar scowled. He turned to face Melibar's shadowy hood. "There are riots in the streets," he said. "Warehouses are being plundered. Already, two passing ships have refused to anchor. When we made our bargain, you did not hint at the turmoil that would result. As elected leader, I also have the responsibility to see that order is restored."

"Assemble and train a new cadre of warriors," Melibar replied. "My need now is greater. The unrest in the Wheatlands may not last beyond the season."

"I did not think that your scheme had any merit." Trocolar shook his head. "It appeared a risk-free means of securing five hundred tokens with which to augment my vote. I had no intention of surrendering such a central element of power after I had won."

"Nevertheless, I provided the skills without which you could not have been guaranteed victory," Melibar replied. "We have an agreement. I have honored my part. You must do the same."

"And I had the clerks, the distribution, and the strategic locations for the glamours," Trocolar snapped back. "I exploited the use of your wares as I would any others'. The triumph is of my own making. No other credit is due."

Trocolar paused for breath and then smiled. "You speak of agreements to honor, but what have you offered in good faith? Worthless disks of metal, five hundred circles of dull steel. And the stones — they have value of their own creation. Intrinsic worth because demand exceeds the supply, independent of the rituals in the confines of my estate. You have given me nothing, Melibar, and expect a largesse in return."

Trocolar licked his lips as if he were savoring the taste of his words. "Nimrod, escort him away," he commanded. "I hold no writ of indebtedness, but this cold one would be well advised to make Pluton no longer a port of call."

"Another lackey's task," Nimrod mumbled. "Will sweeping the dungeon floor be next?"

"It is the fee that binds you to the island, is it not?" Melibar pushed a slender hand palm outward from his cloak as Nimrod hesitated. The imp dance above the cold one's head quickened. Their glow of light throbbed from dull red to robust yellow. "Do you hold the concept of honor the same as your new master?"

"My troop has fulfilled its contract for over four decades," Nimrod shook his head, "through the tenure of more than a dozen councils. And we expect ample bonuses with our recompense for the year just past, as we have been rewarded many times before."

"For the year past." Melibar's voice quickened slightly. "Fees rendered after the service is done, rather than before? What perverse logic you use to conduct your affairs in this realm! Had I known, I would not have even bothered with this Trocolar. Name your price for the year to come, warrior, and it shall be yours."

"There is the matter of custom and tradition," Nimrod persisted. "We have been treated well." He turned a scowl at Trocolar. "Heretofore, the leader of the council has been able to judge between private interest and public need."

"Nimrod, to your duty," Trocolar commanded. "Use the sword you pulled from the rock, if you must. It is the cold one's own folly if he does not move aside when you thrust."

"Then is it the sword that gives you such presumption, trader?" Melibar asked. "Without it, how would you regard the bargain then?"

"Indeed, with the sword and the scentstones, I need little more." Trocolar laughed. "I have enough to handle a simple peddler with a few tricks such as yours."

"Swords and scentstones." Melibar's own voice lowered until Jason could barely hear. "You compare them with the resources of a navigator?"

He whirled and motioned to Holgon, who was still standing near the cavern wall. "Forward, magician. Perform the ritual as you have been instructed."

"But that was before the sword was captured and Trocolar's election completed. He is my master, and now I do not see the need," Holgon said.

"The ritual," Melibar repeated. "Think. Where should your allegiances truly be? With a petty island trader without honor or with one who can show you secrets that none of your kind has ever dreamed?"

Holgon looked at Trocolar and then to Melibar. He stepped backward until he touched the rough wall. He glanced at the wooden box at his feet and shrugged. Stooping down, he dragged the crate to the middle of the

171

floor.

"I will allow no more of your strange games," Trocolar said. "And as for you, Holgon, remember that you are still in my debt."

"If you have so much power, then why do you fear the simplest of your children's toys?" Melibar asked. "Show him, Holgon."

Holgon grunted and pulled out a large box from the crate. With a flourish, he removed the lid.

"Dominoes!" Nimrod snorted. "A game with which my men sometimes wager their rations. I have never seen so many packed together like this before, but nevertheless, merely dominos, nothing more."

"Here the use is even simpler," Melibar said. "A quaint practice of no utility, but somehow of amusement to your smaller minds. Also the rat trap, Holgon and the pig bladder as well."

Holgon started standing the dominoes in a row, one after the next. There were a few hundred in the box and some of those watching began to grumble with impatience. Others shushed them to silence. Several hundred. It would be a sight to see.

When the magician was done, he cocked the trap so it was triggered when the last domino fell, then bound a pin to the hammer that was flipped shut by the spring.

"Finally, the bladder," Melibar directed. "Inflate it and tie a knot. Place it so that it will intercept the sharp point as it flies upward."

"Enough, enough!" Trocolar commanded. "Scoop up this refuse and be away."

"In a moment, it will be done," Melibar said in his soft voice. He projected no strain and only a hint of the need for speed. He drew into a tight ball and huddled to the floor, fiddling with something that no one could see. A minute passed and then another. Finally, he drew himself erect. "The nexus is not strong. It took more effort this time, but nevertheless, it has been done."

"Rest. Do not give them cause." A gentle touch ran across Jason's forehead. Augusta was kneeling beside him. "I am sorry for the blow, but I did not know what else to do. Surely, if you resisted further, you would have been slain."

"But the election," Jason managed to say. "Without an explanation, it is all over. Trocolar has won. Our fate has only been postponed while his attention is elsewhere."

"I said I am sorry," Augusta repeated. "But forgive me the one last weakness in wanting to have someone at my side when the trader finally forces his way."

"The domino, Holgon," Melibar's voice cut through the ringing in Jason's ears. "With the softest touch you can manage."

The magician struck the first wooden block in line. One after another, the rest tumbled in order across the rough floor. The last hit the trigger on the trap, flipping it into the air and hurling the pin into the inflated bladder, which exploded with a loud pop. A smattering of applause broke out.

"And now you will be gone," Trocolar said when the action had stopped.

Again, Melibar collapsed into a ball. Wondering what would happen next, no one else moved. Several more minutes passed. Melibar rose again to his feet.

"Two more simple demonstrations," Melibar insisted, waving off the man-at-arms who moved forward to grab his shoulder. "Two more and then I will depart. "Holgon, clap your hands in the rhythm of the *Adagio for Perpetual Lights,* but as softly as you can muster."

Holgon's face registered confusion, but the magician began to push his palms together. On the final stroke, the ground rumbled. A spout of water coursed up the hole that led to the vault. A great spray of cold and slimy wetness struck the low ceiling and showered down on those nearby. The ground trembled slightly, and Jason thought he heard the grinding of great masses of rock.

"The vault! It is flooded! The weak walls have given way!" one of the men-at-arms shouted as he peered down the hole to see what had happened.

"And now the *Stomp of the Forging Presses.*" Melibar did not pause. "And then a taste of other forms of power."

Holgon complied. Beginning with his third step, the ground shook, this time not in slight trembles, but in great jerks that tumbled Trocolar and those around him to the floor. The basin of water below the landing began to slosh as if it was in a washbowl that had been dropped. With creaks and groans, the moored boats crashed into one another.

"Stop them, Nimrod!" the trader shouted. "Stop them before they collapse this cavern as well!"

"The Maxim of Perturbations." Melibar's voice competed with the shriek of tearing rock. "With it, my minions can shake the earth or skim carpets across the ground. And beyond that, there are other maxims as well. Those of perspective, of penetration, persuasion, and pomp. You speak of power, insignificant mite, but know not one hundredth of all it entails."

"The sword," Trocolar demanded. "Nimrod, use the sword."

The constable snapped shut his gaping mouth and sprang into action. He ripped the blade from the man who held it and slashed at Holgon's legs. The magician's support buckled, and he tumbled to the ground. With eyes wide in fear, he threw his hands across his face, awaiting the next blow.

But the rumbling instantly stopped, and Nimrod hesitated before continuing the attack. He grunted as he saw a crimson stain begin to glisten in the hem of Holgon's robe and turned his attention back to Melibar.

"Yes, the sword." Melibar stepped forward to meet his assailant. "The sword that once sliced through rock. Until a moment ago, it held great power. But now, did it feel all that different from any other when you tried it on the magician's flesh?"

Nimrod stopped in mid-strike and turned the blade aside. It plunged toward the ground at Melibar's feet. With a shriek like a rusted bolt in a latch, it skittered across the rough stone and then snapped near the hilt.

"And the scentstones." Melibar glided to the three bags that Jason had brought to the grotto. "Holguin's stomping has done more than rearrange the structures of the caverns. See also what they have done to crystal impurities."

With a surprising grace, he dumped the sacks to the floor, one after another.

"Cloudy!" someone exclaimed as the stones poured over his feet. "Not even citrine or amethyst. Milky quartz and no more!"

"Look closely, Nimrod," Melibar continued over the din that arose as everyone present began to examine his own collection of stones. "It is with this simple rock that you will be paid for your labor and the past year. Who knows what it will be for the next? Come with me to the wheat fields of the mainland, and there will be plunder enough for all."

The wave of white pebbles spilling onto the floor acted like a catalyst. The voices competing with Melibar's rose in volume. First had come the shock of the now useless tokens and now of their glittering, worthless replacements — financial ruin twice within a week. Traders and vault holders began to push between the men-at-arms to side with trusted comrades. Swords rattled with anger in their scabbards.

"The stones are nothing!" one of the men-at-arms shouted. "And I am in debt! I depended on my fee to settle free and clear."

"Then to the mainland with the cold one," the guard next to him said.

"Enough of dull sentries and shrinking cubes."

"Trocolar is the one at fault," a trader cried. "Without his tampering, this election would have proceeded as all those before."

"To your positions," Nimrod ordered. "We have an obligation still to discharge."

"For what?" one of his men shouted back. "For ballast, good enough only to weight a ship's keel?"

"Divulgents, to your guildsmen. Protect one another until we are safely away."

"Trocolar is not a winner. His clouded gems can be worth no more than mine. Now is the opportunity, vault holders! Seize the records. Once again, the island can be ours."

"Those for the mainland, to my side," Melibar said.

"Do not let them dishonor you more."

"Death to the schemer!" Luthor pushed his way through the crowd and headed for Trocolar, waving a small dagger over his head.

Another trader crumpled as he was hit from behind. A torch went sailing overhead to crash into the throng. Someone screamed, and then one guardsman tried to prevent another from reaching Nimrod's side. In an instant, the scene swirled into a chaos of motion, flashing blades, and flowing blood. The shouts and cries of pain mingled with the echoes reverberating from the walls. Torches were ripped from their sconces. In growing dimness, fists, daggers, and swords flailed at whatever was closest at hand.

A richly robed merchant dropped at Jason's feet, clutching his stomach, with spurts of gore pulsing between his fingertips. Augusta grabbed the blade just before another body fell. She severed Jason's bonds with quick slashes. In an instant, he was on his feet and testing his leg.

"Into the passage." She pointed at one of the tunnels leading from the cavern. "On the way, I can tell you where it leads."

Limping as rapidly as he could, Jason followed her into the opening and away from the fighting.

"It dead-ends after a twist a hundred paces farther along," Augusta said as Jason hobbled after. "There is no other way out, except back the way we came."

"A place of defense, then." Jason grimaced. "I need time to think — time for you to tell me what you saw happening through clearer eyes."

He stopped a moment and thought back over what had just transpired. "From what Melibar said, the sword still held power when I tried to withdraw it from the rock. And then, almost without effort, the laws have changed again. To another node in one of the lattices — and Melibar selected exactly which it would be."

High Tide

JASON FLEXED his back and peered around the corner into pitch-blackness. Except for the soft splash of distant oars, there was no sound. No one had pursued them. For over four hours, they had waited for the chaos at the other end of the tunnel to die away and the last survivors to leave. He had had enough time to reason out what should be done next.

He and Augusta must flee. Clearly, that was the best course of action. Any other was folly. But other currents also had swirled in his mind. Flee into what new uncertainty? How had anything he had done led him any closer to what he wanted? The Postulate of Invariance was only a beginning. The puzzle was only partially solved. With more information, who knew what he might be able to deduce? The urge to work on the mystery had welled up inside. He could not put the feeling away.

"The secret may yet be here," Jason said half aloud. He drew Augusta close. "I cannot abandon the quest. You saw how Melibar so easily changed the laws. And perhaps among the bodies, there is some clue that will explain more. It does no good to understand *what* was done unless we also know *how*. Let's hope that in the confusion at least one boat was left," Jason straightened to full height. "Come. I think it is safe enough now that I can get you out."

"But, what has happened?" Augusta asked in the darkness. "Does one faction now rule the island?"

Jason frowned. He felt a good deal less confident than he was trying to appear. Now it was more than Trocolar's minions they had to fear. No faction on the island would aid the ones who disrupted the election with the magic sword. Likely as not, they could become the common focus for the frustration and anger, an outside enemy that everyone could hate, a catalyst for uniting into a new order out of the destruction of the old.

He ignored Augusta's question and started down the passageway, fingering the cold and damp walls and navigating the rough variations in the rocky floor. Still limping, he guided Augusta back to the landing above the vault. In the entranceway, he stumbled over a lifeless body. He moved to the side, but ran into another. He felt Augusta tense to scream and put his arm around her shoulder.

"It is to our good fortune," he said. "Surely, one of those who remain has a flint and steel."

Positioning Augusta near the wall, Jason gave her a reassuring pat and then on all fours like a baby, began to explore the floor of the cavern. After several minutes of distasteful groping, he found the necessary tools on one of the victims. Soon a single torch illuminated the arching ceiling with its flickering glow.

"Half the wealth holders of the island are gone," Augusta gasped. "Look, there is Cumbrist and next to him Benedict, his principal rival. Beyond them, I think I see even Trocolar among the rest."

Tears welled up in her eyes, as she looked at the form barely an arm's length away. "Poor Rosimar," she said softly. "He came for my sake and now he will play the hero no more." She sank her head on Jason's shoulder and shook with a spasm. "And he was bound, with not even the slightest defense. When I freed you, I should have thought of him as well."

"You have seen enough." Jason tugged her away. "Let us go to the cliff edge to see what remains."

The torchlight cut through the darkness down to the water. Only two skiffs were left. Even Jason's raft was gone. Sprawled over the side of one, with hands dangling in the water, was a trader with a dagger in his back.

"Luther." Augusta squinted through the gloom. "He wears the embroidered leggings from his last trade. And look at the tide. I have never been here when it was so high. Jason, we must leave."

"You go ahead," he said. "You have traversed the tunnel many times, and I am sure you can manage alone. Wait just behind the portcullis that opens onto the bay. At most, I will be a few minutes behind."

Augusta started to say more, but Jason drew his face into a mask of rigid determination. "Every minute we delay, the water rises higher. You help me best by making haste."

Augusta nuzzled closer and then sighed. "I am not so much the dreamer that I would also offer to stay. But, take care, Jason. The events spin too fast. I seem to need your comfort more and more."

She disengaged and descended the ladder. With the precision of an oarsman, she maneuvered the empty skiff away from the cliff and toward the narrow opening in the far wall. As she disappeared from view, she waved a final kiss.

Jason cleared his head. Now he must hurry to find out what he could before the tide rose any higher. He would first explore the other passageways, then whatever remained among the wreckage on the landing floor, and finally the vault itself. He crossed back over the bodies and debris to begin. He entered a side tunnel and examined the ceiling and walls for any trace that Melibar might have left behind. Falling into the pattern of the puzzle solver looking for clues, he investigated to the end of the passage and then started to explore the next, losing track of the time.

An hour later, Jason emerged from the last, as empty handed as when he had begun. He turned his attention to the floor of the cavern and located Holgon's body sprawled across Melibar's toys. In the torchlight, he examined each one: the broken bladder, the sprung trap, and the painted blocks of wood. They felt quite ordinary, and no arcane symbols were anywhere to be found. Nearby was the broken sword of magic. When Jason grasped it, only the sense of cold steel greeted his fingertips. The shocks of electric pain were gone.

In frustration, he rubbed the worn coin about his neck. There was nothing here that told him anything more than he already knew. But somehow, with greater ease than the simplest glamour, Melibar had replaced the substitute magic with yet another.

Jason gripped the broken sword tighter, twisting its strange, unbalanced feeling back and forth. Later, in the light of day, there might be something else that he could not see now. Yes, that would be his plan — take an example of each form of magic and study the connection at a better time. He placed the sword hilt where he could find it again and then scooped up a handful of dominoes that lay next to the guard. He scanned around for some example of traditional magic and saw Benedict's coin changer reflecting the torchlight from a few feet away.

Jason stooped and pried loose the divulgent's stiffening fingers from the device that was still strapped to his waist. He cut it free and tripped one of the levers. A pile of worthless tokens fell into his palm and bounded onto the cavern floor.

Jason continued his search, but found nothing more. Finally, he knelt by the side of the shaft leading down to the flooded vault and peered into the inky blackness. He gathered the tokens he had spilled and dropped one of the coins into the opening. Almost immediately, he heard an answering splash.

The water level was halfway up the shaft. There was no way to see

179

what had happened below. Further exploration was impossible. If any secrets were in the vault, they would forever remain there. One by one, he dropped the rest of the tokens into the dark water, trying to visualize the imagery of their grave.

As the last one left his fingers, he bolted upright with a sudden thought. The tokens in the vault were completely submerged and inaccessible. It might work at that! The thought had no bearing on the riddle of the changing laws, but it could help Augusta, nonetheless.

A rush of excitement blotted out the pain in Jason's leg. He had learned all he could in the grotto. There was no reason to remain. Now the feeling of urgency returned. He must get out ahead of the rising tide, out to safety so he could tell her his idea.

He scurried around the landing, gathering up his loot. Balancing the load precariously, he descended the rope ladder to Luthor's skiff. After a little hesitation, he pushed the trader the rest of the way over the side of the boat and kicked the wares to the bow.

"Forgive my disrespect," he muttered, "but if the grotto is ever used again, you will be given the proper rest."

In a few minutes, Jason was at the tunnel opening that connected to the outer chamber. The water level was far higher than he had seen it the week before. On his first passage, only the narrowest part near the center had been confining. Now, even at the entrance, he had to duck his head.

He paddled forward and peered into the receding darkness. The tide was still rushing in, and each stroke of the oar was an effort. The ceiling hung oppressively close.

As he stroked, Jason concentrated on the small knobs and folds protruding from the tunnel wall ahead, measuring his progress as these landmarks passed by. He ducked to the side to miss a low monolith and then paddled furiously to avoid an outcrop that narrowed the passageway from the left.

For a moment, he stopped rowing and let the stream blunt his forward momentum. Perhaps it would be better to return to the landing and wait half a day for the next tide. No, not that. It might be too high. And who knew what would transpire outside in twelve hours? He had sent Augusta ahead to wait in the outer cavern. He must increase his effort in order to pass through the neck of the tunnel before it was too late.

Jason resumed his rowing. He sucked in lungfuls of air and concentrated on delivering powerful strokes to either side. For a few minutes, his pace increased noticeably, but then another low dip in the ceiling forced him to duck and wait for the obstruction to pass. When he continued, his burst of energy was spent. He felt fatigued and winded. His wound and the confinement in Trocolar's dungeon were taking their toll. It seemed he could just barely make progress against the force of the water rushing in.

The ceiling sank lower, and the walls closed with unrelenting menace. The skiff jammed into a narrow restriction, and Jason had to use his good leg against the wall to break free. He ducked beneath a projection and found that he could no longer sit erect. With each passing minute, he hunched lower and lower, barely avoiding blows against the top of his head.

Eventually rowing became impossible. Jason switched to pushing his oar along the wall, as he had seen the oarsmen do before. He adjusted himself to be as comfortable as possible, lying chest down on the keel, propped on one elbow while he pressed the oar against the rock. His progress slowed, as more and more frequently the skiff became jammed between the confining granite. With each yard forward, the ceiling sloped lower. With each passing moment, the water rose to meet it.

The gap between the side rail and the ceiling diminished to less than a foot. His forehead beaded with sweat as the truth of his situation began to sink in. He was not moving swiftly enough. There would be too little room. Before he reached the narrowest constriction, the boat would jam against the ceiling, and he would be trapped.

Removing himself from a confining tube, he thought. He did know of a puzzle like that! A finger from each hand stuck into either end. The more you pulled the harder you became bound. Instead, by pressing — He growled and tossed the thought aside. Wrong puzzle! That would not help.

Forcing himself to concentrate, he ran through his catalog of standard things to try. 'Divide and conquer', he remembered after the items above on the list did not provide any help — break a large puzzle into smaller and easier ones that could be solved. He enumerated what he needed: transport through the tunnel to the larger chamber on the other side, air to breathe while he was doing it, a boat for the transport of what he had found.

Jason groped around the bottom of the skiff, trying to understand where his thoughts were leading him. Behind the pile of Luthor's leggings lay a coil of the flexible tubing: animal intestines wrapped in cloth and stitched together into great lengths. He frowned and examined the ceiling. He visualized the skiff pressed firmly against the rock and cold sheets of water spilling over the rails on both sides. No, wait. He was smaller than the skiff; he did not need it. That part of the larger puzzle was solved! With a shudder, he convinced himself of what he must try.

He pulled one pair of trousers from the pile and looped shut the waist with some of the twine that held the bundles together, and then one of the legs with another piece. He inhaled as deeply as he could, and blew into the open leg, as Holgon had done with the pig bladder. Again and again, he emptied his lungs, until the leggings bulged like a misshappened balloon. Then he collapsed the hem in his fist and forced the end of the tubing through the constriction. With the last of the twine, he bound the end of the pipe into the opening, sealing it shut. It did not hold much air, but that was all that he could muster. Finally, he grabbed the other end of the coil in his right hand and pushed one of his feet into the gap above the railing.

Struggling awkwardly, he worked his calf through the opening and then his thigh. The splintering wood dragged against one side of his leg and the rough rock ceiling against the other. With each wiggle, he felt the resistance increase.

Using both arms for leverage, he forced his other leg out, ignoring the pain from his wound and then, with a burst of strength, shoved himself clear to his waist. He inhaled again, preparing for one more thrust to push him free. He glanced around the skiff a final time and blinked in surprise about what he had almost forgotten. Scattered on the keel board were the sword hilt, dominoes, and Benedict's changer. If he escaped without them, then it would have all been in vain. He might as well never have come into the grotto. But there was not time to pack them away, and he could not carry them all when swimming.

Then one, just one, part of his mind demanded. If he could take one, from it there still might be some clue with which to continue. But which had the best chance of assisting him toward his goal? The water continued to buoy the skiff upward. The railing pressed harder and harder against his chest. Each breath became a painful effort that could not be ignored.

Jason waved his arms in indecision and then impulsively grabbed the changer, instantly regretting what he had done. What if it was not the best decision? Perhaps one of the others would have been better. He pushed the thought away. There was no more time. He had made his choice, and a decision once made …

He pushed his knuckles against the keel board, trembling from the effort, and somehow squeezed the rest of the way over the side. There was barely a handsbreath clearance between the water level and the rock, but Jason began kicking away from the skiff.

He glided into the dark water, turning his head to the side for gulps of air and then floating forward, pushing in front of him the crude balloon he had made and being propelled by his kick, each alternate thrust accompanied by a stab of pain. With each gasp, the ceiling pressed closer and then finally, it drug along the top of his head. He tipped his neck lower until his chin bore down on his chest. Then he felt the ribs of rock scrape along his back. He could proceed no farther without resorting to swimming underwater. He took one last gasp of air and then thrust the end of the tubing into his mouth. Holding it in position with his hand, he angled downward and continued his glide.

In what seemed like too short a time, Jason was out of breath and he sucked on the tube. The pressure from the leggings was not great. He gasped for air. He felt his lungs expand, but sensed no great satisfaction from the musty smell that filled his mouth. He pulled himself through the water, not quite believing that he had received any nourishment at all, but somehow managing to complete another dozen gliding strokes.

Again, he gasped for breath and received the tainted air from the tube. He banged against one of the tunnel walls in the darkness and angled slightly to the side. He reached upward and felt the ceiling scrape across his knuckles, in contact with the water and just inches from his head.

Onward he stroked, trying not to think of what would happen if the leggings finally collapsed or the hose was too short. In a mindless daze, he paddled through the darkness. Time lost all meaning. Despite his efforts to concentrate only on his swimming, the sense of panic grew until he could contain it no longer. After countless gulps of air, he missed a stroke and floundered, slipping deeper into the water and rolling on his side.

As he tumbled, the tube jerked from his mouth. He reinserted it, but coughed as he inhaled water. He tried pinching off the opening with his hand while he prepared to draw again and then felt a sickening release of tension as he jerked the hose about. It had extended to its full length, and he had pulled it from the leggings at the other end. The air he had in his lungs would be his last.

Jason somehow maneuvered back into a horizontal position and touched the side of the tunnel for orientation. With a spasmodic kick, he floundered a few feet more down the passageway. He tried to resume a smooth stroke for one final try, but his bubbling thoughts swept all coordination away. Like a child splashing in a bath, he jerked forward in uneven spurts. It seemed he could feel each thrusting limb pumping air from his lungs like a piston and replacing it with a foul odor he must expel.

Jason began to feel dizzy. Strange dots of light appeared before his eyes. His diaphragm began to twitch against his will to hold it firm. In a last desperate test, he thrust his hand toward the ceiling and felt the same cold wetness. He was still submerged, and there was no more air.

The dark spots of light grew into fuzzy images of his sister, the golden coin, Delia, the mysterious Melibar. They all began to shimmer and wave in his dimming consciousness. Almost without knowing what he was doing, Jason rolled over on his back. He placed his palm upward in front of his face and walked his fingers along the rock, as his kicks became mere twitches, moving him barely inches at a time. Finally, he stopped moving altogether, letting his fingertips splash in meaningless patterns on the water's surface. With an inward sigh, he released the tension in his body and prepared to sink into oblivion.

Water's surface! He choked suddenly. With a gasp, he thrust his head upward and inhaled the sweet air. There was a sliver of open space between the waterline and the upsloping rock. He had passed the narrowest constriction. Now each length forward would give him more room to breathe, not less. The tide was still rising, and he must not tarry, but at least he had a chance. He would not drown. He would keep the rendezvous with Augusta after all. Lying on his back and inhaling deeply, he floated through the rest of the tunnel into the outer cavern. As his senses returned, he noted almost with amazement that in his left hand he still tightly clutched Benedict's changer.

The Final Tally

FOR A few moments, Jason continued to float, savoring his close escape. Then he rolled onto his stomach as Augusta maneuvered the skiff in his direction, a single torch bound erect in the stern lit her way. He waited, exhausted, for her to draw alongside and provided only feeble assistance to her tugs to get him on board.

"There is a large sloop nearby in the harbor," she said as she resumed rowing. "I saw it through the portcullis. We may as well head directly for it, rather than hide in the hope that it goes away."

Jason did not protest. He lay in a limp huddle in the bottom of the skiff, trying to recover his strength, while Augusta propelled them through the opening to the grotto and out into the bay. In a few minutes, they rendezvoused with the sloop, and eager hands pulled them aboard. Over the far rail, two more ships with the same rigging lay at anchor, and beyond them, a flotilla of many more. On the shoreline, flames still danced among some of the smoldering ruins, although not as many as before. The sky was smeared with dirty browns and grays. A rain of ash covered the rail and deck with a fine powder of grime.

A row of grim-faced traders whispered among themselves near the main mast. The eldest noticed Jason and Augusta coming aboard and broke off from the rest to see what his men had found.

"It was a good thought to wait outside after we departed the grotto," the trader said after he had scrutinized Jason for a while. "Even though the one called Melibar was able to sail for mainland Arcadia with the constabulary on the tide, not everyone responsible for what has happened has managed to escape.

I recognize this one as a sword wielder, and the woman is a fugitive as well," the trader continued. "No matter who wins, there will be a reward for their dispatch. Save their heads so that we can collect a bounty, if one is offered later."

Jason tried to shake himself to full awareness. He remembered in a rush what he had concluded in the cavern. "Wait! You need not bother with such insignificant tasks. I greet you with the news that you can again be wealthy men."

"Tokens and scentstones," the trader said. "I have gambled and lost with both. A bounty will be enough. Even if it fetches only a bowl of gruel, your demise will be well worth the effort."

"But if you have holdings in Augusta's vault, you can have means once again," Jason rattled on as he struggled to his knees. "The tokens in her vault — what if their magic has returned, as if nothing had happened, the way they were before?"

"An easy enough tale to weave," the trader spat out. "No one could prove you wrong."

"Exactly so," Jason agreed. "And why should anyone of wit choose to disagree? Isn't it in your best interest that the value of the token be restored?"

The trader squinted at Jason with beady eyes. He ran a hand across his chest. "The tokens have not been restored to magic. There are some here on deck, and their tingle is gone. The masters of the guilds moan the loudest because their craft is no more."

"Only tokens, and only those in the grotto," Jason replied.

"The token was the medium of exchange. How can it be that, buried under the slime?"

"As it was before. Only rarely were they moved about as you conducted your trades. Far more often, it was pieces of paper that you exchanged — writs that certified the shifts in ownership and the new balances that corresponded to them. It is the ledgers all carefully kept that told the story of your wealth, not the pieces of metal hidden away."

"But I had no deposits in Augusta's vault." A second trader came forward. "There is no gain for me to consider as truth what you claim."

Jason looked about. More of the traders were joining into the conversation. Exhausted as he was, he felt the first rumble in his gut. He took a deep breath. This was different, he told himself. He was not the one at a loss. He had something important to say.

"Dump your tokens down the shaft to join the rest," Jason spoke slowly and carefully. "When they hit bottom, consider their magic restored as well. Again, the ledger books will reflect your true wealth. Things will revert to exactly as they were before."

"It is too illogical to believe," the second trader objected. "Magic restored to the tokens in an inaccessible vault — there and nowhere else!"

"The consequence of not accepting the possibility is to continue the way things are now," Jason said. "The riots, the barter, perhaps the end of Pluton as a port of trade. But if everyone agrees to accept the tokens in the vault as they were before, then what difference does it make what happens with steel disks buried under the water?

"And if you agree in addition to pool the tokens from all of those who died in the grotto and then divide them up among those of you who survived, you will in fact come out all the richer from what has happened."

The eyes of the first trader widened at the mention of additional wealth. "The rates with the other commodities would be fixed as before," he mused. "I could buy from Tobruk and pay my debt to Demson with the usual exchange of writs."

"I could take the cargo from the ship that lies just outside the harbor," the second said. "And credit the captain's account with some of my tokens so that he could buy from others for a return voyage across the sea."

Jason scanned the faces of the other traders. On some, the hints of smiles indicated their acceptance of his scheme to recover their fortunes. Others were blank with confusion, and a few were drawn in stiff lines of rebuttal. He sighed. It would take longer than he had first thought. But even arguing for hours was better than how the traders had suggested they pass the time instead.

JASON SLUMPED down on the deck. Seventeen traders in all had needed convincing, and the last had been the most stubborn. But finally, they all had agreed on the merit of his idea. They could find no better alternative.

"Call the rest of the faction together," the first trader instructed the rest when the last had decided. "We must send signals to the others so that they can agree as well. With that soft-voiced Melibar sailing with most of the mercenaries, almost everyone will have the sense to see that this is the only way to restore order to the isle."

"What about Trocolar's assets?" Augusta asked. "I am in his debt for the pumps in my vault. And he threatened to make the sum due immediately rather than over a period of years, as is the custom."

"Trocolar!" the trader snapped. "He was the one responsible more than any other. His wealth will be pooled and divided just like the rest. And I doubt that anyone will be interested in carrying out his plans. The prudent will disassociate their inclinations from his faction as much as possible. I was a member of that group, but my votes will be cast in another direction. There is little chance that one of his followers will garner anywhere near enough to win a position on the council."

"Then, Jason, you have saved me indeed!" Augusta exclaimed and hugged him close. "With Trocolar dead and none to follow in his steps, I can continue to run the vault as I did before."

"And with considerably more influence." The second trader eyed Augusta critically. "The other vault holders may still hoard gold and other metals that we will need for minor exchanges, but only you will receive the holding fees for *all* the tokens on the island. Congratulations, Mistress of the Grotto. Your future prosperity seems assured."

Augusta tightened her grip on Jason. "The week is over, and your indenture has expired," she whispered. "It will appear unseemly for one partner in the vault to be the property of another."

Jason surveyed the group of traders. On every face was an expression of self-importance. Once they had all agreed, they now were no longer paupers, but holders of great wealth and power. Augusta was no more the fugitive, but again the prestigious vault holder. The fires on the shoreline, the dead in the grotto, and the realities of the outside world melted away. As long as there were tokens, the rest did not matter.

"But Melibar," Jason shook his head. "The power that is at his command cannot be ignored. It is not for a peaceful intent that he leads men-at-arms into the rebelling Wheatlands."

"The mainland can be far away if we choose to ignore it, Jason," Augusta replied. "Concentrate instead on what I have just offered — a partnership in what will become the wealthiest vault on the island. It is not something to be dismissed lightly, even by a dreamer."

Augusta pressed against him. Even through his fatigue, he felt the growth of desire. Perhaps this could be the end of his quest. He had vindicated his worth with his first love. Now she was his for the taking. How important was struggling as a wordsmith anyway, when he could lounge in luxury with no effort expended at all?

Clumsily, he pushed Augusta away. What should he do? He folded his arms across his chest and closed his eyes. He had to think.

"Gently, my sweet." Augusta wrapped her arms around his waist from behind when he stood immobile for more than a minute. "The poisons of your exertions have not yet run their course. Be calm and fight inner demons some other day."

He was sinking deeper into the pit of sand. Removing his block and restoring sorcery were mere pimples on the face of what now was at stake. Melibar was a menace of great power. All of Arcadia could fall to him. Perhaps Procolon across the great ocean as well. Perhaps the entire world. Yes, somehow, the cold one must be stopped.

"The archimage," he said aloud. "Does anyone know when he is due?"

"The archimage will be here when he decides to be so, and none of us have heard any date. It could be tomorrow, a month from now or perhaps even an entire season could pass."

A season, Jason thought. That would be much too late. Something must be done now. But thwarting one such as Melibar was a task for someone else, for someone who could do far more than merely withstand the stares of a small crowd. There must be an alternative. Someone else, someone else who understood what was happening, someone who could solve the rest of the puzzle ...

There was no alternative, he concluded.

Jason turned about and gazed into Augusta's eyes. He sighed and then spoke softly, almost not believing the words as they came forth. "The cold one travels to the Wheatlands, and, if not the archimage, then the high prince must be warned. If the traders and vault holders of Pluton will not do it, then — then it must be me.

"The puzzle of his power must be solved completely, Augusta," he continued. "His menace is too great. We cannot not just stop after removing a few outer pieces from a stack of sliding blocks." He paused for a few heartbeats and then rushed on. "And there is a slave girl who must be freed. The reason is too great, Augusta. I must be gone."

"You fret about a menace to the high prince and mysterious puzzles," Augusta said, "but I wonder, Jason. How much of your quest is for them and how much for this slave girl whom you mention the last of all?"

Part Three

The Axiom of Least Contradiction

1

Homecoming

JASON WALKED down the deeply rutted path, guided only by the moonlight. Little was different in his native village, despite more than a decade's absence. As he walked, he pondered the logic that had brought him home.

Two months had passed since he had left Pluton. Despite his urgency, the lingering winter rains had slowed his journey and the accompanying chill had made travel a definite displeasure. When he had learned that the high prince also journeyed to the Wheatlands, he made the royal party his quarry. The regent should be warned of what Melibar had done and of the stranger's interest in unrest and plunder.

The random factors must have aligned for him to catch up with the prince when the royal party visited the barony of Lord Kenton. Now there was no reason for Jason not to visit his father's hut as well. It was no less than his duty. But what would he say?

Jason recognized a familiar structure and broke out of his reverie. His father's hut stood to the side of the path. It seemed unchanged from the image painted by the wash of memories. As before, the tattered curtain that served as a door fluttered against its lashings in the quickening wind. The feeble wisps of smoke from the tin stack indicated that the fire inside was little more than smoldering coals. The light of a single candle winked through a high window with some of the panes stuffed with rags.

Jason hesitated. Then he gathered his cloak around himself and decided that it was foolish to stand in the unseasonal cold any longer. He sighed and approached the cloth-covered opening.

"Jasonel, Freetoiler Jasonel, are you there?" Jason called out. "The air chills deep, and I ask to share your fire."

A moment passed, and then a hand that was beginning to show the blotches of age fumbled with the thongs holding the curtain closed on one side. The drapery fell open and Jason gazed into watery, blue eyes. The cast of the chin was like his own, but the face was lined with rows of coarse furrows that remained, regardless of the expression.

"Father," Jason said, as the other squinted and did not speak. "It is your son. I have returned home."

Jasonel's face moved almost imperceptibly in recognition and then hardened into steel. He reached out a hand and ran his fingers over Jason's new cloak like a mouse looking for cheese. "Freshly woven, but without the logo of a master. Your status is little different from what it was when you left."

"Father, it has been almost fifteen years."

Jasonel did not reply.

"There is much that I have learned," Jason tried to fill the awkward silence. "Much that I want to hear from you as well. Many a note I have scribbled over that span after I left your brother's bed and board, but nothing have I heard in answer.

Another silence.

"Ah, how fares Mother?"

"She is with your sister, almost two years past." Jasonel motioned toward a small patch of rocky ground to the left of the hut. "Daughter, wife, son, they all have passed beyond the need for me to care."

He turned without saying more and shuffled back toward the dimly flickering fire. Jason watched the hunched shoulders retreating and followed into the hut. "But I am here," he said. "And with a far better future than when I left. Aren't the years enough to mellow the keenest disappointment?"

Jasonel settled onto the small stool before the fire, lowering himself as if the slightest miscalculation would result in a spill. "Your sister gave her life so that you might have a chance, Jason. A chance to find the means for the rest of us to break free from Lord Kenton's bonds. Each year, he has grown more oppressive. Each year, his masters come forth with more abuse of the craft. Before you left, there was only the ripening. Now there are even harvest cages and sadistic amusements in the keep.

"You were to be our way out of all of that. After Milton had passed on, you were to be the one who nurtures the crops for Lord Kenton and ensured his harvest. You were to sit in honor at his table and be our shield.

Jason surveyed the interior of the hut. The painful memories bubbled forth. The little cot was no longer against the wall, but the image of his sister was bright and firm. He clutched the brandel about his neck and swayed from the rush of emotion. He thought of his decision in Pluton and tried to hold firm why he was going on.

"I return with the means to see you away to something better," he said. "A vault holder from Pluton gave me a full purse before I journeyed here."

Jasonel looked at Jason's dress. "A merchant, then. A partner in some trade with the islands. Perhaps it would not be so bad. As long as you managed well, you probably would fare better than your cousin, Anton. He runs a mill now, but is forever in debt, trying to maintain lordly airs."

Jasonel rubbed his hand along his chin. "Yes, it might be possible. These purses you receive — how often does one come and how many coppers do they contain? Do you have a chance of increasing your share if your work is good?"

Jason turned his head aside. "I refused the offer," he answered. "The one purse was a gift. There will be no more."

"A single purse." Jasonel's tone regained its harsh edge. "A single purse for fine cloaks and expensive leggings. And, no doubt, for fancy meals and down-filled beds as well. After it is gone, do you plan to labor twenty more years to get another?"

"No," Jason shook his head. "My next reward possibly could come much sooner. I have tracked the high prince here to warn him of great peril. If I can unravel its cause as well, then an ample show of appreciation might be mine."

Jason paused. "Although that is not the principal reason. It is something that I have decided must be done."

"The high prince!" Jasonel snorted. "It is true that he is here. He shares the bounty of the village's labor with Lord Kenton in his castle on the rise."

"For nearly two months, I have been following his party," Jason said, "up the river from Searoyal harbor and through the midland baronies to the central plains. I just missed him at Lord Burdon's as it is."

"Burdon has accompanied the prince to Kenton's keep. But the movements of the nobility do not matter. You are as likely to audience with the prince there as he is to grace my hearth here in the village."

"He will lead the incantation for the spring harvest in the square tomorrow," Jason persisted. "The winter wheat is to be reaped despite the lingering cold. I hope to have a chance to speak to him then."

"And he feasts with Kenton in the keep come nightfall, as well. But in either case, what will you say to the thaumaturges who will block your path?"

"I will talk to them with these." The desire for forgiveness no longer mattered. If his father could be so unyielding at every turn, then so could he. He reached under his cloak and withdrew his purse. Reaching inside, he scooped out two gold brandels and threw them at his father's feet. "Use them for firewood," he said as he turned to leave. "Perhaps they will warm more than the air in the room."

2

Spring Harvest

JASON GRIMACED as the butt end of the spear jabbed into his back. Like a stew that takes forever, all morning he had simmered over his father's treatment the day before. And now, he had wanted to wait until the incantation was finished before approaching the high prince. But the men-at-arms made it clear that it would do no good to protest. Everyone was to watch. Packed shoulder to shoulder with the others, he shuffled forward against the line in front. He marveled at how calm he felt. No eyes were turned his way, it was true, but he was in a crowd nevertheless.

Like no more than a stray calf, Jason had been herded into the south end of the square, well away from the high prince and the double row of thaumaturges who flanked him on both sides. He remembered the familiar sights of his childhood. The same rough-hewn boards showed through blistered paint, the tattered awnings flapped limply over empty storefronts and the drab signs still signaled little commerce and even less life. Only the thaumaturges carried an air of freshness. The morning sun filtered through tiny clouds to cast pale shadows of their crisply pressed robes onto the cobbles of the square. A hint of wind from the west shook their hems as they moved toward the central fountain in stately cadence.

The high prince wore the robe of a master, although Jason knew that it was only a courtesy for the sake of tradition. The thaumaturges would speak the incantations and invoke the words of power. The prince was an actor, miming the motions for gullible subjects, and no more. He was not the one who brought the crop to ripening at the desired time. It would mature as the thaumaturges directed, whether he gave his benediction or not.

Jason stood on tiptoe to see over the shoulder of the villager in front. The procession stopped its march next to a huge, banded candle. The tallow column was an alternation of white and gray disks that towered

197

well above the tallest head. On the prince's signal, a journeyman climbed a ladder to light the wick. With the first spark, it burst into flame. Faster than one would have expected, the topmost layer burned away.

"Less than a minute for a full day," the swarthy man on Jason's left grunted to his comrade. "They will have to move quickly to ensure that each field is serviced at the proper time."

As the candle began to consume the second layer, the master thaumaturges broke from their precise line and scattered around the courtyard like chickens fleeing a wolf. Each ran to position himself in front of an earthen pot from which sprouted a single long stalk of golden wheat. They began chanting a nonsense harmony, a complicated sequence of phrases and syllables that meant nothing to the untrained ear and disguised the words of power when they were spoken.

While the candle burned through the second layer, the journeyman scampered to the thaumaturge the farthest distance away. He carried a giant lens, and the master grabbed it from his hands when he approached. Carefully judging the distance and angles, the thaumaturge focused the sun's rays onto the ripening plant. He grunted with satisfaction as a small billow of steam almost instantly snaked upward from the drying grain. The master handed the lens back to the journeyman and extracted the kernels, one by one, from the tassel of the tall grass.

As the candlewick began to expose the next level, the journeyman darted back across the square to another waiting master on the other side. The same steps were repeated with the second, while the first thaumaturge recited a solo incantation and then sat on the ground, his task done.

One by one, the masters tended to their singular crops, each one acting within the time span specified by the melting of a single band of wax. When the last was completed, nothing remained of the rapidly burning taper. All the masters focused their attention on the high prince.

"The rocky ground to the east." The man on Jason's left spoke again. "They ripen those fields last because Ocanar and Pelinad are so near. If any fields are to be sacrificed, they will be those."

"Pelinad and Ocanar will be far away when the harvest starts tomorrow," another said in reply. "A large troop presses upriver from Searoyal at the high prince's command. Lord Kenton has convinced him that the threat is more than a brigand's idle boast."

"Yes, that it will be," the first growled, rubbing his stomach. "Kenton again has increased his rents, and the late warming will mean the yield is poor. They call us freetoilers, but the margin between that and bondsmen has grown exceedingly thin. Pelinad might find many more in his camp."

"Pelinad!" The other snorted. "It would be a shame if any of stout heart hearkened to his banner. It is to Ocanar that the support must come. Of the two, only he has the wits to give the high prince any cause for alarm."

"Yes, wits and craft enough to barter his own daughter for advantage, if he saw the need," the first said. "And if he were to win, then for us it would be no better. Kenton or Ocanar, to tithe to one lord is as good as to another."

"You mention a troop from Searoyal," Jason interrupted. He had to seize the moment, no matter what his stomach started to do. "Do you know the names of any who make the trip? Is there a Melibar as well as men-at-arms?"

The two men abruptly stopped speaking and stared at Jason. "The cloak is not the fashion here," the first one muttered. "Not one of our own." The second nodded. "He should ask our good lord himself at the feast tonight. The one to which no freetoiler is invited."

Jason frowned. Perhaps a bribe would help. He reached for his purse but stopped as the words of the high prince echoed across the square.

"Freetoilers of Arcadia," the booming voice said, "again the nobility has granted you a boon. Again, you will harvest fine crops from the plots scattered around your fair plain. And again, the wheat will mature and ripen in the proper sequence so that none is spoiled while waiting for the thrasher's flails. Rejoice in your good fortune. Exult in the high yields. Thank the graciousness of your Lord Kenton that you have the means to be, not slaves, but free."

At the mention of Kenton's name, a low murmur started in the crowd, and the men-at-arms straightened from their slouches to a state of alert.

"Yes, thank your lord for the way that he has analyzed all elements of the cycle." The high prince raised his voice above the buzz. "The seed selection, the fertilization, the water channels, the grain barges, and the pushing back of the harvest of winter wheat to early spring, so that there are two crops a year instead of one. Without his guidance, you all still would be scratching out barely enough to feed yourselves. Instead, you nourish all of Arcadia and even baronies across the great ocean. Tonight in his feasting hall, the millers, the barge captains, the traders, and the grain keepers all come to pay homage to your lord's great use of craft."

"And had he not been so clever," someone shouted, down the line from where Jason stood, "then, at least, we could have starved with some leisure. As it is now, we toil from sun to sun, and our stomachs growl all the same."

"You need not avail yourselves of your lord's machinery and arts," the high prince replied. "Farm your rented land as you see fit. But if you rely only on the natural climate and soil, your neighbor who gives his labor in exchange for the benefits of the art will have a production that exceeds your's many fold."

"And so, only the ones who march in step in the cages will be able to pay the increased rents that rise every year," the man next to Jason muttered.

"And once you miss a payment, you are trapped as a bondsman and forced to labor just the same as the rest," a second replied. "Free or fettered, it makes little difference. We will all be Kenton's in the end."

"But if you owe nothing at the close of the season, unlike the others, you can leave," a third said. "Only if you are in debt are you legally bound."

"Walk away to what?" The first one spat. "A lord rules the plain the mountains to the east, just as one does here. The walled cities will not admit someone who does not have a craft." He shook his fist. "A pox on whomever first applied thaumaturgy to the fields. It has tied us to the land far tighter than any edict ever could."

The hubbub intensified, and so did Jason's discomfort. He put his hands over his ears. The high prince stamped his boot for silence, but no one heeded. A few of the men-at-arms pushed the shafts of their spears menacingly into the crowd. The agitation grew. The prince tried to speak again, but he was drowned out. He paused for a moment more, then whirled about in disgust and waved his arms for the thaumaturges to follow. Rigidly erect, he marched through the small archway that led from the square and disappeared. The thaumaturges hastily shouldered their way after. In an instant, the plaza was deserted by the masters.

The men-at-arms became more aggressive in their pokes and jabs. Without any focus for their hostility, the feeling of the crowd ebbed away. The ranks to the rear started to turn. In twos and threes, they stepped back into the alleyways and disappeared. Those in front shouted one last defiance as they retreated into the space at their backs. Far more rapidly than it had filled, the square was emptied of everyone except the men-at-arms.

Jason frowned. His father had been right. He was no closer to the high prince than he had been at the start. The incantation for the spring harvest had presented no opportunity at all. He could only hope that, if somehow he got into Kenton's keep, his chances would be better. But for that, he needed to accompany a grain trader or a miller.

A grain trader or a miller. Anton. Anton was a miller and forever in debt. Yes, that was it. Jason touched his full purse. Perhaps his cousin would be receptive to a little transaction to the benefit of both.

3

Tread of the Ambulators

THE AFTERNOON passed swiftly before Jason found his cousin. Anton was as his father described, long on appearances but short of coin. Once the agreement was struck, the rest had been surprisingly easy. As darkness fell, Jason found himself in the feasting hall of Lord Kenton and mere yards away from the high prince.

But barely an hour had gone by when Anton drained the last of his fifth goblet and waved it over his head to be refilled. With a lurch, he sagged against Jason's shoulder.

"You cannot empty the kegs alone, no matter how hard you try," Jason whispered in irritation beneath the din. "Pace yourself, Anton. The bargain was a seat at the table against the gold for a feathered cape. I did not offer to carry you home to your mill."

"Nor did I agree to hear pious judgments from a free toiler's son," Anton slurred. His face was puffy, like rising dough. Beads of sweat trickled down ruddy temples, even though the huge room was cold. "Had I not the need to dress to catch Lord Kenton's eye, a sweet doxy would have been my choice for a companion, not a cousin suddenly visiting from afar."

Jason started to reply, but a page arrived with a flagon, and he contented himself with pushing Anton erect. He had far more important things to which attend. His forehead glistened with sweat. The optimism he had felt in the crowd earlier in the day had vanished. The situation now was different. The noise was all about, in front of him, behind him, and on both sides. At any moment, someone could point him out and start the cruelty. He was barely managing to maintain control.

For the dozenth time, he surveyed the large, rectangular room. All four walls were hung with tapestries from floor to ceiling, with cutouts for high doorways that led to the kitchens beyond. In each corner was a

202

treadmill, a belt of wooden planks tied together with rope and looped around two axles in a tight band. An ambulator sat on each, muscular legs dangling over the sides. Long tables defined the perimeter of a central square. Around the outside edge sat over fifty revelers, eating Kenton's fowl and drinking his wine. The table to the south was higher than the rest, and its center was the focus of Jason's attention.

Lord Kenton's loud and commanding presence dwarfed even that of the high prince, who sat on his right. The two men were most unalike. Prince Wilmad's face was thin as a hatchet fish, and his eyes set too high above a razor-sharp nose. His head was always tilted slightly back. From under half-closed eyelids, he scanned the room, daring anyone to relieve a majestic boredom. Kenton's face was round, with full cheeks that pushed his eyes into tiny dots. His chin bristled with a two-day growth of beard. After perfunctory wipes of a gravy-laden hand on a soiled surcoat, he was as likely as not to run his fingers through a tangle of jet-black hair. At his left was some doll furniture, an array of tables and chairs, laid out in a scaled-down replica of the feasting hall.

With a booming command, Kenton slammed down his flagon and beckoned the wine steward for more. Pushing aside Wilmad's hand with a laugh, he grabbed the skein from the steward and filled the prince's cup until it overflowed. With what appeared as an afterthought, he splashed a few swallows into his own.

"Do not be so cautious, my liege." Jason strained to catch Kenton's words. "You are among friends, as safe as in the highest keep in Searoyal. Everyone here is a man of at least some means. Master thaumaturges, barge captains, millers, and sack makers. The last harvest incantation is done. It is an opportunity to enjoy yourself. Even a prince must sometimes indulge in simple pleasure."

"Our interests in a successful harvest are mutual," Wilmad said. "The mood throughout the kingdom would grow more ugly if it fails. I do not deny that. But the whole does not necessarily follow from one of the parts. The crude humor of a misplaced melon peel does not compare with the experiences one can feel on Morgana."

"Yet what will you do next season, my prince?" Kenton smiled. "The rumors have it that sorcery is no more. Perhaps it is time now to cultivate new tastes."

With a wave of his hand, he signaled to the far corner of the room. The ambulator stood up and began to pace on the treadmill. With a fluid kick, the man picked up speed, pushing the planks under his feet faster and faster. The creak of the boards as they rounded the axles added to the noise drowning out the prince's reply.

Jason tensed. He knew the ambulators were one of the ways for providing the energy to an incantation. Kenton would not have started one running unless he intended to exercise the art.

"And now let me see," the lord boomed. "Who is in most need of stretching his legs to relieve the tedium of the feast?"

A sudden blur of motion streaked by Jason's side. He turned just in time to see Anton fall to the floor, his chair tumbling back to the wall.

"Ah, you always were the alert one." Kenton laughed as the miller struggled to regain his feet. The buzz of conversation transformed into a chorus of laughter as Anton stomped on his new cape and fell again to the ground.

Jason put his hands over his ears and clamped his jaws to hold the sudden urge to lose his dinner. The laughing is for Anton, he told himself. It is for Anton, not for me.

The ambulator now panted heavily, trying to rebuild the treadmill's speed. Where was the simulation? Jason tried to focus his attention away from all of the faces looking his way. He scanned the hall for something that would be related to the chair. When he recognized the small model held in Kenton's fingertips, he stopped and managed to feel, mixed with the rest, a small hint of satisfaction of a trivial puzzle solved. A simple case of thaumaturgy, but an exercise of the art nonetheless.

Kenton caught sight of Jason holding his ears. "In the Wheatlands, it is polite to help one's cousin," he said.

With a deft motion, the lord flicked another model chair with his thumb. Jason felt his own seat scoot away. He grabbed for the tablecloth as he fell and crashed to the floor in a pile of plates, flagons, and spilled food. The laughter increased, and even the tapestries could not muffle the roar.

"Two chairs. They account for two of the treadmills," Kenton continued. "But with four ambulators in the hall, there must be additional bindings."

Anton continued struggling to regain his balance, but Jason did not try. He curled into a ball, hands pressed against his ears. But even with them in place, the laughter filtered through like the roar from a great waterfall. It was as it had been before. Everyone was laughing. Everyone. All laughing at him. He had not been able to perform even the most simple of all incantations — to remove a wart from a finger. How could he with all the stares from the other apprentice hopefuls, the pointed fingers, and most of all the laughter, the cruel laughter aimed directly at him?

His heart beat in an irregular rhythm. He gasped for breath but could not get enough air. Limbs trembled and became numb. The dizziness did not hide the feeling in his gut. In an instant, his dinner was spilling down the front of his tunic and onto the floor.

Across the way, a wine cup suddenly jumped from a table, splashing its contents on another of the guests. A turkey thigh rose from a platter and plunged into the beard of a grain keeper on her right. For several minutes, the laughter continued as Kenton manipulated the objects, dashing the chairs into anyone who lost track of where they were, bouncing the cup off heads and elbows, and thrusting the turkey leg into mouths not discreetly shut when it passed by.

Gradually, Jason began to realize that he was no longer the center of attention, but in his misery, he did not care.

"Enough," the lord said finally. The ambulators collapse to sitting, their chests heaving from their effort and their treadmills still. The laughter died away. Jason opened his eyes and sat up, although still clutching his chest.

"Release the bindings," Kenton ordered, and the thaumaturges started to sing as they had done earlier in the day. The lord turned to the prince. "This is just a sample of what the other arts can do to amuse one nobly born."

"It is little different from last year's," Wilmad said. "And a few minutes' entertainment at that. You presume too much, Kenton. Guide your masters in the production of wheat. In that, you have shown much skill. But leave true art to those who have the sense to judge the subtle from the mundane."

"But the goblet," Kenton protested. "Have you no idea the difficulty involved in fashioning a replica on such a small scale?"

"The craft of your masters is well regarded, even in Searoyal," Wilmad replied. "The candles that they carefully build, taking a full day for each layer, are used throughout the plains."

Jason staggered to his feet. Anger broke through the panic of moments before. It was his fault for the laughter so long ago, but this time, Kenton was to blame. "You waste time in debating the merit of foolish games when you should be attending to the responsibilities of being lords," he interrupted, not bothering to wipe away the mess on his tunic. He had come to tell the high prince of an impending danger, not to be the butt of a baron's jokes.

His outburst brought the hall to silence. Jason immediately realized what he had done, but there was no way to turn aside the look that began to etch itself on Kenton's face. The sense of anxiety began to return and mingle with his flash of anger. He plunged on while he still could.

"First sorcery, then magic. Can you not see that even thaumaturgy might be next? How will you harvest all of these ripening fields if the art gives you no aid?"

"The last incantation of ripening has been performed," Kenton replied in a surprisingly quiet voice. 'The thaumaturges stood in the center of the village in exactly the same geometric pattern as that of the fields upon the plain. The crops will mature, each field one day after the next in lock step, just as the representative stalks did in the square." The lord glowered at Jason. "All that remains is to ensure that the labor for the reaping is properly applied to the task."

"Not the cages again," another voice on Kenton's left interrupted. The man stood and faced the prince with his palms spread wide like the senior master of a guild instructing a first class of neophytes. A ring of white hair circled a completely bald crown. Burst veins of blue netted his cheeks, and flesh hung limply from slender arms. "The freetoilers work to their limit as it is. Another fetter will drive them directly into the brigands' hands. Instead of eleven bushels where you used to have ten, you will have none at all."

Jason felt a glimmer of relief as Kenton's attention turned from him, but he did not move, unsure of what to do next.

"I have eleven where you have only six, Burdon," Kenton answered the interruption. Eleven to your six because I know better what effort the freetoilers are capable of exerting. If it is the cages that will increase this year's yield to the desires of the high prince, then cages I shall use." Kenton waved his hand in Jason's direction. "And for everyone that I can fill with legal cause, it is one less that the freetoilers must elect to enter by choice."

"I do not care to interfere with your methods," Wilmad interjected. "As long as the grain is produced in sufficient quantity and my house gets its rightful share, the means are not my concern."

The high prince eyed Kenton down the length of his nose. "They are not my concern, as long as Arcadia remains at peace with itself and I do not have to explain to my doddering father why the royal garrison must be pulled from the coast to the inland plains. One company from Searoyal is quite enough, Kenton. Do not overstep the bounds, so that next year I again must shout apologies about a vassal's conduct to the rabble in the village square."

"The chance of rebellion is not to be lightly dismissed, my liege,"

Burdon said. "Each day the brigands add one or two more to their cause — one or two more cursing Kenton's abuses of the art."

"Abuses!" Kenton snorted. "A weak excuse for those unwilling to toil as they should. Why, of the five arts, thaumaturgy is the least sinister. It has the smallest potential for true harm. There is no opening of a channel to the frightening power of the demons with which the wizards toy. Nor the possibility of lifelong enchantment that can come from a sorcerer's gaze. No awesome weapons, like those from a magician's guild. No salves or philters of evil intent from an alchemist's athanor. No, just two simple principles to aid in the production of our crops."

Kenton paused for breath, but then raced on before Burdon or the prince could speak again. "Even I understand their intent, if not the incantations that invoke their uses. The Principle of Sympathy, or 'like produces like.' Because of it, when I move the model chair, the one in the room responds in kind. A whole field ripens, as does a single stalk.

"And the Principle of Contagion, or 'once together, always together.' Both the full-size chair and its model were made from the same log. The wheat maturing in the square is coupled to the field from which it came and no other. These two concepts, plus the binding of a bit of energy to make it all come about, span the full scope of the art. It is so simple that, as I have told you, no great harm can result.

"And look at what we have accomplished by applying the craft to our fields year after year," Kenton continued. Seeds placed in straight rows to equal depth merely by inserting one. Germination in unison of all that is sown. Accelerated growth, as if each plant were nurtured in the finest of fertilized soils. An entire field ripening at once, while its neighbor is delayed for a day, so our limited tools can be used for each at the optimal time."

"The harvest incantations occur in my villages, as well as in yours," Burdon said. "We all understand that each layer of candle wax was made a single day before the one underneath, and hence lives one more sunset from birth to death, and that each field's ripening is bound to a layer so that it matures in the same sequence.

"All of that is not the point. You see no abuse, yet it is all around you, Kenton. What of those misshapen ambulators? Their thighs are as big as their waists, of no use other than to provide the energies that your incantations demand. If by some chance the art were to go away, to what other craft could they be employed?

"No, the issue is not the principles of thaumaturgy," Burdon continued, "but the degree to which its magic robs our people of their will. Now the freetoiler has little choice. He must volunteer to man the cages in step with the bondsman so that his own field yields as much as yours. If you have your way, ultimately he will be little more than a machine, locked in a grotesque dance that stomps the stems and separates the chaff with jerking steps precisely placed."

"My masters have not yet perfected their craft; it is true." Kenton smiled. "But it is a goal well worth striving for, nonetheless. The cage that you show so much concern about is no more than the logical extension of what we have been doing for years. And the freetoilers need not employ it. As long as they can get eleven bushels from each acre, where last year they harvested ten, how they accomplish the task I do not question.

"Yes, eleven bushels." Kenton turned his attention back to Jason. "For one of the miller's trade, it will be a grand experiment. It is the form by which you will accept the punishment for your impertinence. Eleven days in the cage. Let us see if you are as skillful as the rest when you are done."

Kenton smiled but said no more. He rang a small bell at his side and from somewhere in the castle, a huge gong sounded. He motioned to his thaumaturges and ambulators. The treading resumed. The words of a binding incantation again filled the air. A squad of men-at-arms marched into the feasting hall, carrying shackles and chains.

Jason turned to look at the new arrivals. His panic increased. In the hallway behind the men, he glimpsed iron bars and a steel plate. He heard the rumble of wooden wheels on stone. What they were he knew he was soon to learn.

4

Fugitive's Choice

JASON GASPED when the cold water hit his face, snapping him awake. It was dawn. He was outside Kenton's castle at the edge of a field of wheat. A steel belt and chains fettered him to the sides of a large metal cage. He was the only occupant, although the volume could have accommodated many more. Straining as far as his bounds would allow he came nowhere near to touching one of the walls. Bars were spaced a hand span apart on all four sides. A steel plate formed the ceiling. Underneath, it was bracketed with tools, gears, screens, and other machinery that Jason did not immediately recognize.

The bottom was open. He stood on the rough ground. In each of the four corners, large wooden wheels pressed into the damp earth. Identical cells formed a precise line staggered into the distance, each one placed a cage length behind the one in front and offset to the right.

The man-at-arms who had aroused Jason continued down the row, waking others who hung slumped in their bonds. A sergeant followed behind, tapping each cage with a baton and barking the order to make ready. He stopped at Jason's cell and pointed at the scythe attached just within arm's reach to a bracket on the ceiling.

"You must cut it all," he said. "If any tickles the touch plate in back, the flagella will whirl. And get rid of the cloak, It will get in your way."

Jason did not reply. Only with great restraint had he not resisted being seized the night before, and it had saved him from certain injury. He had been thrust into the cage in such a hurry that he was still dressed for the feast, the smell of his rotting dinner apparent. The sergeant looked at the waving stalks and then turned a crank that led into the top of the cage. As the handle spun, a coarse horizontal screen lowered from the ceiling to about waist level, directly behind Jason. Then, above the screen came a cylindrical drum, its axis parallel to the back of the cage. Long strips of leather coiled around it, and sharp metal brads covered the loose ends that dangled in the air.

The sergeant examined the grain a second time, made a small adjustment with the crank, and then nodded to himself in satisfaction. He tapped his baton once more on the metal bars and turned his attention to the next in line.

As the sky brightened, Jason gazed across the field down the long lines of high-standing grain. In the distance, there were more treadmills like those of the feasting hall but built on a larger scale, with ambulators four abreast. They started the treadmills in motion, and Jason waited for what the thaumaturgical effect would be.

Almost immediately, a strange rustling shimmered throughout the field. Thin tendrils of vapor snaked into the morning air. Triggered by the incantation the day before, the crop had matured and was ready to harvest. Jason's cage lurched and began to rumble forward. Ahead and behind, the rest of the staggered line move in unison. Somewhere, a thaumaturge was guiding a small toy to which all these were bound. Jason stumbled on a rock and missed a step, but the cage continued forward, pulling him by the fetters tied to his waist.

The man in the cage directly ahead entered the field and grabbed his scythe. With a practiced stroke, the prisoner felled the stalks that filtered through the vertical bars in front. His path was such that the left edge of his swath matched the right of the prisoner who preceded him. Jason grunted understanding. The cages were large enough to give each man room to swing, yet they were grouped in such a way that, once they had all passed over the field, no grain would remain standing.

Uncut grain danced into Jason's cage as he reached the field. But his anger of the previous night still lingered. Nurturing a spark of defiance, he folded his arms and stomped on the grain as it came underfoot, letting the growth on either side pass by untouched. He glanced over his shoulder, to see it spring back to nearly full height, almost as if he had not gone by at all.

The tall stalks poked through the screen that the sergeant had lowered into place. As the first tassel passed through the grid, one of the gear trains on the ceiling began to creak. A lever pulled a pawl from a ratchet, and the drum at Jason's back whirled into motion. The leather thongs uncoiled and whipped from their resting place, striking him with a barrage of the sharp metal tips. Hot bursts of pain exploded across his shoulders and neck, staggering Jason almost to his knees.

The sergeant's words suddenly had meaning. Jason grabbed the scythe as quickly as he could. With a slashing abandon, he hacked at the grain that continued to pour through the bars of the cage, toppling all the stalks before they slipped past him to be detected by the screen. The swinging blade tangled in his cloak. With a rip of his free hand, he flung the garment to the ground. He studied again at the methodical sweep of the other prisoners' scythes and tried to imitate their economy of motion. He felt his own cage pick up speed and fell into a rhythm to keep up with the pace.

The rate of progress increased two more times before Jason reached the end of the row. With leaden arms and gasping lungs, he mowed the last few lengths. He was not used to the hard labor. Already he felt his coordination deteriorate from the fatigue. He dropped the scythe to the ground, then thought better of it and barely managed to retrieve the blade as the cage continued to trundle along its predetermined track.

Jason was led to a second field adjacent to the first and placed into another staggered line. While the last of the cages were finishing their swaths and being moved into position, a small, hinged door opened from the ceiling and a cup of dirty water descended on the end of a long rod. Jason grabbed the offered liquid and drank deeply, thankful for a moment of rest.

On the first field, another row of prisoners had begun to move across the mowed ground. Their cages were different, with deep wooden bins hanging along the interior walls on both sides. Through a complex of linkages and springs, the suspended hoppers were connected to a circular disk, faced with two rotating pointers like the hands of a clock. One seemed to circle of its own volition, revolving at a steady but rapid rate. The other bounced and jerked, moving forward through short arcs only whenever another armful of shorn stalks was dumped into one of the hoppers to increase the weight it contained.

Most of the time, the weight indicator led the other, but occasionally it would be passed and lag behind. Whenever it did, the drum behind the occupant of the cage whirled into life, lashing out with the barbs of sharp metal. Snatching and scooping in a fury, the harvesters made sure that little of what had been mowed was left on the ground.

Without warning, Jason's line began to move again. The cup retreated into the ceiling. In an instant, his cage lumbered into more uncut grain. Again, he was late to stop the screen behind his back from being touched, and again he felt the incentive to leave no stalk uncut. Grimly, he swung the scythe and tried to take his mind off anything more than ensuring that his task was perfectly done. Before the sun had reached its zenith, Jason had cut six more rows of wheat. By dusk, he had lost track of the number.

211

With the last rays of the sun, he was allowed to stop at the end of the row he had just worked. His arms, his back, his legs, and every muscle was throbbing in protest to the strenuous labor. His waist bled from a dozen sores where the metal belt had dug into his flesh. He hung like a damp rag in his harness, feet dragging on the ground and arms dangling with no life.

The blankness of his thoughts was interrupted by the sergeant, who placed a bowl inside his cage. The man-at-arms looked hastily over his shoulder, and then scooted a second dish between the bars. "The first day is the roughest, but if you do not eat to get strength, then the next will be your last."

Jason raised his head and eyed the sergeant dully, too tired even to offer thanks. "I earn no favor with the lord if one of the cages stops working during the day," the guardsman said gruffly as he unknotted one of the chains binding Jason to the bars. 'Take advantage of your good fortune so that I can ensure mine."

5

Intertwined Journeys

LATER, WITH food in his stomach, Jason felt a small degree of reason return. Another ten days of this he could not endure. He stood and looked around the cage. With only one fetter, he could reach the side, but rattling the bars revealed no looseness. They all held tight and firm like those in a royal dungeon. Tentatively at first and then with greater vigor, he sawed with the scythe against the linkage that still bound him, but the blade just skittered across the harder metal, refusing to bite and make a notch.

Jason grasped the tool with both hands near the neck where the blade joined the wooden handle and tried to imagine how he might separate the two pieces and turn them into something that would be of use in an escape. He ran his hands over the gears and levers of the ceiling, pulling at protrusions and attempting to break something free. Each object he could reach he studied in turn, grasping for some idea that would help his plight.

But try as he would, all his thoughts were leaden. He was too tired from the labor to think anything more than the obvious. With the certainty of failure, he went through the motions, making the escape attempts that every cage occupant tried.

Finally, he turned his attention to his own possessions. He ran his hands over his newly purchased tunic, now deeply soiled and smelling of vomit and sweat. As he touched his pockets, he felt the reassuring lumps of their contents: his purse of gold, Benedict's changer, and the various curios he had brought with him to Morgana were still there. In the haste to have him confined, no one had bothered to take anything away.

One by one, he removed the items, trying to couple them with something else in the cage. When he reached the changer, he idly thumbed piles of coins into his palm and poured them back into the slit in the top.

As the metal disks slid into the opening, Jason could hear the soft click of some sorting apparatus that directed them to the various columns. But the output of each was a jumble — gold, silver, copper, and steel, diameters of many sizes, coins with central holes and those without, all mixed when a dispensing lever was depressed.

He cycled the coins, letting the soft jangle soothe the soreness from his limbs and back. He found himself watching the pattern of types as they emerged and tried to guess what the next might be. Silver, he thought, fingering the lever for the leftmost column. Silver again, he smiled when his choice proved correct. "And again," he muttered half aloud when he was right a second time. "Perhaps, even without magic, the box can still sort if given enough tries."

Five silver coins in a row fell from the column before a brass dranbot ended the string. "An interesting puzzle," Jason mused, putting the device aside as he tried to visualize what the internal mechanism must be. After some thought, he lifted the changer again. With a rapid series of motions, he emptied the entire contents of coins onto the ground. Then he selected one copper and inserted it into the slit. Trying the dispensing levers one by one, he found that the third column had received the coin.

Two coppers in sequence were partitioned into columns three and four. If they followed a silver, they went instead to two and five. In a rapid series of experiments, Jason used longer sequences of coins, trying to deduce the rule by which they were distributed. He inserted runs of all one coin and then two types interleaved in pairs. Cycles of four, mixed triplets, groups of seven — the various combinations filled his thoughts as he struggled to assemble all the results into a coherent whole.

The sky dimmed into night, and then the first stars twinkled into view. The moon streaked pale shadows of the cage bars onto the ground, but Jason continued, unheeding. He divided the coins into distinct piles that he could locate by feel in the darkness.

"Suppose we limit the problem to five of each type," he muttered. "And the challenge is to choose the order so that in the end they all will be sorted. Yes, I will call it Benedict's problem. The path each one takes from the slit depends not only on its type but on what the columns already contain as well. It cannot be done in one pass. When four coppers are in column one, unless a silver is in both two and three, the last will go to five instead. So one must remove some from the bottom and intermix them with those remaining to be added at the top. Only then can there be a chance."

"With the setting of the moon! Pass it along." A whispered voice broke Jason's concentration sometime later. He had not noticed that another of the harvest cages had moved to barely ten feet away.

"With the setting of the moon. Do not sleep. Pass it along," the voice repeated. "The message comes from one of the Pelinad band. Kenton expects him only to touch the fields in the east, if at all. But it will be tonight. Here, they will make the attempt."

Jason shook himself alert. He frowned at the scatter of metal disks that lay in front of him like buttons from a sewer's tray. He glanced at the sky, now quite different from when he had last noticed it. What had he been doing? Frittering away time on a meaningless puzzle, and one of his own making at that. He must be more tired than he had thought. Disgustedly, he scooped up all the coins and inserted them in the changer. He shook his head, confused about his actions, and thrust the device away. The visions of sliding mechanisms and clinking coins began to fade. He wrinkled his brow and forced his thoughts back to his immediate plight.

"Wait," he said to the occupant of the other cage. "The setting of the moon. Pelinad's messenger. What do you mean?"

"The reward justifies the risk. With common laborers too tired to lift a sword, there was no reason for taking the chance. But two new ones were added to the cages today, and one is a sorcerer from Morgana."

"I am no sorcerer," Jason replied. "I was only on a visit to the island to learn the craft."

"Not you, dolt. The big man farther down the line. Now pass it on, before the guardsmen hear your chatter and come to investigate."

Jason started to ask more, but the other cage began to move away. He cursed himself for not noticing sooner that the messenger had come so close to hand. Sorcerers and Pelinad's rebels, they were far more important than the tinkle of a few pieces of metal. Determined, he made up his mind to recover the time he had lost. He checked the ground to ensure that all the coins had been retrieved and then began to push his cage in the direction of the next in line.

And at the next, rather than returning to his own position, he offered to carry the message farther down the row, At each stop, as he whispered the words, he stared into the darkness, trying to recognize a familiar face. The practice of sorcery in Arcadia had been confined to Morgana. A master sorcerer would have to come from there. But it would not be tradition-bound Farnel and certainly not Gerilac. And why would any of the other masters journey to the Wheatlands?

A dozen stops produced nothing, and Jason felt his fatigued legs begin to tremble from the effort of pushing over the ruts that ran alongside the lines of wheat. But the memory of his mental lapse goaded him on, and he continued to the next. He lost track of how many cages he visited. The end of the line finally came within sight.

As he approached the fourth from the last, a sudden scream jerked him alert. A drum sounded to the left, and the guard fires sprang back to life. Shouts of alarm came from all along the line. Steel clanged against steel three cages away. In a matter of a hundred heartbeats, dark figures ran from cell to cell and keyed open the doors. He heard the jangle of freedom in the back of his own cage and tugged with an energy he was surprised he still had to free himself of the metal belt.

He bolted so quickly to the outside that he nearly knocked down the man racing from the adjacent cell. Together, they flailed to regain their balance in the dimness. As they spun about, the moon on the horizon caught the other man's features. Jason's mouth dropped open in sudden recognition.

"Canthor!" he exclaimed. "Canthor, the bailiff of Morgana Island. Why are you here? You are no more a sorcerer than I!"

6

Which Way To Turn

THE CAMPFIRE was framed by the rising hills. Jason tried to stretch himself into a more comfortable position. His linen tunic, freshly washed, was now bunched in thick creases beneath a vest of stiff leather. Below his knees, the equally fine leggings hung in tatters. There had been no pursuit for over two days. Now Pelinad's band was high enough in the foothills so that the lookouts would be able to spot any activity out of Kenton's castle on the plain below.

The slopes rapidly merged into the higher mountains in the east, and escape was possible in a dozen ways. Not that flight was the only option. Before the attack, Pelinad's brigands had numbered about sixty. Now they were three times as many. Not one of the bondsmen or freetoilers had elected to stay behind. Even the troop from Searoyal would find the rebels more than a mere nuisance.

In small groups of three and four, they huddled around the sprinkling of morning fires. Some sprawled exhausted, still asleep despite the cold and rocky ground. Others talked with loud animation, slapping the arms of old acquaintances and testing the feel of the newly supplied hide-covered shields. Behind them, the silhouettes of craggy spires were just barely discernible in the bright evening sky. Slightly north of where the sun would rise, the dark crestline dipped into the deep notch that was Plowblade Pass.

Jason watched Canthor return from a huddled conference with Pelinad and his lieutenants around one of the fires to the left. The bailiff squinted off into the distance, then looked at Jason and smiled. "Farnel's tyro," he said as he approached. "Who would have guessed it? Returned to his homeland, no doubt to seek his fortune the same as an old soldier who knows that where there is turmoil, there is also the opportunity for gain."

"But the message said that there was a sorcerer among the captives," Jason whispered. "Did you come with someone else?"

"*I* am the master." Canthor patted his chest and laughed. "It is for me that Pelinad staged his raid. And he has just told me why. He is to meet this morning with Ocanar, the leader of the other rebel band, and the village rumors say that this rival has acquired the aid of a master of one of the arts. Pelinad feels that he must show equivalent strength if he is to bend Ocanar to his will, rather than the other way around."

"But you do not practice sorcery. Pelinad has made a mistake."

"And one that I have chosen not to correct."

"But why?"

"Why not? For all intents now, I can weave illusions as well as any master." Canthor grimaced and looked in the direction of the sea. "No need, they told me. No need for a bailiff or men-at-arms. With no art, there would be no visitors. What little order they needed they could manage by themselves. Booted out from the keep with wages a month in arrears! Fine thanks for services almost two decades done. And so, it was either starve or beguile the weak-witted with impressive-sounding chants that I have heard repeated over and over. A wave of the hand, a penetrating glance, a deep-pitched voice in a dimly lighted room. There are enough begging to imagine some fantasy in the air that the coin was easy enough to come by along the way."

"Pelinad rescued us for no less," Jason said. "With sixty men or three times that, he will not directly challenge Kenton's sharp steel and tight mail. The rest are babbling about their good fortune. They think that they have a weapon to use against the catapults and the lord's missiles of war. You had better explain quickly that you are a fighter like them and no more."

"You did not seem so quick to speak when they filled your bowl with a double portion," Canthor remarked. "Even the tyro of a sorcerer rates more than an even share."

"I put forth no such claim," Jason protested. "The forced march was enough after a day in the fields, to keep any man's mouth from wasted chatter."

"Nevertheless, they have accepted my word as to your budding proficiency." Canthor waved down the volume of Jason's voice. "And, as I told you, Pelinad needs to have a sorcerer in his retinue for the parlay. Yes, the rumor of sorcery's demise has been circulating for quite a while now, but how can anyone here in the Wheatlands tell?

"For the moment, it is better that things proceed as they are," Canthor continued. "Besides, with two, we should be able to carry out the illusion all the better. There will be time enough to reveal the reality. And if no harm is done in the process, then what can it matter?"

"My purpose for coming to the Wheatlands was not to fight in a rebellion," Jason said. "Rather, I intended to warn the high prince of the power of a stranger who has mercenaries of his own."

"Oh?" Canthor flicked another branch onto the fire. "Then perhaps you should demand an immediate audience with Pelinad and inform him forthwith where your allegiances lie. I am sure that the others who were released with you would delight in the presence of a representative of the prince."

Jason scowled and looked about the campground. What Canthor said was true. None of Pelinad's rebels would care anything about warning the prince. Perhaps he should slip away when there was an opportunity. But slip away to what? Certainly not back to the toil of the cages or the oppression of Kenton's barony. Was it for the benefit of the Arcadian nobles that he was to offer what he knew? What should he do now? He shook his head in confusion, closed his eyes and tried to think.

"ALERT, TO arms," Pelinad cried. "Ocanar comes for the parlay, and I do not trust his intent." The tall, angular warrior thumped his fist on his chest. The beginning of a bald spot peeked out from a comb-over like bare ground showing through a thin patch of grass. "Stand up smartly now and show them, each and every one, that you are the equal of any whom he has to command."

Jason opened his eyes, groaned and willed his body erect. No solution to the puzzle had come. Without words, he accepted Canthor's nimble fingers tightening and adjusting his leather vest. He grasped the scythe in one hand, wondering how well he would fare against someone who knew how to use a blade. Pelinad shouted orders, drawing his men into a jagged line that faced the direction from which Ocanar would come.

After a few minutes, the trail sounds that had alerted the lookout grew loud enough for everyone to hear. Subsequently, the first of Ocanar's band topped the small rise to the west. Murmurs of surprise arose among Pelinad's own troop as they saw the procession come forward.

"Mail," the rebels whispered. "Some of them are in mail." "Yes,

Ocanar and at least a dozen more." "And the total number — he comes with unexpected strength."

"Silence," Pelinad snapped, but Jason barely noticed the command. He had expected Ocanar's master to be the same as Canthor, another fraudulent sorcerer manipulating the gullibilities about an art that was no more. But instead, what followed the line in front was a shock.

"Melibar!" Jason cried. "And the men in mail. Nimrod and the Pluton mercenaries."

7

Drums and Weights

CANTHOR CUFFED Jason in the arm as a warning. Jason blinked, surprised, and then dropped his eyes from Pelinad's disapproving stare. Fidgeting uncomfortably, he waited with the others, watching the troop pour over the hill and form into another straggly rank, a few pike lengths from Pelinad's own. Jason's father march up with the last, in a clump of older villagers, all with faces set in grim lines.

Jason was already numb from the jolt of Melibar's appearance and gave the second surprise little thought. Both troops spread out to span the depression from lip to lip, each a single row deep, alternating clumps of men and wide gaps. Despite the attempts of each leader to make his following appear the larger, the forces numbered about the same.

"Greetings, brother," the red-bearded man in front hailed. He was short and stout, like a brew master, but his arms were bare and rippled like those of a smith. He alone wore an embroidered surcoat, and the morning sun glinted off a cap of steel. "The hills speak of an increase in your might. Had I not been augmenting myself, then your size might have begun to rival even my own."

"The lord's burden grows too oppressive." Pelinad moved forward to answer the greeting. "Two nights ago my following tripled. Tomorrow, if I approach the village, it will probably double again."

"A day too late." Ocanar laughed. "I have already made the sweep while you were fussing over the harvest of a single field. Look at my legion."

He waved a thick arm to those filling in behind. "At least two hundred, trained freetoilers, and ready to fight. Yes, two hundred. It is clear that the momentum has swung my way. The rebellion is growing, and I am the center. The time for timid confusion is over. I charge you to accept my command, Pelinad. Swear allegiance to me as leader, so that we may strike at Kenton's strength rather than poke with petty irritations at his periphery."

"Command is not measured by mere numbers." Pelinad pointed at Jasonel and those around him. "If I wanted to enlist the old men and the lame, I could have done so a year ago. No, my raid was strategic. Because of it, I have garnered an element of great power." He motioned Canthor to come forward. "Henceforth I battle with a craft far removed from simple thaumaturgy. Here is my sorcerer, Ocanar, and from no less than Morgana itself."

Ocanar eyed Canthor as the bailiff walked forward. He frowned and pulled at his beard as if he were tugging his thoughts to come forward. "The village whispers that sorcery is no more. And this man wears no robe with a logo. His walk is that of a fighter, not the shuffle of the masters I have seen."

"Look me in the eye and we will test the truth here and now." Canthor put his hands on his hips. "Let's see to what extent the village talk is true."

Ocanar took a step backward and threw his hand across his face. "Whatever resources we have should be tested in battle. It is folly to waste them fighting among ourselves."

"Allow me to accept the challenge to your place." Melibar glided forward to stand by Ocanar. "Let the so-called master pit his skills against the powers that are mine."

"Ocanar speaks with good judgment." Pelinad put his hand on his sword hilt. "There is no need for confrontation."

Melibar hesitated. His deep cowl scanned the line of Pelinad's men, all grasping weapons. Like cranked crossbows, they waited for the signal that would release their restraint. Ocanar's troop responded in kind. No one moved. All eyes were on the leaders to see what would happen next.

"A fight here in the foothills sheds none of Kenton's blood," Melibar said at last. "And it is not according to my plan. Perhaps I do agree, Ocanar. The battlefield is best. There is no need to test this so-called master now. Let him show his merits in the pass, and then all can judge the true prowess of his craft."

Jason bit his lip. Melibar knew that nothing remained of sorcery. The stranger was maneuvering Canthor and Pelinad into a position from which they were bound to fail. But right now, he could say nothing. His own position was too tenuous. It was just as well that Melibar did not recognize him as one who had disrupted Trocolar's scheme in the grotto.

Ocanar tugged on his beard, peered at Melibar for a moment, and then glanced across to where Canthor stood. "Yes, tomorrow can be the judge. Pelinad, do you abide by it? The one of us whose power best decides the battle. Then he is to lead us both."

"What battle?" Pelinad asked. "We do not yet have the strength to confront Kenton in his keep, even with both of us acting together. And soon he is to be fortified by a troop of the prince's own from Searoyal."

"It is your good fortune that we have met," Ocanar said. "Your ignorance would otherwise prove quite costly." He turned and forced a laugh that his men picked up in chorus. "This troop from Searoyal. No doubt you have seen some trace?" He turned back to mock Pelinad. "What would happen if they came upon you unaware?"

"We have seen nothing," Pelinad replied. "We have been in these hills, planning for our successful raid."

"You would have seen nothing, even if you had been on the plain!" Ocanar roared. "They do not beat upriver for all to see so that we can melt away." He waved a fleshy palm to the east. "No, they proceed by stealth in the next valley. Through Plowblade Pass they intend to come — to fall upon us in our lairs and thrash us from behind is their plan."

Ocanar sucked in his breath. "But we are the ones who will stage the ambush. It is into our trap they will fall, not us into theirs. And after our victory, the plains will erupt with fire. Not a single man will hold back. Kenton and the others will be swept from the fields. It will be a true rebellion at last."

Ocanar gazed off into the distance, savoring his thoughts, and then fixed Pelinad with a hard stare. "You dispute my leadership, Pelinad. But by the laws, on what grounds? Certainly not your vision. You show as much imagination as an ambulator upon his mill."

"It was I who found the truth," Melibar stated before Pelinad could reply. "Nimrod has many friends in the royal garrisons. Let us keep the importance of my contributions in focus, Ocanar. I have been deceived once by your kind. This time, there is to be no misunderstanding."

"Our agreement still stands," Ocanar said. "I see no reason to change it. You come with a dozen men in mail, trained fighters whom you offer to be my captains. And they have bullied my rabble into fighting shape. I do not deny it. Aid me in plucking Kenton from his keep, and what you ask shall be yours, even if I do not understand why you want it so."

"You find it strange, do you not, that my lust is not for a manor and rows of humble servants? Those trappings, Ocanar, will all come in the proper time. For now, I desire only a halt of all thaumaturgy. After the unlocking, I will need nothing more. And what better way to achieve what I wish than the chaos of insurrection? Unlike sorcery and magic, the craft is too widespread for the contradiction to be effective any other way."

Melibar's voice hardened. "And in the end, we shall see whose fiefdom is the greater. A single valley is not enough to interest even the least able navigator, and among them, I am the first."

"As I have said, it is agreed." Ocanar waved his arm in irritation. "I have heard enough of your mumbled nonsense before. Just make sure that your rock rumblings and strange images are ready when they are needed."

"I begin my preparations for tomorrow now," Melibar motioned back to the hill over which he had come. "It is somewhat paradoxical that the power of thaumaturgy, which makes the transition so difficult, also greatly mitigates the unlocking."

"Your cozy tent provides the catalyst for much grumbling among the men," Ocanar said. "You should sleep on the ground like the rest."

"Warmth?" Melibar replied. "Rest? It is not for those that the Maxim of Perturbations was vitalized in the grotto. Which would you rather? Push a pack train along these trails, or have a single minion effortlessly steer my possessions as they are guided now?"

Ocanar did not respond. At the crestline, a large tent float over the rise. It was Drandor's, the one that had caught Jason's eye in the bazaar on Morgana. Its faded canvas hung in loose folds with coarse stitching bounding swaths of different colors together in jagged seams. But unlike the structure on the island, no guy ropes or stakes were to be seen. The bottom side panels gently rippled over the rock and scrubby plants, like the hem of a woman's dress. All the cloth danced and wavered as the whole structure bobbed along. A single man-at-arms held the end of a rope that ran to a ring attached above an entrance flap. He tugged the structure along without effort into a quickening morning breeze.

No matter the differences, Jason thought. Drandor's tent! Perhaps some more clues were at hand!

"Perturbations," Melibar continued. "Perhaps not as dramatic as a dance which cracks open fissures in the earth, but the guidance of small swirls of air at the right place and time can produce brilliant effects as good as the largest balloon."

With a soft whoosh of the tent, the man-at-arms halted a short distance behind Ocanar's line. Melibar glided into the opening and returned shortly with the drums and weights that Jason had seen briefly when Drandor had shown him the interior of the tent on Morgana.

"These will be used for our common benefit." Melibar waved the drums in Pelinad's direction. "Simple devices that aid me in my craft. Hold your men silent, so that I may receive all that they tell." He eyed Canthor. "If your master has any preparations to make as well, then gladly will Ocanar's legion return the favor."

Pelinad glanced at Canthor and then scowled. He flung his arm to the side in acquiescence and prepared to watch with the rest. Jason tried to concentrate on what Melibar was doing as the cold one set the drums up in a row between the two lines of men and adjusted the tension in the heads, one by one.

"Five drums," Melibar said to Ocanar. "Five drums, excepting those of Wizardry, one for each of the laws."

"I am a fighter, not a practitioner of the arts," Ocanar growled. "The details of your craft are not my concern."

"Perhaps it is a weakness," Melibar replied. "It gives me a perverse pleasure to display my workings for all to see and have none understand the slightest glimmer of what truths they mirror. Well spoken, Ocanar. It is the blind devotion to the narrow perspective of your kind that gives me the greatest assurance that a navigator and his manipulants shall succeed."

Melibar selected a small weight that was not wired to a drumhead and placed it in the center of the first tight membrane. The tare barely dimpled the surface. "The new sorcery. And there are no animations, as the lack of depression shows."

He placed another weight on the next drum in line, and it sagged more deeply into the thin, translucent covering. "The new magic. Because the tent is so near."

Next, he placed weights into two drums simultaneously. The tares snapped from his fingertips and, with what looked to Jason like a force far stronger than the pull of the ground, the weights distorted the planes with deep, cone-shaped depressions. "Thaumaturgy. The presence of the craft is strong, but then that is why I am here."

"And lastly Alchemy," he concluded, as he added a weight to the remaining drum. "It is Alchemy that will be the last, after we are sure of victory."

Melibar rubbed his fingertips together and then examined a collection of small metal rings mixed with the weights. He selected one from the rest and placed it on the warped drumhead that had been associated with the new magic. It disappeared from sight into the depression. "Excellent.

225

The workings of the art are not as nearby as a vault, but they are widespread and strong enough that there can be no challenge. The unlocking will proceed better than I first would have thought."

"Well," Ocanar demanded impatiently, "what does your reading portend?"

"The unlocking will be now," Melibar replied. "Before, I was too cautious. Now I know that I can be much more bold."

Melibar bent to the ground and released the tension in the drumheads. He stored the apparatuses back in the tent and then indicated silently to Ocanar that he would be but a moment more. In a fashion almost as theatrical as Holgon's, he removed from a chain on his belt a small cubical structure that was painted with colors on all six sides with each ruled into a three by three grid.

No, not a ruled grid, Jason realized as Melibar manipulated the solid, twisting faces in a series of rapid rotations. It was a collection of smaller cubes, bound together and yet able to move in several independent directions, creating and destroying intricate patterns as they came together in varying juxtapositions. It was the smaller cubes that were colored. Only when they aligned properly was an entire face of the larger one a single hue.

Jason frowned at what he had seen. It was a puzzle, yes, but certainly of much greater significance than that. What sort of mechanism inside would allow the small cubes in the corners to rotate about three independent axes?

Just as the thought formed, Melibar stopped and displayed the cube for all the onlookers to see. The single color on each of the cube's faces was gone. Now a motley of pigments adorned each of the six sides.

"Now the contradiction," Melibar said as he motioned to the tent.

Out walked Delia, her face a total blank, staring straight ahead. Her arms were burdened with a collection of small rat traps like the one Jason had seen in the Vault in the Grotto. She showed no emotion about the sharp ends of some of the springs that cut into her skin.

8

A Chain Reaction

DELIA! JASON thought. Delia! He had been right. She was here! Or at least partially here, he decided as he searched for some trace of the person inside of her vacant stare. He closed his eyes, but a good idea of what to do still did not come. First, he just would have to learn more. He looked out again and stared. Fascinated, he watched with the others to see what was going to happen.

The slave girl placed the first of the traps on the ground in front of Melibar. Then she backed off a step and put down two more, each a good twenty paces away from the first. She added four more equally spaced in a third row, and then eight in the next.

Delia return to the tent, fetched sixteen more traps and resumed her task. More trips she made, adding to the pattern until some ten paces away over a thousand traps were positioned on the ground, fanning out in a huge array like a sunburst. When she was done, she disappeared again.

"Now some assistance from your men, Ocanar," Melibar said when Delia was no longer in sight. All of these must be connected to act in harmony together. He bent down to the trap nearest, the single occupant of the first row, and from it unrolled two woven cords that had been wrapped into spirals and attached to the hammer. He held up one coil for everyone to see, slowly unwound it all the way and attached the free end to the catch of one of the traps on the second row. Finally, he set the hold-down bar on the trap and returned to stand before the first.

"Do exactly as I have done with the others," Melibar commanded. "Continue until all of them are connected. When each trap is sprung, it will pull the cords and trip two more."

With Ocanar's prodding, several of his troop got up and started to do what Melibar directed. More than once, part way through, one of the traps would be sprung accidentally and the ones that followed would spring as well, forcing all to be reset. It took more than an hour before the entire array had been connected together.

Jason shifted from one foot to the other restlessly while he watched with the rest. Now what? Was there going to be more? And to what purpose this time?

Delia emerged from the tent again, this time carrying tripods, from each of which hung a small weight attached to a release at the very top. She tied a cord from the hammer of one of the last-most traps to one of the releases, and went into the tent to bring forward more of the structures. Melibar motioned, and Ocanar's men started repeating what Delia had done.

After the more than one thousand tripods were in place, Delia began bringing out another armload — small wooden cylinders, each with a rubber bulb attached to one end. Jason frowned, trying to recognize what she was carrying. Delia dumped them all to the ground and then handed one to Melibar, who squeezed its bulb.

It was a duck-call, Jason realized when he heard the dissonant squawk that resulted. Delia took back the lure, centered it under the first tripod-hung weight, and returned to the tent to get more.

When all the duck-calls were properly in position, she brought out small vertical frames. In the top of each hung a sharp blade ready to fall guided by vertical tracks on both sides and held in place by another trigger. At the bottom of each frame, held firm in a half-circular yoke, rested a small sprout of cabbage, barely bigger in diameter than a token from Pluton. If there had been a basket underneath each frame to catch the portion of the cabbage cleaved away, they would have been tiny examples of the devices used by executioners in the southern kingdoms.

Delia paid no attention to what she was building as she ran the second cord from each last-row trap to the frame triggers and then retreated into the tent, not to be seen again.

Melibar signaled for silence and dropped a pebble on the catch of the very first rat trap. The hammer sprung, and an instant later so did the two in the second row. The release of the hammers cascaded through the array to the very last, and then a loud cacophony of duck-calls filled the air. Near simultaneously, all of the sprouts were cut in twain.

"Finally, the relocking," Melibar said to Ocanar. He again brandished the small cube and in a flurry of movements restored it to its initial condition. All the faces showed only a single color.

Jason closed his eyes and folded his arms over his chest. He struggled to make sense of what he had seen. After a long time, how long he did not know, his eyes blinked open. He was surprised about he had concluded. Melibar and the tent were gone, presumably back over the hilltop. Both Ocanar's and Pelinad's bands were in their separate camps. A single man stood patiently before him.

"If you are finished with the dreaming, then I have a suggestion," his father said. "Ask to be that Melibar's apprentice. Perhaps he can teach you a thing or two."

9

Strength in Numbers

EXCEPT FOR Canthor's snoring nearby, the night was quiet. Jason paced in agitation. He had reached a conclusion that had to be flawed. It just had to be. The puzzle had transformed from one of *what* to one of *how*.

For any puzzle, often it does not pay to strive for a solution right from the start. Sometimes, it was better to gather observations and assemble them into order — deduce partial answers along the way.

First — the laws of magic were not immutable. They could be changed. But because of the metalaw, the Postulate of Invariance, there were always seven, no matter what.

Second — Melibar knew how to do make the changes. He kept track of which laws were in force using his two lattices, each node representing the laws that were in place. The frame of stacked cubes kept track of three laws, the flat one, two others. Wizardry was excluded. Evidently, those laws Melibar could not or did not want to change.

Third — the distortion of a drumhead must indicate the degree a craft is being exercised. Yes, that was it, Jason thought. What else could it mean? When Melibar placed a tare on the drum that he said represented sorcery, it remained flat. Reasonable enough, since, except for one of the cold one's followers, there are none who know how to practice it. But the drum for thaumaturgy became a deep cone. Here in the Wheatlands, the art was widespread.

Jason strained to recall more of Melibar's words of yesterday, but he had no Benedict to help him. Thaumaturgy. Something about 'that is why I am here'.

He stopped, unable to unravel any more. Then, methodically, as he had done many times before, he began reviewing what he knew of other puzzles and techniques for solving them.

A picture of many pieces, he counted off eventually. One of his scrolls talked of noble ladies with time on their hands assembling a portrait or landscape out of many irregular small pieces that interlocked together. A well-known technique was to assemble borders with straight edges before attempting the interior.

Jason shook his head. That did not seem relevant. But then, making such pastimes was difficult and expensive, he mused. It was too hard to shape each small piece uniquely. The same pattern for a block of joined pieces was used repeatedly throughout the larger puzzle.

Yes, he though. Another basic technique. 'Look for patterns. See if any of them repeat'. He pondered a moment more and then rushed on. Thaumaturgy was strong in the Wheatlands. More sorcery was routinely practiced on Morgana that perhaps anywhere else. Pluton was awash in tokens of magic. And if an abundance of the craft was common for all three, then what else, what else was the same?

His thoughts raced now. For each location, right when a law shifted, an enactment of the new law was performed. Drandor's rapid projection of a series of images on Morgana, Holgon's movement of the doves and transformation of the chest of sand in the Vault in the Grotto. And even the thousand duck calls earlier today. Even though there was no evidence of it yet, also thaumaturgy probably was no more. It too had been replaced by a new law not quite the same …

No, that could not be right. Because of the Postulate of Invariance, there could be only seven laws of magic at one time.

Unless, unless … he picked up the train of reasoning again. Today, Melibar spoke of an unlocking and relocking. Somehow with the manipulations of his little cube puzzle, the laws of magic could be unlocked. And, and, while they were, for a short while, the Postulate of Invariance momentarily did not hold. There could be viable competing laws in effect, similar but not quite the same. For a while, there could be more than seven magics operating at once. Then with the relocking, only seven would again remain.

But how were the new seven chosen? With the relocking, would not the laws revert to exactly the way they were before, rather than move on to something new? What made thaumaturgy change from what it was to a similar craft that used a duck-call for an incantation rather than the spoken word? And why one thousand and twenty-four? Would not one have been enough?

A very large number, Jason thought. Over a thousand, far more than the contagions for the cages of the thaumaturges. And Drandor's string of images — hundreds of them, far more than the chants of a dozen sorcerers. And for magic …

He had to think deeper. There were thousands of magic tokens in Pluton, perhaps tens of thousands, perhaps more. What could outnumber — the sand! Yes, the grains of sand that transformed from rough granules into perfect little pyramids. Millions of them, outnumbering even tokens in the vault.

In a flash, it all became clear. Fourth — there is a second metalaw.

Of course, if there can be one, then why not another? When the laws are relocked, the ones chosen to remain are those that best explain what is happening. Nature selects those that have the least contradiction with what is going on. Yes, that is it — an Axiom of Least Contradiction or some such fancy name, 'that which explains the most is the best'.

Jason slumped from exhaustion. Such a reach for explanations from so few observations to work with! But it was no different from any other puzzle. If the solution were clear from the outset, then it would not be a puzzle at all.

He should have felt elation. Except for understanding the workings of Melibar's little cube that performed the locking and unlocking, he had solved it all. But he did not. None of this altered the conclusion he had already come to.

He was no warrior, no hero for the sagas. He took a deep breath and went through the logic yet again, hoping the find the flaw.

His inspiration had become blocked, so he had sought out a sorcerer to teach him a spell of self-enchantment. But for that to happen, the craft of sorcery first had to be restored. And for that to come about, it was not a simple trader to be confronted, but a strange being with powers almost unimaginable. Melibar, Melibar, the one responsible for the loss, had to be caught and restrained.

And for that, someone with the means to do so needed to be made aware of the threat. But it could not be the high prince or Lord Kenton; their abuses were too great. Nor could it be the rebels. Melibar was their ally, not their foe!

Who else was left? No one — no one but himself! Like a vice that squeezed his options to fewer and fewer choices, his entire journey was being funneled onto a path with no options. It was a puzzle with but a single solution — one that frightened him far more than a crowd pelting him with cruel laughs.

10

Avalanche

JASON'S GUT rumbled. Anxiety was starting to build. But this was different, not a reaction to an irrational fear, but for something real. Walking boldly into Melibar's tent was an insanity. And then what? But staying in the camp was not an option either. For days, he had done nothing. The troops from Searoyal had come, and now, like it or not, he was about to be swept up into a battle.

The advance scouts had moved through the pass at dawn. The main body of the troop from Searoyal should have marched into the ambush over an hour ago, but the road winding down the mountainside was clear. No cloud of dust or creaking wagon wheels disturbed the serenity of the morning,

The pass itself was still in shadow on Jason's right. A narrow cleft barely four men wide, like a deep furrow in freshly plowed ground. From where he was hidden behind the rocks at the side of the trail, Jason could not see all the way through the notch to the other side. Beyond the crest on the down slope that eventually led to Kenton's barony, Ocanar's band huddled in concealment, waiting for the royal companies to march by. They lay armed and ready, as did Pelinad's men across the wagon ruts from where Jason crouched.

Canthor slumped peacefully beside him and shook his head. "How can you be so calm?" Jason asked. "You understand as well as I that Ocanar has manipulated Pelinad into an impossible position. Melibar is on the top of one of the crags that frame the pass. I have seen his powers before. He will be able to shake the earth and deliver the avalanche on schedule, splitting the royal troops in twain. But you can make no illusion that will terrify those on this side as we fall upon their rear. Pelinad will have no special aid."

"The avalanche will be enough." Canthor stretched and yawned like a great cat from across the ocean. He idly fingered the crude logo of sorcery stenciled to his tunic. "That and the attack from behind will make up for our lack of mail and sharp weapons. I will say some meaningless words and then join with the others pouring onto the trail. And when the swords start swinging, no one will remember whether the hesitation of the opponents was due to surprise or a fanciful image."

"But experienced troops from Searoyal!" Jason said.

"The toll will not be light," Canthor agreed. "Yet there will be enough booty in the end for those who are quick and skillful."

Jason noticed the scythe that was lying nearby and then at the thick-bladed sword in Canthor's lap. "Such a view is perhaps easier for one who has seen combat before. Easier for one who, at least, has the proper tools of the trade."

"Stay close and guard my rear." Canthor shrugged. "You will fare as well as me."

Canthor patted the hilt of his sword. "Even in battle, it is still muscle and bone that determine the final result. Illusions of great monsters or slides of rock perturb the outcome this way or that, but in the end, a blade is in your gut or it is not. It is the warriors who sit on the thrones of Arcadia, Procolon, and the other kingdoms. Warriors are kings and not the masters of the crafts. Why, even the archimage commands only a small guard and a modest house of stone."

A puff of dust billowed lazily skyward like a dust devil vanishing back to his own realm. The royal troop was coming at last. Eventually, the marching column came into view. Triple file across the trail, the men-at-arms snaked into the cleft of the pass. A mounted commander, with pennant bearers stepping smartly at either side, led the procession. In full armor, he prodded his sweating horse up the incline. Behind the leading officers came the first company. On foot and dressed in mail, they breathed heavily like laden oxen from the labor of the climb.

Jason closed his eyes, but it did no good. Even now, he still could not figure out what to do. After the second of the four companies had gone by, the rocks were to tumble. Each of the two outlaw bands would fall upon those on its side of the pass and then come to the aid of the other, if it were able.

The last of the first company entered the notch, and Jason waited expectantly for the next to follow. But just as the pennant bearers of the second group approached, the ground shook. A grinding rumble filled the air.

"Avalanche! Look out!" someone shouted.

The flag carriers threw down their standards and turned to run. Small rocks and then heavier boulders began to rain down from above. Streaks of blurring gray fell from the cliffs. The groans of breaking stone and then those of wounded men sounded over the deep, teeth-shaking rumble. Clouds of white and dirty brown billowed from the saddle of the pass.

One pennant bearer was hit in the shoulder by a rock ricocheting in a flat arc, but he managed to stagger back before the larger boulders smashed him to the ground. In momentary confusion, the marching column stopped in the swell of dust and noise. A horn sounded from the cover on the other side of the trail, and Pelinad's band jumped to the attack. With swords raised high, they thundered into the third company's flank.

"But Melibar was supposed to wait until two companies had passed through!" Jason shouted to Canthor. "And you were to stage your glamour among the wagons from behind! Now Pelinad charges on the side, rather than into the rear."

"A misbegotten plan, to be sure," Canthor said, now alert. "Leave it to a practicer of the arts to bungle what chance we have." He grabbed his blade, bounded around the rock, and looked up and down the trail. "Quickly, follow me. With three companies rather than two, the line is too long. We are blocked from the others. But despite Pelinad's odds, we will fare better on his side of the trail than here. There is no time for a pretense of sorcery. Our hope will be to circle through the confusion of the avalanche if we can."

Jason knew further thought was futile. He scooped up the scythe and ran after the bailiff as Canthor scrambled toward the pass. The attention of the royal troops was focused on the charge of Pelinad's men, and no one noticed them coming from the other side in the swirling dust. With practiced precision, the middle company turned its shields to meet Pelinad's attack, while the ones on either side made ready to engulf the flanks as the ragged line drew closer. Soon the rumble of the rock was replaced by the clang of steel and cries of pain.

Canthor jumped among the boulders with an agility that belied his age. He headed directly for the broken rock that had spilled out of the confines of the pass. The royal troops were giving the area a wide berth. In the confusion, Jason and the bailiff managed to reach the edge of the rubble before they were noticed. Without slowing, they climbed onto the fresh talus and began to scramble toward the other side of the trail.

Three-quarters of the way across, they were spotted by a pennant bearer. Before Canthor could reach him, he cried out an alarm. In answer, half a dozen men-at-arms turned from the rearmost line and started to climb the rubble. As they approached, Jason swung out the scythe at arm's length and struck only empty air.

Two more closed on Canthor, who slashed with his blade, biting deep into the wrist of the one on the right. Undaunted, the other four pressed forward, one waving an axe. Canthor stepped back in order not to expose his side. Watching the bailiff out of the corner of his eye, Jason retreated as well, taking a few steps up the slope.

One of the men-at-arms tried to circle from the left. The remaining attackers continued forward, waving their swords in menacing arcs. Jason found himself retreating farther up the jumble of rocks, swinging the long scythe awkwardly back and forth as best he could.

As he retreated, he jabbed tentatively point first, using the shaft like a pike. The man he faced reacted swiftly. Before Jason realized his mistake, a slashing sword hacked the blade from the head of the pole. Jason jabbed a second time, but his adversary continued forward, this time removing two more feet from the shaft. Jason threw the useless pole aside and turned to look at Canthor to see what he should do. As he watched, the bailiff stumbled on a loose rock and fell onto his back, his sword sailing out of his hand.

The man-at-arms on the left ran forward, seeing his advantage, and swung his axe high over his head for a fatal plunge. Canthor threw his hand upward in a desperate attempt to ward off the blow, his eyes wide with the image of death. Then, like a drowning man grasping at leaves on the surface of a lake, he sang one of the sorcerers' chants. The three recitals tripped from his tongue faster than Jason had ever heard a glamour spoken before. He recognized it as the illusion for a windstorm. Canthor scooped up a handful of dirt and pebbles and threw them in the axeman's face. The distraction was only momentary. The axe arched down and Canthor gasped his last.

"A sorcerer" one of the men-at-arms called to the others. "He should not have shouldered arms. He would have been of value if there is a prisoner exchange." He pondered, staring down at the bailiff's body. "His tyro, then. Perhaps Ocanar's master would see some use in him."

11

Torpordust

PUFFS OF air skittered around Jason's ankles as he approached the tent. The flicker of candlelight escaped from the hem of the canvas as it danced over the uneven ground. From the chatter in Lord Kenton's camp, he had deduced that the battle was a standoff. Pelinad's forces had been annihilated on one side of the pass, and Ocanar, with Melibar's aid, held the other and the crest.

Jason had been hustled to the crestline at sword point, and, in exchange for a man-at-arms, deposited at the entrance of the tent. He had to enter. There was no other choice.

But he could barely think. He had been in this tent before, he tried to reason with himself. There is nothing there that would be new and strange. And it only had room for a few rather than a crowd. But the anxiety of his irrational fears had transferred to the situation in which he was now. Yes, he was the one who had to confront Melibar. But how? With what? The cold one had the power to alter the very laws of nature. He was just a wordsmith, nothing more.

His stomach was long since empty, but the rapid heartbeat, the labored breathing, the dizziness, the trembling would not go away. It was the worst he had ever experienced. With an arm heavy with hesitation, he managed to push aside the flap.

The interior looked much as it had on Morgana. Two small candles provided most of the light. The entrance to the rear chamber was closed. Delia's counter was gone. On the bare ground, Melibar was studying his drums and weights, the two lattices at his side. Except for the buzz of the imps about the cold one's head, there was no other motion.

Jason had no idea of what to do. He grabbed at the first thing that came out of the chaos of his mind.

"You have worked with others before," he managed to croak.

"Drandor, the trader, and Holgon, the magician. Do you, do you desire yet another apprentice?"

Melibar glided forward until he stood facing Jason. A slender hand jutted from the flowing robe and poked him in the shoulder. A wave of intense cold that numbed his arm sent a shiver down his back. His eyes traced from the dark, painted nails, up the draped arm, to the cowl that hid everything but reflections of the candlelight in the eyes.

"But more important than that," Jason blurted, "who are you? From where do you come?"

"Inquisitiveness is not the mark of a good follower," Melibar replied as the cowl moved closer in the dimness. "Obedience is the virtue that will garner the greater reward."

Melibar stopped and studied Jason's face. "I have seen you before. You were the one who tried to imitate the magician in the grotto."

"The Postulate of Invariance," Jason replied without thinking. He was starting to reel. He would not be able even to remain upright much longer.

"The Postulate of Invariance is not the concern of any manipulant," Melibar said. "To him, such information is of no use. And the fact that a metalaw holds interest for you harms, rather than abets, your suit."

Melibar studied Jason more closely. "Your distress at even being in my presence is evident. A healthy and respectful fear. I like that. And Drandor's usefulness is drawing to a close. Hmmm, I must consider this."

The cold one stared into the distance for a long while, then turned his attention back to Jason. "Follow me," he said and threw back the flap that closed the entrance to the rest of the tent.

Jason could no longer stand. He fell to his knees and meekly crawled after Melibar into the other compartment. The light was even dimmer than in the first.

"Delia!" he exclaimed as her slender form caught his eye. Despite his anxiety, his heart filled with a surge of pleasure. "You are here, as I suspected. And Drandor —"

Jason stopped short as he examined more closely the trader, now standing beside a small lantern and a scatter of transparent images on the floor. One arm dangled at his side, flat and shapeless, like an empty sleeve. His face sagged to the side, lips curving down to where the firm line of the jaw should have been. The cheek was only a loose bag of flesh — like a sack of fat from a slain pig.

Jason's eyes darted back to Delia and scanned her body from head to toe, searching for similar disfigurements, but except for the vacant stare, she apparently was whole. She wore the same gown in which he had seen her last, and a band of iron still circled her wrist. Finally, he looked back at Melibar.

"What has happened to him?" he asked, pointing at Drandor. "Was he exposed to the fighting as well?"

"My helpers, my manipulants?" Melibar responded. "No, they are too precious to waste in such a manner. But negligence cannot go unpunished." He swept his arm in Delia's direction. 'This second one should never have been allowed to get away. Nor did the pet I gave the first thrive under his care."

"By all the laws," Drandor slurred, "stop him. The cave beneath the tent, the sleepers, the sucking! I can feel the dissolving inside. Stop him before there is more."

"Silence," Melibar commanded. "Silence or the manipulants shall have fresh marrow before it is needed."

He turned and faced Jason, his voice now soft and quiet. "You spoke of apprenticeship."

He waved his arm over his head, and imp light twinkled into tiny points of brilliance. The air in the tent grew chillingly cold like the insides of a house built of ice. "I demand complete obedience. When lithons soar close to one another, there is no margin for less. The three metalaws are for my concern. You must forget what you have learned."

"Your plan is to change everything, isn't it?" Jason managed to ask. "One by one, until only your minions can perform any of the crafts. The thaumaturges, the alchemists, the magicians, the sorcerers, the wizards, even the archimage, all will be powerless against you. Despite what Canthor says, it is not men-at-arms who hold the balance of power in their hands. One who has exclusive command of unknown crafts would rule the world against the sharpest blades."

"This world, the stars, your entire realm," Melibar said. "Ocanar sulks with the stalemate. But for me, the battle has accomplished almost as much as I had planned. Tomorrow, with the help of some simple animations, the villagers will believe in a setback of the royal troops, despite whatever else this Kenton may say. The timing is right. The passions will be inflamed. In a fortnight's time, the plains will vibrate to the stomp of thousands of scythes and flails. More than four companies from Searoyal will have to come.

"I will have gone from a single greedy trader, from a dozen men-at-arms, to a whole kingdom at my command. Alchemy will be next. In the end, everything will be mine."

Melibar paused and jabbed Jason on the shoulder. "Yes, be my apprentice. The choice is a wise one. Serve without failure, and you will be rewarded well."

Even in his dizzy state, Jason knew what he must say. "No," his voice as soft as Melibar's own. "It is too much power. The laws were not meant to be altered."

"Whence I came, the laws were not meant to stay the same." Melibar stepped forward. "But no matter. By one means or another, you will serve. Seize him, Drandor. If he chooses not to offer his mind and muscle to me, then the manipulants will enjoy his marrow."

Jason crawled backward, cringing. As he did, the imp light about Melibar's head brightened to a fiery incandescence. Too late, he tried to dodge a handful of dust that Drandor somehow managed to splash onto his face. He felt the beginning of a numbing torpor. Then nothing.

12

Manipulants and Rock Bubblers

JASON FELT a gentle touch on his forehead and forced open his eyes. A bouncing glow of reddish light and strands of golden hair filled his view

Delia!" he exclaimed weakly.

Jason rose to sitting. His mouth was dry as abandoned cotton and the taste rancid like water from a flat of alkali. He felt as if he had been awakened from the middle of a drunken sleep. Hovering a few feet from his head was a large, glowing sprite, its bony arms crossed in front of a shallow chest and its legs coiled into a knot. The forehead bulged with bumps and mounds. Tufts of coarse hair protruded from tiny ears. The nose lay smashed across a broad and pockmarked face. Except for the whine of rapidly beating wings, it seemed like the well-preserved remains of a grotesque child.

Jason ran his hands over his leather vest, touching the reassuring smoothness of the coin about his neck and the lump of Benedict's changer underneath. He placed his palms down at his sides and felt a tingling from a surface that was glassy-smooth. As his senses returned, he detected the same vibration through his thighs. He looked around in the sprite light. Rock everywhere. He and Delia were enclosed in a perfect sphere, centered on the small demon and showing no seam or exit. As if from the polished face stone of some great palace, specks of quartz and mica cast back pale reflections of the flickering luminescence. He did not panic. The scene was strange, but there was no crowd, and Delia was here.

"A rock bubbler," Delia explained. "That little demon can maintain a void several arm spans about itself in all directions, even at the greatest depths. He is one of the score or so that keep open a pit under Drandor's tent."

She shrugged. "Apparently, I have some degree of control over this one. He responds to my bidding, as long as it does not conflict with his other instructions."

"The Law of Dichotomy," a small, squeaky voice radiated from the bobbing devil. "One of the two upon which wizardry is based. 'Dominance or submission.' There is no other choice." One small eye cocked to the side and stared at Delia. "I have a master, and I must obey. If I fulfill your request, it is because it does not contradict and it is my choice."

"By whatever justification, the end result is the same," Delia said. "I instructed him how to trick two others of his kind with which he had a petty feud. And now he has kept his sphere out of tangency with the others so that the manipulants could not find you, Jason, before you awoke." Delia stopped and shuddered. "Although with the fighting that will eventually happen above, they will have many from whom to pick."

"What has happened?" Jason shook his hands at arm's length to restore the circulation. Any excitement from being with Delia was muted by the remains of a deep lethargy. "Where are we? The last I remember is Drandor somehow managing to cast some powder in my face."

"Torpor dust," Delia answered. "Something that can be made with the new magic. He uses it to slow prisoners for the manipulants."

"I thought it might have been a freezing."

"The cold does not come from Melibar. It is generated by the imps that circle his head. Without them, he would have to sleep with the rest. I suspect he can barely tolerate moving among us as it is. When he must concentrate deeply, he requires it to be even more frigid."

"Then where is he from?" Jason asked. "From what he has said, not across the ocean or from another star in the sky."

"No, not another star." Delia shook her head. "Somehow, it is farther than that. J asked him once and he laughed. He said that on all our worlds the laws are the same. It was only through the demon's portals that one could journey whence he came."

"The realm of demons," Jason mused. "It may well be the lands beyond the flame from which the djinn appear when they are beckoned."

"My master forbade me to speak of it, or I would tell," the sprite interjected. "But even in sleep, I must honor his will."

"These manipulants?" Jason asked. "Are they demons too?"

"No, I think not. Even demons would not behave as they do."

"But if not djinns, how can they exist behind the flame?"

Delia reached out and grabbed Jason's hand. "There is little else that I know. Little else except for some of the workings of Drandor's animations. Melibar has been teaching me the craft and has made sure that I remained unharmed. The cold one wants the trader to know he can be replaced if he does not continue to comply. There is nothing with which Drandor can bargain, not even the exercise of the new sorcery."

"And I?" Jason studied the featureless sphere. "What did I have to offer that was any better?"

"For four days you have slumbered while I kept the rock bubbler apart from the rest." Delia ignored the question. "Now you must use your wits to aid me as you have done before.

"Come," she said as she turned until she was on hands and knees. "Follow the sprite. You will see what else lies in the rock under Drandor's tent."

Jason frowned as the small demon turned in Delia's direction and began to drift away. Before he could ask more, he felt the sphere rotate beneath him, pushing with increasing firmness behind and then finally toppling him forward to sprawl by Delia's side

As Jason scrambled into a crawling position, a tiny opened formed in the curved wall directly ahead. The circle grew, revealing a larger cavern beyond. Sliding his hands along the smooth surface and pushing with his feet on the slope behind, he managed to keep up with the slow rotation of the sphere.

In a moment, the opening had expanded to the maximum extent. The rear of the bubble that contained Delia and him became a hemispherical bulge on a larger volume. Like a sealed chamber in a dungeon, the bigger void in the rock was heavy with damp air and the smell of decay. The floor was shaped like the crate for an array of eggs, a lattice of shallow depressions that matched a similar set of indentations in the ceiling above. In between, in a more or less geometrical precision, hovered other rockbubblers, eyes closed, and arms and legs crossed.

Jason studied what he was seeing for a moment and deduced how the expanse had come about — a merging of many separate globes into a greater whole. Like a rag doll flung aside, Drandor lay in the center-most depression. The trader's eyes were mere slits and his chest heaved with deep breaths. Occasionally, he lashed out with his good arm, swatting the empty air. Dots of light showed where imps, much smaller than the hovering rock bubblers, flitted above him, dropping a fine mist of sparkling sand.

"More torpor dust," Delia said. "It keeps the trader in lethargy until Melibar requires his efforts." She swallowed. "And except for those, the manipulants, it would not be necessary."

Jason followed the sweep of her arm. On a large sled with rounded runners that fitted the curve of the floor, six humanoid forms, dressed only in loincloths were all lying prone in apparent slumber. They were tall and slender, more suited for the dance than for wielding blades. Their skin was an almost translucent gray. Beneath the tough elasticity, Jason could see the course of the major arteries and veins, half wore massive ornamentation, nose rings, necklaces, and anklets, their fine black hair coiled in elaborate swirls. Sharp planes of bone defined blocky faces. Filmy lids covered opalescent eyes. Below the bulge of the nose, each had large pinkish lips like the suction cups of an octopus or squid. Cupped in each left hand was a can with holes in the lid. On a chain from the waist dangled small picks like those used in gemstone mines.

"I have seen them before!" Jason exclaimed, "On Morgana, in Drandor's animation the night of the storm, the one that shifted the Rule of Three to the Rule of the Threshold."

"Too close," one of the nearest sprites interrupted Delia's reply. "First, you move away, not even maintaining contact. Now you press in on my space, my innermost core. Back whence you came, prickly one. I would rather you not support my flank than push with so much pressure on my chest."

"Pox blisters," the sprite above Jason's head shot back. "For you, there is no distance that pleases. You would be better off as a solitary. Always bickering, trying to force the swarm to your own natural harmonics. Never just accepting what resonates with the entire clutch."

"You are no better, mint breath," the other replied.

"Your wings must have been unbalanced in the egg. They have vibrated your brains to mush. You have no frequency that stands above the noise. You keep flitting like a djinn in heat around the soft and golden one and not even your master."

"Vibration is what makes the lips quiver and the foolish noises issue forth," Delia said sternly. "It is strange that you would be one speaking of balance."

A high-pitched whine bounced around the room. Jason guessed that the other sprites were twittering at what she had said. The demon directly ahead snapped shut his mouth and, except for the hum of wings, the pit plunged into silence.

For a moment, nothing more happened. Then one of the manipulants stirred and crawled from the sled, lethargically groping over the dimpled floor. Like a newborn puppy, he seemed to flounder instinctively toward food and comfort. He bumped against Drandor, and then with uncoordinated jerks, closed around the trader's boneless forearm. Drandor's eyes flickered, and his face contorted into a mask of strain. With glacial slowness, he struggled to crawl away, but the manipulant was slightly quicker and pinned him where he lay.

In staccato bursts of motion, the left hand with the shaker positioned over the trader's elbow. A fine powder fell onto the pliant flesh, and then, after several misses, the large lips contacted the glistening surface. A loud slurping noise blended with the demons' hum. Drandor's entire body trembled. He opened his mouth with an ear-piercing scream.

13

Growing Rebellion

"AS MELIBAR would look without his hood," Delia pointed towards the manipulant next to Drandor. "They suck the marrow through the skin after somehow dissolving the bone. That must be what keeps them alive as they wait. Apparently, this place is so warm that they languish like lizards in a desert sun.

"Melibar let me remain awake so that I could avoid the manipulants," Delia continued. "He did not suspect that I would influence one of the sprites as well." Her voice shrank to a whisper. "I could have dragged the trader away, just as I did you. But each time I thought of it, I also remembered his crude sketches of my disfigurement, his tongs and pinchers, and the fact that it is because of him that I am here."

Jason wondered anew what he should do. Drandor had released the beast after them on Morgana. He had abducted Delia to this oppressive tomb. He felt the line of his own jaw and then the reassuring firmness of his forearm. Delia shuddered, and he drew her close. She did not resist, but rested her head on his shoulder. The touch of her cheek was cold.

While Jason wavered, the manipulant released its grip with a loud pop, like that of a bursting bubble. Drandor struggled away to collapse in the bottom of an adjacent sphere. His eyelids snapped shut. His chest resumed its slow and steady cadence. The rnanipulant groped over the cupped floor, bumping into Drandor a second time and then one of the walls. Eventually, it found the sled and crawled listlessly back into its space.

"Their needs are minimal," Delia explained. "It will be another week before that one ventures forth again. Drandor is safe until the next arouses in perhaps the length of a day."

Jason let out his breath and patted her on the shoulder. "This is horrible. How did you manage to survive?"

"I am in command of my own spirit. Nothing would be served by succumbing to despair."

Jason gazed into Delia's eyes and then back around the entombing rock. Laughing crowds were insignificant compared to this. "That is a spirit I must admire," he said. "There are few who could keep their minds intact when faced with such as this."

Delia rubbed his hand on her shoulder. "And when I was summoned above and saw it was you, I felt the first real hope since I was confined."

Jason smiled. "It has been an eventful quest. Let me tell you what I have learned while we were apart."

He related all that had happened. To his surprise, he found that mentioning Augusta made him feel awkward. With a wave of his hand, he passed on to talk in more depth about meeting Melibar and the discovery of the two metalaws.

Somehow, as the words came out, the driving force of his quest seemed to be more for Delia and less because of the fate of Arcadia and Procolon across the great ocean. But she listened quietly and did not contradict. With an intense concentration, she absorbed everything that he told her.

"And now that you understand Melibar and his threat," she whispered when he was done, "what is your plan?"

The bubbling in Jason's stomach returned. "We must escape and defeat him. Then restore the laws to what they were. Prevent them from changing anymore."

"Yes, yes, I agree. Melibar must be thwarted, but how?"

Jason frowned. He clutched the coin about his neck. He still had absolutely no idea.

While he pondered yet again, a flicker of light broke through the ceiling. One of the small imps appeared and the rock bubbler in the center of the cluster rose to meet it.

"Curse the binding," it grumbled as it rose. "With any normal master, my decisions would be my own while he slumbered. But no, I am to bounce like a ball every time an imp flits into view. Such was his last command before he drifted into slumber."

A column of rock rose beneath the ascending bubble and a hemispherical void pushed into the ceiling. At the apex, a tiny iris of black widened into a larger circle. Through it were glimpses of stacked crates and flickering light beyond.

"Another compartment of the tent," Jason mumbled as he recognized some of the contents. "The one behind the counter where we first met.

This pit was beneath it all along and I did not suspect."

Delia grabbed his arm and pointed at the opening. Two boots draped over the edge to dangle into the void and then the rest of another body crashed down into the sphere. The sprite increased the beat of its wings in response to the load. Slowly, it reversed its direction, settling back to the same level as the others.

Jason shook himself out of what remained of his lethargy. He groped his way from one circular depression to the next, reaching the slumped form and turning him face up.

"Burdon," he said over his shoulder as Delia followed. "One of the lords at Kenton's castle when I was there. Melibar grows bold indeed if he can snatch away the nobility as well as bondsmen."

Jason eyed the sleeping lord and rubbed his chin. "He may know something of value. If we secure him away as you did me, how long until he can speak?"

"It took you four days. For someone older, who knows how long it would be?"

"We can ill afford to wait." Jason frowned. "How deep is the sleep?"

"If you stimulate him enough, he might respond, but only in long snatches and they could be incoherent, at that."

Jason reached down to roll Burdon over but felt a numbing twinge in his shoulder. One of the dusting imps was hovering overhead, and he sprang aside.

"Drag him back into my sprite's sphere," Delia said. "We will withdraw from the rest."

Jason grunted and pulled at Burdon's bulk. "Rebellion," the lord mumbled. "The archimage, wizards, and wine."

Jason ducked to the side as the imp made another pass and then heaved Burdon from one sphere to the next. In a few minutes, he had crammed the lord into Delia's globe. Awkwardly, he squeezed in beside her and tried to keep his balance as the giant ball of emptiness rolled away from the rest.

"Thirty years," Burdon mumbled. "Who would have thought of treachery by my steward after thrice a decade? They have all lost their senses. Drugs in the wine. Swinging scythes like madmen, not caring whom they struck down."

"Where is the high prince?" Jason shook the man's arm. "What did Kenton do after the battle in the pass?"

"Kenton, Kenton." Burdon's eyes flickered open in a glassy stare.

"Of his, I am not surprised. So hard. He pressed them so hard. But my own. My very own, along with the rest. As if ensorcelled, although that can no longer be.

"And now it is full rebellion," Burdon continued. "There are thousands upon the slopes. No matter how many the high prince and the others muster, they will not easily storm these cliffs against the flails and rakes. They have even taken the cages and dragged them up the mountainside for all the plains to see. They are a symbol, a measure of their defiance, and a taunt for the high prince's men to mount an attack."

"Another battle!" Jason exclaimed. "I would think the high prince would move with caution after what happened at Plowblade Pass."

"The pass. The battle," Burdon wheezed. "This is far graver than the skirmish of a few companies. Far graver, no matter which side you believe was the final victor. Now all the baronies and all their minions are drawing together to put down the insurrection. But what if they fail? Yes, what then? Everyone is afraid to uncover what he knows to be true. If the leather vests carry the day, there is nothing standing between them and the palaces in Searoyal.

"And I saw the gravity of the situation, even if no one else did." Burdon waved his arm, suddenly more alert. "I sent for the archimage. It is not only catapult and shield that we are dealing with. The wizards and alchemists and all the rest whom he can muster will be needed as well. I rode with an escort of six to where he had agreed to meet at dusk. A few swallows of wine from the flagon on my saddle horn quenched my thirst. There is something wrong. I feel dizzy. I must sleep."

Burdon's face relaxed. His arm fell to his side. Eyes snapped shut. Lips vibrated with the beginnings of a snore.

"The archimage!" Jason said. "Of course, the archimage. The Master of the Five Magics. He must finally have arrived across the sea. The archimage. He would listen. He would understand about metalaws. He would take on the burden of defeating Melibar. Far better than Kenton or the high prince."

Jason surveyed his surroundings in a new light. The great weight melted away. Its magnitude had made him ignore one of the basic rules for puzzle solving. 'Always look for a second solution.' He did not have to face the cold one alone after all. "Exactly where are we now? How far to the archimage and in what direction?"

Burdon did not answer. Jason shook his arm and then both shoulders with more vigor, but nothing happened. Frowning, he let the lord slip back into the bottom of the sphere.

"Each passing moment is time in Melibar's favor," Jason said. "We must be away." He studied the small bubble again, this time more critically, searching for some clues that would lead to an escape. Yes, that was the way to frame the puzzle. It was like detaching interlocking rings from a slide. He studied the walls in the hope of seeing a fissure and then stared up at the ceiling, trying to imagine exactly where they might be. He closed his eyes and descended back into thought.

"Delia, your sprite," he said after a while. "How can it be that you can order him about? You are no wizard. I know the basics of the theory. There is no gratitude or courtesies with the likes of an imp or a sprite."

"I do not dominate him as would a wizard. He already has a master." She shrugged. "And despite whatever you say is the theory, he states he has done what he has for favor received."

"You were able to persuade him to pull this sphere away from the rest."

"Just a little distance was far as I could convince him. And for that, even in his misshapen face, I could see the struggle not to comply. He says he can act only insofar as it does not conflict with the instructions of his master."

"But to give him instructions at all, somehow you must."

Jason halted and snapped his mouth shut. He frowned as he felt his thoughts begin to race off to solve a new riddle. There was no time for that now. Their escape was the important matter at hand. With resolution, he forced his concentration back in the proper direction.

He turned his attention to the walls, judging distances in the featureless surroundings. "The void seems larger in area than the tent that rests upon it. Did you try sending the sprite upward as well as to the left and right?"

"To what purpose?"

"We might not be that far beneath the surface."

"I thought of that myself," Delia said. "Even if the demon were to break through to free air, there would be no way for me to climb. The curved walls are too smooth."

"Not the walls, but my shoulders. I saw the distance Burdon descended. It cannot be far. Yes, that is it, Delia. We must burst through to the surface and escape. Tell your sprite to ascend above as the one in the center did."

"A moment." Delia grasped at Jason's arm as he squirmed to turn around. "Have you thought it all the way through? Suppose I were to get to the surface. What then? More likely than not, I would find myself in the middle of some armed camp. And even if I could escape and flee to the opposition what tale would I tell? How could I do better than you at Kenton's feasting?"

"But there is no time, Delia. Yes, I do like to think everything through to the end before I act, but not this time. I will, I will think of more as we go along."

"As no doubt, you did before charging into the Vault in the Grotto with the magic sword?"

Jason opened his mouth to rattle off a rebuttal, but then stopped and frowned. "Those are hard words for one whose intent was to save you from your fate. Despite what I said to Melibar above, the quest was at least in part for you."

"You are like the raw elixir of the alchemist, Jason." Delia reached out and stroked his arm. "The power of your thoughts fumes and sparks. You show a great talent for seeing the solution where for others the goal is unclear. But sometimes, the puzzle you solve is incomplete."

"I cannot help how I think." Jason pushed her arm away, irritated. "And it has served you well on more than one occasion already. It was not detailed instructions that confronted Drandor's pet."

"Nor was it your forethought that brought the dagger when the beast was at your throat."

Jason scowled and grabbed at the brandel dangling about his neck. He ran his tongue over his lips, formulating what to say. He gazed into Delia's eyes. She moved her hand forward a second time but stopped short of placing it on his arm. Palm upward, it rested on the curve of the sphere halfway between where they knelt.

Jason let out his breath. He rubbed the brandel between his fingers. The hint that she was a piece of the puzzle ricocheted through his mind. She must have some feelings for him. Why couldn't she be more like Augusta, warm and friendly, rather than meting out favors only in exchange for some gain?

Jason gazed back at Delia. She was patiently waiting, her face a pleasant mask. For a moment, there was silence.

"You are right in that the solution to any puzzle can be improved if it is studied again," he said at last. "The number of steps until the pieces disentangle can be lessened, or the beauty of how one manipulation logically follows another enhanced.

"It is Burdon we must free from this pit. Burdon, more so than you or I. He was the one who has called the archimage. We must wait until he awakens — until the right time when he can make good his escape."

"So it would seem to me as well," Delia replied softly.

"We must stimulate his recovery as best we can and then tell him everything we know. Give him a plan, something he can carry back and put to work against the magics that Melibar will employ. We can use the time while we wait to explore all the details of what we will do."

"Then let us begin with formulating the message to the archimage."

Jason released the coin about his neck. The tension was gone just as suddenly as it had come. For a moment, he regarded Delia's outstretched hand. "Anything else?" he asked.

14

The Door into Elsewhere

JASON WATCHED impatiently as the ceiling dissolved. Under Delia's direction, the sprite in the bubble rose slowly, creating a void above its head, pulling all three of them upward and collapsing the one below. Eventually, the surface was pierced and sunrise poured into the sphere.

"A little bit more," Jason called out. "We need at least the length of a forearm for the diameter of the opening at the surface of the ground."

The sprite halted at Jason's words and folded his bony arms across his chest. "You are not the one who took my side against the mushbrains who babble so," it said. "It is to the golden curls that I choose to show my favor."

Jason waved his arm in exasperation and motioned Delia to come closer. In a few moments, using words hardly different from his own, she directed the passage to the surface to be in the desired proportion. Without saying more, she climbed on his shoulders and raised her eyes above the level of the ground. She looked in all directions and then stretched to full height, scrambling out of the hole. A short while later, a crude rope made of belts and torn clothing snaked back into the pit. Jason fastened a crude harness around Burton and climbed to the surface. Together, they hoisted out the lord.

They were on a flat ledge on the slopes of one of the mountains. The folds of Melibar's tent stood to the left, quietly flapping in a midmorning breeze. Excited shouts came from a second ledge above. Much wider, it ran out of sight around the curve of the mountain in both directions. All along its length was packed with men, some dressed in leather, some with helmets of horn, others in bare-sleeved tunics, waving flails in the air.

With hoarse shouts and cheers, they rained abuse and taunts down on the valley below. Everyone's attention was turned in that direction. No one bothered to watch what was happening near the tent.

Below the lower ledge, the ground fell rapidly away. Like a blanket covered with crumbs, the slope was littered with boulders. Cracked rocks and gaping fissures laced the slanting ground in intricate patterns. Halfway down the incline were tangled masses of steel bars and dented plates. Next to them, still undamaged cages sprawled to the ground. In twos and threes, they formed a line of demarcation that divided the high terrain from the plain.

Sweeping to the horizon were the wheat lands of Arcadia, all scoured black and sending wisps of smoke into the air from still smoldering flames. In the near distance, the humps of thatch and precise lines of stone marked the village of Kenton's barony. Approaching the very foot of the slope was a vast army of armored men. Squares of marchers, their mail gleaming brightly in the sunlight, stood ten rows deep. For every four companies on foot, there was a squad of richly decorated cavalry. Even from the distance came the nervous whinnies of the horses as they approached. In the very center flew not one royal standard but two. The rebellion had become far too grave for the high prince to handle without the presence of his father.

Behind the front ranks were arrayed rows of catapults and ballistas. Pressed close together, they look like the wall of a huge fortress that kept the mountain from creeping further down the plain. Robes of brown busily flitted among the throwing machines, adjusting tensions and making ready the arsenals of stone arrayed by each.

The first contingents of the army were already climbing the slope, breaking precise formations and picking their way among the loose jumble of rock that littered the surface. A gentle cascade of smaller stones started to rain down on them from above. With a start, Jason realized what that must mean. It was a warning. 'Avoid traps that ensnare' snapped into his mind.

"Come along!" he shouted. "It is an unfortunate time to have emerged. We must get to safety now."

Without waiting for an answer, Jason broke for the edge of the cliff and began to scramble down the slope. Delia called out, and he reached back to grab her wrist, pulling her after. Burdon, puffing from the effort, clambered over the edge into the cloud that marked Jason's path.

Down the incline, Jason dodged, dislodging small streams of pebbles that cascaded in front and bounced off the larger boulders in the way. Barely in control of his motion, he careened between two rocks and then cut sharply to avoid another directly ahead. Delia stumbled and tripped. Only Jason's grip kept her from tumbling to the ground.

A small stone whizzed past Jason's ear, and then a shower somewhat farther away. The throng on the ledge above were not sure who the runners on the slope were, but the targets were much closer than the ones at the base.

Then there was a sudden rumble in the ground. Jason missed his step and skidded to his knees. A large rock on his right began to pitch back and forth in its shallow depression. The shower of pebbles from Jason's feet was joined by additional rivulets across the entire face of the cliff. A stone the size of a child's head skittered down to follow.

Bigger rocks began to move, crashing into those in front and dislodging them from their rest. Two large boulders rumbled from their moorings on the left and plowed smaller debris down the cliff to augment the cascade.

The quaking increased in intensity, so much that Jason could barely move forward. Like a drunken man, he stumbled down the mountainside, tripping on the obstacles thrust in his way. He gritted his teeth to ignore the sharp pulses of pain, as small missiles hurled into his ankles and legs.

"Avalanche!" Delia shouted, finally realizing what was going to happen. Her cry was drowned out by the grinding sound on the ledge as massive monoliths began to lumber downward.

Over Jason's shoulder, a dense, wave of dust had masked the shouting rebels. The hillside was alive in a fusillade of hurling death. "To the cages!" he yelled. "Farther down the hill. I see three that are undamaged. One for each of us. It is the best that we can do."

With a wrench of his arm, he spun Delia after and scampered down the slope toward the wreckage of Kenton's machines. He heard Burdon trip behind him, but now there was no time to turn back. Without thinking about how he would stop, Jason vaulted a stone in the way and skated on a wave of pebbles for a good thirty feet. Regaining his balance, he twisted past a boulder bounding by on the left, whipping Delia to the side.

The roar of the falling rock became deafening as they reached the first of the cages. Without dwelling on how close they were to loosing balance, Jason thrust Delia inside, snapped shut the belt around her waist and closed the door.

"Keep your arms and legs inside the bars!" he yelled. "Hope that the chains prevent you from slamming into the sides."

He turned to grab Burdon's tunic as the old man tumbled past, completely out of control from the motion of the dancing mountain.

"Into the next!" he shouted, jumping out of the way, as a large rock sailed past his shoulder and then bounced off the bars of Delia's cage. Without looking to see how the lord fared, Jason dove for the last cage in the cluster. Fingers numb and unresponsive slid on the belt.

Just as he did, the wave of dust engulfed him completely. Small pebbles and rocks sailed through the bars and struck his head and back, producing painful welts. Larger rocks clanged off the bars and continued down the slope. A huge boulder crashed into one end of the cage and spun it around. A second hit broadside, bending the bars with a shriek of protesting metal like the final groan from a fatally wounded dragon, and then, under the nudge of a boulder, it joined the stream tumbling end over end, another piece of debris in the sweeping storm.

Jason gasped from the tugs of the belt. He shut his eyes to block out the dust and the swirl of rock. All sense of orientation vanished in the dizzying tumble. He was barely aware of the cries of men and panicked whinny's of horses as the avalanche roared through their lines.

Then, as suddenly as it had begun, the tumbling stopped. A sudden quiet replaced the roaring cascade. Jason opened his eyes and peered through the dust. His cage was upended in a pile of granite, one end crushed within inches of his head and the steel ceiling plate pitted with dents a foot across. He reached out and grabbed a bar to steady the whirl in his eyes. After a few moments, he was able to release the grip of the belt and scramble out onto the mound of stones.

He blinked in dust-sprayed sunlight. Where there once had been an army was now an area marked only by a few shards of mail scattered amidst the piles of rubble. To Jason's left were what remained of the rows of catapults. Half were splintery rubbish. On others, thick-beamed spars dangled like broken arms. All were immersed in a sea of stone that extended farther back onto the plain.

One or two of the machines had survived unscathed. The thaumaturges hastily cranked back the great arms to release their flights in retaliation.

"Wait, wait," he heard one yell. "The incantation. Something is wrong. The small sliver is not bound with the whole. Sympathy and contagion. They no longer seem to work."

Jason searched the slope through the haze, searched the rubble for signs of Delia and Burton. He sucked in his breath when he glimpsed a few twisted bars poking out from beneath a boulder the size of a small hut. He ran to examine the wreckage, not daring to think of what he might find.

As he drew closer to the monolith that must have crushed flat whatever had stood in its way, he heard a faint, high-pitched hum and the squeak of a tiny voice.

"The time has already been many heartbeats. At this distance, I can remain no more. I must return and fulfill the obligations to my master. I am to maintain the void under the tent. Little else do I have leave to do."

Jason ran around the rock and blinked at what he saw. Delia huddled inside a shimmering transparent sphere that was centered about the rock bubbler sprite.

"Nevertheless, you have saved my life," Delia told the demon. "You see where the cage came to rest in the monolith's path. There was barely enough time to get out and call for your aid before it hit."

"Your thoughts were compelling and clear." The sprite unfolded its arms from its chest. "I do not understand truly what made me come. But no matter. In a few heart beats more, I must —"

The imp stopped, and then a spasm ran through its body. "The packing of the spheres has shifted. The others have told. My true master calls. He has been awakened and commands that I return." The demon closed its eyes and pivoted, pointing a thin arm up to the ledge from which it had come. "See, he walks among you mortals and has summoned another to do his bidding as well."

Up the mountainside, the rebels were quiet, stunned by the awesome power of the avalanche. A small flash of white-hot flame suddenly cut through the swirling dust and then a blur of motion, fiery oranges and burning reds. The patch of color soared up into the air. In a breathtaking glide, it arched down to where he and Delia stood.

"A djinn!" the rock bubbler cried. "Master, have pity on one who has honored the letter of your law. I have kept open the void under the tent. I left only when the others were so positioned that I contributed nothing to the total volume."

The dance of color formed into a large demon. Unlike the sprite, its limbs were full and bulged with muscle. Thick, overlapping scales covered its entire body except for the tenuous membranes of bat-like wings and the pockmarked cheeks and forehead. Without effort, it descended from the sky, its long tail dangling far below its cloven hooves, testing the ground for a place to land.

Jason followed the trajectory with a mixture of fascination and dread. "Not since the agreement between the archimage and the demon prince has one been summoned," he muttered. "The wizard who conjured him is either a fool or a true master."

The djinn drew closer, carrying a bundle in each arm. One was dark-cloaked Melibar, the other a manipulant, now fully alert.

"Have him release me." Melibar coughed as they settled to the ground. "A moment of heat will not destroy you. For months, you have been peacefully resting. It is only fair that you should carry some of the hardships as well."

The manipulant motioned with his arms and then collapsed to the ground as the djinn released its grip. Melibar momentarily staggered, but quickly regained his balance and drew himself to full height. He looked at the sprite that had moved away from Delia and then at Jason.

"In the grotto, and now even one of my manipulant's sprites you have subverted," he said. "Your persistence begins to mark you as a captive of some quality."

For a moment, Melibar looked back down the chaos of the hillside. "I do not have the time now to unravel how you did that. Instead, I will put you in a safer place. Your marrow still will touch the lips of no less than the first among the navigators, but not just yet."

Jason grabbed Delia and closed his fist defiantly. "Numb us again if you will," he heard himself say. "Somehow, we shall escape as we did before."

"The torpor dust is insufficient for one such as you. That you have already demonstrated." Melibar waved his cloaked arm through the air. "But now there are only alchemy left. I will meet this so-called archimage of yours, and then the victory will be complete. You will be the first I will savor when I have gained control of them all. In the meantime, I will place you where I can be more sure you will stay."

Melibar kicked the manipulant huddled at his side. "Send them away. Back whence we came."

Jason tensed as the figure on the ground somehow managed to start a small fire from implements tucked into the waist of his loincloth. He tried to ignore the sense of helplessness that welled up within him. He faced no less than a long-tailed djinn that could slice him in two with the snap of its claws. No mortal who was not its master could stand against one such as that. There was no point in even trying to resist. With round eyes, he watched the demon step forward and spread its blood-red wings. As its arms closed around him and Delia, the smell of burning sulfur made him gag.

"Why?" Delia blurted. "Why are you doing this?"

"Elsewhere," Melibar commanded. "Send them to elsewhere. Let them see if they can fare in my realm as well as I have in theirs."

Part Four

The Verity of Exclusion

1

Skysoar

JASON COULD not judge the passage of time. There was a moment of disorientation and then sharp cries of surprise. The wings of the djinn unfurled. As quickly as it had engulfed them, the demon stepped back into the flame and vanished.

A blast of numbing cold air ripped at Jason's uncovered hands and eyes. A sense of weightlessness rose from his gut, and his feet slowly left the ground. He felt like he was a balloon filled with a light gas that was just launched. He blinked, surrounded by a vast expanse of reddish sky, not the robust oranges of sunset reflected in clouds, but a soft color that washed from horizon to horizon, full of a diffuse light for which no source could be seen. In the far distance, spanning across the ruddy glow were dim hints of long, straight lines, a trellis of triangles like the facets of a gem.

He spun his head. The trellis was all around him — extending below the horizon in front, behind, on the left and right, and even directly overhead. Far away triangles everywhere *encased* him, all the same size and equilateral, connected together with repetitious precision like one of the models he had seen so long ago in Drandor's tent.

Where was he? It was a scene that could not possibly exist in the experience of man. Everything was alien: the colors, the smell of the air, and the sound of the whistling wind. The shock hammered at Jason's senses and froze him in place, a mute statue without any comprehension of what he saw.

A hand grabbed his shoulder from behind. He was thrust into a shallow pit carved from solid rock. Delia was pushed to his side. Long, slender fingers pointed to small indentations in the walls, and he understood what to do. Gripping tightly with his hands and feet, he prevented himself from floating upward and away.

For the longest time, Jason remained huddled in the pit, pressing against Delia to share her warmth and feeling the wind whip over his back. He kept his eyes screwed shut, all muscles tensed to lock him into position, not wanting to move, trying to will away what he had seen as part of a flawed glamour. But the thought of what must have happened bubbled in his mind, gathering strength and dripping with desolation and helplessness.

Finally, he had to be sure. He opened his eyes, extended his head from the pit as far as he could while still holding on and looked about. A dozen figures, dressed in loincloths like Melibar's manipulants, huddled in depressions similar to his own. They were arrayed in a circle about a deeper pit that contained the last flickers of the fire, a set of mirrors mounted on swivels, and a flat table-like stone with strange glyphs marked around its periphery.

Farther to the right, at the end of what might be a safety rope, looped through a series of metal eyes, was a large indentation in the rock. Steps lead down into an interior and the hint of torchlight cast dull shadows on the roughly hewn granite. Except for these features, all else was bare, a gently curving expanse with sharp ridges hammered and polished away, the texture of the sea frozen in sculpture's stone.

Like Melibar's manipulants! Jason's sagging spirits plummeted even more with the thought. Like Melibar himself! Here the beings appeared to move about in comfort, to be the norm. He and Delia were the exceptions, the outcasts trapped inside a geometric structure far away from home. The strange one had made good his threat.

"Where are we?" Delia came to life at his side. "Is this the realm of demons, the world behind the flames?"

Jason scanned the horizon again. They seemed to be on the top of a rocky mound. The terrain fell away in all directions. But the proportions were all wrong. Except for the distant trellis, there was nothing in the distance beyond the curve of the hill, no plain stretching away or other mountains, only reddish sky and the distant lines.

"No," he answered slowly. "It is unlike anything that the wizards have recorded in the sagas."

He peered again at the men clustered about them. They talked in a soft chittering and ignored him completely. In the pit with the tablestone, one obviously older than the rest and cloaked in gray spoke in hoarse whispers, gesturing commands. His sleek black hair had turned pale, and deep wrinkles furrowed a caved-in face. Pus ran from one half-closed eye.

At his side were what looked like simple toys for an infant's crib —

two vertical arrays of horizontal copper wires and on each a brightly colored bead that could be slid back and forth. Beads on the left most wires could occupy one of three indentations, those on the right only two. More simple, certainly, Jason thought, but they reminded him strongly of Melibar's lattices.

The old one wiped pus from his eye and gestured at the horizon. A new line of hills appeared where there had been none before. The crest line grew taller and extended farther to both sides. The undulations of the peaks were ripples on a more gentle curve that bowed up into the sky.

Jason was confused by what he was seeing, but in a few heartbeats more, the rising ground began to fill his view, and in a flash, he understood where he was. They were riding a boulder, a large one to be sure, over a thousand strides in diameter from what he could see, but no more than a mere hunk of rock, slowly rotating and hurtling toward a larger orb that was directly ahead.

Jason realized dimly that he should have some reaction to the impending collision, at least a sudden flash of anxiety — this time from the primitive fear of falling — but he felt instead only the huge weight of his increasing despair.

Details of ragged peaks and scarred valleys grew on the bigger sphere as they closed. Here and there were small craters, and in other places, long slashes gouged the surface. Calmly, the manipulants went about their tasks, seemingly oblivious to the danger of a collision. Two sighted the approaching body through a telescope and sextant while another moved two pale blue stones across the top of the tablestone closer together in response to what they called out. "Chirrrpen, raspparn, chittterardd", said one.

Through his good eye, the old one squinted up at the approaching planet. He glanced at the markers being adjusted on the tablestone and nodded. Reaching into one of the pouches bound around his waist, he removed a small pyramid, each side covered with triangles colored much like squares that marked Melibar's cube. Without pause, the strange one began twisting the faces of the solid, permuting the triangles on the surface in a pattern that was hard to follow.

After a few heartbeats, he stopped his manipulation and nodded again to those carefully watching. The original markers on the tablestone were swept away. A quartet of other manipulants replaced them with new pairs of brightly colored, fist-sized rocks, each one abutting its twin. Clasping each stone with coiled fingers, the four began to pull them apart slowly.

The old one again manipulated the pyramid, and then suddenly, there

263

was a ground-wrenching lurch, a groan in the granite that vibrated the entire mass on which everyone rode. Jason felt a deceleration, a resistance in the direction in which they sped.

In the pit, like a shopkeeper with a tally-counter, the ancient being slid one of the beads in the left-most column all the way along its wire to the right as far as it would go. Without pause, he then moved three more in the second column from right to left and finally, three in the first column from their central positions to the left side as well.

The pyramid was exercised a third and fourth time, and another of the attendants performed complex motions on the tabletop with a pair of like stones, this time with sparkling crystals of pale violet. Again, the boulder shuddered and responded. The rotation of the rock slowed, and the uprushing ground was now directly overhead.

The whispering chatter became more intense. The ancient one began working with his pyramid almost continuously. Like gambling in a complex game of chance, the manipulants alternately placed small colored stones on the table, maneuvered them briefly and then shoved them away. With each pair of pyramid reconfigurations, the old one shuttled beads back and forth on his lattice to keep track of what was being done.

Suddenly, the one with the sextant waved his arms, and all activity stopped. The old one slumped down beside the tablestone, exhausted. The ground rushed closer, but not quite as fast as it had before. More importantly, it also began moving to the side.

Beyond the large pit stood a scaffolding and next to it a line of crudely built wagons, wheels of solid wood and tongues with handholds rather than yokes. Behind them were several hoists, complicated constructions of levers, pulleys, and slings. Shovels and coarse woven sacks piled everywhere battened down under tightly stretched nets.

The rate of closure became less and less. The lateral motion increased until the features on the ground streaked by in a rush. Finally, they seemed to stop falling altogether and flew over the surface at a blistering pace, skimming along over the ground faster than any bird could fly.

"What just happened?" Delia asked.

Jason shook his head. He was a puzzle solver, but all of this was too much to comprehend at once. He did not understand. "Only a part of this echoes what I have learned before," he said.

For a moment, nothing more happened. Then the sextant holder shouted, pointing to the left and far ahead. The old one directed one more manipulation, and they resumed their descent towards the surface.

Smaller features resolved as they grew closer, the wrinkles of mountain slopes, the canopy of individual trees. Jason held his breath as they skimmed over a small ridge and then above a marshy plain. He recognized the grazing animals as like those that had appeared in Drandor's initial animation and, stalking them behind the cover of tall grass, strong-jawed dogs.

A net billowed from the scaffolding to catch the wind. Working two-handed cranks, the manipulant at the scaffolding let out enough line so that each end of the net skimmed along the ground. With a hoot of panic, the grazing beasts saw it coming and began to stampede out of its path. However, the race of the boulder was too swift. In an instant, two or three were caught and scooped from their feet. With a soft, tinkling laughter, the manipulant next to Jason beat his thigh with his palm in apparent delight.

Crank handles spun, slowly drawing the trapped beasts from the surface up onto the rock. The distance between the boulder and the surface began to widen. They had passed the point of closest approach. Gradually, the lateral motion turned into one of recession. As quickly as they had come, they now were speeding away back into the reddish sky.

The tension seemed to dissolve from among the manipulants. They all gestured at one another with a curious contortion of the fingers of the right hand. While two hauled in the catch, three others helped the old one out of the pit and into the opening that led inside the rock. Another manipulated the mirror linkage, and coded bursts of light radiated out in all directions. Finally, one returned to where Delia and Jason lay still, huddled in their pit. He brandished a short sword of copper and motioned them to follow the others inside.

Jason eyed the manipulant's face and slowly released his grip. The sword he did not mind. What disturbed him most was the smacking of the thick, pulpy lips. Perhaps it would have been best if their encounter had not been a near miss after all.

2

Saga of the First among the Navigators

JASON STARED at the pile of coins in his lap. He put them back into the battered changer, one by one. Playing with Benedict's problem was what had kept him sane. Besides Delia, it was his only contact with the world from which they had been cast.

On a rock barely a thousand strides across, they had been marooned in Melibar's realm. There was no doubt about it. And time must be running out back in their own world. Burton did not survive the avalanche. The archimage had not been warned. There was no easy way to measure time here, but the chance to act was slipping away. Over two score times, they had slept while nothing else seemed to have changed.

In his mind's eye, Jason was able to visualize almost every feature of the lithon. Honeycombed with caverns like a giant ball of cheese, it would have been an impressive monolith on an Arcadian plain. But here it was a mere speck, smaller than most of the others in the sky.

Despite what he had suspected after the encounter with the larger sphere, he and Delia had not felt the sharpness of the copper blade. Instead, they were shown to small caverns carved from the rock. And once cautious tastes of meat from herd animals produced no ill effects, their basic needs were provided for as well. The manipulants were even friendly in an offhanded sort of way. Teaching each other their languages had begun almost immediately. He had learned much after a few sessions of struggling with the basic concepts.

They were not prisoners. Like curious visitors from a foreign land, they could come and go as they chose. But as Jason had soon learned, their freedom meant very little. Melibar had been right. Isolating Delia and him on a hunk of granite was a perfect prison. There were no exotic powders with which to summon the stronger demons. He and Delia were trapped, hopelessly trapped, far more removed from freedom than in any pit a few feet beneath the ground.

Jason studied the sky. And even if they could escape, escape to what? One speck of rock, a lithon as the natives called them, was no better than any other. If they were able to make the transition back on their own world, would that be in time, before whatever they returned to was lost?

He pulled his leather vest tighter and massaged one cold hand with the other, but it did not help. They were brittle like icicles that might snap off. At least their worst fears had yet to be realized. The old one and the others seemed to have enough marrow from the grazing animals to keep them satisfied. There was no need for either hibernation or feasting. Other than a few appraising leers and teasing grasps, he and Delia had been left alone.

Jason examined the changer at his waist. He had mused over the facts so many times that even the critical nature of the situation could no longer stifle the undercurrent of boredom that mingled with the threat of ultimate doom. It was fortunate that he still had the collection of coins to divert his attention when the level of frustration was particularly high. Not that Benedict's problem was proving any easier to unravel. With his latest sequence for loading the changer, the five coppers came out of a single column, and the silver did, too. But the brandels were interleaved with the rest. The initial condition still was not set right. And any small change in the order with which he inserted the coins made the confusion worse. Perhaps there was no solution-a bad omen for the other more important puzzle he somehow had to solve.

A shadow crossed the doorway. One of the lithon's inhabitants entered and settled cross-legged on the other side of the floor. His face was old and, save for the operator of the pyramid, more leathery than any other in his small band of colleagues. In large patches, the translucence of his skin had dimmed to milky opaqueness. Deep wrinkles surrounded his eyes like waves lapping on a shore. His black hair was streaked with white on a head that peaked in a slight ridge running from the brow to the base of the skull like a tight roll of hardened dough. He held his token of leadership— a small shovel with a long and deep blade— in stiff fingers that did not completely curl about the shaft.

"The other, the one you name a female," the visitor said, "She is tired. Tired of teaching to me your speech."

"Anything tires with repetition, Ponzar," Jason clawed his way through the accent. The skyskirr had shown an amazing aptitude for vocabulary and syntax, but his diction distorted and was hard to understand. "Delia has spent many of our hours with you over two score of our days. She probably is as bored as am I."

"Repetition?"

"To do something over and over, again and again," Jason explained.

"Ah, then life is repetition," Ponzar said. "Forever we drift in the sky. Swoop to the larger lithons. Trade for water. Fly away from the air that is foul. Harvest the lodestones that have the power. The skyskirr have done this since-since the great expansion. Until the great right hand wills a change, we will do so forever."

"And yet you show an interest in our tongue. Perhaps the time between encounters does not pass so swiftly for you either."

Ponzar twirled the shovel in what Jason had learned was the equivalent of a shrug. "It is the talent of a captain. To be such, one must speak with all who soar. And I am counted with the quickest. My memory is almost perfect. I can learn in a few sleeps what takes a common mason hundreds."

"And there is more," Ponzar continued. "You have traded thoughts with the outcast, Melibar. Many lithosoars fear that he will return. It is worth the effort to talk so that I might learn."

"Lithosoars?"

"Smaller stones like this one. With little mass and easily manipulated. The larger ones we call lithofloats. Big and cumbersome, they are difficult to move. The lithosoars visit them rather than the other way around."

Ponzar slumped forward in thought. "I no longer trust the others. I do not believe the silvered words they flash by mirror. The more I can speak of your lithon, the more Valdroz will pay me honor when we meet to trade." He paused for a heartbeat. "Also, it is to your advantage to tell me all. You will last longer if others think you have value more than common marrow."

Jason thought of Delia's last words before they were transported here. 'Why?' she had asked. 'Why are you doing this?' He smiled grimly. For him the question had always been 'How?' How does one solve the puzzle, never 'Why?' And perhaps her question was the one that should be answered first.

"I seek knowledge as well," Jason said. "Tell me of Melibar. What are his powers? What has he done? Why does he despoil a realm foreign to his own?"

"You are only property," Ponzar replied. "You do not have the honor to question those who harvest what has been provided by the great right hand." He twirled the shovel through several full circles. "And I do not know if your words are true, if you are not another of Melibar's manipulants. Sent back to help his return. A manipulant of one people who resonates with the navigator of another."

"But I may be of help," Jason said. "I have deduced two metalaws. Melibar said that there is a third. If I know them all, I might be able to thwart his plans."

Ponzar threw back his head, and the small cavern echoed with his tinkly laugh. "You against Melibar? Against the one who navigated a course with nine changes in the laws?

"Even old Utothaz, may the great right hand make his bones tasty, could not keep the coupling tight. Keep it tight if Melibar chose to break it. Speak. By your own telling, you have faced his power. How well did you fare?"

Jason frowned and waved his arm in irritation. "If Melibar is so powerful, how did he become an outcast?"

"He is the greatest of the navigators," Ponzar said. "The first among the first. No one in the vastness of the 'hedron that encloses us says it is not so. But he reached too far. He studied his craft above all else. Studied it instead of the greater needs of the skyskirr, of our people."

Ponzar looked toward the sky. "Each lithon must have its turn. It is the way of the great right hand. Every sphere, no matter how small, has the right to unlock the laws. The right to change which of the stones of power have the force of attraction and repulsion. The right to choose which are without power like common rock. Each lithon must be allowed to avoid collision. Each to harvest from the larger, to explore where no other has gone."

Jason leaned forward, listening intently. The more he could learn about these strange beings the more clues he would discover-more clues to solve the puzzle of how to get home.

"But Melibar had eyes only for other things," Ponzar continued. "Eyes for the strange laws which have nothing to do with the walls of the 'hedron or the magical minerals within it. He would unlock the binding when there was no need, demanding many strange rituals be performed until he discovered what would move the laws to other unknown vertices of the lattice.

"Each uncoupling made him stronger, more able to force a translation, even if other navigators wished it or not." Ponzar's eyes took on a faraway look. Like an orator reciting from memory an ancient tale from the sagas, the old skyskirr's voice began to boom, even though in a language not his own. "And every new vertex of his lattice, each scintilla of knowledge, increased his hunger for more. His thoughts became less and less about the soaring of the skyskirr. For his own lithon, he planned

269

fewer and fewer changes of course. To his own captain, he would not answer. Except for his manipulants, he cared for none at all."

"Course changes," Jason blurted. "You mean like what happened when Delia and I first arrived? How you manage to direct your-your lithon to skim bigger orbs and harvest what you find there?"

"Finally, his perturbations conflicted with another's," Ponzar ignored the interruption and continued his story. "A conflict, even though there was no real need. Azaber's lithosoar was in trouble. They wished to close with a watery orb and break a long drought. But the lodestone, yellow orpiment, was with power at the time-and repulsive rather than attractive.

"Both the wet sphere and Azaber's lithon carried many large stones of the deep yellow. With strong force, they were being pushed apart. Azaber's manipulants saw boulders of cairngorm on the orb. If their navigator could change which laws were in effect — to give the brown stone its attractive power while turning off the repulsiion of the yellow, then they could converge in time."

"Lodestones?" Jason asked. A glimmer of understanding began to form. "Lodestones, but of more than one type?"

"And so the manipulants signaled by mirrors to all the lithons," Ponzar again ignored the outburst and like a wagon running away down a mountain trail he raced on. "All others agreed not to work the craft until Azaber's navigator was done. A common request that is always honored. When one is far away from other lithons and moving swiftly, it does not matter which of the laws are in effect."

The skyskirr twirled his shovel and pounded it on the ground. "All agreed, that is, except Melibar. His sphere was one of the largest, a huge lithofloat, far grander than the one that soon we will see. And he had thoughts only for his own searching. He held the lock tight against Azaber's navigator. The bond did not break. Slowly the smaller lithon was pushed away with no chance to choose speed or direction. It drifted into a region of poisonous vapors. A region with no lodestone strong enough to alter its path for a return. Only the gentle force between the faces carried it along."

"I don't understand," Jason said. "Lodestones that attract and repel seem similar to ones in my own realm, but what are faces?"

Ponzar waved his arm absently out to the dim lines in the distance. He started to form a reply, but then shook his head and continued his saga. "For far too long, the ones who soared with it were without the means of guidance. In the end, they all gave their marrow to one another. The last reflections said they were drifting out of mirror range, and resigned to their fate.

"Azaber's navigator took a great chance when he ran their course so close to a void, it is true. It is one of the risks for the lithons that soar rather than float. But if Melibar had loosened his grip, as was his duty, then the lithon would have spun around its target. Spun around and returned to better air."

"After all the skyskirr learned of what had happened, the rest of the lithons sailed as one. United, they manipulated the laws to converge on Melibar's orb. Never since the great expansion has so many been in one small portion of the 'hedron. Ten times a hundred swords of precious copper were drawn. A thousand were ready to ride the smaller lodestones down upon the floater. To seek the vile one out, to break his bones and scatter his marrow to the twenty faces."

Ponzar drew his wheezing breath. "But Melibar and his manipulants escaped. Through the laws of what you call wizardry, he conjured a lodestone that was not made of rock. A strange being that whisked him and his manipulants away out of the boundaries of our 'hedron entirely, to some other place whose nature we can only guess."

Ponzar stopped speaking and slumped, exhausted from his oration.

Jason struggled to make sense of what he had just heard. Ponzar said that Melibar was a navigator. Here, the title must refer to one who locks and unlocks the laws of magic. One who used lattices to keep track of which held power and directed others to create examples of what the new laws were to be.

Insight came in a lightening stroke. The old one he had seen on Delia and his arrival, he too was a navigator! He too used lattices to keep track of the laws. How was it at the beginning? A single bead in the left-most indentation, and six more in ones far to the right. Seven at the extremes in all.

And after the deceleration, four beads to the right indentations in the left-most column and only three at the farthest right. Again seven beads in positions of importance. Seven! Yes, seven exactly, just as required by the first of the metalaws. Although in a completely different realm, the Postulate of Invariance still held true.

The others around the old one, Jason's thoughts bubbled on, the ones followed the navigator's directions, moving stones together and farther apart on the tablestone so that the desired new laws came into effect. An exercise for the Axiom of Least Contradiction. Reality was different here, but, nevertheless, it was governed by the same fundamental principles.

"The laws you mentioned that are strange to you," Jason offered after a moment of silence, "I know them well. They are the Law of Dichotomy, 'dominance or submission,' and the Law of Ubiquity, 'flame permeates all. "

"So well that after thirty-seven sleeps, you are still here." Ponzar laughed softly. "If you can do this wizardry, why not return? Return by commanding the strange being which brought you here."

"I-I have never attempted the detailed workings of the craft."

Jason hesitated and then rushed on. "Besides, a true djinn will not come in simple flame. He needs the burning of special powders, and you have none of it here on this rock."

Ponzar did not immediately reply. He again slumped. "Most interesting," he said after a moment. "I will add that to what I will tell."

"You speak with some apprehension about this rendezvous," Jason said. "Why bother if it gives you any concern?"

"Utothaz calculated the course long ago." Ponzar looked back at Jason. "And once we spun past the sphere with the grazing beasts, the path was set. Only when we near the lithofloat will there be another chance to alter our track." Ponzar twirled his shovel and tapped the ground. "Our caverns are overflowing with harvest. The floaters are too big to move as swiftly through the sky as we, but they have minerals that we could well use. If there is trust, the trade will be good to both sides."

"And if there is not?"

"Valdroz is a greedy captain. He is not at peace that his Iithon is so big and slow. Were it not for the way of the great right hand, I fear he would plunder all that I have. Plunder all and give nothing in exchange. I also think of the strength of the lodestones. Valdroz's lithon has huge boulders of positive cairngorm. Our own are not small. As long as its law remains inert, it acts no differently than baser rock. But if we shift to a vertex where it has power, we could be hurled to only the great right hand knows where.

"But my heaviest thoughts are about the portion of the sky in which we meet. Behind the floater is a great sea of base stone lithons. Some are larger than the greatest floater, great enough for hot rock to flow and clouds of poisonous vapor to hurl in the air."

"Why should that be your greatest concern?" Jason asked. "If lava flows on the surface, you need not swoop close. And the fumes should dissipate on the currents of the air. It sounds not so very different from what I would call a volcano."

"There are few enough winds in the 'hedron except for those made by our flight," Ponzar said. "Only in time is the foul mixed with the pure.

The poisons move out slowly from where they were born. And the vapors of which I speak fill a very large volume. Even though a lithosoar can fly for many sleeps on a drifting course if its supply of marrow is high, no skyskirr can hold shut his lips for as long as it takes to pass through such a cloud."

Ponzar waved his small shovel in front of Jason's face. "The great right hand guides. It is the duty for all the skyskirr to follow. Whatever happens is by his design. And I have a duty, as shown by my token of office. The navigator uses his key for the unlocking. The manipulants chip precious lodestones from baser rocks with their picks. The others, the scribes, the smiths, the skinners, all have their duties and tokens as well. And the captain of a lithosoar must scoop the treasures from the skies and provide for his people so that marrow is for feasting and not survival in the voids."

Ponzar sank into silence, oblivious to the fact that Jason was even there. Then he rose abruptly, satisfied with the conversation. In the doorway, he shifted his shovel to his left hand. He extended his right index finger pointing at Jason, thumb upward and middle finger bent to the side. Jason returned the signal as he had been taught.

When the captain had gone, Jason sighed. "Which would be worse: return to a world with no apparent future, or stay here to be mere property, perhaps the dessert for a skyskirr's dinner."

He turned his attention back to the coin changer, stared at it for a moment, and then shook his head. No, that puzzle was an unimportant one. Instead, he should be devoting all of his time to the mysteries of this realm. He must probe every cranny of the lithon and look in all directions of the sky. The fact that inserting three dranbots before a galleon caused the last coin to go into the first column was something to be pondered later.

273

3

Attraction and Repulsion

JASON FELT the slight tremble as their small lithosoar began to slow in its passage rather than continuing to hurl past the larger sphere. Compared to the agonizing slowness over at least a dozen sleeping periods when their target had come into view — first as an indistinct speck and then growing into a discernible disk, the motion now seemed rapid. He knew that soon they would reach a perilith, and then loop back in a long ellipse. Ponzar had said that the trade delegation would come when they were almost skimming the surface.

Now, the other lithon blotted out a good portion of the sky, fissures and crags becoming more distinct with each passing moment. Details were more regular, indicating the effort of intelligent minds. Larger squares of greens and blues checkered a relatively flat plane like a fancy quilt. Upthrusts of rock were sculptured with spiraling steps. Hundreds of lights blinked in small clusters that covered the orb like a great pox.

Jason and Delia stood with the skyskirr, awaiting the arrival, crammed among sacks of bones, twisted branches of trees, wagonloads of sparkling rock, and other objects that Ponzar's group had scavenged in their trek across the sky.

Jason twisted restlessly as the large sphere drew closer. He had been able to deduce some additional facts about his surroundings, but even more time in his own realm had been lost as the lithons converged. With no periodic repetitions in the heavens, he could not be sure how much. But at least, Melibar's djinn had not reappeared. Now, with contact with other skyskirr imminent, perhaps he could find something more than bare rock to bridge the gap to the demon realm and then home.

"I still do not understand the forces between the special stones," Delia said at his side. "How do their attractions affect the direction in which we will go?"

Jason smiled at the sweetness in her voice. For most of their journey, she had remained to herself, gladly accepting a separate cavern when it was offered. Now, like a weathervane, her charm was again pointing his way.

"It is the construction of this realm," Jason answered. He grabbed a shovel from her hand and with its blade scratched a crude figure in the surface of the rock. "Ponzar is reluctant to say much, but by watching Utothaz and the others closely, I have figured out much of their laws."

"You know the third metalaw?" Delia's face brightened. "Does it provide the means to see us back?"

"Just laws, not metalaws," Jason shook his head. "It all began to make sense when I finally recognized the pattern of the distant lines in the sky."

He looked upward and nodded. He had walked all over the surface of the lithosoar and seen them all. There could be no other answer.

"We are in a box, Delia — not a rectangular box, but a giant icosahedron, a magician would call it, a regular solid with twenty triangular sides. All that the skyskirr know to exist lies within the walls of this crystal. From the triangular surfaces, they get light and heat. The closure of the 'hedron keeps the air from whirling away to whatever is beyond."

"Like the edges of the world in our own sagas?" Delia asked. "If you sailed too close, you ran the risk of falling over the side."

"Here the risk is not one of falling off," Jason said, "but of never being able to return. I suspect that the faces of the icosahedron are covered with the lodestones that the scavengers find so dear."

"It is these rocks that pull them through the air?"

"Exactly so. Cairngorm is either attracted or repulsed by two faces on opposite sides of the 'hedron. Even when it is near no other orb, a lithosoar can be accelerated by the forces from the walls.

"There are twenty faces in all — ten opposite pairs. For each pair, there is a corresponding rock: black sphalerite, violet spinel, rusty cairngorm, orpiment, realgar, anatase, chrysocolla, epidote, beryl, and serpentine. I have seen the rocks on the tablestone and as they have spilled from the manipulants' pouches, ten types of lodestones in all. And for each type, there are two laws that can be invoked, one that creates a force of attraction between the rocks and one that creates a repulsion. The force falls off with some power of the distance.

"Actually, it is a little more complicated than that." Jason contorted his hand in the sign of greeting. "An additional force interacts with each type of lodestone as well. It is much weaker than the primary one and only is felt by a lodestone when it is moving at an angle to one fixed direction. It is the meaning of the right hand."

"If the thumb points in the direction that runs from the face called the 'top' to the opposite one, the 'bottom'", he continued, "and the forefinger in the direction the lodestone is moving, then the additional force will be in the direction of the other fingers. The extended fingers of the hand are a simple aid from a distant past to help in the calculation of trajectories."

"But our flights are anything but so simple," Delia said. "Utothaz maneuvered us almost at will."

"There are other bodies in the 'hedron as well, each with its own complement of rocks that attract and repel."

"But what of the control? He maneuvered our lithosoar over the other as if we were a docile bird."

"It is the — the metamagic. Yes, that is the word for it," Jason said. "The laws of attraction or repulsion for the stones can be turned on and off at will. To approach a target, you invigorate the law that attracts the two bodies together. To break before collision, you switch instead to one that repels. Far away from any lithon, you rely on the forces between the faces."

"That is the role of the metamagician in this realm," Jason rushed on with his explanation. "He is the navigator who calculates the courses and steers the scavengers through the sky, guiding them from one stone to the next to collect whatever of value they can.

"The laws themselves are simple," he concluded. "Attraction or repulsion, falling with distance, and a second force at right angles to the velocity. Once a law is in effect, it permeates the entire realm, but with a few observations, anyone can calculate the trajectories that result. There is little of the arts as we know them here, Delia. No complex rituals or incantations that only a master can control. It is metamagic instead that is supreme."

Jason broke off and pointed skyward. A swarm of small figures rose from the surface of the larger rock and accelerated to catch their lithon as it hurled past. When the visitors grew closer, they looked much like Ponzar and the rest, dressed only in loincloths, despite the stinging cold. Each carried a huge pack on his back, and a copper sword dangled from his side. Arms extended directly forward. In one hand, each held a fair-sized stone of blue that seemed to pull its owner along. In the other was an inert crystal of red.

"When they get close, they will deactivate the attraction of the blue stone and change to the repulsion of the other," he said. "When they arrive, their relative speed will be almost zero. Then the law will be shifted to another type of rock, and the lodestones will have no special powers until they are reactivated for their return."

In a few minutes, Ponzar climbed with a slow, careful step to where the first visitor had landed. He grimaced slightly as he forced one of his fingers to bend into the proper signal and offered the security of a well-anchored rope. The new arrival accepted the hospitality with a quick patter of soft tones. Ponzar pointed in Jason's direction, and several members of both parties approached to view him better. He scowled back at the rude stares and put up his hand when one reached forward to rip away the front of Delia's gown.

"Careful, faraway one," Ponzar warned so that Jason could understand. "Your value is less if you are no better than the beast."

"Far away, a man is valued by the keenness of his mind," Jason answered.

"As it is here," Ponzar said. "And in your case, there is perhaps a little interest. It would help if you would show them how one conjures up a demon."

Jason's scowl deepened. "As I have told you, I do not know the craft. There would be nothing to see, only empty flame."

"Then something else."

What the captain had said was true enough, Jason thought. As long as he and Delia had some value, they had remained away from the sucking lips. And on a bigger orb, they might have a chance to find something that would help them effect the return to their own realm. But what to demonstrate? Something that would appear impressive. He closed his eyes.

"We are waiting," Ponzar prodded.

Jason spotted the various items stacked for trade nearby and began rummaging. Nothing seemed to be relevant, but after a few more tries, he dug his hands into one of the nearest sacks. Saleratus, he realized. Bicarbonate of soda from the edge of a great salt lake. He surveyed the small collection of bottles obtained from some previous trade and sniffed for one that had a vinegary smell. Saleratus and vinegar. Where had he read about them in his library scrolls? 'The novice's first day.' Yes, that was it.

"Alchemy." Jason turned back to face Ponzar as he prepared. "A craft governed by the Doctrine of Signatures, or, simply stated, 'the attributes without mirror the powers within.' These powers are invoked by writing a formula, a series of arcane symbols in a precise order, a formula only known by the practitioners of the craft, such as, well, such as me. I will make a Foam of Wellbeing by mixing what I have found.

"As you probably know, when saleratus and this liquid with the pungent smell are mixed together, they react. Confined, they could produce an explosion as a result. But with the aid of alchemy, instead the reaction is gentle — an elixir for reducing pain.

"Although marvelous results are possible, the craft is not always certain. Not always will the result be what is desired. It all depends, we alchemists say, on whether or not the random factors align."

Delia translated what Jason had said while he jotted some nonsense on a nearby hide. What he scribbled did not matter, but it would create the impression that he possessed some special knowledge. He opened the stopper in the flask and tossed in a handful of saleratus. Then he plunged back the cork and hurled the bottle up into the sky.

It sailed away, easily escaping the feeble grip that held it to the lithosoar. All eyes followed the trajectory upward, and then with a sharp pop and the glitter of tiny shards, the bottle disappeared.

The visitors shrugged. Their placid expressions showed that if the container had not come apart they might have been interested, but when it did as expected, all interest evaporated away.

"If properly done, the bottle does not burst," Jason tried to sound as competent as he could. "As I have told you, in alchemy there is no guarantee."

Ponzar slowly twirled his shovel of office with his stiff fingers, looking at Jason for a long while. "I cannot be sure. You still may be one of Melibar's. But if Valdroz's traders accept, you will be their problem and not mine. Wait with the rest of the harvest. I will see what agreement the great right hand will provide."

Jason clenched his fist. Ponzar's attitude was no surprise but it grated nonetheless. Certainly, he and Delia should be regarded differently from a bundle of sticks. Defiantly, he would speak out despite Ponzar's instructions.

But before Jason could respond, Valdroz's traders suddenly began racing as fast as they could manage in the light gravity towards the assembled scavenging. As they ran, they emptied crystals of black sphalerite from their packs onto the lithosoar's surface. When they reached the bags and crates, they started refilling them with the sacks scattered about along with the blue lodestones that had repelled them from their lithofloat.

Ponzar slapped his shovel against the rock in alarm. "We are

278

betrayed," he shouted. His own followers snapped to attention and scurried after the plunderers. More poured out of the cavern entrance, waving their copper blades and yelling in high-pitched shrieks. Utothaz tottered to standing in the tablestone pit and grasped hold of his pyramid, holding it tight with both hands.

Jason grabbed Delia about the waist and pulled her away from the skyskirr as they dashed about. One of the visitors cried in shrill pain as a blade cut into his shoulder from behind. Ponzar's skyskirr ran in among the others, hacking to the right and left, trading blows with whoever turned to resist. But Valdroz's followers were too well rehearsed. Despite Ponzar's rush, in a few moments most of the goods for trade were bundled away.

The laws changed. Blue lodestones on the lithofloat began attracting rather than repel. The visitors leapt into the sky, hands wrapped around the ropes binding the crates, and streaked away, back to their home.

Utothaz screamed. The pyramid tumbled from the navigator's hands, wisps of smoke coming from the smaller vertices as they whirled. Ponzar watched the stricken metamagician for a moment and then the skyskirr shooting away. "Hang on, hang on," he commanded as he struggled toward the pit. "The lithofloat. The sphalerite. There is too much of it there, and its activation is the next vertex in line."

Jason pushed Delia down into one of the many depressions on the lithosoar's surface. He knelt beside her, and as he did, the rock almost tore from his grip. An audible sound like the groan from a waking wyvern filled the air. Desperately, he reached again to grab hold of the surface as it seemed to slip away. He jammed one hand into the indentation and flung a leg across Delia while she struggled to catch on. His body move sluggishly as her home so many days gathered speed.

His legs slipped from where they were braced, and he hung only by his arms. The wind began whistling around his head. Small bits of wood, sacks, and ropes seemed to come close and whip out of sight, falling behind. Jason gritted his teeth and pulled with all his strength, trembling from the effort, somehow drawing himself closer to the receding rock. Using all the muscles in his back, he gradually drew his legs parallel to the curving surface. With one great lunge, he touched the granite, and his foot caught in the proper indentation. Straining from the effort, he pulled Delia in front of him to the safety of the pit. Firmly braced with all four limbs, he dared to chance a look at where he had been.

He gasped in surprise. The other globe was shrinking. Like the shot of a catapult, it was hurling away. Their own lithosoar was soaring into the unknown far faster than he had ever travelled before.

279

4

Foul Air

JASON TURNED his head away in disgust. Utothaz's body, sprawled on the tablestone, could barely be seen beneath the huddled forms of his manipulants bending over him. The smacking of lips like pigs at a trough competed with the whistle of the air. He turned into the direction of the wind. In the distance, he could just discern a tiny speck against the reddish background and, around it, the shading to brown that indicated the concentration of toxic fumes. They had soared for another dozen sleeping periods, and the careful observations through the telescope had long since confirmed that there were no deviations in their flight. By whatever chance, none of the lodestones they carried had a repulsive counterpart on the poison-spewing rock. And no other lithons were anywhere in sight. Still, it seemed little enough reason for Utothaz and the others to abandon hope so quickly.

Ponzar appeared at Jason's side and tapped him on the shoulder. "It is no more repulsive than the way you tear the flesh from the bone with your teeth. And if he is not a criminal, we leave the skull — leave it so that the features remain when the body is cast off into the sky."

"The air is not yet so foul that it cannot be endured," Jason replied. "Utothaz has not yet breathed his last." He shook his head in amazement that the captain still spent his entire day in language drill. Even the accent showed hints of fading.

"He may just as well." Ponzar twirled the shovel blade. "The struggle to hold the laws bound was too great. He knows that he will unlock and move to another vertex only a few times more. It is better for him to give the rest the sweetness of his marrow while he is still fresh."

"But the manipulants," Jason protested. "They bicker on who is to be fed upon next. What have they done to deserve such a fate?"

"It is our way. Without the navigator to guide them, their lives are as lost. The bonds will be broken. There will be no resonances. It is for few others that they can manipulate the stones."

"It seems to me that the last thing you would want to do is rid yourself of the only talent that has any hope of reversing your direction."

"We will hold trials for another navigator. Although, even if we find one in those who remain, it will little matter. Our flight is swift. There are no other lithons nearby."

"How can you be so calm?" Jason growled. "Your very life is in peril. This may be your last soar across the sky. Why are you not straining to invent a scheme, some plan that will save us all?"

"It is the way of the great right hand. Valdroz wanted us repulsed after he had plundered our harvest. But I do not believe that he would want us to be pushed where the air hangs foul. No, we must have been touched by the great right hand as well. Life is repetition, but skyskirr do not fly forever. For each comes the time when the tugging lithons are far away, and the drift leads without change to the walls. For this small stone, that time is now, and we must accept. Our duty is to give our fellows the pleasure of the feast before it is too late to be enjoyed."

The captain eyed Jason speculatively. "And as to your own marrow — we have treated you well. Better than some of the other lithons might. It would be to your honor if you do not wait before offering yourself and the female for the benefit of the rest."

Jason drew his arms back to his chest. "I am not Delia's owner. Anymore than you are of me. She will decide in her own mind how she will face the end if it is to come."

Ponzar pondered and then pointed with his shovel at the speck in the distance. "The question is not if, but when. Make peace with the great right hand in your own 'hedron. We would prefer your gift freely given, but will not wait long for it."

Jason scowled and turned his back. The helplessness of their situation tore through him like stinging acid. More time had slipped through his fingers. Now it was possibly too late for his own world. He regarded the growing cloud of dull brown. And soon it would also no longer matter here.

He heard Utothaz cry in discomfort again and clutched at the brandel around his neck. Ponzar had refused to tell him more of metamagic, even after the treachery of Valdroz's floater. In total isolation from the rest of the skyskirr, the captain still was taking no chances regarding Melibar and his suspected return.

Jason felt the battered coin changer at his waist and fingered a dozen coins into his palm. Looking down at the mixture of metal, he smiled ruefully. Benedict's puzzle of the twenty-five mixed coins was probably the last conundrum he would solve — a meaningless pastime instead of the foundation of the universal laws. He glanced back into the sky and shrugged. A child's puzzle or keystone to the realms. In the end, was either more important than the other?

A hacking cough at his side broke Jason out of his reverie. He turned to see Delia leaning against the safety rope and clutching her other fist to her chest. Her skin was pale. Her golden hair hung in limp snarls. Deep wrinkles had appeared under her eyes, and her cheekbones cut sharp angles on her face.

"The air affects you more than the rest," Jason said. "You should remain in one of the caverns. Perhaps we can rig up a seal so that the most foul will not as readily mix."

Delia snapped closed her lips and tried to gain control of her spasms. She settled to the rock surface and motioned Jason to follow. "It is so cold," she muttered. "So cold. I wonder which of the perils will get me first."

"Do not talk that way. I have not given up like Ponzar and the rest. Perhaps some other navigator will change the laws in a way that will repulse us from this outgassing lithon. Perhaps we will manage to sail on through to greater possibilities beyond."

He pounded his fist into his palm. "If only I had the wit to master wizardry! Even an imp might give us more resource than we have now."

Delia managed a wan smile. "You have saved me twice. I have no right to expect more. And if it is to proceed to an end, I could have done far worse than to share it with one such as you."

Jason drew her close.

A few times before, they had huddled together for warmth. But this time, she melted into his arms in a way that he knew was different. The passion that he had held in check since the rebuff in Farnel's hut flamed anew.

"You are not without virtue yourself," he said. "A gambler in the markets of Pluton, the organizer of Farnel's presentation, a survivor of the confines of Drandor's tent, the seducer of a rock bubbler sprite.

"That is another part of the mystery." Jason continued. "I had put it out of my mind. How could you possibly get the demon to do as you commanded? He was bound to one of Melibar's manipulants. A master he already possessed. Perhaps wizards can wrest control of demons, just as the metamagicians contend for the unlocking here."

"I did not seek you out to push small tiles about a puzzle," Delia said.

"There is little enough time. Come, let us go into one of the caverns while the skyskirr are occupied with their feast."

"I thought it was my analytical bent that had finally worn down your resistance." Jason laughed.

Delia did not smile. "As I said, there is little enough time and certainly no other choice. Let us make the best of it that we can."

Jason frowned at her serious tone. "But what if I were the one with a heavy cough and you the more able-bodied?" he asked. "Would you still seek me out? If somehow we return, what then of your closeness?"

For a long while, Delia was silent. "I do not know, Jason." She sighed. "Abstract conjectures no longer matter. We are here, and the time is now."

Jason pulled Delia tighter, and she kissed him on the cheek. He ran his hand down the length of her arm and felt his pulse quicken. But what she had said also began to gnaw at the back of his mind. Like a grain of sand in the corner of his eye, the words detracted from the anticipated pleasure. He thought of Augusta and the way she had looked when he decided to leave. He remembered the contrast of Delia's coldness when he tested her intent in Farnel's hut.

"It is because you have a need, isn't it?" Jason stiffened and pushed Delia away. "On the cliffs of Morgana, beneath Drandor's tent, speaking the charms for Farnel. In each case, you gave because of a necessity. An even exchange, one favor for another. And when we soared through sweet air, you were sufficient unto yourself. It is only when you desire a windshield against the cold or the cradle of an arm at the last that you come slithering back. Farnel, Gerilac, Burdon, whoever's comforting presence, it would not matter as long as you get what you want."

"Your pleasure will be as great." Delia's tone hardened. "I do not take that for which I cannot provide adequate compensation."

"Nor do you give without expecting payment in return," Jason snapped. "You are a woman with many skills, Delia. I am attracted to you in a way I cannot explain. But my thoughts were not of grateful favors when we raced down the cliffside in Morgana or struggled into the cages above the Arcadian plain." He placed his finger under her chin, raising her face to his. "You might try an unfettered gift once. There is more than one way to interact with another."

"That is easy enough for you to say." Delia pushed his hand aside, her eyes flashing. "You did not have your innocence ripped away by dirty-handed traders only too eager to offer so-called advice in the token exchanges. You were not the slave of foul-breathed ruffians who delighted in making you a gaudy display. I have done my share of giving and learned quite well what is the result."

"And have I been like the others?" Jason asked. "When we huddled for warmth, were my dirty hands misplaced?"

Delia turned away from his stare. She caught her breath and twisted the iron bracelet around her wrist. Jason waited, breathing rapidly despite the tainted air.

"No, they were not," she whispered. "From the first, you have acted as would a hero from the sagas, just as I visualized in the dreams I have long since thrust aside."

She glanced up at him and then darted her sight away. "You state that I deliberately stayed apart. Indeed I did, Jason, indeed, I did. But not because of what you think. It has been so long, yet I am still afraid. You are soft and tender. I felt the walls I had so carefully erected melt away. But I cannot be so foolish. Even at the end. What if you turned out to be no better than the rest?"

Jason's anger melted. Beneath the exterior barrier, there was feeling for him after all. He reached out but halted before he touched her arm. "I thought that no one's anguish was greater than my own," he said softly.

Delia took his outstretched hand and pressed it to her cheek. "Your insight pierces more than the interior of lifeless puzzles," she gave him a small smile. "You are right, Jason, I have used you as I have many others, and even now I came to use you still."

She placed her finger across Jason's lips. "No, say no more. There is too little time left to be so ill met. I wish to try again. But first, I must think of a gift, a gift freely given without any obligations attached."

Delia dropped her hand. The passion ebbed away. Jason took a deep breath and then joined her in a chorus of coughs. The air had a distinctively metallic taste, with hints of sulfur, like the breath of the djinn that had transported them here between the realms. He tried to think of something more to say, but the words would not come. In silence, they stood to face each other, with the foul wind whistling between them and tugging at their clothes.

After a few moments more, Jason felt a tap on his shoulder. He whirled to see Ponzar and two others standing in a row.

"Yes," Jason snapped. "What do you want? If it is our bones, you have come too soon. We are not ready yet to give ourselves up."

"It is the matter of Utothaz's final peace." Ponzar ignored the tone. "It seems that the removal of the ribs gives him some pain. And at the convergence, you had mentioned a Foam of Wellbeing."

"That law is not operative here," Jason confessed. "I would produce only a minor explosion as before."

"But if there were an unlocking, and you attempted the formula within the confines of Utothaz's palms."

Jason frowned and then nodded in understanding. "With the laws uncoupled, it might be a least contradiction. We are far away from any other lithon so the effects of the others will be quite small. It might work at that." He glanced at Delia, then eyed his coin changer and tugged the brandel around his neck. "And I might just as well while away the time with one puzzle as with the next. Yes, lead on. I will run through the formula once again."

Ponzar and the others turned and headed toward the pit with the tablestone. Jason started to follow, then hesitated and looked back at Delia. She held her head downward, avoiding his glance. "Get out of the wind," he said. "I will work on a seal when I am done with the alchemy."

5

The Metamagican's Key

JASON EYED the navigator lying on the tablestone and tried to hide his revulsion. Both of the skyskirr's legs dangled over the edge of the rock like limp rags. The hands were folded across the stomach in a tangle of pliant fingers. The chest spread over the stone far wider than natural proportions should allow. Beneath the skin, Jason could see the weak throb of the heart. Crowded behind the navigator was the entire population of Ponzar's lithon. Manipulants, weavers, smiths, and scribes all waited respectfully to see Utothaz's last.

"How can he work the pyramid to perform the decoupling?" Jason asked.

"A manipulant will assist," Ponzar said. "Signal when you are ready."

Jason checked off the materials at his feet. Ponzar had produced a larger flask of vinegar than before. The captain had even rummaged and found a purer sack of soda. Jason fingered the sharp piece of charcoal for writing the formula and brushed his knuckles over a finely tanned hide on which to make the symbols.

This time, random scribbles would not do, he thought. But luckily, the tale of the novice's first day had the real formula transcribed in his library scroll. Normally, alchemists guard their formulas with fierceness, but occasionally some leaked out. The one for a novice's traditional first day was short and simple. It had a success rate greater than ninety-nine times out of a hundred so that a beginner's confidence would be boosted. And the mild painkiller that resulted was harmless enough not to be of great value.

Jason ran through the symbology one more time just to make sure that it was all still fresh in his mind. "Ready," he called to Ponzar. "When he has performed the decoupling, I will scribe the formula and then add the ingredients together."

Ponzar nodded to Utothaz, and, like one telling his last wishes on his deathbed, the metamagician chittered instructions to the manipulant at his side. The fleshy fingers were pressed against the pyramid, and the faces' colors were changed. All eyes turned to Jason, expecting the flourish of the formula.

"The alchemy," Ponzar spoke in his ear. "You must hurry. Utothaz must also unlock for the succession testing, and there is very little time."

Jason coughed and wrinkled his nose. The smell was tangibly worse, like the spray of a skunk that was caustic as well. This time, he wrote each of the symbols carefully on the fresh leather rather than dashed nonsense. Then he added the two ingredients together into a bottle and, for safety flung it again into the air. He did so gently so that it would not escape the lithon's pull and that waiting skyskirr could catch it when it returned.

The bottle sailed upward, reached its apex and started to descend. But before it had fallen a skyskirr's body length, it exploded in a shower of glass, the same as the one before.

"It might not have succeeded anyhow," Jason said before Ponzar could speak. "Perhaps some other contradiction forced it away."

The captain closed his eyes and did not respond. After a moment, he stood to full height in the wind and pounded the handle of his shovel for attention. He pointed at Utothaz, still managing to labor on the table, and motioned all the skyskirr who were not manipulants to form into a line.

"We will use the unlocking instead for the test." Ponzar turned to Jason and explained. "It is unfortunate that the last breaths of the navigator will not be without some pain." He paused and then spoke in a whisper that Jason could barely hear. "And I think it is best that you try for possession of the key as well."

Jason puzzled at Ponzar's words, then he understood why. The captain was giving him a hint on how to increase his value, now that the alchemy had failed. He pulled himself along the safety rope to the rear of the line. From the way the queue snaked around the uneven surface of the lithosoar, he had an unobstructed view of the tablestone. The procedure was simple enough. The first in line swung down into the pit and listened to Utothaz's hoarse commands. Starting with brown carngorm on predetermined marks, the skyskirr moved the stones over calibrated trajectories chiseled into the rock and then he was done. For each one who tried, the sequence was different. Some traced out hyperbolas, and others looped the stones in ellipses or circles about a common focus. But all were able to do as directed. Ponzar indicated success by dipping his shovel after each had completed his task.

Finally, Jason's turn came. He listened while Utothaz wheezed his instructions and then waited for Ponzar to translate what had been said.

"Blue chrysocolla," the captain explained. "Two stones motionless a hand span apart. Move them together on a straight line. Accelerate their motion as they draw closer and collide."

Jason climbed down into the pit and reached into the scatter of stones. He coughed once and then shook with a spasm that made his eyes water and blurred his vision. With a feeling of sudden doubt, he closed his fingers around the nearest stone.

"No, not serpentine — chrysocolla," Ponzar said. "Two stones of the same type with a force that is to attract."

Jason squinted at his hand. Somehow, he had picked up the wrong rock. Staring at the tablestone, he closed on the proper targets and then studied the carved inscriptions to see where they should be placed. A forest of crosses, squares, and tangled lines swarmed before his eyes. What had been so obvious standing on the edge of the pit was now a hopeless confusion. He stabbed blindly with his left hand and felt the stone on contact slip from his cramped grip like a sardine fresh from the sea.

One of Utothaz's manipulants slipped past Jason and moved the stones in the manner prescribed. The last of the tests had been completed. The old one performed a relocking. The laws once more were in effect. They all had succeeded in the simple exercise. All except Jason. The simple magics of Melibar's realm were beyond his ability to master.

Ponzar extended his right hand with the index finger pointing at Jason, thumb skyward and middle finger to the side. Jason whirled to look at the rest. They were all doing the same.

"By the grace of the great right hand, homage to the new navigator," Ponzar said. "Homage to the new navigator, or as he would say in his own tongue, homage to the metamagician, master of all the laws."

"What do you mean?" Jason asked. "I failed. Of all of these, I was the only one who could not pass the simple test. If I cannot master the basic principles, what hope do I have of controlling the metalaws as well?"

"You are not Melibar's manipulant." Ponzar rose and pounded his shovel on the ground. "He would never have sent a possible rival if he knew of that one's power. There is an instinctive distrust that grows as awareness unfolds. No, faraway one, the test has confirmed it. There can be no doubt. You are a metamagician. May the great right hand make you strong."

"Two metalaws," Jason protested. Two metalaws is all I know."

"There is only one more," Ponzar said. "The Verity of Exclusion is the third."

"As Melibar had mentioned, there is a third." Jason nodded. "After the battle in Plowblade Pass."

"Exactly so," Ponzar agreed. "The Verity of Exclusion, or, as the skyskirr say, 'if skill with the key, then none with the stone.' You can be a mover of the stones or the one who uncouples, but not both. The great right hand does not permit such talent to reside all in one."

Jason gasped as the words hit him. The implication was staggering if it were true. He closed his eyes and wrapped his hands around his chest. That would explain why he had been unable to perform the most simple of alchemies. It was not a rare failure after all.

His thoughts began to roar. That also explained why he could not use the magic sword. It was not because he was unworthy. He could not use it at all regardless of his merit!

And the failure to cast the enchantment in the presentation hall on Morgana. It was not because he was overwhelmed with anxiety. He could not, regardless of how calm he might have felt.

The final realization tore through him with the stunning impact of a charging bull. Thaumaturgy! His trial to be an apprentice when he was ten. It was not a failure to be ashamed of. He could not have succeeded no matter what. He grabbed at the brandel around his neck. For fifteen years, he had worn a badge of guilt, a burden that need not have been born.

And, and rubbing the coin for reassurance whenever he was stressed was the wrong thing to do. At some deep level, it reminded him of the failure, for having to stand helpless and endure the cruel laughter with no place to turn and hide.

Jason reached out and grabbed Ponzar's arm. "I want to believe, Ponzar, most certainly I do. It would explain so much." He stopped and frowned. "But this is unbelievable — like a poorly written fancy, the unlikely hero with unique capabilities he never suspected rising to the occasion and saving the world."

"It is nothing unique and unlikely," Ponzar twirled his shovel. "There are fewer navigators than manipulants, it is true. But there is always one or more on every lithon, ready to assume his duties when his predecessor falters. In your realm, there may be even more, I do not know.

"Many skyskirr are unable even to perform manipulations within the laws," Ponzar continued, "but those also with the proper temperament have a desire to always study and ponder before deciding what to do — those are the ones who navigator. Our laws are simple here, but with even the smallest error in calculation or in planning, a disaster could result."

"You say that there are only three metalaws, and now I know them all," Jason said. The constraint of seven I understand and the manipulation of least contradictions as well. But for the uncoupling?" He shrugged. "I know nothing of the working of Melibar's cube or even Utothaz's pyramid."

"Those are only crutches," Ponzar replied. "The key to bring forth the powers the navigators possess inside. They are bound to the gradual awakenings, the growing understanding of the working of the laws. For each navigator, it is different, something unique to his own being, something that resonates with what molded him into the power that he is to be."

"I have no such device," Jason protested. "The only thing remotely resembling it would be this old coin changer I carry and the puzzle that …

The thoughts still were coming clear and fast. "Benedict's puzzle. Twenty-five coins," he mumbled. "The trick is to insert them in such a way that each column ends up with only one type. I have done the best I can but have yet to come up with the solution. There is no way with twenty-five already in the chambers to set the initial state properly before I make any discharge. I would need something else, another from the outside. A twenty-sixth to have it right."

Jason's eyes blinked as it all rushed together in a flash. With trembling fingers, he removed the leather thong from around his neck and untied the knot. Slowly, he slid the worn brandel from the loop. Holding his breath, he inserted it into the changer.

The coin tinkled into the innards. "Dranbots," Jason announced as he fingered the leftmost column. He pressed the lever and five identical coins then glittered in his palm. "Galleons," he continued with more excitement as he pushed the next. "Regals, coppers, and finally gold brandels, the last of all."

Jason pushed the final lever, holding his lips in a tight line. He felt the strain of a stretched rope and then a sudden snap as the realm started to drift. Ponzar and the others resumed their reverent bows. It was true. Jason had no doubt. He had unlocked the laws.

No one spoke. Jason felt dazed from the staggering immensity of what he had learned. *He* was a metamagician, master of the three metalaws. At first, he had thought he was pursuing a sixth magic, but now he understood that that concept was wrong. Although only seven could have power at one time, there were a countless number of magics, each governed by its own laws. Metamagic was something entirely different, with three metalaws of its own. And the metamagician was able to deactivate the underlying principles of an entire realm and replace them with others at his command.

Without thinking, Jason reached back to the tablestone and fiddled with the small rocks so that the laws would re-engage. One of the manipulants scrambled forward and, with a slight bow, pushed aside his hand.

Jason frowned and then laughed. "Of course, I cannot perform the craft. It will take some getting used to. Um, black sphalerite, moving in a single line. Bring them to touching with increasing speed."

The manipulant looked back at Ponzar and heard the translation. Soon the laws were reestablished and relocked. Jason sagged to the table, the intense wash of emotion robbing the strength in his legs.

'The manipulants?" he asked Ponzar. "You told me before that they must be attuned to the metamagician's power as well."

"As it is to be," Ponzar said. "The one who rushed forward has felt the urge more so than the rest. Perhaps because of our differences, he may be unique." For a moment, Ponzar watched Utothaz, still wheezing on the table, and then the speck now more apparent in the sky. "But how many you have does not matter. The transition has been accomplished. Utothaz may give his last in peace. I have done my duty as a captain. The great right hand will be pleased."

Ponzar turned to go, but Jason grabbed him by the shoulder and held him back. "Wait, I feel that there is still more. How does one select the manipulants? How do I know when we are well met?"

"Their dexterity is enhanced by a navigator's nearness. Like you, they have inherent skill. But close to your side, they are able to act far better than they could alone. The stronger the navigator, the more powerful are those who serve with him as well."

Jason's face brightened. "Not only the pushing of the stones, but any craft."

"Any of the laws. Why do you ask?"

Jason did not reply. He turned and scampered as fast as he could along the safety rope toward the entrance to the caverns.

"Delia," he called. "Delia! I know why you were able to receive so much aid from the rock bubbler and to say the glamours for Farnel with such little drill. At the very least, you are a sorcerer and a wizard. It is you who will find the pathway home."

6

A Gift Freely Given

JASON HELD his hands to his sides. He willed himself to take short swallows of air through his nose, but it did not help. The metallic smell was pervasive. The sulfur made him want to gag. Any deep draw burned his lungs. His eyes watered as if filled with salt, and he felt a tingling in his hands and feet. Delia nurtured the flame to life for the dozenth time, and he knew that she would not last much longer. Her hands trembled as she manipulated the spark. Jason wanted to grab the flint from her grasp, but restrained himself, because he knew it would do no good. Delia had to summon whatever devil she could. At best, he could only be near and watch.

He eyed the stairway leading outside to the reddish sky, now visibly dirty and gray. A fine ash swirled in the air, leaving a dark powder everywhere. He could hear the deep-throated hacks of a dozen of the skyskirr, even though they were less affected than Delia and him. Two more had already submitted themselves for the feasting of the others. Jason had noticed a ruddy glow in the cheeks of those that remained. Despite the foul air, their stomachs were distended from the offerings of their comrades. Occasionally, they would look into Delia's chamber and smile encouragement, assuming that, even near the end, their new navigator was trying to save them.

Delia coughed again, and her outrushing breath blew out the beginnings of a flame. She looked up at Jason with the helpless eyes of a sick child, but he managed a smile to encourage her to try again.

"Even if I start a blaze, it will be the smallest of imps," she rasped. "Without any powders, there is no way to summon a djinn."

"Relax and let whatever augmentation I bring mix with your own power," Jason said. "And if you are truly enhanced, a small devil might be enough to carry at least you back. And in benign air, you can conjure what is necessary to come after me.

"You are doing the best you can. The way you laid out the sticks in a row and had the flints ground to uniform size are things I would not have thought of. You are indeed a worthy manipulant."

A small smile tugged at the edges of Delia's mouth. She pulled her stringy hair out of the way and bent low to try again with the flame. Jason moved to cut out what flow of wind he could but then tensed as he felt something begin to stir inside. Since he had finally understood the metamagic and the changer had worked correctly for the first time, his sensitivity had increased.

"Another unlocking," he muttered. "And somehow I feel that I must withstand this one." He grasped the changer with both hands and jammed his fingers under the levers to prevent their accidental release. But the strain built faster than he could resist. The laws uncoupled, and almost at once, there was a distant flash of light.

Jason stood and peered outside. To the left, perpendicular to their direction of travel, another flash darkened the red to crimson and then there was a third. A sudden increase in pressure stabbed at his ears. The lithosoar shook and bobbed like a pebble churned by a wave.

A second pulse followed and then the last, each one more violent than the one before. And with the final wave of pressure, although it made no sense, the wind seemed to shift direction. Jason scrambled outside, looking around to reestablish his bearings. The lithon to which they were rushing was still directly ahead. They were close enough now that it was more than a mere dot in the sky. On a visible disk of blacks and browns, he could see dense clouds of smoke spewing forth to form a dirty halo around the orb.

He watched until he was sure. They were still flying to their fatal encounter. Nothing had changed their momentum, and yet the wind came from another direction. A swirl of debris caught his eye where he was sure there had been none before. It slammed into the lithosoar a little above his head, ricocheting off and then continuing on in the breeze. A circular eddy whipped past, and then another that tossed their boulder back and forth in a gut-wrenching jolt.

Ponzar appeared over the horizon, pulling on the safety rope and motioning Jason to come to the tablestone.

"The laws have been changed again. I have felt it," Jason said as they met. He had to shout as the wind tore at his clothing and whistled around the rock.

"It is Melibar returning," Ponzar replied. "The signal mirrors tell of it. Control of one 'hedron is not enough. His manipulants work some new art that whips the air into swirls. He plans to let none of the lithons soar as they choose until they have submitted to his will — until every navigator has broken his key and can manipulate the laws no more."

Ponzar started to continue but gagged on the flux of foul air. He sank to one knee and let his shovel clatter on the hard ground. The stifling breeze pushed against the blade. In an instant, it was sailing away.

Another flash and shock wave shook the boulder. Jason felt his feet leave the ground. He reached out and snagged the safety rope in the crook of his elbow, just as he flew past. He twisted around to grip the line with his other hand and hauled himself back onto the surface. Ponzar wrapped his legs around one of the stanchions and sagged. He made the sign of the right hand and slumped to the surface of the rock.

"Follow the other metamagicians," he croaked. "As you gather strength, you will feel their presence more. Acting together, you might have a chance to stop Melibar as he tries to twist things farther away from the proper laws."

Jason glanced up into the air. Turbulent winds ripped at the bubbling brown gasses from the other lithon. In great gouts of dirty cotton, the fumes exploded across the intervening distance, filling the sky.

"But the chance may be better back in my own realm," he shouted over the roaring wind. "There, wizardry and alchemy might provide some weapon better than attracting stones. I must help Delia conjure her passage back, to get to the archimage as we originally intended." He gagged and spat bitterness from his mouth, trying to shake the taste from his tongue.

"No, no, your duty is here." Ponzar shook his head. "You are the navigator, and must act for the skyskirr."

Jason tore himself free and pushed against the wind, back in the direction of Delia's cavern. His vision began to swim and his knees felt rubbery. He wanted to breathe deeply, but held his chest tight, hoping to reach the pocket before his senses slid away.

The roar of the air increased to a blistering intensity. The cold stung his lips. His knuckles turned white from their grip upon the rope. Hand over hand, in one strength-draining tug after another, Jason pulled toward the opening that loomed just ahead. Deep browns enveloped him and made it hard to see more than a few feet in front of his face.

He shut his eyes to keep out the sting. From memory, he crawled the last few paces. With a gasp, he tumbled into the entrance and squinted to see how Delia fared. She was curled in a tight ball in the far corner of the cavern. Her skin was pale and her breath came in short pants. He touched the coldness of her flesh and recoiled from the clammy feel. She smiled weakly and, with jerky movements, pointed across the chamber.

A dance of light in the brown cloud that flowed in after him sputtered in the last embers of a flame. A small, squeaky voice sounded somewhere above the roar.

"Better make it snappy, bub. I can only manage one, and my master said that it was to be you."

"No, you are to transport Delia," Jason choked.

"In another minute, it will be nobody at all," the imp squeaked. "I am not sure I can manage one of your size as it is, and that excuse for a flame doesn't give me much room to maneuver."

"Navigator, your duty," Ponzar called from outside. "You will serve the skyskirr, even if I must carry you to the table myself."

Jason looked at the darkening sky and back at Delia's crumpled form. Ponzar entered the cavern with a drawn sword. "Delia and quickly," he commanded the imp.

"No, I said it is to be Jason," Delia managed to say.

"I shall follow my master's orders, bub," the demon said. "There is no other way. A gift, she said. A gift unfettered, with no obligation to repay. One free passage to the archimage in the domain of men. Now give me a finger and cut the chatter. It's going to be a tight squeeze."

7

The Archimage

THE PASSAGE through the flames was a chaos that Jason could not understand. When the demon left him, he struggled to pull his senses back into focus on patterns that his mind could comprehend. In the distance, the morning-blue sky had the pink of hope on the horizon. To his right stood rows of tents behind emblazoned standards. On the left, squads of armored men were converging into formations. Directly in front, about a dozen startled men-at-arms scrambled to their feet as he emerged from their breakfast fire. He had arrived in the camp of the archimage on a day of battle.

"Take me to the archimage, and quickly," Jason commanded. "He must send a large djinn to the place whence I came." His heart raced with urgency. There was so little time.

"It looks human enough," the sergeant said to his men after a moment of shock. "And the little imp with him has already disappeared. Surround him with care. If he resists, we will see if he is full of blood or green ichor."

"The archimage," Jason growled. "There is no time for petty debate. What I have to tell him of Melibar will be well worth his time."

Jason felt a sudden prick of pain at the nape of his neck. The drawn blades closed in from all sides.

"Yes, the archimage it will be," the sergeant said. "He has a standing order to report anything out of the ordinary, even if it occurs just before the rebels attack."

One of the men brought forth hinged bracelets of iron with a short chain in between. Jason tensed, but then he emptied his lungs. "Anything to speed the process," he thrust out his arms. "Travel behind the flame is but the least of what I have to tell."

In the middle of a cluster of six, Jason was hurried across the campground toward the group of silken tents with high pennons snapping in the morning breeze. He darted his eyes to either side as they trotted along. To his left, expanding almost as far as he could see, men-at-arms were dousing the last of their morning fires, slipping on their byrnies, and adjusting swords at their sides. Sergeants barked orders. Horse-borne pages waving standards called for where each group was to position itself in line. The faces of the men were grim. Tight-lipped, they did not engage in easy banter. When the eyes of their comrades were not watching, they cast furtive glances toward the hill to the north.

The foreground of the rising landscape was empty. Cracked branches and trampled greenery indicated where the army must have marched the day before. Farther up the slopes was a motley of colors and glints of flashing metal that ran to the summit and stretched far to either side. It was the rebel army, packed shoulder to shoulder and marching in lockstep down the hillside almost like unthinking automatons. Jason tried to estimate the number but gave up after he counted more than a dozen rows. He squinted to see the ragged end of the line on the east. Oceanside cliffs defined the other edge.

Behind the moving wave, at the very top of the hill, were the smoldering ruins of Searoyal, — a pile of jumbled rubble — where once had stood a walled city that could be seen leagues out to sea. Among the tumbled stones flapped the shabby canvas of the metamagician's tent. The sun glinted painfully from huge cubes of metal scattered to its left. Their covers gaped open into featureless interiors like empty crates tipped on their sides. The tops of unneeded siegecraft were just visible over the crestline.

Jason glanced back at the men-at-arms. They all wore mail and carried shields of gleaming steel. Besides the standards of Arcadia were the pennants of Procolon across the great ocean and even those of the southern kingdoms mingled with the rest. Barely two rows deep, the royal forces formed up, their thin line stretching to match the length of the one that approached.

On his right, richly surcoated nobles emerged from their tents, testing the weight of their armor and slashing broadswords through the air. Squires tightened the girths on nervous horses and added the final polish to shiny helms. Behind the line of canvas, Jason could hear the pounding of the surf. He smelled the salt in the air. The royal forces were making a last stand. They had their backs to the sea.

In the center of the row, at the entrance to a modest tent beside the pavilion flying the royal colors of Arcadia, the sergeant pushed Jason's shoulder to duck and enter. Inside, along the opposite wall, had been erected a crude table of crates and planks. Along one side of the makeshift structure was a queue of pages that snaked through another opening at the rear. Seated behind the boards was a slight man in a robe of deepest crimson. His face was narrow and topped by fine yellow-brown hair. Wrinkles crept from the sides of eyes that had not known sleep for many hours. The furrows of concentration above the nose were no longer shallow with the smoothness of youth. Jason grunted as he studied the robe. Along one sleeve were the logos of all five of the crafts.

"To Standall." The seated master set down his pen and ripped the parchment from the roll. "He is to use the ticklesprites only if lord Feston's elite guards falter. We call too much upon the demon world, as it is."

The page at the head of the line took the message and disappeared through the opening. As the rest moved up, the master thought a moment and then began scribbling another note. "Melthon should continue trying the formula, for the chance that alchemy might return. He is of no help otherwise, and the attempt cannot hurt."

"Archimage Alodar," the sergeant said in reverent tones. "I realize that all of us must make the final preparations for battle, but something has transpired that I think you should know." Alodar looked up from his writing as Jason was jostled forward. "He stepped from a flame just as a demon would, although, as you can see, he is quite normal in form."

"Not wizardry as well!" Alodar muttered. "If this is a portent that it too withers away, then we truly are lost. It is the only craft left that we can use."

"It remains unaltered as long as Melibar desires to conquer not one realm but two," Jason said quickly. "He needs the means to travel between. And the laws do not just wither away. They are replaced by others. The Maxim of Perturbations instead of the Maxim of Persistence. The Rule of the Threshold rather than the Rule of Three."

Alodar's eyes narrowed. "What babble is this? Neither magician nor sorcerer anymore can ply his craft."

"In place of those arts, there are two others. By the perturbations, Melibar has brought down the walls of Searoyal. With animations, he has enslaved the rebels to his commands."

"Yes, the minds of the people are clouded. That we have learned from the few who have been captured," Alodar agreed. "All our men are on guard to avoid any inducements that pull at their sight. And we abandoned the fortress and chose to fight on the plain, rather than be crushed by tumbling rock."

"With thaumaturgy and alchemy gone, Melibar will unleash even more strange forces against you," Jason said. "You should prepare for them as well. His powers come from understanding metamagic, the Postulate of Invariance, the Axiom of Least Contradiction, and the Verity of Exclusion."

Alodar's frown deepened. He rubbed his hand across his chin and pondered what Jason had just said. Then his eyes brightened. With a wave, he sent the pages away. "As good a course as any for the final preparations. Why not a gamble rather than filling chinks in a weak and tottering wall? Sergeant, release those fetters and be on your way. This man indeed might have things of value to tell us."

"Everything I will share," Jason implored as the bracelets fell away. "Everything that I have learned. But first, I need a djinn. We must send one to Melibar's domain and save Delia from the fumes."

"A djinn? For your own personal use?" Alodar shook his head. "To save the life of one, when here thousands are in peril? You saw the forces arrayed against us outside. Wizards and demons will be our only hope to even the odds. And we have conjured all that we dare. Any more and the careful balance forged almost two decades ago might no longer be secure. It will do us no good to avoid one jeopardy, only to fall prey to another."

"Everyone knows full well how you became Master of the Five Magics," Jason tried to wave the words away. "That is not the issue here."

"You should understand that the battle today is no less important than the one on the Bardinian plain," Alodar replied. "This Melibar has swept all before him. The kingdom of Arcadia has crumbled. And with the moving pictures that twist the mind, devil-borne agents have stirred up the peoples of Procolon and the southern realms. The baronies are just barely able to keep order with all the troops they have. The one I hold dearest, Aeriel, strives to coordinate a defense across the sea. The balance is a precarious one. If Melibar wins here, the world will erupt in revolution. Everything will be his."

Alodar came around the table. "If you have something to offer, then help us defeat this strange one. Save the many. After victory, we will offer aid to the few."

Outside reverberated with the sound of horns, the beat of drums, and the staccato march of men. How long had it already been? How much longer could Delia survive the fumes? He touched the changer at his waist and stared back into Alodar's unflinching eyes. It was clear the archimage's mind was set. He had a goal and would not be deterred.

"Very well." Jason sighed. "First the battle and then the djinn. As long as the one immediately follows the other. I will aid all I can." He squatted to the ground and began to speak quickly. "I was on Morgana when sorcery failed. It happened the night of the grand celebration."

"No, from the very beginning." Alodar glanced at the sand running from a glass as he reached for a pen. "Leave out no detail. The most insignificant might be important."

Jason sighed again. "My father wanted me to be a thaumaturge," he said. "He gave me his last gold brandel for the testing fee."

"AND SO mobilizing all of the alchemists to manufacture sweetbalm in preparation for battle was to our determent." Alodar paced around the confines of the tent like a caged wyvern, his hands behind his back. "They had to stop their normal productions to convert their facilities, and in the lull, when no formulas were being written, this skyskirr changed the law. What you say is hard to accept, Jason, even if it does explain what has come to pass better than the tale of any other."

"Exactly so." Jason nodded. He wanted to rattle off everything at once, but the archimage would not be rushed. He had asked questions about all aspects of Jason's quest, and with each answer, Alodar had grown more introspective, concerned with something else besides the working of the metalaws.

"These unlockings. You say that I cannot perform them." Alodar rubbed his sleeve with the logos. "The power has been awakened in you and no other of our kind."

"As it would appear," Jason agreed. "The Verity of Exclusion prevents a practitioner of the arts from doing so."

Alodar nodded. "Then what do you propose?"

"Well, I would —" Jason sucked in his breath in surprise. "*You* are the archimage. Why do you ask *me* what to do?"

"You state that my crafts are of no use," Alodar persisted. "What is it that you propose?"

Jason closed his eyes and wrapped his arms around his chest. He thought for a long while, but in the end, reached the same conclusion that he had before. He was still the one who had to confront the cold one. The feeling of relief that he felt when the archimage was mentioned in Drandor's tent melted away. But at least, this time, there was something that he *could* do.

"I would—I would have to challenge Melibar with manipulants of my own," he said at last. "I see no other way."

He took a deep breath. "I would bring about an unlocking. Direct the enactment of rituals, incantations, and formulas that are our own. Have the laws move in a direction that favors our cause rather than his. And then, perhaps with the cold one unfamiliar with what our crafts can do, his power would be small. Men-at-arms could secure his capture."

"Can you really do this?" Alodar asked.

"I am not sure," Jason said softly.

Alodar resumed his pacing. He stopped at the desk and fingered a magic ring that was now stone-cold. Finally, he turned back to Jason.

"I must," the archimage concluded. "We have too few choices left. I have decided to give you command of the alchemists, magicians, sorcerers and thaumaturges who are here. Only the wizards must be withheld for more critical tasks."

"But, but —"

Alodar did not wait for Jason to continue. He went to the flap at the rear of the tent and ducked outside. Jason hesitated and then hastened after. They jogged to a shallow depression nearby that was packed with men, more than one hundred robes crammed together with the implements of their non-functioning crafts. Near the far lip, a single squad of men-at-arms snapped to attention as they saw the archimage approach.

"You have all trusted my judgement in the past," Alodar orated. "And there is little time to explain my decision now." He waved his arm back towards Jason. "Accept this one as your leader. Follow his commands as you would mine. He may send you into danger, but surely that is to be preferred to waiting for rebel blades to come slashing into your midst."

Before Jason could decide what he should now do, a great shout echoed from the plain. Trumpets blared an opening charge. "The archimage! Where is the archimage?" voices shouted. "Up on the hill behind their lines among the metal boxes! He must come and see. A circle of flame!"

Alodar did not wait for any reaction from the masters. He bolted away and headed for the battle line. Jason felt all the eyes now boring into him, waiting for what he would say, what his first command would be. He had hoped that, since he now understood the root of his panic attacks, he would not have any more. Apparently, that was not the case. Getting rid of them would take more work at some other time — if there were another time. He was facing a crowd, a large one, and all were masters of their crafts. The racing heart, the shortness of breath, the dizziness and nausea began again.

8

Counterattack

JASON STRUGGLED to keep thinking clearly. When the archimage had asked what he proposed, he had thought it through. Melibar had had only six manipulates under Drandor's tent. Six or seven masters might be enough, to tip the laws back to the way they were before — no need for over a hundred watching him, judging him, laughing at him when he could not do what was expected.

He waited for the verbal onslaught to begin, but there were no catcalls or cries of derision, just the anxious shuffle of many feet. Jason managed to take a deep breath. Get them all occupied with executing the plan, he thought, something to turn their attentions away from me.

"You with the flasks and powders," he said at last. "And over there, the sad-faced ones mumbling in the mirrors." He spread out his arms. "There is not time to worry about resonances. The archimage commands. All of you follow me. We will get as close to the fighting line as we can."

Jason ran out of the depression, not looking back to see if any would comply. But soon he heard the swish of robes and the clank of paraphernalia as he sprinted across the marshy ground around Alodar's tent. The word of the archimage carried enough authority that they followed even one such as him without hesitation.

As he cleared the pavilions, Alodar was not to be seen. Instead, up the gentle slope, the two angry lines closed on each other and the battle began. The grate of steel shrieked from a thousand collisions. Like a pair of mating snakes, the two armies writhed across the tilted plain. The men-at-arms with thick shields and shining mail slashed their swords right and left, cutting through leather and hacking off the blades of scythes. But onward the rebels came. Mindless of the hurt, unflinching under the rain of blows, they whirled their flails and stabbed with their poles, borne forward by their comrades who pressed from behind. In two or three places, the royal line thinned, and in one, a salient broke through to circle from the rear.

Above the combatants' heads, the sky crackled and sparked. Pungent smells filled the air. Glowing sprites and tiny imps streaked down on bare heads, ripping away tufts of hair in their talons or dropping trails of itching powders in their turbulent wakes. Fox-sized devils sprayed their repulsive odors and radiated the feeling of unquenchable thirst and will-sapping pain.

Towering over them all, larger demons roared in aerial combat against their brothers, commanded by Melibar's manipulant-wizard. Veinous wings of turgid green beat for altitude, trying to elude glowing globules of sputtering sparks that blackened on touch and sizzled away the pulpy flesh. From gnarled fingers shot bolts of piercing reds and violet that ripped the air into a hot incandescence.

In the rubble of the hillside, the circle of flame that had brought the page running to Alodar shown with an intensity that was difficult to watch. Next to the tent, a huge djinn, far larger than the one that had carried Jason and Delia away, was twisting his body into an arch twice the height of a man, his cloven hooves and fingertips barely touching the ground. All along his scaly legs, his humped back with the furled wings, his forehead, and upper arms, they all danced an angry red flame that shot high into the morning sky. Framed in the arch was the cloaked form of Melibar, the navigator, Melibar, the cold one, Melibar the metamagician; about his head a blur of fluttering imps.

As Jason bounded over the terrain, the royal flank farthest from the sea crumpled and dissolved like a clod of dirt in a storm. A group of bondsmen swung with blades rather than with scythe and flail, trading the thrusts of the men-at-arms blow for blow, battering forward like rutting stags in spring. Because of their superior number, they had forced the corner back.

Most of the rebels' swords appeared to be made of wood. Only about one in ten was true steel. But all the weapons, metal or not, were clanging off the soldiers' shields as if they were of the finest temper. One slipped underneath a dropping guard and crashed against links of mail, popping ringlets and spewing blood.

"I would call the law something like 'same shape, same function'", Jason shouted over his shoulder. "No doubt Melibar's replacement for thaumaturgy provides his followers with more than harvest tools." He glanced at another spot where the freetoilers had broken through. Women and children behind the fighters lofted blobs of a purple tar onto the backs of the men-at-arms. Everywhere they touched, the metal glowed red. Drops of molten iron sputtered to the ground. Burning sizzles mixed with howls of pain.

"A new alchemy," Jason said as he signaled for a halt some twenty yards behind the struggling fighters. "Perhaps 'the base drives away the good.' No matter. We are close enough to try. Alchemists, concoct foul smelling odors, foul enough that even imps will find them repulsive. Thaumaturges, enclose the gasses in fragile shells and propel them to the swarm of imps hovering above Melibar's manipulants. We want the small devils to scatter so that his minions will feel more of the heat and collapse into sleep. Work more of your magics than they. You others, assist as best you can."

While the masters exercised their skills, Jason emptied the coins from the changer into his palm. He sorted through the collection and reinserted them in the slit in the top. He held his breath as he fingered his old worn brandel last and it slipped away. Working the five levers one by one, he emptied the sorted coins back into his hand.

Jason felt the tension of the parting rope and imagined the creak of the fibers as they strained to breaking. For a moment, the line groaned and twisted, but then, suddenly, it was again slack.

Jason frowned as he reloaded the changer. There was resistance. As Ponzar had said, metamagicians could struggle over the state of the coupling. Jason cast a hasty glance in the direction of the hilltop. It was too far to see more than the skyskirr's outline, but he felt his presence nonetheless.

Jason grasped the changer. He tried to visualize the rope again growing taut. Mentally, he tugged on the line, straining against a force he could not quite comprehend. He placed his feet wide apart and arched his back, swinging both fists to the side. Then he tried to bring himself erect, imagining the rope tied to his collar and tugging him from behind. His muscles tensed and then trembled from the effort. With eyes closed, oblivious to the noise and swirl of battle, he brought his arms forward and then his head. In his mind, he saw the rope spring tight and, with a snap, burst in twain.

"Look at that!" an alchemist exclaimed. "The yield is about half. The formula works, one that has failed ever since the craft went away.

"The coupling is weak; just the pollen in the air and the flowers from which they came," a thaumaturge said. "But at least the globes are arcing to the vicinity of the desired targets."

The imps above Melibar's manipulants scattered when the shells hit the ground near them and broke open. The magic making skyskirr slowed and then toppled to the ground, deep in slumber. Closer down the slope, a glob of tar solidified in midflight and bounced harmlessly from a shield. Wooden swords began sliding without effect across metal shields. A great cry of confusion went up from the pressing rebels. The men-at-arms answered with a cheer. With tired arms, they held back the attack, stopping the onrushing momentum.

Jason smiled. "Melibar has only a half-dozen manipulates," he said. "Six or seven may have been enough, but our numbers make sure." He poured the coins back into the changer and worked the levers. Inside, he felt the tension in a new rope that indicated that the laws had been relocked. The masters stopped their spell casting and began to dance. The laws of alchemy and thaumaturgy were back to where they had always been.

Jason looked up the slope. The counter-attack began to push upward. He still felt some anxiety, but perhaps, just perhaps this was not going to be so hard after all.

9

A Portal between Realms

JASON'S SAVORY of the moment cut short. He clutched his changer. He felt the hint of a tug and then a growing strain and jammed his fingers under the levers, cradling the device close to his chest. A dull pain shot through his head. He sank to his knees. Walls of force around his mind seemed to ripple and tear apart into sinuous tendons. Like stubby fingers in massive gloves, they probed his thoughts, sending numbing jabs into deep recesses of his awareness. He felt his hands twitch on the changer and then, with an involuntary spasm, his left hand fell away, trembling with fatigue. In his mind, he saw the coarse fingers surrounding him, fumbling with his own, prying them loose and pushing them aside.

Almost in helpless fascination, his other hand hurled free. A shower of coins tumbled into his lap. He felt the laws accelerate away. With a rush, they sped to the next vertex in the lattice, back to where wooden swords and obnoxious tars held power, but they did not stop there. Like a peg counting score in a game of cards, the next vertex was reached and then the one after that. The fabric of existence wrenched onward, taking the laws several more steps away.

"Catapults," someone suddenly yelled. "They are using the siegecraft. Hurling missiles on friend and foe alike."

Jason shook himself out of a daze to see stones streaking across the sky. In a heavy shower of gravel, colorful pebbles and rocks cascaded down upon the line of fighting. Like hailstones hitting a slanted roof, they bounced from upraised shields and skittered across the ground. A few careened in Jason's direction — pale green of epidote crystals, not individual rocks, but conglomerates of smaller pebbles loosely held together by a sticky glue.

Jason felt the laws relock. Instantly, he realized what would happen next. "To cover," he yelled. "Stay away from the rocks! The laws will change. The small pebbles in each cluster will suddenly repel one another."

He glanced about and dove for a small hummock that he hoped would be free and clear of the deadly rain. As he did, in a series of loud pops sounded all down the battle line, the grenades exploded into jagged shrapnel and high-velocity shot. Small missiles propelled apart from one another whistled through the air, tearing through flesh and ricocheting from metal that stood in its way. Men and maces, shields and swords, shirts of mail and leather vests, all danced along the ground, battered back and forth by the blows that struck from all sides. In an instant, the discipline of the fighting line vanished into a pool of wounded and dying men.

For a short while, the insurgents in the rearmost rows were silent when they saw the carnage in front. But they quickly realized that now only a few remained to oppose them — isolated men who staggered dazed among the bodies of their fallen comrades. With a triumphant yell, the rebels clambered over the bodies and headed for the wizards who still directed their imps with harassments from above.

Jason climbed to his feet. The battlefield was dissolving into a rout. Some of the wizards bravely stood their ground, concentrating on the demons they commanded while others kicked over their fires and bolted back toward the sea. A flurry of pages exploded from the royal pavilion. Knocking shoulders, they jostled the king and the high prince on jeweled litters, tugging against one another over which way to go.

Up the hill, the arch of fire still framed Melibar. But there were others as well. Coming out of the red background beneath the demon's span were more skyskirr with heads bowed and moving slowly toward the metal boxes.

Jason paused, but only for an instant. No time for new puzzles. The enormity of what had just happened began to sink in. His plan was not going to work. It did not matter how many manipulants he had, no matter how many times he unlocked the laws and marshalled the masters to change them to the familiar. His idea of dispersing the imps hovering over the heads of Melibar's manipulants did not matter so long as a single one remained alert. The cold one was too strong, a master of the metalaws.

On the other hand, he was a mere wordsmith. He had no skills in magic. He could never exercise the rituals. And he was too inexperienced in metamagic. He could not prevent another unlocking. Melibar could pick the time to do so at will and which laws to be then established when he did.

Jason's heart increased its pounding. He could not get enough air. Acid gurgled up into his mouth. Dots like imp light seemed to dance in front of his face. The conclusion was still inescapable. It still would have to end between him and Melibar. And despite what he now knew, it would be no better than the time he had met the cold one in Drandor's tent. He still had no idea at all what to do, how to stand up to one on his way to the control of, not one, but two entire realms.

He could not continue much longer if his feelings grew any worse, Jason realized dimly. In a moment, he would falter and fall. The presence of the masters now that they were distracted by his commands did not bother so much. It was the confrontation with Melibar that was to come that fueled his panic ever higher the closer that he came to him.

But somehow, defeat him he must. 'Move in the direction of the goal', he thought. Perhaps an answer would present itself if he just continued on the one path that had been set before him, doggedly continue, because there was nothing else to do.

"To the metamagician. He still is the key," Jason shouted. "Charge through the confusion of the rush. We must get as close to him as we can."

'If a technique works on part of a puzzle, then apply it to the whole', he thought suddenly. Distracted. The masters were distracted by his commands. Then he should command himself as well. He was in a battle and should behave as a warrior as best he could. Push away other thoughts until they really mattered.

Jason ran forward and picked up a shield from the ground. He ducked to the side to avoid the down swipe of a rebel racing past. Scrambling on hands and knees, he retrieved a sword. Just in time, he raised it upward to send steel grating down his blade to the hilt.

"Masters, rally to me," he yelled. "Men-at-arms, ready your weapons and coalesce the craftsmen into a group. Isolated, they are certain to fall."

Some of the masters hesitated. The rebels running through their midst cut two to the ground, despite widespread arms and empty palms. Most turned to run, but a few came forward, dodging blows and scrambling to Jason's side. The men-at-arms formed into a disciplined line, curving around Jason and the others. With swords drawn and shields locked, they began to move up the hill.

Ahead, the onrushing rebels dissolved into an undisciplined mob. Like angry bees, they swarmed onto the isolated remnants of the royal forces, hacking away at those who still stood and charging after the ones who ran for the sea. A few saw Jason's squad and tried to reform, but for most, their eyes were on the struggle around the royal pavilion and the glint of plundered jewels and gold. A few blows were struck in token resistance, and then the rebels backed off to attack more promising targets with smaller risks. Like a great ship sailing out of the harbor, Jason's wedge parted through the confusion of the battle and continued up the hill.

As they grew closer, Melibar's guard become alert. About twenty men in mail, all heavily armored, formed into a line to contest the advance. Behind them were two of Melibar's manipulants, staggering in drunken circles from the heat among the metal boxes, but still managing to stir pots of tar. A third chipped away at a boulder of orange-red realgar, dropping the shards into globular molds.

At the hillcrest, Melibar was accepting the unlocking keys from other skyskirr as they passed through the portal formed by the flaming djinn. With his tinkly laugh, the navigator directed them to the boxes and watched them crawl inside the massive structures twice the height of a man.

Jason commanded his wedge into the waiting warriors. With a slash of axe and blade, his squad began hacking at limbs and crashing into upraised shields. He knew he did not have the skill to swing his sword with any effect and contented himself with raising his protection right or left to ward off blows. Two assailants on either side of Jason went down, and then another on his left. As Melibar's guards surged through the opening, Jason forced himself into the gap, feeling the numbing jolt of blows against the shield as he lumbered past. He managed to duck by the slow-moving manipulants and staggered towards the ring of flame.

10

Memory's End

FLINGING ASIDE the sword and shield, Jason grasped the changer at his waist. He steeled himself for the confrontation. A magician and two alchemists managed to slip around the flanks and scrambled to his side.

Melibar slowly turned, while Jason tensed in readiness. The metamagician gestured to his manipulants, and they stopped stirring the tar. One picked up a small pipe from the ground and whistled a short tune. Immediately, the air swirled into violent funnels. The masters accompanying Jason cried out as they began to spin in a vortex, feet off the ground and arms flung wide.

Jason clutched at the changer and ground his teeth. Without someone to work the arts, he was powerless. Regardless of where he might shift the laws, it would do no good unless there was someone to exercise them when he was finished.

"So it is you." Melibar stepped back from where the djinn crackled and burned. "My misgivings were properly placed. You are more than a bungler, one who merely adds grains of sand to the joints of my grand design. Far more than the likes of a Drandor, who gave even his skull to my other manipulants."

The skyskirr laughed and waved his hands back toward the portal and then down to the plain. "Far more, and yet not enough. You were able to unlock the laws when my attention was distracted to my own 'hedron. But it was nothing to wrench control back from your grasp. And now it is almost finished."

Melibar pointed back at the portal. A cool breeze tainted with wisps of brown filtered through the opening. A high-frequency shriek bubbled from around the djinn's limbs. Its muscles twitched and trembled. Beads of dark sweat dripped onto the ground.

"A new use for the demons," Melibar said. "One that tries the strength of even a djinn. On his left side are the laws of your domain; on the right are those of mine. The shriek is their discord as they meet at the boundary in his scaly hide. But through the portal comes the refreshing breeze that allows my manipulants to shed the torpor of hibernation.

"Through it, I have received the other navigators, one by one. They tried in concert to move the laws from where I had locked them. But my sojourn here, where, except for you, there are no others, has made me strong. A mere step in the portal was enough to resist all they could try. And now, as I have commanded, they surrender their keys so their lithons might not be crashed together or stripped bare by the buffeting storms.

"I have conquered them all. And without the means to unlock, they are powerless. I can crush their bones and mix their marrow with common dust. They have no means to shield away the disgrace. All except for Utothaz. His lithon, curiously, does not respond. But even now, my manipulant is directing the window there. I will keep it open until he can step onto the rock. It cannot take long to search, and then I will have the last of the navigators' keys."

Through the opening, Jason saw Ponzar's lithon grow in size in a sea of brown. Tendrils of hazy vapor snaked through the portal. He began to gag on the smell that was growing stronger even in his own clean air. Behind him, down the slope, the rebels in the row of royal tents, pulled away the silken panels and shouted with each discovery of hidden wealth. Here and there were pockets of resistance still. A few wizards about the archimage and a company of reserves standing their ground in the surf. But the outcome was clearly decided. Melibar was marching towards them. The battle could last only a little more time, and then everything would be lost.

THE FLASHES of memory faded. Jason's thoughts jerked back to the present.

Melibar's manipulants had blown him like an autumn leaf into one of the shrinking cubes. The lid had slammed shut. The cube was magic. There was no way to escape.

11

The Final Puzzle

JASON'S THOUGHTS exploded in tatters. All parts of his mind shrieked at once. The cube rumbled and shook, pushing against his back and thrusting him into the others. And not just a cube, but a cube of magic. There was so little time before it would crush everything together. Nothing would be left, only a pulpy ooze that drained away in the end.

Think, he commanded himself through his panic. It is just a puzzle. How does one escape from a box that has no escape?

Yes, escape from the box, but escape to what? Outside, victory was within Melibar's grasp.

The walls vibrated and contracted another step. Jason's forehead beaded with sweat. He bumped into one of the alchemists and smelled his fear.

Confronting Melibar on his own terms was not the way to do it. He did not have the skill, let alone the experience. He must somehow pose the problem in a way that he could figure it out.

Methodically, he examined the events that had led to his capture — all the images that surrounded Melibar in his camp upon the crest and each previous encounter that might give a clue how to proceed. He recalled all the detail of his last images before the lid slammed shut. Melibar walking down the hill, the manipulants, and the portal touching Ponzar's lithon.

The minutes passed. Jason felt an elbow push painfully into his side. The incoherent babble of the magician rose to a deafening wail. One alchemist repeatedly pounded the walls, and the other had retreated into silence. Jason examined all the alternatives that his imagination pumped into his awareness. He reviewed his list of the simple rules that aided him to tackle the puzzles that were the most difficult:

'If a possibility does not work try another'

'Move in the direction of the goal'

'Consider the possibility that the peculiar are related'

'If a solution works on a similar puzzle, try it on the one at hand'

'When a new opportunity presents itself, try it'

'Similarities are a clue'

'Always look for a second solution'

'Divide and conquer'

'If a technique works on part of a puzzle, then apply it to the whole'

'Look for patterns. See if any of them repeat'

'Avoid traps that ensnare'

.

.

.

'Think outside of the box'

"Think outside of the box! Yes, that is it," Jason said aloud. His thoughts rushed in a new direction. Outside, outside the box. Trying to escape from the inside was futile. The box was magic. If there were a way, it would have to be from the outside. Even though it was completely dark, he closed his eyes and wrapped his arms around his chest.

IN A moment, it all came to him and fell into place, There was nothing more to think about. The chance of success was small. He did not know if it would work, but at least he had calculated it out; this time, all of it calculated out to the very end. He shook himself out of his introspection and groped in the darkness for the crying magician. He slapped the master's face sharply and grabbed his cheeks.

"Listen closely," he said. "Your only hope now is to continue to follow as I command. Remember the words of the archimage. To do otherwise is certain doom."

The magician stopped his babble and did not resist as Jason stood him up and placed him in line next to the silent alchemist. He boxed the remaining master in the ears to attract his attention, then laid a hand on the master's fist to stop the pounding.

"Now, imitate me exactly," Jason commanded, "while the cube is the proper size for what we must do."

He crouched with his back against the wall. With a yell, he sprang across the volume and crashed into the metal plate near the lid. The cube shuddered from his impact and tipped slightly on the small platform that supported its base.

"All of us together! We can do it," Jason shouted. "If we can topple the cube, then we will have a chance."

The silent alchemist grunted, and then the other two masters nodded as well. As one, the four slammed into the side of the cube and felt it tumble forward onto the ground.

"And again," Jason yelled. "Before Melibar returns. Before his manipulants deduce what we are trying to do."

The masters squirmed and pressed together, shoulder to shoulder with Jason against the wall. Again they leaped to collide with the cube, rolling it forward another quarter turn.

"To what purpose?" the magician gasped. "We only make more unbearable the conditions at the end."

"Just follow my commands," Jason snapped back.

"No, not that side. Now we have to change direction. There is a need for explanation only if we succeed."

The box shrank again, leaving barely enough room for the masters to maneuver according to Jason's orders. They collided into the wall with a jolt that spun them over three times more.

As they struggled, the cube continued its contractions.

They managed two additional rotations before it pinned their limbs in a tangle so that they could no longer spring. One of the alchemists gasped with pain as the other tried to pull free a leg twisted to the side.

"Once more," Jason shouted. "Rock back and forth where you are. I think I can hear the whine."

Jason moved one foot from where it pushed against the magician's stomach until it rested high on the rear wall. Twisting his torso so that both hands were more or less angled forward, he oscillated his hips back and forth above the masters. He felt the box rock in response to his motions as if balanced precariously over a slight irregularity in the slope. With a savage lurch that sent stabs of pain into contorted wrists, he tipped the cube over for a final time. He hoped his memory had been accurate. There would be no chance to maneuver again if he had misjudged the distance or orientation.

As the cube tumbled, the walls vibrated once more. With a shudder, the box groaned and contracted. Like children wrapped in a blanket, none of the occupants could move any longer. With a bone-jolting crash, they came to rest against hard and solid ground.

The magician again began his incoherent babble. One of the alchemists added a mournful cry. Jason slowly twisted his head, gasping for air between sandaled feet that raked across his cheek. There was no time left. Either his assumptions were correct, or the next contraction would be one of crushing pain. Almost afraid to find out, he held his breath and began to extend his foot past a fleshy resistance, searching for the smoothness of a metal wall. Finally, he made contact and pushed with what little leverage he could muster.

For a moment, nothing happened. Then, with a pop, the panel fell away, allowing everyone to tumble out. Jason collapsed onto unyielding rock, barely able to see a hand span in front of his face because of the toxic brown vapor that swirled everywhere.

"Where are we? What has happened?" one of the masters managed to cough. "By what glorious accident are we set free?"

"We are in Melibar's realm, on Ponzar's lithon," Jason said. "And it is no accident that the box no longer works. We moved the cube through the opening — to where the law that contracts it does not work. I was not sure, but it was our only chance. Here it is a mere box of metal, unable to respond to the commands of magic."

"Melibar's realm," the master gasped. "Then back through the arch and let us flee, before he returns and confines us again."

Jason hesitated. He peered through the haze, trying to spot the opening to where Delia must be lying beneath the surface of the lithon. But then, he clenched his fist and peered back at the djinn. "No," he said, more to himself than to the others. "First, it will be the tent," he commanded. "That is the pathway to the solution."

Jason did not waste any thought on how close had been his escape. He tugged at an alchemist's sleeve and whipped him through the portal. Like dazed sheep, the two other masters followed as he ran toward the flopping canvas.

When he drew close, Jason grabbed the faded panels in his free hand. With a burst of strength, he ripped them away from the poles and rigging. Running around the structure, he exposed the contents to the air, kicking the tatters of cloth aside.

"Unpack all the crates and examine what they contain," he yelled. "Make ready to use whatever you find the most familiar."

Jason glanced at a realgar boulder. Three of Melibar's manipulants lounged listlessly like arctic bears emerging from hibernation. They awaited the navigator's return. He scanned down the slope over the bodies of the fallen masters and men-at-arms. The metamagician and the remains of his retinue, about a dozen warriors, walked with majestic slowness to confront the Arcadian king.

"Duel!" Jason cupped his hand to his mouth and shouted. "Duel of the metamagicians! Let us see the extent of your power, Melibar, when evenly it is contested."

12

Duel of the Metamagicians

MELIBAR STOPPED and turned. He looked up the slope and waved his arms in annoyance. The warriors reversed their march. At a trot, they started back up the hill.

"Tambourines and knotted ropes," the magician called out to Jason from a nearby trunk in the metamagician's tent. "Not like those for any ritual I know, but somehow similar, nonetheless."

"And potions and powders," an alchemist shouted. "Condensing columns, grimoires with arcane symbols, none like any I have ever seen."

"Get them all out and look for more," Jason called over his shoulder. "But do not manipulate any until I have given the command. Wait until Melibar begins his unlocking and I appear to resist. I am betting that he will try to handle things swiftly with the realgar. He cannot ignore us while we are here. The threat is too great that I might attempt an unlocking on my own."

Jason nodded as the metamagician reached for his unlocking cube and waved his arms to signal his manipulants. The navigator's followers stirred from their rest and began to pull some of the smaller pieces of the rock in helical trajectories. Jason searched for the pile of keys that Melibar had collected from the other metamagicians when they passed through the portal to surrender, the twisted remains of his changer lying on top. He ran over to where it lay and hefted the hunk of flattened metal that could hold coins no more.

And as he did, he felt the snapping jolt of an unlocking. While Melibar's men-at-arms rushed forward with swords drawn, the metamagician's laughter carried over their heads on the stirring of a breeze. Jason grabbed the battered changer and concentrated on resisting the unlocking, but he never had a chance from the start. He felt the fury of Melibar's power knocking his feeble strength aside as if it were a leaf in the wind. The metamagician's rage, caused by his continual

319

annoyance, bubbled in Jason's mind. The laws unlocked with a burst, not gradually drifting, but vibrating with the energy of the navigator's frustration.

"Now," Jason shouted to the magician. "As many elements of ritual as you can. Better and faster than you have ever enacted them before."

The magician reacted swiftly to Jason's words. He grabbed a tambourine and flung three cuttings of rope onto its flat surface, dancing them about with a tap of his hand. Immediately Jason felt the laws pause in mid-shudder and a gentle acceleration away from a node of the lattice.

"And now the alchemy," Jason shouted. "It does not matter what, as long as there is enough."

The alchemists responded by dumping a sackful of sparkling powder into an uncorked bottle of some fuming liquid. Sparks flew from the mixture, rising into the sky.

The manipulants struggled with the realgar. They still moved sluggishly, and their precise motions were not enough. The laws were drifting in a direction different from the one Melibar had intended. But the metamagician sensed what was happening as well. He waved his arms, and his attendants quickened their pace, hurling showers of rocks towards the tent.

The laws kept drifting in the direction of the new magic and alchemy. Melibar stopped in his climb and huddled into a tight knot, the imp light above his head suddenly alive. For a moment, the drift continued uncontested, but then Melibar stood erect.

Jason felt the metamagician reassert his strength, this time attempting to relock the laws where they had just been anchored. Melibar had decided that working with the magic and alchemy he had was better than giving them up, even in the hopes of activating the realgar. Again, Jason offered resistance, grasping the changer and straining to force the fabric of existence farther from its mooring and increase the rate of drift.

But Melibar was far stronger. Jason felt the drift begin to slow and then reverse direction, heading back to the node of the lattice from which it had sprung. He sensed the laws gaining momentum, tugged by Melibar's desire to complete the locking, overwhelming any tendency to wander away.

"Now, stop the ritual and the formula," Jason commanded. "Start others that are completely different. Use more exotic wares. Quickly, before Melibar completes the relocking!"

The magician dropped the tambourine and reached deep into another crate. He brought forth a collection of silken handkerchiefs and an empty tube into which he proceeded to stuff the squares, one by one. The alchemists broke the bottle of brewing chemicals, letting its purple stain soak into the ground. They began picking apart delicately preserved spider webs and pressing each of the strands onto some sticky paper that unwound from a bulky roll nearby.

The laws lurched again, heading in a new direction unlike the one before. Melibar fidgeted with his cube, mystified by what his adversary was trying to do.

"Now again, the knots and mixing chemicals," Jason said. "Only this time, twice the activity as before."

The magician grabbed two tambourines, one in each hand. The alchemists scooped powder from the sack into a waiting row of vials. The laws spun, heading back in the direction they had been traveling, but with a speed twice what it was before.

"And again the silks and spider webs," Jason commanded. "More intensity. You must make it more."

The masters responded with precision. Like puppets with two sets of strings, they alternated between the rituals and formulas, sending the laws first one way and then the other, soaring past the original node with ever-increasing speed. And with each pass, the tug of Melibar's attempt to relock fed more energy into the system. The amplitudes of the oscillations became greater and greater. No longer in a straight line, they careened about the lattices in an unpredictable way.

Upward rushed Melibar's soldiers. Wider became the undulations. Jason felt the fabric of existence overshoot the next node of the lattice in one direction and then roar past two more as it came tearing back. He sensed Melibar exerting his maximum power to grab at the laws as they swung past, but the effort was not enough. The momentum could not be checked. With one final filling of the vials, the laws plowed through the lattice like a derailed train, past all the nodes that were recorded, into a region that Melibar had not explored before.

The imp lights winked out, one by one, from around Melibar's hood. He turned to see that the arching djinn stood on the hillcrest no more.

"What have you done?" Melibar strained his voice above the trample of the onrushing men-at-arms. "The laws, the laws, they are new and strange. Even for wizardry. No one knows what their manipulations might be."

"It is as I planned," Jason shouted back. "Now the three who serve you will have no advantage over mine. We are equal in the crafts that we can command."

Melibar was silent. With twitching spasms, he ran a hand over his cube. Impulsively, he knelt, but then immediately stood again when there was no buzz of imps. He looked at his men-at-arms closing the distance to the crest and laughed.

"Yes, equal," he said, "equal for the moment. Soon the balance of manipulants will be three to none."

Jason did not reply. He turned back to look at the perplexed masters. "Vinegar and oil of vitriol, whatever you can find. Do not bother about the alchemy. Toss everything you can."

The masters hesitated and frowned. Jason ran into their midst and pointed to two flasks at random. One of the alchemists nodded. He mixed the contents and then hurled the containers at the men-at-arms. The first shattered harmlessly off an upraised shield, but the second hit the ground and brewed a minute longer before exploding into knifelets of glass. Two men yelled in surprise and tumbled to their knees with dozens of tiny cuts oozing blood.

The alchemists waved for the magician to join them. With inspired abandon, they concocted the remaining ingredients of the tent. Some became simple missiles that clattered off blade and mail, others, deadly grenades that cut into flesh. A bottle of oil, splattered against the middle of the advancing men, with a flaming torch thrown after, sent an explosion of fire along the line. One by one, the remaining soldiers went down, until only two were left.

Jason looped behind the masters. He tightened his grip on the changer. The outcome had to be exactly right for his plan to succeed. He pawed among the tumbled crates for some more of the ingredients that had produced the smokiest reaction. Just as the warriors rushed upon the masters, he threw the chemicals into their midst.

One alchemist went down from the slash of a blade, but the other circled behind and felled the man-at-arms with a blow to the head. The smoke billowed from the mixing brew, dimming what anyone could see. Jason rushed into the opaqueness and aimed a swift kick where the soldier's groin should be. He heard a gasp of pain and then a dull thud as another of the alchemist's blows struck home.

Jason backed out of the smolder, and his masters staggered after. Surprisingly, he grabbed one by the collar of his robe and banged his head into the forehead of the other. Like sleeping skyskirr, they slumped to the ground.

Jason took another step backward and held his breath, waiting for the reaction to run its course and the fumes to clear. When they had dissipated enough for him to see Melibar down the hill, he stepped forward slowly, shoulders slumped and with a dragging step.

The metamagician did not immediately react. He stood frozen, looking at Jason up the length of the slope. Then the navigator threw back his head, and his laugh rang across the hillside, the loudest that Jason had ever heard.

"You did give me pause," the metamagician shouted. "A closer contest than I would have thought. But in the end, the result is the same. Your manipulants fall, and you have no more resources, while I still have three in this realm and three more guiding the storms in the 'hedron beyond. It will take some time to probe and find where you have spun the laws, but you are powerless to stop my search. Eventually, I will restore things to the way they were. You may as well come forward now and hand me your key as token of surrender. All you can do is wait and watch the enveloping of your fate."

Jason continued his cautious motion forward. He scanned down the hillside at the remains of the battle still in progress and saw that Melibar took no notice. The metamagician had not moved. He waited with arms crossed, chuckling with his soft laughter.

Jason walked down the slope, moving with the gait of a man going to the gallows. With each step, he tightened his grip on the changer, holding it close to his chest, not wanting to give Melibar any reason to do other than stand and wait.

"Finally, you caused a significant perturbation," Melibar said when Jason halted about a man's height away. "But it is a perturbation nonetheless. It still ends according to my plan."

"Perhaps according to mine as well," Jason replied. "You are the keystone about which all else hangs. If you are felled, I can free the other navigators from the cubes that have now stopped contracting. Together, we can navigate to laws that will aid both our causes, coerce your manipulants to our bidding, reestablish the portal, and rescue Ponzar and the others on his lithon.

"And with no demons to oppose him, the archimage can summon enough devils of his own to escape from the battlefield. Without a leader, the passion of the rebels will dissipate into brawls for plunder. There will be no message across the sea to fan other rebellions. It will take some time, but order can be restored."

"You speak like a villain from one of your sagas," Melibar hissed, "prattling his entire plan before he is thwarted. But as I have noted, there is a difference between your design and mine. I am the one who has succeeded, the one who has brought his to full fruition. I still possess manipulants. I still have a basis of power, where you have none."

"There is more to my plan," Jason answered. "It hinges on differences just as you speak. Differences between you and me. Differences besides your greater experience, your well-thought-out plot, your strength that gives you the title of first navigator.

"Your whole existence has been one of metamagic," Jason continued, "one of living each day with the three metalaws, steeped with the reality of the Postulate of Invariance, the Axiom of Least Contradiction, and the Verity of Exclusion. But for me, it was different. I did not know of their existence. I struggled instead to master the manipulations, to work the crafts for myself, rather than command the use of others."

"This prattle is of no consequence. Give me the key."

"I fully intend to. But first, think of the meaning of the difference. To you, a metamagician without his manipulants is powerless. There is nothing he can do. You would let one approach within a few feet, confident that he must meekly wait until your base of power returns."

Jason lifted the changer in his hand. "But for me, the possibilities are not the same. You are without any crafts to command. For the next few moments, there are no rebels close enough to come to your aid. Think of it, Melibar. Our duel has just begun. And I have thought outside of the box."

Melibar eyed Jason's changer and then glanced over his shoulder. He took a cautious step backward. But Jason did not hesitate. With one swift motion, he flung the heavy mass of metal at the navigator, crashing it against the skyskirr's skull with a bone-cracking snap. He watched the navigator crumple to the ground and grunted with satisfaction. As simply as that, it was over.

13

A New Beginning

"AND AS a group, the other metamagicians were able to force an unlocking, using Melibar's little cube," Jason said, "even though it was not as familiar as their own keys." Automatically, he touched his coin changer, now restored through the efforts of the magicians and metalsmiths.

The onshore breeze was refreshing. Around the assembled court was a mixture of expressions. The old king sat stone-faced, and the other nobles, clustered behind the makeshift throne, registered neither gratitude nor relief. Prince Wilmad's empty seat on the monarch's right was draped in black. The newer barons on the other side of the barn squirmed uncomfortably in their fine silks and linens. Jasonel, a new seneschal, had to keep reminding himself not to slouch. Augusta smiled as Jason spoke, and even Farnel's stern visage was without some of its customary tightness.

Jason squeezed Delia's hand where she lay on the cot at his side. He smiled as she grasped his arm closer to her cheek. Her rescue had barely been in time, but the vapors that had spilled through the portal had lessened in density around Ponzar's lithon. The sweet air that drifted back in exchange was of benefit as well. With all the skyskirr helping to rediscover wizardry and reopen the passage, they had been able to scoop her and the others away from the vapors before it was too late.

"And it is well they took the first among navigators to the 'hedron before the opening was closed a second time," the archimage interrupted before Jason could continue. "For our realm, one metamagician is quite enough."

"If Melibar was so easily defeated, why did we waste precious arms and place our very presence in peril?" the old king rumbled. "This Jason struck him down unassisted, aided by neither sword nor master."

"With Melibar in control of the laws, there was no way you could reach him by the arts," Jason said. "And the rebel army kept away the men-at-arms. Indeed, when I rushed upon him in Trocolar's dungeon, and he thought me a thief, he commanded the guards to effect my seizure. In the tent, after the battle of Plowblade Pass, he directed torpor sand my way as he would to any errant manipulant. But when he saw me as another metamagician, one who worked his will through the direction of others, it did not cross his mind that I could carry any threat without attendants. He let me approach unhindered, calling no one to give him aid."

"Perhaps it is best we end all the threats while we are about it." The king frowned at Jason through rheumy eyes. "We have seen ample evidence of what havoc can be wreaked by one with powers such as Melibar's." He turned his head in Alodar's direction. "And I think, archimage, that you will agree. Prudence dictates putting this one immediately to the sword."

Several of the nobles grunted agreement. Jason's eyes widened, but Alodar waved the comment away.

"Then who will protect us from the next?" the archimage asked. "What if another comes from some other realm by stealth and attempts to move the laws away from where they have been restored? Who do you suggest to detect the unlocking, to struggle to keep the anchoring where it is?"

The old king frowned. He stroked his chin and stared at the archimage.

"I will add him to my retinue," Alodar continued. "His major task will be to keep the laws securely bound. If he does nothing else, it will be bargain enough." He returned the king's stare. "Let me worry about what is best for those with talent in the arts. You will be busy enough rebuilding a kingdom from what is left."

"Selection of the new barons from those who fought against him was a wise first step," Farnel added. "Men who have sweated in the cages will much less likely subject others to them."

"And the vault holders of Pluton are willing to make the loans that lubricate the reestablishment of order," Augusta chimed in. "It is in peace that we prosper, not the anarchy of war."

"The masters of Morgana need the tranquility of their thoughts," Gerilac added. "Without inner peace, no glamours of greatness can be cast. The possibility of losing our crafts again is not one we wish to consider."

The king turned his eyes back to Jason. "I am told that Melibar had a taste for exploration. If this one has the same talents, how would he be any different? Why should he be content with waiting to hold the laws firm against some future attack when he could send everything drifting instead?"

Jason cut off Alodar's reply. "I can speak in my own defense," he said. "No one here knows the feeling of an unlocking more than I."

He ran his tongue over his lips, frowning as he tried to put his feelings into words. "For me, the pursuit of the metalaws was like untangling interlocking rings or removing the beads from a knotted rope. But now, that puzzle is solved. The mystery, the enticement, the allure — all are gone. Moving through the lattice only means boring repetition. I crave the familiar, not the unknown. The desires that pushed Melibar are not mine."

"Then what is your demand?" the king asked. "How many brandels a year to bribe you from unlocking the laws?"

"My basic need has been satisfied," Jason smiled. "My mind again is abuzz with ideas that I must put on the scrolls — tales of enchantments, hidden caves under the sea, rotating cages, and even rocks that sail through the air. I will be satisfied for some time to come. And after those ideas are used? Well, I have learned that it does pay to get out and about every once in a while."

"It is a wonder what saving the world will do for one's self-esteem," Alodar said wryly. "But I do not plan to let you stay idle while you walk the garden paths of my retreat. You have the insight to construct the general from the particular. Even though you cannot work any of the crafts, I expect you to aid the masters in formulating extensions of their powers. You are unique among all the practitioners of the arts, Jason. Even though you profess no longer to have a desire for fame, I suspect that it will come, nevertheless."

"It was not one realm but two," Delia said. "The skyskirr are as grateful as I am for Jason's gifts."

Gifts. The word resonated in Jason's mind. He remembered what Delia had done on the lithon. Without her, despite all his bold words, no success would have been possible. And she had done it for the benefit of him alone. In the end, saving her had meant more than anything else.

Jason turned from Delia and gazed at Augusta, just to make sure. Yes, even in that he had chosen the right solution. The vault holder of Pluton would not lack for suitors, and there was only one with whom he wanted to share his destiny.

"I expect you to teach Delia in those crafts as well," Jason said to the archimage. "She has shown talent in more than one and, close to me, her skills will prosper." He looked back at the former slave girl. "Perhaps, I presume too much, but our pasts have been too intertwined for our futures to be far apart."

Delia rubbed the pale band of skin on her wrist where the bracelet had been. "You do show some promise." She nodded. "I think I will keep you around."

Author's Afterward

MASTER OF THE FIVE MAGICS (MFM) was published in 1980 under the Ballantine/Del Rey imprint. After the final manuscript was submitted and waiting for publication, I did not start working on another novel. I felt I had achieved my goal of producing what one could call a 'hard' fantasy — definitive laws of magic with limitations and constraints.

A couple of years went by. Finally, Lester del Rey asked if I would be interested in doing a sequel.

The prospect of another book had never occurred to me. But what to do? MFM is a novel of setting. The plot and characters are standard fantasy fare. The prospect of there being a sixth, seventh, and so on magic did not appeal. I began thinking about the physical laws in our own world. Perhaps there was an inspiration there.

The pursuit of the postulates of reality

The ancient Greeks modeled the cosmos as being composed of four basic elements: earth, air, fire, and water. Everything else was combinations of these four. Centuries later experimentation had resulted in the atomic hypothesis — at a microscopic level all mater consisted of molecules, and all molecules were an assemblage of atoms. There was a distinct type of atom for each different element, although by this time the number had expanded from four to around one hundred.

In the nineteenth century, the chemist Mendeleev noticed the similarities between some of the elements and arranged them all into a periodic table, (or if you will, a lattice). One could even predict the existence of more elements with properties that filled empty slots in the table.

Then in the beginning of the twentieth century, it was discovered that the atoms of all of the elements were composed of just three 'elementary' particles: the proton, electron, and neutron. The structure of all of the atoms could be explained by just these three. The advent of quantum mechanics in the twenties even went so far as to explain why different atoms fell into the columns and rows of the periodic table that they did.

Now, in general, science in its quest to explain all of our reality is guided by reductionism — seeking the fewest possible postulates that are needed to explain everything. Having just three 'particles' as the foundation rather than approximately one hundred was very satisfying. The basis for our reality was much more simple than it had been before.

But the new model did not quite explain everything. Yes, the pion particle was discovered and seemed to fit the role of enabling what is called the strong force interaction that keeps most atomic nuclei stable despite the repulsive electrical force between the protons, but there were other discoveries as well.

"Who ordered up that?", the physicist Isaac Rabi quipped when evidence of the muon particle was discovered in cloud chamber traces from cosmic rays. And there were other revelations as well. The positron — identical to an electron but with a positive charge rather than a negative one. The neutrino, with hardly any mass at all, but apparently necessary to conserve one of nature's laws. And there were other particles given the label 'strange' because of how long they lived before decaying into more stable ones of less mass — the lambda, the three sigmas, the two xis.

By the mid twentieth century, our fundamental list of elementary particles upon which everything else was built had grown once again to be a major part of one hundred. The simple reductionism model no longer applied.

In the 1960's, Murray Gel-Mann and, independently, George Zweig, introduced the concept of quarks in three varieties: up, down, and strange. Protons, neutrons, and most of the other original elementary particles were composed of just these three. For a third time, the basis of reality was simple again.

But then, once more, you guessed it, it was discovered that there were three more types of quarks, eight (or nine, depending on how you are counting) gluons, more exotic types of neutrinos, …. As of this writing, the hadron super collider at the European Organization for Nuclear Research (CERN) is poised, among other things to search for 'super symmetry' particles that could increase the number of the latest batch of fundamental particles even more.

Will this search ever end? Is there an ultimate final core of the onion, a foundation on which everything rests? Or are there an infinite number of layers, each one the basis for the one above?

No one knows, of course, at least for our reality. But in a fantasy at least, the answer can be clear. Just like the hundred or so elements or the like number of protons and its kin, there can be many laws of magic. But underneath them all is another structure that explains everything.

OK, I thought. I can run with this idea. Have many more magics than five, and underneath them there are metalaws, a deeper explanation of reality that is the structure for everything above. And like what happened in our own reality, this structure was discovered by observations and then deductions from them. So I started writing the sequel to *Master of the Five Magics* that I tentatively entitled *Metamagic*.

Changes in the second edition

In the original, the protagonist had an ability to solve puzzles. This is why he was able, just like with our own scientific history, to use mathematical induction to discover the metalaws. For this second edition, I have made this thought process more visible. And, as part of that, made some of my favorite classic puzzles more visible as well.

Getting published

My original title for the book was *Metamagic*. But just as with MFM, Lester del Rey had other ideas. He thought, correctly, that Metamagic did not tie well as a sequel to MFM. He wanted it to be *Secret of the Sixth Magic* instead.

But that was the exact opposite of what I wanted to do, I protested. There is not just a sixth magic as one would expect in a sequel, there are hundreds of them. The title is very misleading. The book is about a deeper layer in reality, not the number of magics at all.

Just add a few lines in the book somewhere, del Rey directed, where the protagonist says something like, 'Hmmm, I wonder if there is a sixth magic operating here. ... No, that's not it ...' and continue the story as you have it.

And so I did, and SSM saw the light of day in 1984, four years after MFM.

A final note

At the time that SSM was written, I was using the word-editing program Wordstar, running on a Morrow desktop using the CPM operating system. (The operating system was so small, that each floppy contained a complete copy of it.) All communications with the publisher, however, were on paper. I would print out all that I had written, and mail my draft to del Rey. He would mark it up and then give it to a copy editor who would mark it up some more. This then would go to the typesetter, galley proofs would be generated, and a copy of the proofs mailed back to me for a final edit. I would mark up the galleys, send them back, and then the typesetter would make these final corrections.

In one of my correspondences with del Rey, I mentioned the idea that perhaps all of this would be easier if I just mailed him the four and one-half inch floppies (each holding 200 kilobytes) to him. He could put them on another computer in his office, and then his and the copyediting could be done electronically, the edited floppies sent back to me ...

Del Rey replied that the publishing industry was very conservative and it would be one of the very last to adopt the computer revolution that was gathering momentum at that time. What I suggested would probably happen but it would take a while.

We have come a very long way since 1984.

What's next?

From *Riddle of the Seven Realms*

Prologue

KESTREL LOOKED past the flame toward the cabin door and estimated his chance of escape if something were to go awry. Like the lairs of most wizards, there were no windows in any of the walls; the distractions of the outside could well be done without.

He glanced back to the center of the room at the figure standing in the chalk-drawn pentagram that surrounded the firepit. Phoebe was not reputed to be a wizard of prowess and it was no simple devil that she was trying to summon.

If only she had been as greedy as the rest! The price he asked for an entire wagonload just like the branches he waved in front of their faces was usually low enough to hurry all of their thoughts away from testing what they were to receive. Some stored it all in their larders without even bothering to examine any of the leather sacks. Usually he was well into the next kingdom before they learned that a simple woodsman had gotten the better of the bargain rather than they.

But this one chose even to doubt that the sack he brought inside contained only anvilwood and nothing else. She had insisted upon a test to see that more than just the merest of imps was contacted through the realms, once the fire was lit.

Kestrel looked around the cabin. Thick beams bridged stout walls of white plastered mud. On the left, a bed of straw with room for only one stood underneath a shelf sagging with rolls of parchment. Behind Kestrel and extending along the wall on the right were tiers of wood-framed cubbyholes rising to the high ceiling, a scrambled collection of nailed-together boxes and wide mouthed bins.

In most of the openings Kestrel could see the contents stuffed nearly to overflowing and spilling onto the wood planked floor with goat-bladder sacks, vials of deeply colored powders, dried lizard tongue, sunflower seeds, licorice, and aromatic woods; this was as well stocked a wizard's larder as Kestrel had ever seen.

Kestrel looked again at the wizard staring intently into the flame. He had sought her out because of the tales of her wealth. All the practitioners in the Brythian hills, though they thought little of her skill, admitted that she was the richest. But if not for that, his interest might have been piqued anyway. Rather than in ratted tangles, her well-groomed hair fell in a cascade of shiny black down the back of her robe. The broad and youthful face was clear and unwrinkled. It carried the open simplicity of an unspoiled peasant girl, rather than the somber broodings of one who dared to thrust her will through the fire. The sash of the robe, adorned with the logo of flame, attempted to pull tight a waist a bit thicker than the current fashion. But at the same time, it accentuated curves that would otherwise be hidden. Despite her caution, her manner had been quite warm. She did not display the disdain that vindicated in part what he did.

Kestrel ran his hand down the back of his head, feeling how well the thinning hair still covered the beginning of a bald spot. He imagined how he must have appeared to the wizard when he had knocked on her door barely an hour ago-brown curls on top, what there was of them, deep-set eyes about a long slash of a nose, and wide lips in a sincere-appearing smile. His clothing was plain but still fairly new. The road dust on tunic, leggings, and boots had just been applied around the bend from the cabin, rather than being the result of a three day journey, as he had said.

How much had his ease in gaining entrance, Kestrel wondered, been because of other thoughts in Phoebe's mind, rather than the possibility of acquiring some of the rare anvilwood that peeked from the rucksack on his back? He savored the mental image which suddenly sprang into his mind. What would it be like to offer a wagonload of true potency instead of the disguised snags and rotten branches and to ask a fair price, rather than display an apparent ignorance of the value of what he possessed, or not to hurry away before his deception was discovered?

No. He shook his head sadly. He could not take the risk. He had to take advantage of the base impulses of others. It was his only defense. Long ago, he had trusted-and the scars still remained.

Phoebe suddenly stiffened. "I am yours to command, master," she said.

Kestrel immediately sensed that something was wrong. The air above the flame shimmered and danced. A hand emerged from nowhere, and then a head with features more plain than bizarre. The demon was no towering giant with menacing fangs and crackles of lightning, but Phoebe's jaws went slack, and her hands fell to her sides all the same. She had not won the contest of wills; the demon had done so, instead.

Kestrel made a step to the left and then hesitated. The demon might be content with domination of the wizard and pay no attention to him as he slowly glided past. It was still morning. He could be well away before nightfall and anyone else suspected. On the other hand, he would be abandoning what little anvil wood he had remaining with nothing to show for it. In mixed fascination and fear, he watched as the demon continued to tear apart the fabric of reality and emerge into the realm of men.

Available in Trade paperback, Ebook,and Kindle formats.

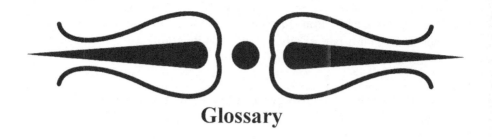

Glossary

agoraphobia

An anxiety disorder in which one feels uncomfortable in particular environments.

Wikipedia: http://en.wikipedia.org/wiki/Agoraphobia

115,000 Google results

alchemist puzzle

Of the three puzzles mentioned in chapter four of Puzzles for the Wordsmith, the one about the alchemist, imp, flask of acid, and bag of silver coins is the easiest. Children in elementary school routinely solve it.

The puzzle

An alchemist restocking his laboratory comes to a river that he needs to cross. He is carrying an imp tethered to a rope, a flask of acid, and a bag of silver coins. A boat is available for the crossing but it will hold only him and one additional item.

If he takes the bag of coins, the unsupervised imp will remove the cork from the flask of acid, and maneuver a loop of his restraining rope into it. The acid will then eat through the rope, freeing the imp who can then fly away.

If he takes the imp, mischievous children playing nearby will pour the acid into the bag of coins, dissolving them completely. There is also another group of like-minded children on the other shore. Neither group understands that a bag of silver is a valuable commodity and would run off with it if it were unattended.

How does the alchemist get all three items transferred safely across the river?

The solution

First, the alchemist takes the flask of acid across the river. The imp has no interest in silver coins, and the mischievous children stay away because of his presence.

Second, the alchemist returns and takes the bag of silver coins across the river.

Third, the alchemist returns, but not with an empty boat but also with the flask of acid he had originally ferried.

Fourth, the alchemist takes the imp across the river and refetters him there.

Fifty, the alchemist returns, takes the flask of acid across the river and continues on his way.

Wikipedia:
http://en.wikipedia.org/wiki/Fox,_goose_and_bag_of_beans_puzzle

400,000 Google results

alchemy

On earth, the root of the word comes from the Greek for transmutation. In the Middle Ages, alchemy focused on changing baser metals into gold, finding an elixir of life and a universal solvent. Some alchemical practices ultimately became the basis for modern chemistry.

In Master of the Five Magics and its sequels, alchemical procedures were described by formulas of arcane symbols kept in grimoires. Formula success was governed by probability; the more potent the result the less likely it was to succeed.

On earth, the most similar craft is that of a chemist.

Wikipedia: http://en.wikipedia.org/wiki/Alchemy

3,790,000 Google results

ambulator

A human who walks on a treadmill to create the energy needed for thaumaturgical spells.

anatase

Anatase is one of three forms of titanium dioxide.

Wikipedia: http://en.wikipedia.org/wiki/Anatase

632,000 Google results

archimage

A master of all five of the crafts of thaumaturgy, alchemy, magic, sorcery, and wizardry.

athanor

A furnace used by an alchemist to provide uniform and constant heat.

Wikipedia: http://en.wikipedia.org/wiki/Athanor

247,000 Google results

axiom of least contradiction

Spoiler Alert

You may not want to read the following until after you have finished the book.

The axiom of least contradiction, or 'that which explains most is the best' is an example of a metalaw, a law about laws.

This metalaw is the least well understood of the three. The basic idea is that a metamagician can unlock the laws of magic in a realm. While they are unlocked, different laws can compete for dominance. Then when the metamagician relocks the laws, the winner of the competition becomes the law in effect.

A contradiction in the metalaws?

Wait a minute, you say. Doesn't the first metalaw, the postulate of invariance prohibit such a thing from happening? Unlocked or not, there can be more than seven operating.

Well, yes, such a law as the postulate of invariance, or, in this case, a metalaw, is a 'conservation' law. Other conservation laws are things like the conservation of energy or the conservation of electrical charge.

Conservation laws are important aids in solving problems. They provide a shortcut that saves a lot of computation. In billiards, if one shoots the cue ball at the eight ball, with its speed and direction noted both before and after the collision, the speed and direction of the eight ball afterwards can be deduced using the law of the conservation of momentum without resorting to any additional measurements. One does not have to measure exactly at what angle the cue ball strikes the target, how loud the sound of the impact was, determine if there was some sliding friction between the two balls on contact, etc.

Physicists devote a lot of time and effort to discovering new conservation laws and testing to see if they really work in all circumstances. And in fact, it has been determined that even something as hallowed as the conservation of energy is not absolute. Things break down in both general relativity and in quantum mechanics.

In quantum mechanics, the amount of energy and the time over which it applies cannot both be determined to an arbitrary accuracy. The uncertainty of one times the uncertainty of the other cannot be less than a physical constant.

Wikipedia: http://en.wikipedia.org/wiki/Uncertainty_principle

1,690,000 Google results

Among a lot of other things, what this means that if the time interval for the measurement of energy is short enough, its value cannot be determined accurately. For sufficiently short time intervals, energy need not be conserved.

Despite its definition, the vacuum of space is not always empty and devoid of any energy. Particles and their antiparticles are continuously being created and then annihilated in a quantum foam that forms and collapses so quickly that we cannot measure what is happening.

So, apparently, the same sort of quantum effect occurs for the laws of metamagic too! For some period of time while the laws are unlocked, more than seven can have potency. And judging from the tale in the text, whatever the governing constant is, it has a value significantly larger than a tiny fraction of a second.

Additional mysteries

There are other aspects about the axiom of least contraction that we just do not yet have a full understanding. What really determines which law dominates? It would seem that quantity of spells is important, but is that the only thing? The proximity of these spells to the metamagician performing the locking and unlocking is a factor as well, but how close do they have to be? If a metamagician leaves the laws unlocked for longer and longer, then what happens?

Fortunately, metamagician researchers throughout our realm, and perhaps others as well, are studying these problems as we speak.

Logo for the second metalaw

343

The metamagicians who practice their craft based on the metalaws do so with knowledge of all three. They do not wear multiple logos, one for each metalaw on their robes, as would an archimage. But if they did, it might be a seesaw that was symbolic of the competition between competing laws.

Keeping track of where you are in metaspace

There are a lot of magic laws, not just seven. Which ones are in effect at any given time can be difficult to determine. After all, there are no overhead road signs with the title 'These laws are in effect today until further notice."

It is hard even for experienced metamagicians to keep track of exactly what the operative laws are. They use memory devices to help them keep things straight. Melibar used two lattices: one for three of the laws and a second for two more. The nodes or, as sometimes called, vertices, of the lattices were color coded to indicate which laws were in effect, and he wrapped a braided coil of gold around the ones that indicated where things were at in metaspace.

Melibar needed the laws of wizardry to remain where they were for all of his travels, so did not have to keep track of the two laws associated with the craft as we know it. It was only when Jason orchestrated a wild ride through the metaspace that, for a while, even wizardry went away.

The two figures below illustrate what travel along each direction in the lattices corresponded to which laws of magic would change.

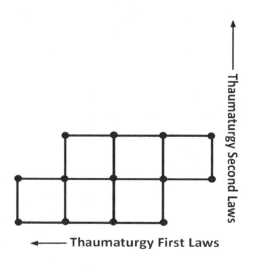

Thaumaturgy Second Laws

← Thaumaturgy First Laws

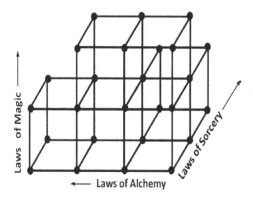

Laws of Magic

Laws of Sorcery

← Laws of Alchemy

ballista

A siegecraft that used the principle of a bow and arrow to hurl large projectiles.

Wikipedia: http://en.wikipedia.org/wiki/Ballista

1,200,000 Google results

bartizan

An overhanging turret projecting from a tower or curtain wall on a castle that allows defenders to hurl weapons down upon attackers. The walls were usually rounded so as to deflect bombarding missiles and minimize damage.

Wikipedia: http://en.wikipedia.org/wiki/Bartizan

60,000 Google results

bastion

Part of a castle's fortification that juts out from the curtain wall.

Wikipedia: http://en.wikipedia.org/wiki/Bastion

520,000 Google results

beryl

Beryl is a mineral of beryllium and aluminum.

Wikipedia: http://en.wikipedia.org/wiki/Beryl

18,100,000 Google results

byrnie

A waist-length coat of mail

Wikipedia: http://en.wikipedia.org/wiki/Mail_(armour)

5,660 Google results

cantrip

On earth, cantrip is a word that means a spell of any kind. In Master of the Five Magics and its sequels, it means the sorcerer's charm for prophecy.

Wikipedia: http://en.wikipedia.org/wiki/Cantrip

100,000 Google results

ceremonium

A lecture hall in a magician's guild of substantial size so that large scale rituals can be exercised.

chain reaction

Although not quite the same thing as Melizar's exercise of over a thousand thaumaturgy incantations, rat, well mouse, traps are used in a classic illustration of what happens in nuclear fission.

A single neutron hits the nucleus of, say, U235, and splits it into several parts, several of which might be additional neutrons. These neutrons split two more atoms, producing four projectiles and so on.

I remember watching such a display on the Walt Disney television program more than a half century ago. Since then, thanks to YouTube, you too can see such a simulation with a click of the mouse.

Nuclear fission simulation: https://www.youtube.com/watch?v=vjqIJW_Qr3c

charm

On earth, a synonym for spell in general. In Master of The Five Magics and its sequels, a sorcerer's spell in particular.

Wikipedia: http://en.wikipedia.org/wiki/Charm

chrysocolla

Chrysocolla is a mineral of copper.

Wikipedia: http://en.wikipedia.org/wiki/Chrysocolla

740,000 Google results

crenellation

A series of usually rectangular notches in castle walls that permit defenders to hurl missiles at attackers. A single notch is called a crenel.

Wikipedia: http://en.wikipedia.org/wiki/crenellation

76,200 Google results

demon

Resident of another realm different from that of the universe containing the earth and the world of Master of the Five Magics. With the exception of djinns, of limited physical power in our realm. Synonymous with devil.

Wikipedia: http://en.wikipedia.org/wiki/Demon

Wikipedia: http://en.wikipedia.org/wiki/Devil

Wikipedia: http://en.wikipedia.org/wiki/List_of_fictional_demons

14,200,000 Google results

devil

A synonym for demon in Master of the Five Magics and its sequels.

Wikipedia: http://en.wikipedia.org/wiki/Devil

Wikipedia: http://en.wikipedia.org/wiki/Demon

Wikipedia: http://en.wikipedia.org/wiki/List_of_fictional_demons

20,300,000 Google results

disentanglement puzzle

There are many puzzles with entangled parts that are to be separated by a sequence of manual steps.

Wikipedia http://en.wikipedia.org/wiki/Disentanglement_puzzle

57,300 Google results

In our world, a classic one is known by the name of the Chinese Ring Puzzle.

Wikipedia: http://en.wikipedia.org/wiki/Baguenaudier

464,000 Google results

The solution to the puzzle involves getting the most entangled ring off first, then the next most, and so on until only the 'first' ring is left. You can get clues for how to do this by watching:

https://www.youtube.com/watch?v=aXmb2ijxe0g

divulgent

A buyer and seller of information on the island of Pluton.

djinn

The largest and most powerful demons physically, and a considerable challenge for any wizard to dominate.

Wikipedia: http://en.wikipedia.org/wiki/Jinn

1,580,000 Google results

enchantment

On earth, to cast a spell over someone. In Master of the Five Magics, a sorcerer charm in which the sorcerer takes complete control of the enchanted.

Wikipedia: http://en.wikipedia.org/wiki/Enchantment

3,980,000 results

ensorcellment

On earth, bewitchment. In Master of the Five Magics, the sorcerer charm of moving the consciousness from one animate object to another.

Wikipedia: http://en.wiktionary.org/wiki/Ensorcellment

5,640 Google results

epidote

Epidote is a mineral of calcium, aluminum, and iron.

Wikipedia: http://en.wikipedia.org/wiki/Epidote

496,000 Google results

glamour

Many meanings on earth: a magazine title, appearance of attractiveness, a shape-shifter, and others. In Master of the Five Magics, the sorcerer's charm of illusion.

Wikipedia: http://en.wikipedia.org/wiki/Glamour

icosahedron

One of the five so-called Platonic solids. It has twenty triangular faces, twelve vertices and thirty edges.

Wikipedia: http://en.wikipedia.org/wiki/Icosahedron

85,000 Google references

imp

The smallest of demons and mostly just pranksters.

Wikipedia: http://en.wikipedia.org/wiki/Imp

5,130,000 Google results

jigsaw puzzle strategies

Separate and connect the edges

Use the picture on the box cover as a guide

http://www.dailyjigsawpuzzles.net/jigsaw-puzzle-strategies.html

471,000 Google results

keep

A fortified tower within a castle that is the defense of last resort.

Wikipedia: http://en.wikipedia.org/wiki/Keep

57,700,000 Google results

lattice

A set of regularly spaced points.

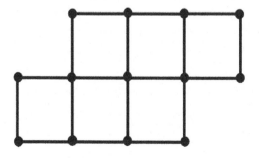

A two-dimensional lattice

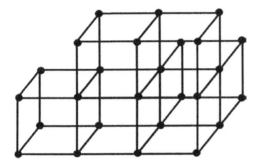

A three-dimensional lattice

Google 48,000,000 references

magic

The use of means outside of normal availability to affect change. On earth, the terms magic, sorcery, thaumaturgy, and wizardry are roughly synonymous.

In Master of the Five Magics and its sequels, each, along with alchemy, have distinct meanings. Magic is performed by the exercise of rituals, the steps of which are derived from extensions of rituals deduced previously.

The goal of these exercises is the production of magical objects, things that are perfect in what they do, such as mirrors, daggers, swords, and shields. Once created, with few exceptions, they last forever.

The power of magic is limited by the time and expense involved in performing magic rituals. Some take several generations and the involvement of many participants. Because of the time and effort involved, magical objects are quite expensive.

On earth, the most similar craft is that of a mathematician.

Wikipedia: http://en.wikipedia.org/wiki/Magic

63,900,000 Google results

magician puzzle

Of the three puzzles mentioned in chapter four of Puzzles for the Wordsmith, the one about the five magicians and the chest of coins is the hardest.

The puzzle

Five magicians on a journey from one guild to another stumble upon a chest full of gold coins. The sun is setting, and they decide to divide the treasure the first thing the next morning.

One of the magicians wakes up in the night. He is suspicious that one of the others might do something magical in the morning to take all of the gold and decides to take his fair share immediately.

He divides the gold into five equal piles but discovers that there is one coin left over. This he sets aside under a bush, hides his share as well, and returns the remaining coins back into the chest. (Evidently, magicians are fast counters and very heavy sleepers.)

A second magician then wakes up and comes to the same conclusion as the first. He divides the remaining coins into five equal piles and discovers there is one coin left over. This he sets aside under a bush, hides his share as well, and returns the remaining coins back into the chest. (Evidently, magicians are fast counters and very heavy sleepers over extended periods of time.)

The third, fourth, and fifth magician wake up in sequence and repeat the process — divide into five equals piles with one left over, hide his share and the extra coin, and return the rest to the chest.

In the morning, the five magicians divide the remaining coins a final time and give one coin left over to the neophyte who was carrying the baggage. Each one must have seen that coins were missing, but all kept quiet because of their own duplicities.

How many coins were in the chest originally?

The solution

There is not a single answer to the puzzle. Regardless of how many coins are a solution, one can add 15,265 to that number and get another answer that also works. This is because 15,265 is 5 x 5 x 5 x 5 x 5 x 5, a number that can be successfully divided by 5 six times — the number of times that the coins are split into equal piles. So, properly stated, the puzzle is to find the smallest number that works.

Actually, finding the smallest number that works is not quite right either. One wants to find the smallest *positive* number that works.

Of course, you say. How can one have a negative number of gold coins?

Well, thinking hypothetically, as magicians are wont to do, just suppose one could have a negative number of gold coins. How about minus four!

The first magician hides one positive coin so that the total in the chest becomes minus five. He then divides these coins into equal piles of minus one and takes his share leaving minus four again.

The other four magicians do the same. After each one is done, minus four coins remain in the chest. The following morning, they give one coin to the neophyte and divide the minus five coins equally among themselves. So minus four is indeed a solution to the puzzle.

But we can always add 15,256 to any solution to get another valid one. Minus 4 plus 15,265 gives us 15,261 coins which is the smallest positive integer solution.

Amazon:
http://www.amazon.com/Scientific-American-Mathematical-Puzzles-Diversions/dp/0226282538

manipulant

A magic worker in the realm of the skyskirr who follows the instructions of a metamagician.

maze

The wall following method can be used to solve what are called simple mazes, i.e. those that have all walls connected to the outer boundary. After entering the maze one places a hand on a wall and keeps it there no matter what. The path taken is not necessarily efficient but eventually the goal will be reached.

In the example below, if you place your right hand on the vertical wall as you enter, you get through the maze quickly. But if you happen to use your left hand on the horizontal wall, it takes a while longer.

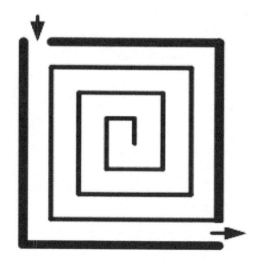

Wikipedia: http://en.wikipedia.org/wiki/Maze_solving_algorithm

14,100,000 Google results

metamagician key

Spoiler Alert

You may not want to read the following until after you have finished the book.

The metamagician's key is a mechanical device that channels his focus and energy on unlocking and relocking the laws of magic in a realm.

In an amazing coincidence, the key Melibar uses, is, on our world, a mechanical puzzle invented by Ernö Rubik.

Wikipedia: http://en.wikipedia.org/wiki/Rubik's_Cube

7,320,000 Google results

orpiment

Orpiment is a deep orange-yellow arsenic sulfide mineral.

Wikipedia: http://en.wikipedia.org/wiki/Orpiment

16,100 Google results

portcullis

A vertically-opening, latticed gate

Wikipedia: http://en.wikipedia.org/wiki/Portcullis

52,500 Google results

postulate of invariance

Spoiler Alert

You may not want to read the following until after you have finished the book.

The postulate of invariance, 'seven exactly' is an example of a metalaw, a law about laws. Implicitly, the laws of magic are not immutable. They can become inoperable, completely failing to work at all. But if this does happen to one, it will be replaced by another one. There will always be seven; the number is invariant. (But see also the glossary entry for the axiom of least contradiction.)

The metamagicians who practice their craft based on the metalaws do so with knowledge of all three. They do not were multiple logos, one for each metalaw on their robes as would an archimage. But if they did, a candidate for the postulate of invariance would be the regular geometric polygon of seven sides, the regular heptagon, or, as it sometimes called, the septagon.

One of the endeavors of plane geometry is finding out what can be constructed using only a compass and a straightedge — a ruler without any measurement marks. Constructing a regular pentagon is easy enough that the steps were included in my high school geometry text.

Wikipedia: http://en.wikipedia.org/wiki/Heptagon

1,840,000 Google results

The great mathematician, Carl Friedrich Gauss, at the age of nineteen, proved that polygons with even more sides — such as the heptadecagon, a polygon with seventeen, also can be constructed with only a compass and straightedge! Gauss was so pleased with what he had done that he requested at a regular heptadecagon be inscribed on his tombstone.

Procolon

A kingdom west across the great ocean from Arcadia. Actions take place there in Master of the Five Magics.

rat trap

It always amazes me how even the most trivial mechanical devices have parts with definite and distinctive names.

http://www.physics.drexel.edu/~gyang/How/mouse_trap.pdf

realgar

Realgar is an arsenic sulfide mineral.

Wikipedia: http://en.wikipedia.org/wiki/Realgar

347,000 Google results

realm of the skyskirr

The entire realm of the skyskirr is confined to the interior of a giant icosahedron, one of the five so-called Platonic solids. This solid has twenty triangular faces and thirty edges with five of the edges meeting at each of its twelve vertices.

Wikipedia: http://en.wikipedia.org/wiki/Icosahedron

675,000 Google results

Faces on opposite sides of the icosahedron are composed of a single mineral, ten minerals in all for the twenty faces. One face carries a 'plus' charge and other natural occurrences of the mineral within the volume also carrying a plus charge are repelled from it. The opposite face carries a 'minus' charge and attracts. These charges are analogous to the plus and minus charges that dictate electrical forces in our own realm.

The skyskirr uses these forces to propel their homes called lithons throughout the 'hedron in order to harvest and trade. A particular type of mineral only feels these forces when the associated magic law is in effect. By carefully turning on an off which laws are operating at any given time, the skyskirr are able to perform necessary maneuvers.

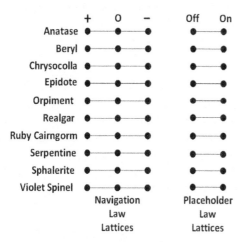

	+	O	−		Off	On
Anatase	●	●	●		●	●
Beryl	●	●	●		●	●
Chrysocolla	●	●	●		●	●
Epidote	●	●	●		●	●
Orpiment	●	●	●		●	●
Realgar	●	●	●		●	●
Ruby Cairngorm	●	●	●		●	●
Serpentine	●	●	●		●	●
Sphalerite	●	●	●		●	●
Violet Spinel	●	●	●		●	●

Navigation
Law
Lattices

Placeholder
Law
Lattices

Of course, the Postulate of Invariance dictates that when one law is turned off, another must turn on in its place. Although not mentioned in the text, it must be that the skyskirr have other weaker, 'placeholder' laws that can be turned on when one that moves lithons is turned off, and hence the status of the other lithon moving laws are not disturbed.

The Right Hand Rule

Just as moving charges in our realm creates magnetic forces at right angles to the electrical ones, so do moving minerals are also affected by lateral forces in the 'hedron.

Was this complication necessary? Well, of course not. But I thought that a closer analogy to electromagnetism in our realm was a good concept, even if things are not exactly the same.

As an amazing coincidence, the direction of this second force, as every high school physics student knows, is given by the 'right hand rule'. In our realm, extend the index finger in the direction that the current is moving from plus to minus and the middle finger in the direction of a magnetic field that is also present. Then, the thumb points in the direction of the corresponding force that is felt.

It is even more amazing that both realms use the *right* hand rule. In fact, when I was in high school I was taught the *left* hand rule instead.

Things working out correctly with the right hand depends upon the arbitrary designation that electrical current flows from positive to negative.

As we learned more and more about what electricity flowing in wires really was — negatively charged electrons moving from one place to another, scientists realized that there really was not any flow of charge from plus to minus. It was the other way around. One of the consequences of 'fixing' this by pointing the index finger in the direction that electrons moved was that the right hand now gave the wrong answer for the direction of the magnetic force. One had to use a left hand instead.

Eventually, cooler heads prevailed. Regardless of what was actually carrying charge in a wire, current was considered to flow from plus to minus as it had from the get-go. The importance of the right hand was restored.

robe

Practitioners of each of the five magics are distinguished by the capes and robes they wear.

Thaumaturges wear brown covered with what is on earth the mathematical symbol of similarity.

Alchemists wear white covered with triangles with a single vertex bottom-most symbolizing the delicate balance between success and failure when performing a formula.

Magicians wear blue with the palest for a neophyte and the darkest for the master and covered by circular rings symbolizing the perfect mathematical object.

Sorcerers wear gray covered with the logo of the staring eye symbolizing the ability to see far in time and place and into another's inner being.

Wizards wear black covered with wisps of flame symbolizing the portal by which the realm of demons and the realm of men are connected.

rusty cairngorm

Cairngorm is a variety of smoky quartz found in the Cairngorm Mountains of Scotland.

Wikipedia: http://en.wikipedia.org/wiki/Smoky_quartz

92,400 Google results

serpentine

Serpentine is a mineral of magnesium and silicon.

Wikipedia: http://en.wikipedia.org/wiki/Serpentinite

21,400,000 Google results

situation puzzle

Situation puzzles are riddles that cannot be solved by thinking in isolation by oneself. Instead, a group is involved. One person, the host, narrates a puzzling event or sequence of actions. The task for the others is to figure out the explanation for what happened.

The host knows the solution for the strange behavior. The others can ask yes/no questions — questions than can be answered only with a 'yes' or a 'no'. All other questions are disallowed.

Gradually enough facts are uncovered so that the solution can be pieced together. In a common variation, a kindly host can also reply 'immaterial' when a 'yes' or 'no' does not give the guessers any helpful information.

A classic example is the following. A man lives in a high-rise apartment building on the seventeenth floor. Every day that he goes to work, he rides the elevator down to the street and then proceeds to his work place. In the evening when he returns home, he rides the elevator only up to the tenth four and then climbs the last seven on foot. Why does he do this?

My personal favorite is:

A man walks into a bar and offers a drunk $50,000 dollars if he agrees to have his arm amputated. The drunk agrees. The two go to a doctor's office where the operation is performed, and the drunk is paid, never to be seen again.

The first man, now in possession of the severed arm, wraps it up carefully and sends it to a second man. The second man opens the package, sees that it is an arm, rewraps it, and sends it to a third man. The third man opens the package, sees that it is an arm, and throws it away. What is going on here?

Wikipedia: http://en.wikipedia.org/wiki/Situation_puzzle

829,000 Google results

skyskirr lattice

A lattice used by a skyskirr navigator to keep track of which laws of magic were in force.

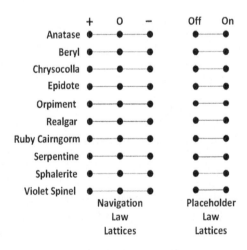

sorcery

The use of means outside of normal availability to affect change. On earth, the terms magic, sorcery, thaumaturgy, and wizardry are roughly synonymous.

In Master of the Five Magics and its sequels, each, along with alchemy, have distinct meanings. Sorcery is performed by the recitation of charms, the steps of which are revealed from self-enchantment.

The power of a sorcerer is limited by the fact that each casting takes some of his life force, and eventually he succumbs when he has no more to give.

On earth, the most similar craft is that of a psychologist.

Wikipedia: http://en.wikipedia.org/wiki/Sorcery

5,070,000 Google results

spell

On earth the terms cantrip, charm, enchantment, glamour, incantation, and spell are synonymous — the performance of an act of magic.

In Master of the Five Magics and its sequels, except for the word spell itself, each of the others have particular meanings, and the word spell is a generic umbrella for any of them.

Thaumaturgy — incantation
Alchemist — formula performance
Magician — ritual exercise
Sorcerer — charm recitation
Wizard — invocation

sphalerite

Sphalerite is the chief ore of zinc.

Wikipedia: http://en.wikipedia.org/wiki/Sphalerite

503,000 Google results

sprite

A demon that is larger than an imp but smaller and less powerful than a djinn.

Wikipedia: http://en.wikipedia.org/wiki/Sprite

3,590,000 Google results

subordinate

The first four crafts have named subordinates in Master of the Five Magics and its sequels.

Thaumaturgy — Journeyman, Apprentice

Alchemist — Novice

Magician — Neophyte, Initiate, Acolyte

Sorcerer — Tyro

sweetbalm

A salve made with alchemy that speeds recovery from wounds and provides an anesthetic.

thaumaturgy

The use of means outside of normal availability to affect change. On earth, the terms magic, sorcery, thaumaturgy, and wizardry are roughly synonymous.

In Master of the Five Magics and its sequels, each, along with alchemy, have distinct meanings. Thaumaturgy is performed by the reciting incantations that bind together objects at a distance that once had physically been together and with a source of energy that can perform work.

The power of thaumaturgy is limited by the fact that all incantations must conserve energy or, as sometimes stated, the first law of thermodynamics.

On earth, the term derives from the Greek for miracle and the most similar craft is that of a physicist.

Wikipedia: http://en.wikipedia.org/wiki/Thaumaturgy

118,000 Google results

tonguetwister

A phrase that is difficult to speak without error. For amusement, sorcerers challenge competitors with tonguetwisters that are not parts of longer charms.

Wikipedia: http://en.wikipedia.org/wiki/Tongue-twister

64,500 Google results

vault in the grotto

The inspiration for this came from the Blue Grotto tourist attraction on the island of Capri in Italy. Part of its appeal was that boating into it for sight-seeing was not guaranteed. When the tide was too high, the narrow passage way from the entrance was underwater. High winds could also made entrance to dangerous. Only lucky ones on a tight travel itinerary could boast that they had seen the Blue Grotto.

Wikipedia: http://en.wikipedia.org/wiki/Blue_Grotto_(Capri)

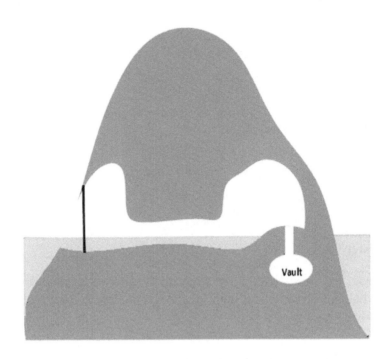

Low Tide

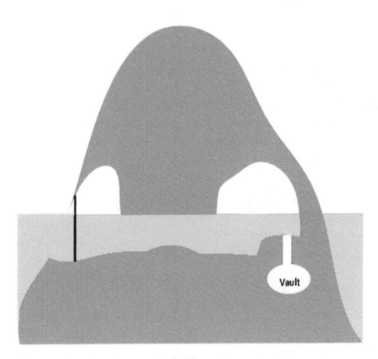

High Tide

verity of exclusion

Spoiler Alert

You may not want to read the following until after you have finished the book.

The verity of exclusion, or 'if skill with the key, then none with the stone' is an example of a metalaw, a law about laws. This, or course, is the translation of the metalaw from the original language of the skyskirr who had a narrow outlook about what the laws of magic really were.

Most beings are proficient in none of the magic crafts or any of the three metalaws on which they ultimately are based. If one is able to practice one of the crafts, then they cannot unlock or relock the laws in their realm. Correspondingly, if they do have the inherent makeup of a metamagician, they cannot perform even the simplest magical skills.

The metamagicians who practice their craft based on the metalaws do so with knowledge of all three. They do not were multiple logos, one for each metalaw on their robes as would an archimage. But if they did, it might be the magician's symbol for the 'union' of two things with a diagonal slash through it to signify that such power united in a single individual was not possible.

violet spinel

Spinel is a gemstone of magnesium and aluminum.

Wikipedia: http://en.wikipedia.org/wiki/Spinel

4,590,000 Google results

wizard puzzle

Of the three puzzles mentioned in chapter four of Puzzles for the Wordsmith, the one about the wizard covering a square box of nine dots with four connected straight lines is of medium difficulty.

The puzzle

In a contest of wills, a demon gives a wizard the following challenge. If the wizard can solve it then the demon becomes under his dominance; if he does not, the wizard is the one enslaved.

Construct a grid of nine dots, three rows of three dots each.

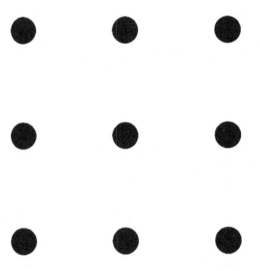

Link the nine dots using four straight lines without lifting the pen and without tracing the same line more than once.

The solution

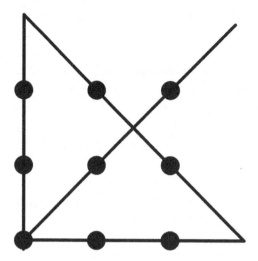

The regularity of the nine dots tends to confine our thinking to staying entirely within the box structure that is implicitly implied. But the instructions do not prohibit going outside. Once this possibility becomes apparent, the solution is easy.

The popularity of this puzzle rests on the accompanying clue of 'Think outside of the box'. It is a metaphor for one way to go about solving any puzzle; think of ways that are not obvious or that come immediately to mind.

By an amazing coincidence, 'Think outside the box' is also a puzzle-solving prod in our own world.

Wikipedia: http://en.wikipedia.org/wiki/Thinking_outside_the_box

7,470,000 Google results

wizardry

The use of means outside of normal availability to affect change. On earth, the terms magic, sorcery, thaumaturgy, and wizardry are roughly synonymous.

In Master of the Five Magics and its sequels, each, along with alchemy, have distinct meanings. Wizardry is performed by the invocation of demons from another realm from that of the earth.

The potency of a wizard is limited by the power of the demons that he can dominate.

On earth, there is no such craft as such, although one could argue that the practices of witches and warlocks is similar.

Wikipedia: http://en.wikipedia.org/wiki/Witchcraft

3,050,000 Google results

word ladder

Word ladders were invented by Lewis Carol, author of *Alice in Wonderland* and *Through the Looking Glass* in the late 1800s. The idea is to transform one word into another by changing just one letter at a time to intermediate words.

A trivial example is:

Dog
Dug
Hug
Hag
Hat
Cat

Wikipedia: http://en.wikipedia.org/wiki/Word_ladder

1,120,000 Google results   370

Among many other things, word ladders and software to find them automatically are described in a book on graph theory:

Amazon: The Stanford Graphbase, by Donald E. Knuth, Stanford University (1993)

Knuth focuses on a database of 5757 five-letter words. Among the things he briefly talks about are:

examples of the 671 words that do not word ladder with any other word,

the two words, bares and cores, that each have the most other words differing from them by a single letter, twenty-five,

the seventeen words that ladder with the word pound,

and so on.

wyvern

A two legged winged dragon.

Wikipedia: http://en.wikipedia.org/wiki/Wyvern

1,920,000 Google results

Made in the USA
Coppell, TX
22 December 2021

69919608R00229